RENEGADE HEART

A woman on a mission, one moment Sarah Maravich is a student of the American past, and the next moment she's *in* it. Mysteriously transported back to the teeming streets of post-Civil War Washington, she arrives too late to change history—and too near to the brilliant, courageous, devastatingly masculine journalist, Tyson Stone.

RUNAWAY TIME

The cannonfire of Antietam and Fredericksburg didn't shake Stone as deeply as the extraordinary arrival of this beautiful, sensuous stranger. Surely she *must* be a spy—yet one so intoxicating and desirable, his soul cries out to possess her. But though she burns for his touch, Sarah knows she must flee Tyson's passion. For surrendering to ecstasy in the past will cost her everything she loves in the future.

“ONE OF TH

New

Other Avon Books by
Deborah Gordon

RUNAWAY BRIDE

If You've Enjoyed This Book,
Be Sure to Read These Other
AVON ROMANTIC TREASURES

A KISS IN THE NIGHT *by Jennifer Horsman*
LADY OF SUMMER *by Emma Merritt*
PROMISE ME *by Kathleen Harrington*
SHAWNEE MOON *by Judith E. French*
TIMESWEPT BRIDE *by Eugenia Riley*

Coming Soon

MY RUNAWAY HEART *by Miriam Minger*

DEBORAH GORDON

RUNAWAY TIME

An Avon Romantic Treasure

AVON BOOKS NEW YORK

RUNAWAY TIME is an original publication of Avon Books. This work has never before appeared in book form. This work is a novel. Any similarity to actual persons or events is purely coincidental.

AVON BOOKS
A division of
The Hearst Corporation
1350 Avenue of the Americas
New York, New York 10019

Inside cover author photo by Bill Santos
Published by arrangement with the author
Library of Congress Catalog Card Number: 95-90097
ISBN: 0-380-77759-2

First Avon Books Printing: October 1995

Printed in the U.S.A.

RA 10 9 8 7 6 5 4 3 2 1

For my friend and fellow author Maggie Osborne. I've always loved time travel stories, especially Jack Finney's *Time and Again* and Isaac Asimov's *The End of Eternity*, but it was Maggie who suggested that I write one of my own, and her wonderful novel *The Pirate and His Lady* (written as Margaret St. George) that inspired me to actually do it.

Runaway Time

Prologue

Berkeley, California
January 3, 2085

The first time Shelby Maravich communicated with her mother Sarah, Shelby was a restless eight-month fetus.

At eighteen, Sarah was little more than a child herself. She was trying to juggle college, marriage, and motherhood, and felt she was failing at all three. Earlier that day, she had skipped her breakfast and only picked at her lunch, and that was bad for the baby. She'd done poorly on an important exam in her major, history, because her brain was foggy from lack of sleep. And later, for the first time in her life, she had yelled at the husband she worshiped.

He hadn't answered, merely kept on working. It was two in the morning now, but he was still closeted in his study, a brilliant physicist doing science only a few people in the world could understand.

The baby thrust a hard heel against the top of Sarah's womb, and she winced. Shelby did that so often now that Sarah's flesh was red and tender to the touch. She shifted positions, but it didn't help. And then, out of nowhere, her emotions—loneliness, frustration, and fear—suddenly rocketed out of control, and she burst into tears.

A sense of raw astonishment shot through her. It was followed almost at once by intense distress. The feelings were deep inside Sarah's head, yet completely alien. They weren't an ambiguous, complicated tangle, as Sarah's thoughts always were, but simple, direct, and emphatic.

Frowning, she changed positions again. Either her mind was playing tricks on her, empathizing with her baby and fabricating what the baby might be feeling—or the emotions in her brain had come from outside. From Shelby.

Sarah told herself it was the first. It was easier to believe she was hallucinating than to accept the alternative, that she and Shelby shared a mother-child telepathic bond. After all, that particular form of telepathy was extremely rare. And then she felt it again—that naked call of distress—and she began to worry. What if it was real?

She decided to experiment. *Teli me what's wrong, Shelby.* She didn't speak the words aloud, merely thought them. But she thought them with such intensity that she might as well have screamed them. *Feel it to me. Try to explain. I know I can make things better.*

Confusion. Frustration. Fear.

Sarah continued thinking. *That's good, honey. I'm hearing you better now. Tell me more. The only thing in the world I want is to help you. I love you, sweetheart.*

Sarah's eyes filled up. She did love the child, with a fierceness that suddenly overwhelmed her. It was incredible. She'd never held the baby, never even seen her except as a false-color image on a screen, yet she felt this overpowering sense of connection . . .

A wave of need and love came back the other way. And then Sarah's mind was pierced by a scream of pain, and she realized that she was sitting in a pool of blood.

Chapter 1

Virginia City, Nevada

The photograph was in black and white, and it looked very old—as old as the hand-etched silver oval that framed it, an antique from the 1860s. A fair-haired woman and a dark-haired girl were standing solemnly side by side. The woman was five-foot-seven and very pretty, but so slender she appeared almost ethereal. The girl was an inch taller and glowed with beauty and vitality. Both were dressed in historical costume, the woman in a dark, flare-sleeved silk gown appliquéd with contrasting ribbon, the girl in a light spotted muslin with lace trim on the neck and sleeves.

The woman was Sarah Maravich, the girl was her daughter Shelby, and the photo had been taken in Bigley's Antiques, a shop that carried books and knick-knacks relating to Virginia City's heyday in the nineteenth century. The proprietor also did a thriving business in period portraits. After decades of effort, he had perfected a process that gave his photographs the stiffness, flatness, and shading of an authentic Mathew Brady, and they were in great demand.

Sarah stared at the picture in wonder, but Shelby

wasn't impressed. "Yuck. I look about ten. That dumb corset thing squashed me flat as a pancake, and those stupid curls . . ." She rolled her eyes. "It's like I have strings of giant RNA sprouting out of my head."

Nothing was quite so withering, Sarah thought in amusement, as the contempt of a budding adolescent. "You're right, Shel," she said softly. "It was a silly hairstyle and I'm sorry I had to inflict it on you, but I told you before, it was the height of fashion in 1865, and—"

"And a doting mother like the character you're going to play would dress up her daughter in the latest style. You didn't want me to look stupid, just young and authentic, because nobody could look at a picture of a war widow and her cute little kid without turning to mush and doing whatever you want. I know, Mom. It's okay."

"But it's a lousy deal, right? You should be able to sulk and complain, to think I'm ignorant, unreasonable, and hopelessly behind the times, the way your girlfriends do about *their* mothers, but you can hear me too well." Sarah hugged her. "And you have too good a heart not to listen."

Shelby shrugged and walked to a rack of costumes. Her mom's illness would have stopped her from acting too bratty even if the telepathic link between them hadn't, but it was better not to say so. Sarah liked to pretend she was healthy. As if Shelby couldn't see her getting thinner and less vibrant all the time. As if she couldn't feel her slowly slipping away.

Yes, she knew what her mother felt. She always knew. And sometimes she hated it. Her mom was right about that. She did wish she were more like her two best friends, Kanisha Lamb and April Fong, at least at times.

Like Sarah, their parents worked on the Wells Project, but Kanisha and April thought they were studying the nature of matter. They didn't know the Project's scientists were manipulating space and time. They had never seen someone vanish into the past as if they'd been sucked into a black hole or pop back into the present with a sparkling flash of weird blue light. It was one thing for a grown-up to keep the biggest secret since the first alien landing, but Shelby wasn't even twelve yet. She envied them their ignorance.

She envied them their fathers, too. Her own dad had burnt up his brains with a laser gun two years before, and she couldn't understand why he'd done it, couldn't accept the loss. After all, there wouldn't have been a Wells Project without him. He'd taken the physics of time travel and turned it into a practical reality. It should have been enough.

And the worst thing of all was that she could have stopped him now. Her gifts had been growing stronger lately. She could hear Sarah better, and every now and then she picked up strangers' bursts of emotion. It was scary. Suppose she started hearing everyone? She'd taught herself to shut out her mother unless she sensed Sarah wanted her to listen, because anything else would have been an invasion of Sarah's privacy. But how could she learn to shut out the whole world?

She had another new power, though, one she was fiercely grateful for. She could affect people's actions. Steal into their brains and plant ideas in their heads. She'd first suspected it last year, when she'd wanted snooty Pami Graham to give a dumb answer in history class, and Pami had. Then, the very next week, she'd caused the cutest guy in school to change his mind about playing the piano for her at her voice recital.

She hadn't told a soul, though, because it would have terrified people, the knowledge that she could mess with their minds. Her powers weren't boundless, but it hadn't mattered. Things had gone exactly the way she had planned. She hadn't been able to stop her father, but she was going to save her mother. Sarah would have a normal lifetime now, not just the year or two the doctors had said.

Shelby glanced across the room. Sarah looked tense and a little sad, and you didn't have to be a telepath to know why. She hated to see Shelby unhappy, especially about her gifts. Besides, she was leaving tomorrow morning for two whole weeks, and it was the first time she and Shelby had been apart. She was worried about how Shelby would do.

She was worried about making it back, too. The act of jumping wasn't dangerous, but things could go wrong when you visited another time. A tempronaut had even died once. But most of all, she was worried that the jump wouldn't cure her. That she would die anyway, leaving Shelby all alone.

Shelby sighed, hating the sickness and fear, wanting the lively, laughing mother of her childhood back. With anyone else, she could have prodded them into a better mood, but Sarah would have felt the mental invasion immediately.

Still, there were other ways to get her mind off her problems. Shelby took a dress off the rack, a scarlet gown with an off-the-shoulder neckline. "Hey, Mom, how about another picture?" She smiled slyly. "That stuff about taking up writing 'cause you were broke and had a kid to support is sort of boring, you know? But suppose you had a little sister who got seduced and abandoned and ruined, and it launched you on a crusade against vice? That's much more interesting, don't you think? Everyone in Washington would want to meet you."

Sarah looked dubious, and Shelby's smile widened. "You can't say I wouldn't fill out the top, either. My breasts are bigger than yours are now. I would have made a great dance hall girl. But then, I guess they were actually—What did they call them in those days, anyway? Women who had sex for money, I mean.''

Sarah knew she was being teased, but that didn't stop her from blushing. She'd been raised not to speak about sexual subjects, but it was different for Shelby. Over the past four years, a series of dazzling genetic breakthroughs had put a permanent end to almost a century of deadly disease, and all hell had broken loose. As a historian, Sarah understood that these things went in cycles—that the staunch repression and extreme propriety of the twenty-first century were bound to explode into wild excess the moment sex was safe again—but that didn't mean she'd adopted the change for herself. She hadn't, not by a long shot.

Still, she didn't let her discomfort show. If Shelby wanted to distract her, she was willing to go along. Anything to take her mind off the jump. ''Hurdies. Pretty waitress girls. Soiled doves. The fair but frail. Parlor-house girls. Or just plain whores.'' She looked at Shelby's chest. ''You really think you're bigger than me? I doubt it, Shel, but since I haven't seen you naked in almost a year, it's hard to be sure. If you want to take a picture, you can, but I want to inspect you first.''

Shelby threw her arms around Sarah's waist and thanked her. ''I can't wait till it's ready. I want to show the kids at school.''

She started toward the back room, but Sarah caught her arm to stop her. ''Not so fast. Tell Mr. Bigley to go easy on the makeup. And I want that neckline to stay where it's supposed to, okay? No cleavage. You're too young for a picture like that.''

Shelby giggled. ''Okay, Mom. Boy, talk about living in the Dark Ages . . . You and 1865 were made for each other.''

Shelby darted away with the dress and Sarah walked over to the glass-fronted bookcase where Bigley kept rare titles and new arrivals. Her eyes lit up when she spotted a reprint of a book from the 1920s analyzing the influence of the California Dream on writers like Mark Twain, Noah Brooks, Ina Coolbrith, Tyson Stone, and Bret Harte. She'd first read it when she was researching her dissertation.

She took out the volume and ran her hand over the cover. For over a century, pundits had been predicting the demise of printed books, but it had never happened. People enjoyed them too much—the look of them on the shelves in their homes, the feel of the crisp paper pages, the act of jotting handwritten notes in the margins. Downloading a volume into your bookfile just wasn't the same thing.

She turned to the section on the journalist Tyson Stone. She admired most everything he'd written, but three articles stood out. The first was a call for equality for men of color, the best of many such columns he'd published over the years. It was a stirring but tightly argued plea of the sort she believed Lincoln would have made if he had lived.

The second, from 1878, was a scathing attack on *Wallace* v. *Robinson,* the Supreme Court ruling that had legalized racial segregation. Stone had made many of the same arguments that would later be used to overturn the decision, in 1971.

Finally, in 1906, Stone had composed what Sarah considered the most detailed, poignant, and brilliant firsthand account ever published of the San Francisco Earthquake and Fire. She started to reread it—the rolling and shaking, the panic and chaos, the death and destruction—and began to tremble. Her parents had died in the Anchorage Quake of '75, when she was nine. It hit too close to home.

She heard Shelby call to her and looked up. Her daughter looked fifteen if she looked a day, and utterly exquisite. Bigley was walking by her side, visibly pleased with himself.

"Damn, but I'm good with makeup," he said. "The girl's a beauty. Would have made a fortune off the men in the old days." He grinned. "On the stage, I mean, not naked on her back. Sings like an angel. What have you got there, Sarah?"

Sarah was about to tell him to watch his language when Shelby intervened. *Forget it, Mom. He talks without thinking. Besides, he did a great job on my face.*

"Oh. The Crawley book," Bigley rattled on. "That reminds me, Sarah, a new one just came in. Ordered it months ago, then forgot all about it."

Bigley unlocked the bottom drawer of an old chest, pulled out a folio-sized volume, and struggled to his feet. The title was *We Built This City: Photographs of San Francisco from the Gold Rush to the Earthquake and Fire.* "Extraordinary work. They used a new computer process on the originals. Even I can't spot the repairs. About a third of these photos are new discoveries." Bigley set the book on a table and gave her a wink. "Check out 217, Sarah. Let's go, Shelby. We've got a picture to take."

Sarah turned to page 217—and gaped. She'd written her doctoral dissertation on Tyson Stone, on how his work had influenced the civil rights movement of the early twentieth century. Only two pictures of him existed, a hazy image of a young soldier and his comrades before Second Manassas, and a photo of a white-haired, white-bearded man standing amidst the rubble of a devastated city. Or so she'd thought.

In this one, Stone was sitting at his desk, smiling up at the camera. The caption read "Tyson Stone at the *San Francisco Chronicle,* 1886. McClure Papers, University of Hong Kong." The reference was to Melanie and Alex McClure, close friends of Stone's who were famous for their Hong Kong detective agency and for their social work in the same city.

Sarah knew from a letter Stone had written to his

sister that the injuries he'd suffered at Chancellorsville in May of '63 included a minié ball strafing his face, and she could see the scar in this photo, taken when Stone was fifty. It ran diagonally from the center of his chin toward his ear, and was about two inches long.

According to the letters and diaries she'd read, his contemporaries had considered him handsome, and the photo confirmed it. Something fluttered inside her stomach. Looking at this picture, aware of the charm, passion, and intelligence that shone through his letters and published writings, she could understand why female after female had become his mistress. They hadn't been able to resist him.

What she didn't understand was the reverse. Why all those women? Tyson Stone had been a young newspaperman in Nevada City, California, in the years before the war, taking care of his orphaned younger sister. He'd mentioned his desire to settle down and have a family in some of his letters, but he'd never referred to any love affairs.

But the postwar letters were different. The references to women were discreet, passing remarks about activities like escorting a lady to the opera or taking her to the races, but the women had been more explicit. More than one of them had poured out her heart in writing, either in a diary or in a letter to a confidante.

Some historians attributed the change in Stone to the war, saying the agony and death he'd seen had destroyed his ability to love. Others felt something dramatic had happened during the so-called "missing years," when he had seemingly dropped off the face of the earth. From July of '63 to August of '65, there were no writings at all, not even letters, and no mention of him in the writings of others.

The only clue to his whereabouts was in an army document from 1866 saying that a "Lt. Colonel Tyson Stone" had been discharged in May of '65. Stone had entered the war as a Pennsylvania volunteer and been mustered out because of his wounds. Historians assumed he had been commissioned as an officer in the regular army after that. He might have been captured by the South, then trapped in some hellish prison.

Sarah was still gazing at his picture when Shelby strolled over, dressed in her own clothing again. "So that's what he looked like. Not bad for an old guy." She turned around. "You were right, Mr. Bigley. She's obsessed with the man. He's her favorite historical figure next to Lincoln. I bet she'll buy the book for that one picture alone."

Sarah riffled through the pages. "I would if I could afford to," she said wistfully. The price was $575.

But you've got the money, Mom. I know you do. Treat yourself for once.

I wish I could, but things could go wrong tomorrow, Shelby. I want to leave you as well provided for as I can.

Bigley's voice filled the apparent silence. "I'll give you a ten percent discount," he said, walking to Sarah's side. "It's the least I can do for a fellow book lover."

Sarah smiled at him in surprise. The emergence of Bigley's generous side was a rare and wondrous thing. "That's very nice of you, but it's still too expensive. Thanks for thinking of me, though."

Shelby sidled up to him. "Nobody will appreciate it the way my mom does, Mr. Bigley. Couldn't you let her have it for less?"

"I'm afraid not, young lady. Business is business." He hesitated. "Then again, Sarah, if you want to think it over . . . I know you're going away for a few weeks, but I could hold it for a while. Give you more time before I . . ." His voice trailed off. He looked at Shelby. He stared into space. And then he seemed to lose himself in thought, frowning so intently that a dozen new wrinkles appeared in his face.

Finally he muttered, "Well, hell, Sarah. Take it at cost. Three hundred even. Your daughter is right. You'll see things in these photos that no one else will. All the little details. You should own the book."

Sarah knew she was being offered a bargain. She thanked him, then ran her fingertip over his scanner. Her mind was on all the errands she needed to run, so it wasn't until a few minutes later, when she pulled into traffic, that she realized how odd his behavior had been. "Okay, Shelby. Tell me how you did it."

"Did what?" Shelby asked, looking puzzled.

"Don't give me that innocent look. You changed Bigley's mind. You got him to give me the book wholesale."

"I didn't. I couldn't. You know that." Shelby settled back in her seat. "You know what would be awesome? If you could track down Tyson Stone while you're gone. You've always wondered about the missing years, right? You could ask him about it—find out what he was doing."

It was Sarah's favorite fantasy. "That *would* be awesome, but it's probably impossible. I'm arriving almost a week before Appomattox. If Stone was in a Southern prison, he wouldn't have been released yet. And if he was still fighting somewhere, he would be beyond my reach."

"But you will ask about him, won't you? Gosh, Mom, maybe Lincoln would know where he was. You could ask *him*. Wouldn't that be incredible?"

That was when Sarah realized she'd been had. Shelby was gifted, but she was also only a child. She had overplayed her hand. "Yes, but not as incredible as what you did a few minutes ago. I repeat: how did you get Bigley to give me the book so cheaply? And don't keep trying to weasel out of answering. It won't work."

Shelby only told the truth because her mom always sensed when she was lying. So she explained how her gifts had been growing, but stopped short of admitting how she'd used them. Sarah might not have liked it, and anyway, she couldn't usually tell when Shelby had left things out.

As she'd hoped, her mother's shock gave way to intense interest. "Let me get this straight. You can't plant a new idea. There has to be a germ first. A leaning. Then you can bring out what's already there and expand it."

"Right. I can push people harder in the direction they're already headed, or influence them if they're thinking about something but can't make up their minds."

"So Bigley was inclined to be generous, and you—increased his generosity."

Shelby nodded, admitting it was a relief finally to talk about it. Listening to her explain, Sarah realized that when she returned, she would have to inform the proper authorities so formal telepathic training could begin. Shelby's new powers, if they grew to maximum strength, would confer new and very heavy responsibilities.

For now, however, her priority was the coming jump. Her mission, the most ambitious to date by far, had been in the works for over a year. According to the government's giant history computers in Washington, the loss of Abraham Lincoln had been the single greatest tragedy the nation had ever endured. Saving him would reduce much of the violence, injustice, and suffering of the next two and a half centuries. Still, nothing fundamental would change. The basics of world history, both good and bad, would remain the same. Given those facts, the Project's scientists had asked permission to prevent the assassination.

President Young had refused at first. She was a cautious woman, and it was a daring mission. But then the cities had erupted in another round of racial conflict, and she had changed her mind. She had told them to move ahead.

Sarah was the Project's historian, not a tempronaut, but in one important way, she was more qualified for the mission than anyone else. She was an expert on wartime Washington. She knew the places, events, and people, including Lincoln, in a way that couldn't be learned from briefing books. But if that was why she had first been considered, it wasn't why she had ultimately been selected.

Jumping was enormously expensive, and so complicated it took two weeks in turnaround to recalibrate the equipment and generate sufficient energy to bring someone back. The Project's budget permitted two missions a year at most. From the beginning, then, it had been standard practice to maximize the government's investment by doing missions with multiple goals.

Thanks to Shelby, Sarah represented a unique opportunity. All mother-child telepaths could function across vast distances, even across the void of space. Scientists wanted to learn if they could function across time, too, and Sarah and Shelby would give them the answer.

As for the final, sentimental reason for giving Sarah the assignment, it was never mentioned directly. Her colleagues talked about her health, not her death. But cell by cell, her body was slowly failing. The disorder she suffered from wasn't contagious; it seemed to be linked to an extreme reaction to environmental pollutants. The only treatment, to boost the patient's immune system, had kept her going, but it would never be able to cure her.

But jumping might. They had noticed from the very first jump that traveling in time somehow strengthened the human immune system. Tempronauts rarely got sick, but when they did, or when they got hurt, they recovered amazingly quickly. There was every reason to hope that jumping would enable Sarah's body to heal itself. If it did, they could study the cellular changes and replicate them in other victims.

Still, with billions of dollars and the fate of a nation at stake, sentiment had no role. It was Sarah's knowledge of Lincoln and wartime Washington that mattered, and the experiment with Shelby. Saving her life was only a bonus.

It wasn't until she was lying in bed that night, drifting off to sleep, that she suddenly realized it wasn't a bonus to Shelby. It was everything in the world.

Her heart began to pound. Wide awake now, she reached into the next room. *Shelby? Are you still awake?*

Yeah, Mom. I can't sleep. I guess I shouldn't admit it, but I'm nervous about tomorrow.

Me, too. Tell me something, Shel. I need to have the truth. Was it you? Did you prod them into sending me back?

Alarm. Defiance. Resignation. *Oh, well. I figured you'd work things out if you saw what I could do, but they wouldn't have gone along if they hadn't been thinking about it already. They do love you, Mom, but it was the medical research angle that did it.* A pause. *Are you mad at me?*

For trying to save my life? Of course not. I don't want to leave you any more than you want to leave me, and if jumping can save me . . . Besides, I'm going to pull this off. I swear I will, Shel. They won't be sorry they sent me.

I know they won't, Mom. If anyone can do it, you can.

Thanks for the vote of confidence. I love you, you know.

Yes. I love you too, Mommy.

Chapter 2

The Wells Project complex was buried deep in the bowels of Mt. Davidson, to the west of the Comstock Lode. Sarah spent the hours before the jump in the compound's prep room, surrounded by the senior staff. The jump pod was charged and ready to go, and so was she, but first she had to undergo a final round of testing.

In the past, she had attended these sessions as the Project's historian, and it always impressed her how cool the tempronauts were. They never lost their patience when they had to answer the same questions over and over again. Personally, she was tired of being drilled, nervous about the jump, and distressed about leaving Shelby, who was sitting directly across from her.

Sam Chapelle, the director of training, had once remarked that nothing short of the promise of resurrection could have torn her away, and he'd been right. "One final time," he said. "When and where are you going to arrive, and what are you going to see when you get there?"

Sarah forced herself to concentrate. At least she'd been spared the history exam she always inflicted.

"Two in the morning on Tuesday, April 4th, 1865, in Washington City." She automatically used the terms of the period. "I'll be in a room on the fifth and top floor of Willard's, facing Fourteenth Street, about a hundred feet in from the Avenue."

She meant the Willard Hotel on Pennsylvania Avenue. She would alight, in short, only a block from the White House grounds. It was the opposite of inconspicuous, but it was the best they'd been able to do. The war had been winding down in early April, but paranoia was still rampant. Travel had been difficult or even dangerous. If you aroused the wrong suspicions, you could be arrested without a warrant and left in jail indefinitely.

Placing Sarah directly into the city had seemed the safest course of action, but the scientists needed detailed records before they could send someone back. Willard's was a capital landmark, at the same location now as in 1865, albeit in a different structure. Registers dating to the 1850s were on file in the Smithsonian Institution. The hotel had been booked to capacity in the spring of '65, but a single room on the top floor had been vacant from April 2 through April 7 because of a leaky roof. Old pictures and architectural drawings combined with recent measurements had enabled them to pinpoint the room's coordinates.

"The room might be empty and it might be furnished," she continued. "We don't know what they might have removed while they were fixing the roof. There's a door leading into the hallway on one side of the room and a double-hung window in the wall on the other side, opposite the doorway."

Sam nodded. "Good. What's the first thing you're going to do when you arrive, Sarah?"

"Activate my shield. I'm wearing it on a ribbon around my neck." She couldn't engage it beforehand because its field played havoc with the Project's machinery. "It looks like a cameo. I should touch it with my right index finger."

"And the next thing you should do?"

"Check the window. Make sure the shade is lowered and the drapes are closed."

"And next?"

"I'll be holding a light source in my left hand. It looks like a lamp from the period." Both inside and out, with one exception. The fuels of the period could explode during a jump, so the lamp ran on a solid synthetic. "I should turn the switch to light it, then set it on the floor in the middle of the room. I open my carpetbag next. It will be sitting on the floor by my feet. Inside, right on top, I'll find two white cubes with raised buttons on top. There's a red arrow on each button . . ."

And so it went, item after item in minute detail. There was a good reason for this numbing level of preparation. Jumping caused fatigue and disorientation. It didn't matter how alert and rested a tempronaut felt in the chamber; when he arrived at his destination, he was always confused and extremely sleepy.

The first tempronaut had gone back only two days. He'd reeled like a drunkard for twenty minutes and lapsed into what looked to be a coma, but awakened a few hours later feeling fine. Traveling farther back intensified the symptoms. A stimulant administered before the jump ameliorated the confusion, but nothing had proved effective against the exhaustion. Unfortunately, Sarah's illness would cause her to pass out more quickly than usual, then sleep for much longer, probably for twelve hours or so.

When the rehearsal was finally over, she and Shelby walked arm in arm out of the prep room. The nights in Washington would be chilly, so she was wearing a heavy robe over her nightgown. She'd taken a throw along in case the bed had been stripped, but she knew she might collapse onto the floor before she could even unpack it.

The chamber itself resembled a huge amphitheater. Massive machines ringed the central pit where the jump pod sat and descended deep into the earth below. Mission control was in a gallery at the top, above and behind the machines.

Sarah's colleagues were waiting by the pod. One by one, they hugged her good-bye, then retired to the gallery to view the jump. Finally only Shelby and Sulee Fong, the Project's physician, remained behind.

Shelby and Sarah embraced, talking silently of their intense love for each other, their hopes and fears, and their sadness at the thought of being apart. *I want us to keep in touch for as long as we can,* Shelby thought. *I need you to help me. Let your emotions overflow. Please, Mom.*

The plea was contrary to Sarah's orders. Sarah and Shelby were to attempt to maintain a link, but not at the cost of the larger goal. Tempronauts were supposed to stay calm and focused before a jump.

But Sarah suddenly didn't give a damn about official orders. *I will.* She hit Shelby with a rush of maternal love. *If we lose touch, I'll miss you every moment I'm gone.*

Sudden amusement. *Oh, really, Mom? Even when you're talking to Lincoln?*

Well, maybe not ***then****. I love you, Shel.* After a final hug, Shelby walked away, but the link between her and Sarah remained strong.

The pod itself was a large tube enclosing a hydraulic lift. Cameras and monitors enabled the tempronaut and those in the gallery to maintain visual contact with each other. Sarah stepped onto the lift. Her carpetbag, trunk, and lamp were already sitting there.

Sulee followed, carrying a hypo in her hand. "Sarah . . . I want you to know—whatever happens next,

Shelby will be able to cope. She's amazingly well adjusted, thanks to you.'' She infused Sarah with the stimulant. ''Believe me, you don't have to worry while you're gone. She'll do fine.''

Sarah smiled as the two women hugged. ''Thanks, but she's in telepathic contact, remember? I hope she agrees.''

Shelby answered at once. *Of course I do. You're the best mom in the world.*

Sulee walked away, and Sarah picked up the lamp. *And you're the best daughter.*

The lift descended and clicked into place. Sarah spotted Shelby in the monitor and felt a wave of love and encouragement. Her eyes filled up. She had hemorrhaged and almost died giving birth to this child, and she wasn't going to quit on her now. *See you in two weeks,* she thought. *And don't worry—I plan to be around for a very long time.*

The stimulant exploded in her body, and she grew light-headed and shaky. A tone began to sound, the ten-second warning before the field popped into existence. The time flew by. The link with Shelby remained strong. Then the tone stopped, and blackness descended.

The field was on now, rending the normal fabric of space-time. Energy was wrested from the past and trapped in the present. Whether in year one of the universe or in year one hundred billion, the total amount of energy and matter had to remain constant. The discontinuity couldn't logically exist. The universe rebelled. At the exact same instant, matter from the present was pulled into the past.

Sarah couldn't have said when the link with Shelby was severed. One moment the world was utterly black, and the next there was a flash of shimmering blue light. Then the blackness turned to ordinary darkness, and Sarah's knees buckled. Somehow, she kept herself from falling. She suddenly felt cold, befuddled, and very tired.

She screamed out for Shelby, an anguished mental cry, but Shelby wasn't there. And then Sarah's training took over. Reeling with fatigue and confusion, she pressed her finger to the cameo around her neck. Look for the window, she told herself, and squinted into the darkness.

She saw a faint strip of gray to her left, parallel to the floor at a level above her head. It was light seeping in at the top of the window, she realized. The shade was drawn and the drapes closed, but a dim band of light was stealing in from outside. There was nothing she could do about that.

She turned on her lamp for a better look, then simply stared, suddenly confused about where she was and what she was supposed to do. This was a hotel room, evidently, a lovely one full of antiques, but why was she here? There was a four-poster bed with a landscape hanging above, she noticed, with a washstand to one side and a table with a lamp on it to the other—an oil lamp, of all things. How odd. It was just like the one she was holding. Oh, right. She had jumped. She was in Washington in 1865.

She slowly turned, absently placing her lamp on the floor, and saw a wardrobe, a small fireplace, a bureau with a mirror and a clock on top, and two wing chairs with a small, marble-topped table between them. There was a patterned rug on the floor, predominantly red, and—

She yawned and frowned at the ceiling, then couldn't remember what she was searching for, only that she was supposed to open her carpetbag and take out—something or other. She knelt, yawning again. She could barely keep her eyes from closing.

She looked into the carpetbag and saw a pair of white cubes. A mental bell went off. Oh, yes. The security system. A tempronaut had been attacked and killed. They'd used these ever since. She had to get them in place.

She took out the cubes and tried to stand up—once, twice, three times. It was hopeless. Her knees wouldn't support her. She collapsed into a heap on the rug, wanting nothing so much as to curl up and sleep.

Something prompted her to fight the feeling. She put the cubes in the pocket of her robe and began to crawl. *First do the door,* she thought, and dragged herself over. She took out a cube, set it near the wall with the arrow facing away from her, and pressed hard on the button on top. The field the cube radiated was invisible, but when she ran her hand along the wall, she could feel its slick warmth.

One down, one to go. She studied the drapes and recalled that she was five stories up. Nobody was going to come in through a fifth floor window, so why bother? But her training was so deeply ingrained that her body did what her mind resisted, laboring across the room, putting the second cube in place, and turning it on.

The effort exhausted her. She propped herself against the wall and looked longingly at the bed. It was no use. She didn't have the strength to move. She closed her eyes and felt herself nodding off.

'Night, Shel, she thought muzzily. Nobody replied. Where was Shelby?

She jerked awake and screamed into the night. *Shelby!* ***Shelby!*** There was still no answer. Panic tore through her, unfogging her mind and energizing her body, and she remembered what she'd temporarily forgotten. Shelby was far away, in another time and a different place.

Acting on instinct, she crawled to the carpetbag and took out the old-fashioned photograph of her and Shelby. Then, exhausted all over again, she staggered to her feet and stumbled to the bed. She had just set the portrait on the table when fatigue overwhelmed her.

She forgot she was supposed to turn off the lamp. Although she managed to pull out a pillow, she couldn't summon the energy to slip under the covers. She simply dropped onto the bed, still wearing her slippers and robe, and drew her knees up to her chest. Within seconds, she had fallen into a deep sleep.

Washington City
May 22, 1865

For almost two years now, Lt. Colonel Tyson Stone had been known as Thomas Jefferson Reid, a lobbyist for the wealthiest bankers in the country, and he was thoroughly sick of the role. Reid was popular enough—he was charming and amusing—but nobody respected him. He was an opportunist, after all, a man who had remained neutral during the war, a fellow with no other aim but to make money.

As Reid, Ty had spent the past week trudging from one reception to another in honor of the victorious troops, keeping his eyes and ears open for possible subversion. The job, a tiresome one, was made slightly more tolerable by the company of his friend Joe Willard, one of the few people in Washington who knew he was a government agent. Joe, along with his brother Henry, owned the hotel where Ty lived, and their cooperation had been extremely helpful. Still, not even the Willards knew the name "Reid" was an alias. In Ty's line of work, one couldn't afford slips of the tongue.

The two men left their final gathering of the night shortly before two, walking home through a steady drizzle. They were standing under the eaves by Joe's front door, talking quietly, when Ty noticed a bright flash of blue in a window across the street, on the top floor of Joe's hotel.

"Did you see that?" he asked with a frown. The light had been extremely odd, a strange violet blue that seemed to shimmer with diamonds. "What in the world—"

"I don't know." Joe stared across the street. "That room should be vacant, T.J. I cleared out a block of three today, for some last-minute guests of General Grant. The occupants offered to double up elsewhere. Most of the party arrived this afternoon, but the family that belongs in the middle was delayed for a day."

A strip of light appeared along the top of the window, above the drapes. Someone was definitely inside. There was a time when Ty might have shrugged and gone to bed, but not now. Six months before, Confederate agents had slipped into New York City and set fires in ten hotels. On April 14, a villain enraged by Appomattox had taken the president's life. And two weeks later, in the waters near Memphis, the steamer *Sultana* had exploded, killing more than a thousand Union soldiers newly released from the pestilent prisons of the South. Some said Rebel spies were to blame.

"We've got hundreds of thousands of troops in this city for the Grand Review," Ty said, "and I wouldn't put it past some Rebel madman to try to blow them all up. I want a look inside that room, Joe."

The two men strode into the hotel, going directly to the front desk. The room, the clerk confirmed, was supposedly empty. None of the keys was missing. Whoever was inside must have stolen his way in, because he hadn't registered.

More concerned than ever, they climbed to the fifth floor. Ty could see a strip of light under the door, but there was no answer to his knock and the door itself was locked. Joe inserted his passkey. The lock released and the doorknob turned, but the door opened only about two inches before stopping, creating a quarter-inch crack down the side.

Ty peered into the room, but all he could make out was the fireplace. It was as if a heavy chest had been pushed against the door to keep it from opening farther, but if a chest had been blocking the way, he wouldn't have been able to see that unbroken strip of light.

Puzzled, he lay down on his belly and peeked under the door. There was some baggage on the floor, a trunk and a carpetbag. He described them to Joe, who insisted that no bellman would have helped take the trunk upstairs without being summoned by the deskman first.

More baffled than ever, Ty slid his fingers under the threshold to see what he could feel. To his amazement, he was stopped by what appeared to be glass. He ran a finger back and forth. The glass was oddly warm and unnaturally slick, not to mention impossibly transparent. A prudent man, he had Joe kneel down to confirm the observation.

Visibly unnerved, Joe pulled away his hand like a man touching fire. "I suppose you should report this to your boss," he said, "but don't ask me to join you."

Ty's superior, at least on paper, was General Lafayette Baker, the head of the National Detective Bureau. He had arrested people right and left during the war, allegedly as spies, deserters, and traitors, and left them in prison indefinitely—including Joe's wife Antonia, who had been a Rebel spy before their marriage.

Ty hesitated before responding. In fact, he worked for Edwin Stanton, not Baker, but only two people here knew that, a colonel in the war department and an old friend of Ty's from California. Still, if he could trust anyone, he could trust Joe Willard. "Tell me something," he said softly. "If you were Secretary Stanton, would you trust General Baker?"

Joe's eyes narrowed. He'd been a Union officer when he had fallen in love with Antonia. Though he had vouched for her future loyalty, Baker still had kept her in the Old Capitol Prison for seven long months, destroying her health. "No. The man is a power-hungry, self-important despot. Only a fool wouldn't watch him—" He cut himself off, his eyes widening with understanding. "Good God," he whispered. "Are you telling me that Stanton is your real superior? That keeping an eye on Baker is part of your job?"

"Exactly. We've got a mystery here, Joe, an unprecedented and frightening one. Stanton wouldn't trust Baker with something this sensitive, and neither do I." He smiled sardonically. At the reception they'd just left, Ellen Stanton had mentioned that her husband would be at his office most of the night, reviewing paperwork. "Unfortunately, if I walk into the War Department alone, I'm as likely to be arrested as permitted upstairs. I would like you to come along."

Joe nodded. To Stanton, neutrality was the same as treason. He detested Reid, or so he had always pretended. "I'll get a pair of my bellmen to guard the door. They'll detain anyone who tries to leave. Besides, if Stanton hears the story from both of us, perhaps he'll even believe it."

Chapter 3

Ty and Joe left the hotel some five minutes later, walking quickly up the Avenue to the War Department. Ty received hostile looks from the soldiers on guard in the lobby, but Joe and the officer in charge had served together in the army. They were directed upstairs as soon as they had stated their business, possible subversion at Joe's hotel.

They found Stanton alone and got to the point at once. The secretary had no patience for small talk. He listened with his usual, impenetrable gaze, showing no reaction to a tale that the men found almost preposterous, now that they were actually telling it.

When they finally finished, he straightened and continued to stare. "Is that all, gentlemen?"

Joe colored. Ty shifted uncomfortably. Both said yes.

The secretary nodded, then delivered a series of crisp orders. "You're to gain access to the room, Colonel Reid. Interrogate the intruder, search his belongings, and detain him if you think it's warranted. I want a report as soon as possible. Send it to my home." He looked at Joe. "Please excuse us, Mr. Willard. Colonel Reid will be out directly."

"Yes, sir." Joe executed a dazed salute, a remnant of his days in the army, and took his leave.

Stanton permitted himself a small smile. "He's badly shaken, Ty, unlike you. Unless I miss my guess, the chief matter on your mind is why I'm having you investigate this incident."

Ty admitted as much. "Given the sort of job it is, my identity as an agent could easily be revealed. Why take the chance, sir?"

"Because you're the best man for the job. You'll do it discreetly and well. I'm pleased you came to me rather than Baker, even though it meant telling Joe the truth about who you work for. In any event, in only a few days, T.J. Reid will die in a drunken fall from a train. Then Tyson Stone can reappear." Stanton leaned forward a little. "I finally have some news about the Beechams."

Ty stiffened a little. The Beechams were old enemies. George had tried to kill him. Ned had assaulted his younger sister. He wanted both brothers dead.

"A landlady in Sacramento recognized Ned from the portrait your sister drew," Stanton continued. "She knew him as 'Sam Potts.' He has red hair and a beard now. He'd left town by the time my agent arrived, but a broker there thought he was going to Colorado. My agent will try to find him. George was with Bedford Forrest at the Battle of Selma and might have been killed during the fighting. General Forrest didn't surrender until May 9, of course. We're checking his records, but they're far from complete."

Ty nodded, hiding his impatience to leave the city and bring the Beechams to justice. "Thank you for investigating the matter, sir. About Reid's imminent demise . . . Does this mean you've decided to approve my request for a discharge?"

"Exactly, Colonel. I understand that you have wrongs to right, and that waiting hasn't been easy for you, but you had a higher duty to answer to and you responded brilliantly. You've sacrificed yourself for over a year now, and I commend you for it, but the troops will be going home in a few days and your presence here will no longer be required. You can leave for New York on the cars and fall to your death as soon as the review is over, but I want you to clear up this matter at Willard's first."

Ty flushed. You didn't expect praise from a man who demanded perfection. "Thank you, sir. For, uh, your generous words and your decision to let me resign. About the intruder at Willard's. . . . I was wondering . . . Are there rumors of a possible attack? Indications of a conspiracy?"

"No more so than usual, but I expected something like this—something bold and unprecedented. Most of the fighting may be over, but there are Rebels who will resist until the day they die. With our two largest armies in the area, it's a logical time to look for vengeance." Stanton fixed him with a steely gaze. "The room in Willard's was reserved for friends of General Grant, people who are allegedly traveling and can't be reached. For all we know, they've been kidnapped or even killed. The intruder may be part of a larger plot. I want him stopped and broken. Nothing can be allowed to disrupt the Grand Review. Johnson isn't Lincoln, and I have little faith in his ability to guide us through any additional turmoil." The secretary leaned back in his chair. "That will be all, Colonel. I'll expect to hear from you within a few hours."

Ty saluted and let himself out of the office. Joe was waiting for him by the stairs. The two men returned to the Willard at a brisk pace, through a light but steady rain. The city was usually quiet at this time of night, but now, with the review only a day away, numerous revelers were still out and about, getting a jump on the celebration.

Joe dismissed the two bellmen standing guard on the fifth floor, while Ty went down to his suite. He returned with a box of tools, dressed in the shirt and trousers of a workman, but a workman didn't normally carry a Colt's revolver and a pair of handcuffs in his pockets. And since Ty's long hair and full beard were well-known in this city, he had taken the precaution of tucking his hair under a broad-brimmed hat, wearing it low on his forehead to hide his face in case anyone wandered by.

The hotel was well enough constructed that little noise could penetrate the thick walls and wooden doors, but the quieter he was, the better. Sawing through the door from the bottom, he decided, would be wiser than whacking out a hole with a hatchet. He slipped a file under the sill about an inch in from the hinges and went to work, switching to a saw when he had the room.

Joe, meanwhile, was squinting around the edge of the door, watching and listening for any movements that might presage an attack from inside. The invisible barrier allowed little clearance, so the sawing was tedious work. Even with the two men spelling each other, it took them over half an hour to reach the top.

The bullet Ty expected never came, but he took out his pistol all the same. Then Joe removed the door and set it against the wall.

There was someone on the bed, Ty saw, curled up like a child, facing the window. He noted the brocade dressing gown, embroidered slippers, and wavy blond hair, and decided the intruder was a female. That was unusual but not unique. Both sides had used their share of female spies.

He put out his hand, feeling for the limits of the barrier, and found that it covered the entire doorway and extended in all directions. Testing its strength, he put his shoulder against its slick, warm surface and pushed hard, but to no avail. Then Joe began to help, but they might as well have pushed at a giant redwood. Finally, telling Joe he had no choice, he swung his hatchet as hard as he could against this wall that he couldn't see.

The hatchet bounced silently off the surface like a blade made of India rubber. The recoil threw Ty backward. He had survived the horrors of battle, the agony of betrayal, and the dangers of a double life, but this barrier was more unsettling than any of them.

"There was no sound," he whispered. "What in the name of God *is* that thing?"

A white-faced Joe simply shook his head. Collecting himself, Ty pressed his nose against the barrier to search for additional intruders. He saw no one, though a conspirator could have been hiding under the bed, but he did spot a small white cube to the left of the doorway. There was a button on top, with a red arrow pointing toward the wall. He lay down flat and extended his arm. Probing at it, he found that it sat on the other side of the barrier.

He stood and looked at Joe. "The invisible barrier . . . I don't know how, but it seems to emanate from that cube. And if it does . . ." He pointed across the room. "There's another cube just like it over there. The window must be blocked the same way the door is."

Faced by things he had never encountered and didn't understand, Ty took the only course open to him and applied logic to the situation. The cube contained a button with an arrow pointing toward a transparent wall. What purpose could the button serve except as an on-and-off switch? The woman had evidently pressed it, which meant it was accessible from inside the room. If he could press it again, it would probably turn the barrier off and end the woman's protection. Then he could find out who she was and what she was up to.

He watched her for a minute, noting the deep, regular pattern of her breathing. She was an exceptionally sound sleeper. His gaze drifted to the fireplace, which was diagonally across from the cube and free of any debris. The chimneys at the Willard were too narrow for a man to climb down, but if he could manufacture a long, hinged stick . . .

He memorized the positions of the fireplace and cube, then eased the door back in place and wedged his hatchet beneath. A few minutes later, in a workroom off the kitchen, he collected the materials he would need to make his tool—nails, cord, wire, and some long strips of wood—and went to work. He left the instrument in three sections, saving the final assembly for the roof, and then returned upstairs.

"I know," he said, as he showed the tool to Joe. "You think it's hopeless, but humor me. It's better than knocking a hole in one of the walls. We wouldn't want everyone within earshot to ask questions."

"Not to mention inconveniencing the people next door." Joe looked resigned. "I suppose you want me to stand guard. Open the door and watch you through the crack. I don't mind telling you, I almost hope that you fail. God knows what will happen if you knock that damned cube on its side. I could reach to turn it off and wind up trapped by something we can't see."

Ty didn't argue the point. "I know. If you do, I'll break through a wall. I'll get you out, Joe, even if I have to terrify our female spy into telling me how to do it."

It was raining more heavily when Ty reached the roof, but the first rays of dawn were glowing through the clouds, providing some light. He hammered some nails into his tool to assemble it, then threaded a cord from the end of the hinged extension through a series of wire loops to the very top. With luck, he would be able to maneuver the extension quite deftly.

He scaled the chimney, now slick with rain, and perched precariously on top. Then, with the extension dangling straight down, he lowered the tool through the opening.

Pulling gently on the cord, he raised the hinged extension. The tool dropped lower into the chimney as the extension angled and slid along the floor. Then it stopped, and Ty realized that the end was caught in the edge of the carpet. He drew the tool upward to free it and lifted the extension higher, above the level of the carpet. Then he rotated it toward the cube and continued.

One story below, Joe was watching in amazement, thinking that Reid's crazy scheme might actually succeed. He couldn't see much more than the fireplace from his vantage point in the hall, but he didn't dare remove the door. Guests had been known to rise at the crack of dawn to visit the bathroom. There was only so much a man could explain.

He caught his breath. Reid's tool was a perfect *L* now. Joe could see it protruding from the fireplace, about two inches above the floor. Reid raised the extension higher, forming a *V*, and dropped it. Joe flinched at the sudden thud—but it was the sound of lumber landing on carpet, and the cube was sitting on the bare wood floor. Reid's angle was off, a few feet short of the cube. The invisible barrier was still there.

If and when it vanished, Joe was supposed to enter the room and push up the tool as a signal. Reid waited for half a minute, then rotated the tool a fraction toward the door. He knew why he'd failed, Joe thought. Once again, he raised the extension up, then abruptly dropped it. And once again, the barrier remained in place.

There was a second pause and a third attempt—and then a fourth and a fifth, the final one wood against wood. Reid tried again and failed, and Joe began to wonder what he was going to tell Grant's friends. With the Grand Review coming up, there wasn't a room to be had in the entire city. And then he heard a new sound—the sound of something skittering across the floor onto the rug—and felt for the barrier, and found that it was gone.

He eased the door open, stepped inside the room, and peered at the cube. It was lying upside down on the rug. He ran his hand over the carpet. It felt like ordinary wool, not glass. The woman in bed, meanwhile, was still sleeping soundly. Shaking slightly, Joe walked to the fireplace and pushed hard on Reid's tool, driving it upward.

Directly above him, Ty felt a flash of triumph, then a rush of relief. The woman downstairs didn't know it, but she was going to talk and talk fast. He had barely slept for the past few nights and was soaked to the skin. His patience was totally exhausted.

He yanked his tool up the chimney and left it on the roof, then trotted down to his suite to pull on something dry. Within minutes, he had joined Joe on the fifth floor.

He peered at the woman in bed. "It's incredible, Joe. She's sleeping like a vampire in the daytime. I've never seen anything like it."

"Maybe she's sick. I got a look at her face. She's too damned thin. I think she has a daughter, by the way. There's a picture on the night table." Joe pointed wearily at the overturned cube. "As for that . . . Either you turned it off or it won't work in that position, so I left it alone. But you were right about what it is. There was the same sort of barrier against the window. I pressed the button on the other cube—it didn't give easily—and the barrier vanished. And her lamp . . . It doesn't spit or hiss. When I shook it, I didn't hear any fuel. I can't figure out what the hell it's burning. If I weren't so tired, I'd be scared to death."

Ty admitted he wasn't any more eager to fiddle with the first cube than Joe was. "Just one thing more, and then I'll get her out of here so you can replace your door. Can you bring me some stationery? I thought I'd check through her baggage, then write up my findings for Stanton."

Joe said he would fetch some paper from his office and left the room. Yawning, Ty walked to the bed and looked at his prisoner. She was stretched out on her side, one leg curled and the other extended. Her nightclothes had ridden partway up her body, revealing a slender ankle and calf—too slender, as Joe had said. Her right hand was tucked under her head, and her left hand was dangling over the edge of the bed near the bedpost. She wore a plain gold band on her ring finger and a cameo choker threaded onto an ivory velvet ribbon around her neck. The girl beside her in the photograph had different coloring, Ty noticed, but there was a definite resemblance. He wondered why the woman didn't travel with a picture of her husband, as well.

He studied her face. Full lips, a small nose, honey-colored lashes and brows, a complexion like fine porcelain, and too little meat on her bones, adding a poignant delicacy to her beauty. Looks like that made him want to protect a woman. In fact, with her sun-streaked honey-blond hair, she reminded him of someone he preferred to forget—Peggy Beecham Moore, another Rebel spy, the woman he had loved and wanted to care for, the woman he had expected to marry.

He pulled a pair of handcuffs out of his pocket. The sleeping woman might look like an angel, but that wouldn't stop her from struggling and spitting when he woke her up. It was only sensible to restrain her first, before she was lucid enough to resist him.

He gingerly snapped a handcuff around her left wrist—the one that was dangling over the edge of the bed. A deft capture of her right wrist, a gentle tug to bring the two together, and it would be over before she could fight him.

He slid his hand under her pillow and found her right

arm. At the same time, he pulled at the handcuff circling her left wrist. Two things registered at the same moment. Her right arm felt exactly like the barrier, unnaturally smooth and strangely warm. And her left wrist didn't move even a fraction.

He touched her face, then cursed softly. It was just like her wrist—warm, smooth, and utterly lifeless. Glass rather than flesh. In other words, there was another damned cube somewhere, protecting her. There had to be.

He looked under the bed, but saw nothing but a chamber pot. He checked the pockets of her dressing gown, but they were empty. He unbuttoned the gown and patted her through her nightdress, but all he felt were the contours of her body. Thin or not, she had lovely breasts, but there was nothing erotic about discovering their shape. He might as well have touched marble. All that mattered was finding the third cube and turning it off—but there *was* no cube. Something else was responsible for the barrier. He wasn't puzzled or afraid now, just aggravated and bone tired. Things like this weren't supposed to exist.

He slid his hands under her body, hoping he could lift her up, but the result was exactly what he had feared. The barrier stopped him cold. He grasped the material of her gown and tried to slide her sideways, but she didn't move. It was a stalemate, then. He couldn't budge her, but he'd been able to get a cuff around her wrist, and her hand wasn't so small or slender that she could slide it off. With any luck . . . He grabbed the open circle of the handcuffs and pulled it toward the bedpost, above the frame and below the headboard. It just reached, gouging the wood slightly as he forced the ends together.

Joe returned as the cuff clicked closed, and Ty explained about the barrier around the woman's body. ''But she can't sleep forever, Joe. Sooner or later she has to wake up, and I'll figure out a way to get her downstairs. Refuse to let her eat until she cooperates, and so on."

"From the look of her, food isn't exactly a priority," Joe said glumly. "I want the room by three, but I doubt I'm going to get it. I've got a door on the way up—an old one, from before the '60 renovation. I can't let a workman see one of my guests chained to the bedpost, so I'd appreciate your helping me install it." He handed Ty some stationery and a pen and ink. "Send the note to my office, and I'll take it over to Stanton for you."

Joe was right about getting the room back. The doors were exchanged within minutes and the new one was painted the proper color by the time the first guests began to stir, but the woman kept sleeping as if she'd been drugged.

Joe went down to nap and Ty began to write, noting what he'd found and done. Then he put the letter aside to search the woman's belongings. The carpetbag held a pair of hand-sewn boots, a light cloak, toilet articles and jewelry, an empty, colorfully decorated revolver, and dozens of twenty-dollar gold coins. Either she'd been paid in advance for her work, or money wasn't one of her motives.

The trunk contained a blanket, a variety of fashionable garments and sundries, a locked metal strongbox, and two letters of introduction. Both were from well-known San Francisco editors, Joe Lawrence of the *Golden Era* and Charles Henry Webb of the *Californian,* and both were addressed to President Lincoln and dated in mid-February.

They introduced the woman as Mrs. Sarah March, a talented writer whose work they had published in their journals. She had come to the capital to do a series of articles on the city and its most notable residents, writing from her perspective as a female, a war widow, and a mother. Lincoln was entreated to grant her an audience. Several clippings were included in the envelope containing the letters, examples of her work for the journals in question.

But Ty subscribed to both those publications, and he didn't remember any Sarah March. He didn't remember the articles she'd supposedly written, either, and he should have, because they were very good, and because female contributors were unusual enough that he took special note of them. It was another mystery.

So was the strongbox. He went downstairs for a picklock and pry, but he couldn't get the damned thing open, either by skill or by brute force. As for the lamp, it ignited without a match and produced the brightest, steadiest flame he had ever seen. There was no fuel in the chamber, only a slender silver bar of some hard, mysterious material.

Ty added the information to his report, then asked Stanton to telegraph San Francisco to have Lawrence and Webb verify their acquaintance with Sarah March. "Until I hear otherwise," he concluded, "I'll assume the letters and clippings are forgeries. Given the devices Mrs. March possesses, I regard her as extremely dangerous. I see no alternative but to wait here until she wakes up. While she's exceptionally well protected, she's also unable to leave, and I'm confident I can induce her to talk."

He sealed the letter in the envelope Joe had provided, then rang for a bellman to take it downstairs. As he closed the door, it occurred to him to try to move the lady by moving the bed, but Mrs. March stayed exactly where she was, giving the impression that she was sliding upward. The barrier was like an invisible shell around her body. Defeated, he returned the bed to its original position.

Reeling with fatigue but too cautious to lie down beside her, he made a bed for himself from a pair of wing chairs and went to sleep. He was jerked awake by the sound of rapping. He looked across the room. Mrs. March was still asleep. A glance at the clock told him it was four in the afternoon. He dragged himself to the door and found Joe outside, dressed in a crisp dark suit, looking rested and alert.

Ty invited him in. "If you're here about the room, it doesn't look good. I'm sorry, Joe."

Joe shrugged and handed him an envelope. "It's only what I expected. I persuaded someone with a sitting room to give it to Grant's friends. Actually, I came to give you this. It's from the secretary." He nodded at the sleeping woman. "If I were her and I woke and saw *you,* I wouldn't be impressed. You look like a bum, T.J. Why don't you take a long, hot bath and put a decent suit on? I'll have a meal brought up and keep an eye on her while you're gone."

Food sounded good. A bath sounded better. Ty gave Joe his pistol and returned to his suite to open Stanton's message. It said precisely what he had expected, that neither Lawrence nor Webb had ever heard of a Sarah March.

His suite contained only a water closet and sink, but there was a tub down the hall in the men's communal bathroom. It was located in a separate chamber behind a set of swinging doors, and was mercifully unoccupied. Ty took his time bathing. After all, the woman could hardly leave.

He dressed in his sternest black suit, the one he used when he was meeting with New York bankers. It wasn't until he looked in the mirror that he remembered the last time he'd worn it, which told him he was even wearier than he felt. April 19. He swallowed hard at the memory. He'd stood in a line with thousands of others that evening, filing slowly into the Capitol rotunda and walking past Lincoln's casket. He blinked back tears, wondering if the day would ever come when he could think of that moment and not want to weep.

And that brought him back to the woman upstairs. No deed he could imagine would ever beget the grief and outrage that Booth's had, but whatever she had come to do, it was obviously something nefarious. He unlocked a polished wooden box, took out a small silver badge—the emblem of the National Detective Bureau—and pinned it inside his coat. She belonged in the Old Capitol Prison, and one way or another, he was going to put her there.

Chapter 4

Ty yawned and rubbed his eyes, then eased himself out of his makeshift bed. When he looked across the room, he saw exactly what he had seen the night before, after he had stripped to his drawers and settled down to sleep. Mrs. March was on her stomach now, evidently oblivious to the manacle around her wrist, but nothing else had changed. She had slept round the clock and more.

He was beginning to think she was spellbound or ill, but if she was, there was nothing he could do to help her. Stretching the stiffness out of his joints, he walked to the window, which was higher than any of the structures to the east and afforded an excellent view of the Avenue. He tied back the drapes, then raised the shade.

It was only a little past seven, but the streets were already lined with people, some holding American flags, others with banners representing a state or regiment they had come to cheer. The city fathers had closed the schools for the two days of the Grand Review, so there were children everywhere, the youngest ones on their fathers' shoulders or in their mothers' arms. Ty smiled at the sight. After all the suffering and death, it was good to see the future again.

He opened the window and took a deep breath. After two days of rain, the sky was a bright, clear blue, and the air was crisp and fresh. The rutted dust storm that was usually Pennsylvania Avenue had settled during the night, creating a fine thoroughfare to march down. It was a splendid day to celebrate a victory. A splendid day to pay tribute to the Union and the men who had saved it.

Ty would have liked to walk among them—to parade proudly down the Avenue with his old regiment. That was impossible, of course, so he had arranged to watch with some of his clients. He would have to send them his regrets, then eat, dress, and compose a second report for Stanton.

The review was scheduled to commence at nine o'clock. The troops would start from the west steps of the Capitol, parade a mile and a half down the Avenue, and disband after passing the reviewing stand in front of the White House, where the president and other dignitaries would be sitting. If he had to be trapped somewhere, he supposed, the fifth floor of Willard's was as good a place as any.

Sarah awoke to the sound of music—a band playing "The Battle Hymn of the Republic" somewhere in the distance. People were singing along, and in her current muddled state, half-awake and half-asleep, it all made perfect sense. She was in the Willard Hotel in 1865. Julia Ward Howe had written those words in this very place in 1861, so why *wouldn't* people nearby be singing them?

She joined in, her eyes still closed, her body still heavy with sleep. ". . . where the grapes of wrath are stored. He has loosed the fateful lightning of his terrible swift sword. His truth is marching on!"

Humming the chorus, she yawned and stretched. But when she tried to straighten her left arm, something stopped her. She opened her eyes to see what it was—and came fully awake. She was handcuffed to the bedpost. Her heart jumped, and she frantically looked around. A well-dressed man, by outward appearances a gentleman of the period, was standing with his back to the window, staring straight at her.

Her first reaction was astonishment. In the world she came from, people didn't enter each other's bedrooms without permission, especially men and women. It was no different in 1865. And how had he gotten in here, anyway? Had she made a mistake in the haze of her postjump confusion? Forgotten to set the cubes? Set them incorrectly?

Fear quickly followed. Fine broadcloth suit or not, he couldn't possibly be a gentleman. Gentlemen didn't chain women to bedposts. He was a criminal, then. A thief or a rapist or worse. It took her another couple of seconds to calm down and remember that he couldn't harm her. The metal of the handcuffs wasn't biting into her wrist, which meant that the field was in the way. She had activated it before she fell asleep, and exactly for this reason—to protect her from the unexpected.

She struggled to sit, winding up with her left arm crossed awkwardly in front of her body. She could see the two cubes now, one in the middle of the carpet, the other below the open window. Neither, obviously, was working.

"Who are you?" Her voice was unsteady. "What are you doing here?"

The man took a few steps forward. "I was about to ask you the same questions, Mrs. March. You aren't a registered guest in this hotel. You broke in two nights ago. Who are you, where do you come from, and why are you here?"

Two nights ago? She had slept for more than twenty-four hours? She looked at the clock on the bureau. It was five past ten. Almost thirty-two hours, to be exact.

None of the other tempronauts had been out for that long.

She grimaced. Then again, none of the other tempronauts had been slowly dying. Her debilitated state must have resulted in an even longer sleep than they'd anticipated. But she didn't feel debilitated this morning. She felt—normal. And very hungry. Maybe the extra sleep was responsible for her appetite, but it was probably the jump.

The tests she was supposed to run would have to confirm it, but still, a shock of hope and excitement tore through her. All she could think about was telling Shelby the news. She called out her daughter's name, silently but with fierce emotion, praying and pleading for a reply. Emptiness came back. The tie was still severed. She ached at the loss.

Then her long hours of training took over and she realized she was responding blindly, speaking before she thought and acting before she analyzed. She was in a horrible mess here. Some local had broken into her room and immobilized her. He knew the name she was using, which meant he had searched her belongings. There was no way he could have opened her strongbox, but what he *had* seen and felt was damning enough. He must have touched her skin and encountered glass. He might have fiddled with her cubes and created a mystery. If he had tried to move her, she would have seemed infinitely heavy. Naturally he wanted answers.

The Project's trainers had devised a number of options for a situation like this, but the truth wasn't among them. She was here to change the past, but only by executing the single specific act analyzed by the computers and approved by the president. She couldn't talk about what she was without introducing a dangerous wild card into the equation. Her presence might provoke a decline into superstition and a new round of witch trials, or a spurt of scientific advancement in a society not yet ready for it. Something she said or did might change the future for the worse.

Her first option was to explain the seemingly impossible in terms of the technology of the period using technical double-talk. Unfortunately, the man in front of her didn't look like he was inclined to believe her. He was standing with his legs slightly apart and his arms across his chest, waiting for her answer, giving her a stare that would have frozen a hot spring.

He seemed familiar, somehow, with that long tawny hair and the full beard that covered almost everything but his cold blue eyes, but she couldn't place him. Since she had studied photographs of all the figures she was likely to encounter, she assumed he was somebody peripheral, a minor personage who had appeared as part of a large group.

But minor or not, he appeared suspicious, determined, and intelligent. Judging by his dress, he was also affluent and educated. Hardly your typical felon, she thought. Scientific mumbo jumbo went only so far with a man like that.

She quickly decided on her second option, to attack. "My name is Sarah March and I come from California. But you already know that, since you've violated my privacy and searched through my belongings for no legitimate reason whatsoever."

She was about to add that she had important friends who wouldn't take kindly to her being abused when a great cheer roared through the open window and startled her into silence. For a moment, the historian in her took over. The patriotic music, the clopping of horses' hooves, the blaring trumpets, the wild cheering . . . There was evidently a great parade going on outside, but nothing of the sort had taken place on April 5. The only such event of the period had occurred on May 23 and 24, the Grand Review of the Union Army.

She felt the blood drain from her face, but if her first reaction was horrified shock, her second was disbelief. It was impossible. The timing had never gone wrong before, not even by a minute. The physics of time travel didn't permit it. The math and the settings had been checked repeatedly. No mistake could have been made. It had to be April 5.

But in the street below her, a band was playing "Tramp, Tramp, Tramp! The Boys Are Marching," and a great assembly was singing along. Then a great cry rose up, sweeping up and down the Avenue like a wildfire. "Custer! Custer! Custer!"

She paled even more. Everyone who had read about the Grand Review knew the story—how the twenty-five-year-old general, the youngest in the army, had thrilled the crowd with his dashing appearance and his dazzling riding; how an admirer had flung a huge wreath of flowers over his horse's neck, causing it to rear and bolt away; how the crowd had repeatedly roared his name after he had controlled the animal and returned to the head of his division.

Her gaze swung to the man by the window. "That's Custer they're cheering. General George Armstrong Custer. The Army of the Potomac is parading down the Avenue."

He watched her impassively. "Yes. As I told you, you slept for over twenty-four hours. It's Tuesday morning."

Then the impossible was true. It was May 23, not April 5. She was overwhelmed by grief. From the moment President Young had approved this mission, in Sarah's heart and mind and soul, Lincoln had been alive again. He was the kindest, wisest, strongest leader the country had ever known, and she admired him to the point of veneration.

He had died 231 years ago—or thirty-nine days ago, to the people of this time and place—but to Sarah, the loss was as fresh as if it had happened the moment before. She had failed to save him.

Weeping was out of the question. The field allowed gases like oxygen and water vapor to pass back and forth, but not bodily fluids, which could accumulate inside and result in drowning. But even knowing that her tears would cause the field to automatically shut down, putting her in danger, she couldn't stop them from falling. She moaned softly, an anguished, ''Oh, God,'' then turned her face into her pillow and sobbed.

Watching her, Ty's first impulse was to jerk her around and shake her. He didn't know which was greater, his fury or his repugnance. It was one thing to spy for one's country, even when one's country was the so-called C.S.A., and another to hate the Union so profoundly that you wept uncontrollably at the very symbol of its preservation, the Grand Army of the Republic. Only one thing kept him immobile—he knew it was pointless to try to touch her.

Only with great difficulty was he able to curb his emotions and do his job—to analyze and strategize. From the moment the woman had awoken, her reactions had been puzzling and contradictory. She had begun by humming a Union anthem and ended by weeping bitterly at the thought of a Union victory. In between, she had appeared to be confused and disoriented, acting by turns surprised and fearful, exultant and devastated, and horrified and grief-stricken.

She had appeared, in short, to be mentally unbalanced. That wasn't a bad tack to take when you were in a spot as tight as she was—it had worked like a charm on him, causing him to abandon his planned attack in favor of further study. So maybe she wasn't unbalanced at all, simply an accomplished actor. Spies invariably were.

And when those same spies were females, they were often uncommonly lovely. Sarah March might have been far too thin, but it didn't diminish her beauty. Fully awake, she was the picture of fragile innocence, and that, too, had sidetracked him. As it had no doubt been meant to.

He decided to continue as he'd begun, at least for a short while longer. You didn't march into battle without a plan, and you couldn't develop a plan until you assessed your enemy. Besides, if he allowed her sufficient opportunity to reveal herself, she might trip over her own lies.

He walked to her bedside. "Why are you crying? Is the parade painful to you for some reason?"

Sarah heard him as if from a distance. His voice wasn't icy now, merely devoid of emotion. She rubbed her eyes and tried to pull herself together. Lincoln had died, but he had always died. She had arrived too late to save him, and perhaps she would always arrive too late. Her mission might have been lost from the very beginning, made futile by the nature of the universe. Scientists knew a great deal about such matters, but they didn't know everything.

It was a comforting thought. She sniffed and dried her eyes, then reactivated her shield. Grief was a luxury she couldn't afford. Emotion was a deadly enemy. She was trapped by a man who wanted answers she couldn't give him. If she ever wanted to see her daughter again, she had to allay his suspicions and secure her freedom. Then she could think about getting home. Her comrades would try to retrieve her on April 12, but it was over a month beyond that date. She had to put a message in the *National Intelligencer* telling them where she was.

She finally turned around. One of the first lessons she'd learned was that the most convincing lies were woven from strands of the truth. "It wasn't the parade. It was President Lincoln. He should have been here, celebrating what no other man could have accomplished, the preservation of the Union. But he's not, and it tore at my heart."

The man's expression softened a fraction, then went blank again. Still, it was progress. "Do you remember what General Sherman said about Lincoln?" she asked quietly. "It was in late March, after he and Grant conferred with the president aboard his steamer. He said, 'Of all the men I ever met, he seemed to me to possess more of the elements of greatness, combined with goodness, than any other.' "

"Yes. Everyone knows that quote. What about it?"

"Just that I believe Sherman was right, and that history will bear him out. I was a great admirer of Abraham Lincoln. I was thrilled at the thought of meeting him. I know it's been over a month, but I still can't accept the fact that he's been taken away from us."

Ty looked into the woman's clear green eyes and saw the same pain and anguish that had faced him so often in his own mirror, but he knew better than to trust them. It was an old spy's trick, one he had used himself. You gained your adversary's sympathy by pretending to share his opinions.

"Even if that's so," he said, "it doesn't explain your presence here. This room doesn't belong to you. You aren't registered at this hotel. How did you get inside?"

She looked bewildered. "Of course I'm registered. I arrived late at night and the desk clerk gave me this room." She shook her head incredulously, as if his suspicions were astonishing. "Good heavens, how else would I have known it was free? Do you think I knocked on doors half the night? With the review about to take place, this was probably the only empty room in the entire hotel."

She was right. It had been—but not because Stanton's theory about a conspiracy was correct, at least not insofar as it pertained to the possible detention of Grant's friends. They had arrived the previous afternoon and were staying in a sitting room on the second floor.

"That's very interesting, but Mr. Willard's desk clerk doesn't remember checking you in, and there's no record of a Sarah March on the register." There was also a full key box, Ty recalled. "Obviously you were given a room key. I would like to see it."

"I suppose I was, but I honestly don't recall." She glanced around, frowning slightly. "I'm sure it's around here somewhere, but I have no idea where. I was exhausted that night. I recall that a bellman took my carpetbag and walked me upstairs, then unlocked the door for me. He said he would go back for my trunk, and then he left. That's the last thing I remember until just now, when I woke up."

"So you fell asleep before the bellman returned."

"Apparently so. Perhaps he forgot to leave me a key." She gestured with her free hand. "Anyway, look at the size of my trunk. Do you honestly believe I could carry it up myself? I assume you're some sort of hotel policeman, so why don't you stop questioning me as if I'm a dangerous criminal and do your job? Talk to the other desk clerks. Talk to the bellmen. I'm sure someone will remember me."

"We have." Or Joe had. He had interviewed everyone on the staff. "Nobody recalls you."

She looked more baffled than ever and claimed she couldn't understand it. Her story was so rife with inconsistencies that Ty decided to tear it apart. Cutting the legs out from under her would soften her up.

"You're dressed for bed, Mrs. March, but I don't see the gown you arrived in. And where were your nightclothes? Your carpetbag was full to the brim when I opened it, but you didn't have your trunk until the bellman brought it up. If you were asleep by then, how did you manage to change?"

She nibbled her bottom lip, then gave him a guileless

smile. The effect was something like being punched in the solar plexus by an angel. "Perhaps it was somnambulism, Mr. . . . Uh, what did you say your name was?"

"I didn't. It's Reid." Reid would disappear as soon as the woman was safely jailed, so there was no harm in using the name he was accustomed to. "If you're a sleepwalker, Mrs. March, you're an exceptionally tidy one. The contents of your trunk were in perfect order."

Sarah gaped at him. *Reid?* As in T.J. Reid, the lobbyist? What would a glib hireling who had never cared about anything but his own wallet be doing in her room? But it had to be. She had never seen his photograph, but she had read descriptions of him. Just as Custer had been famous for his flowing golden curls, Reid had been known for his long tawny hair and bushy beard. And like the man in front of her, he had been tall, handsome, and physically imposing.

Astonished, she murmured, "I, uh, yes, Mr. Reid. You're right. About my being tidy, that is. A place for everything and everything in its place, that's what I always say."

She was babbling. She couldn't help it. She was a historian first and foremost, and she was looking at a living enigma. She couldn't blithely ignore it. "If you don't mind my asking, what on earth are you doing in my room? Shouldn't you be out flattering bureaucrats and bribing congressmen on behalf of avaricious New York bankers?"

His lips twitched. "Not today or tomorrow. They're watching the parade. Tell me, how did you know who I was?" He held up his hand before she could answer. "Wait a minute. Let me guess. Crack journalists such as yourself make it their business to know about men like me."

The dry irony in his tone was becoming dismayingly familiar. It surfaced whenever he had set a trap and was about to snap it shut. "Why, Mr. Reid, modesty is a quality I hadn't previously associated with you. One doesn't have to be a crack journalist to have heard of you. I'm only a simple essayist, yet I've seen your name in the newspapers many times."

"The California newspapers. That's where you're from, isn't that what you said?"

He was setting another trap. Insofar as she recalled, he'd seldom been mentioned in the California press. "No, the Eastern papers. I realize we're somewhat provincial in my state, to take so little notice of any politics beyond our own, but we're not totally uncivilized. Our libraries subscribe to any number of publications."

"As do your friends Mr. Lawrence and Mr. Webb."

The irony was even stronger now. "It's possible," Sarah said warily. "They've published my work, but I can't honestly claim them as friends. Getting back to your presence here, Mr. Reid—"

"We wired Lawrence and Webb." *Snap!* "Neither of them has ever heard of you. Despite those very impressive clippings you carry, neither of them has ever published your work. Would you care to explain that?"

Everything fell into place. Reid was a government agent. As incredible as it seemed, it was the only explanation for his presence. Her own presence, or her very arrival, must have triggered someone's suspicions. He would have gone to the authorities, who had ordered Reid to investigate. And he was making a damned good job of it, too.

The historian in Sarah was fascinated, but the tempronaut knew better than to question him. Her first priority was to weasel out of his trap. You had only one real option when you were faced by irrefutable proof that you had lied: to cut your losses and admit it, and audacity worked better than remorse.

She gave him a sly smile and did some fast improvising. "All right. You've caught me. The clippings are from a weekly in Sacramento and the letters are forgeries. I'm a shameless fraud, but I wanted to meet President Lincoln and I hoped they would help."

"So you said. In fact, your admiration for the late president was so boundless that you traveled all the way to Washington to talk to him. How, Mrs. March? By steamer?"

She knew what he was getting at. The transcontinental railroad hadn't opened until 1869. In 1865, a traveler would likely have taken the steamer to Panama, crossed the isthmus by rail, caught a second steamer to New York, and taken the train down to Washington. All in all, it was a journey of about a month.

That was a long time, but not long enough. Sarah's letters were dated in mid-February in anticipation of an arrival on April 4, but Lincoln had been shot on April 14, and it was now May 23. The timing was all wrong.

"You're wondering why I bothered to come," she murmured. "With President Lincoln already dead, that is."

He shifted his weight. "The thought did enter my mind."

She racked her brains for a convincing explanation. "I was planning to depart in February, but my daughter—she suddenly took ill." She glanced at the night table. "That's Shelby in the photograph. I miss her al—, uh, terribly." Sarah's eyes misted over, but not enough to affect the field. "Anyway, I stayed home to nurse her, and it was early April before I could leave. Grant was still outside Richmond then, and Lincoln was still alive. I took sick in Panama and was forced to remain there for several weeks—"

"Why? Wouldn't it have made more sense to go directly to New York City, where competent doctors were available?"

Inspiration struck. "Perhaps, but I couldn't keep any food down." She smiled weakly. "Well, barely any. You can see how thin I am. Everyone knows how rough the Atlantic can be. Seasickness would have made me even weaker.''

''And besides, Panama is so healthful this time of year. And it has such fine hotels.''

''It was healthier than a packed steamer, and I was invited to stay with an English businessman and his wife. She cared for me until I was well enough to travel.''

''By which time you must have known about Lincoln's death. Tell me, Mrs. March, if you were so heartbroken—if you missed your daughter so much—why didn't you return to San Francisco? You could have waited until school was out and taken her along. Used the extra time to fatten yourself up, not to mention coming to terms with your excruciating grief.''

Sarah squared her shoulders. Reid was a human interrogation program, and a damned sarcastic one at that. She was hungry and clammy and in dire need of a bathroom, and if he didn't back off soon, she was either going to faint from lack of food or soak the blasted bed.

''Because I'm a writer,'' she snapped, ''and because I have a daughter to support and no husband to help me. My creditors don't care a whit about my health, Mr. Reid. Their only concern is their money. There are—''

''So pay them, Mrs. March. Those gold coins in your carpetbag are worth thousands—or did they steal their way into your baggage without your knowledge while you were ill or asleep or busy concocting outrageous lies?''

''I'm not lying to you,'' Sarah said irritably, ''and the gold doesn't belong to me.'' *Damned coins,* she thought, and scrambled for a plausible party to consign them to. ''It, uh, it was donated by the people of Sacramento for the treatment of our wounded soldiers. I agreed to bring it to Washington City and convey it to the proper authorities.''

"So you're a courier, too. I'm impressed." Reid would have looked amused if he hadn't been so bitterly skeptical. "That no doubt explains the extraordinary precautions you've taken to protect yourself. Where do the devices come from? How do they work?"

"Scotland, and I really don't know. I'm a writer, not a scientist. The fact is, there are a great many interesting stories in this city, and I want to write them and sell them. I intend to make a name for myself as a journalist. I'm a loyal Californian, not a Rebel spy or a deranged assassin. And now, if you're finished hounding and attacking me, I would like to bathe and dress and order myself—"

"I'm not even close to finished." Reid walked to the head of the bed and touched her face. Though the field was in the way, she flinched convulsively. "You have boxes that produce invisible walls. A lamp with no fuel that produces the steadiest light I've ever seen. A strongbox I couldn't open, and I can open just about anything. And a barrier around your body that prevents me from touching you and makes your skin feel like glass." He bent over her, a hard look in his eyes. "You want to bathe, Sarah? You want to eat? Then stop stalling and tell me how that bloody barrier around you works—and then turn it off."

Sarah stared at him, feeling intimidated, resentful, and physically uncomfortable. T.J. Reid was a paranoid bully. A sarcastic snake. An agent more than worthy of the man he so obviously worked for, Lafayette C. Baker.

She was frustrated enough to burst into tears and angry enough to flatten him, something she surely could have done if she hadn't been chained to the bed. She might have been skinny, but what was left of her was pure muscle. She had been trained to fight and fight well.

And then she remembered something else about T.J.

Reid. On May 24, after the Grand Review had concluded, he had taken the train to New York on business. He and his friends had begun drinking, apparently much too heavily. Walking between cars, he had stumbled and fallen, pitching headlong into the Delaware River.

She was looking, in short, at a dead man.

Chapter 5

November 1, 2096

Something had gone drastically wrong. The Wells staff knew it within hours, when a shooting in South Central Los Angeles triggered what the Global News Network labeled "the third serious riot in a week"—but there hadn't *been* any riots in the week before Sarah's jump. Ten days of research confirmed the Wellsians' worst fears. Something Sarah had said or done had changed history, almost disastrously so.

Again and again during that time, Shelby tried to contact her mother to find out where she was and what had gone wrong, but nothing except silence came back. Shelby's loneliness was excruciating, her sense of failure, devastating. After three days, she stopped going to school. She couldn't bear to be surrounded by people with no memory of any past but the one that had come into being after Sarah's jump. That was the way the changes always affected people, though not even her father had understood why. Only the individuals in the chamber, the ones who had witnessed a jump, remembered both versions of the past.

Since jumping took a heavy toll on the body, a decision was made to intercept Sarah as soon after her arrival as they safely could—hopefully before she had affected the past. The giant generators were recalibrated and recharged in twelve days, a Project record. Now, on the morning of November 1, Shelby was sitting in the control room, waiting for the field to pop into existence. She reached out hard with her mind, determined to contact Sarah the moment she returned to the present.

The tone began to sound. Shelby ticked off the seconds in her mind, then looked for the sparkling blue flash that would accompany her mother's return.

It never came. The pod remained empty. A technician called out a reading from her instruments. The energy from 1865 was still in the chamber. The exchange had failed to take place. Sarah was lost in the past.

May 23, 1865

In the twenty-nine years of Ty's life, nobody had ever looked at him the way Sarah March just had. He had seen horror equally intense in the eyes of his comrades and pity even more profound, but never both at the same time. He was a monster, the look said, but she still felt grievously sorry for him. It was damned unsettling to be stared at that way, especially by a woman he was holding prisoner.

He wanted to ask her what she was thinking, but didn't. He had finally established some authority over her, and the question would have been an admission of weakness. Besides, his job was to break her, not to understand her.

He leaned closer, looming over her, and she pressed herself deeper into her pillow. Her eyes dropped, but not before he saw distaste and fear take over her face.

He touched the collar of her dressing gown to get her attention and felt a stab of guilt when she recoiled.

He didn't mind inspiring fear in a suspect, but not *that* kind of fear. It was despicable.

"Let's be sure we understand each other," he said evenly. "It's true that I can't touch you or move you, but I hold all the other aces in this game. Unlike you, I can eat when I'm hungry and drink when I'm thirsty. I can visit the bathroom or take a stroll to stretch my legs. If I get restless, I can watch the parade or read the papers. You, on the other hand, can do none of those things unless I permit you to. And I won't permit you to until you stop telling me lies about how you got here and why you came, and until you explain how the devices you brought with you work."

She didn't answer, but her body grew taut with resentment. He decided it was time to ease up, to exchange the stick for the carrot. It was an old ploy, one that Baker had polished to perfection and used time and again on suspects in the Old Capitol, usually with great success.

"Let's take this one step at a time, Sarah." His tone was gentle, almost amiable. "Answer one of my questions and you'll earn one of the privileges I've denied you. Surely that's not unreasonable."

She slowly raised her eyes. "They aren't privileges. They're basic human rights. You're a barbarian, Mr. Reid."

He gave her his most charming smile. "I promise you, cooperating with me will gain you far more than insulting me. Why don't we start with something simple? Tell me how you got into this room, and I'll give you the chamber pot and allow you to use it in private."

The suggestion met with reproachful silence. Nettled, Ty was about to inform her that persecuting a female was hardly his favorite assignment when she lifted her hand and began to awkwardly unbutton his coat. It was the damnedest thing he had ever experienced, like being touched by a creature made of metal. Still, she was a beautiful woman, and he had a weakness for green eyes and hair the color of sunflowers. It didn't matter that he couldn't feel her flesh. He could see her face. He could remember the shape of her body. His manhood stirred.

His exasperation gave way to amusement. Women were all the same. They had more weapons at their disposal than the army, and if the first and second didn't get them what they wanted, they tried a third and even a fourth. He wasn't about to be swayed, but he had to admit that her latest plan of battle was more pleasant than any of the others.

He also had to admit that when he didn't feel like tearing out his hair at her intransigence, he found her uncommonly captivating. She had intelligence, spirit, and a sly quick wit, and even if she was stubborn, the women he liked best were all the same way. Maybe she'd even been honest about her feelings for Lincoln and the Union, although the odds were greatly against it. If her purpose here had been harmless, she wouldn't have been so evasive.

She reached the final button of his coat. She wasn't glaring at him now, just concentrating on undressing him. "I'll be happy to let you seduce me," he drawled, "but it's only fair to warn you that making love to me won't change my mind. I'll still keep asking you questions, and if you don't answer them to my satisfaction, I'll still keep you chained to the bed. You'll give up long before I do, Sarah."

Ignoring him, she pulled back a side of his coat, gazed at it for a moment, and dropped it. Then she turned back the second lapel and fingered the small silver badge that was pinned there. "Just as I thought. You're one of Lafayette Baker's men." She released his coat. "I don't much care for your leader. He's a pompous tyrant who sees traitors under every rock and bush, and his jail is an intolerable pesthole. As bad as *you* are, he makes you look like Clara Barton.''

Ty smiled at the gibe. ''Then you were looking for my badge? You weren't trying to seduce me into letting you go?''

She reddened. ''Hardly, Mr. Reid. I'm not—I wouldn't debase myself that way.''

''You wouldn't? What a pity. About the badge . . . Very few people have ever seen one. How did you recognize it?''

From a museum, Sarah thought. ''I read a description once. I don't remember where.''

He stood. ''You don't remember because none has ever been published. No photographs have ever been made. I'd lay odds you have friends who have been our guests in the Old Capitol—that one of them saw a badge like this one and described it to you.''

Sarah hesitated. Reid would label her a liar if she denied it and a traitor if she agreed. ''Now that I think about it, it was one of your fellow detectives. It had slipped my mind. I'm still very tired.''

''The only place you could have met one of my colleagues was in your dreams, Mrs. March. You've been sleeping since the night you arrived—or did that slip your mind, as well?''

It was several seconds before she could think of a plausible response. ''Not at all. It happened in New York City.'' She racked her brains for the right hotel. ''I was staying at—at the Astor House, right next door to Baker's New York office. The detective was trying to impress me. He wanted to take me to dinner.'' She gave a disapproving sniff. ''Married, too. I saw him with his wife. You and your cohorts aren't only barbarians; you're philanderers, too.''

Reid smiled and shook his head. ''You're quick with a likely story, I'll give you that. They spout out of you like water from a geyser. In fact, if you ever told me the truth, I think I would faint from sheer astonishment.''

Sarah was surprised he had stopped pressing her. ''If that's the way you feel, you should let me go,'' she said. ''Think of all the frustration you would spare yourself.''

''Believe me, nothing would please me more than to walk out of this room and never return, but I was ordered to investigate you, and I mean to do it.'' He reached under the bed and pulled out a large covered vessel. ''Here. I'll be back in a little while.'' He walked to the door and turned around. ''By the way, you were right about Baker's jail. It *is* a death trap. Obviously I can't take you there, but if you continue to evade my questions, I'll have to treat you in a way that's almost as bad, and I think neither of us would enjoy that very much. So if you're as intelligent as you seem to be, you'll give me some answers when I return.''

He left the room, closing the door behind him. Sarah waited a few seconds to make sure he wouldn't come back, then gave in to what was by now an urgent need and used the chamber pot. She slid it under the bed afterward, then examined the handcuff around her wrist. It was locked tight and wouldn't open.

She sighed. Her carpetbag was in the middle of the room, far beyond her reach, so there was no way to get at her pistol. She didn't want to cause Reid any pain, of course, only to put him to sleep. Then she could search him for the key to the handcuffs.

Trying the only other approach she could think of, she began gouging at the bedpost with the metal of the encircling cuff. The wood was very hard, evidently mahogany. She cursed under her breath. At the rate she was going, it would take hours to gain her freedom. There was little chance of escaping before Reid reappeared, but she had to try.

After fifteen minutes of largely fruitless carving, it

struck her that she had disturbingly mixed feelings about her imprisonment—and about the man who was holding her captive. Reid wasn't without charm, no matter how calculating that charm was, and his sense of humor, so well-known to students of the period, could be very engaging. He also possessed a high degree of intelligence and direct knowledge of dozens of important figures. The historian in her would have loved to pick his brain.

As for the woman in her, she was alternately fascinated and repelled. She couldn't fault him for wanting answers; he had a duty to perform. And when he smiled in a certain way, it was easy to forget that his friendliness was a mere technique, the good cop and the bad cop rolled into the same clever agent. But like Baker, Reid was fundamentally appalling, a man who ignored human rights and rode roughshod over the Constitution in order to enforce his personal notion of the law. He had threatened her and he had meant it. If her shield hadn't protected her, there was no telling what misery he would have inflicted to force her to talk.

In the end, though, it wasn't the historian or the woman who decided how to proceed, but the tempronaut. Sarah's duty came first, even before her life, and it prevented her from talking about her mission. She had an unbreakable set of rules to follow, and they would determine her final fate.

But just as surely, those rules would determine the fate of T.J. Reid. They compelled her to lie and hedge, a tactic that would keep him at the Willard, asking her questions. They required her to escape as soon as she could, to minimize any harm she might do, but if she succeeded, Reid's ego—and his duty—would drive him to track her and try to recapture her. In either case, he was unlikely to leave here tomorrow on the train, as history had originally recorded.

So Sarah was confronted by a paradox. Any action

she took short of telling Reid the truth would affect history in ways she couldn't predict, but confiding in him was out of the question. In other words, although he would never know it, she was about to save his life.

It was a huge responsibility—to change the past that way. The thought of it left her shaken, desperately hoping that her arrival was part of some grander plan. If Lincoln had been meant to die, maybe Reid had been meant to live. Maybe that was why she had jumped to this time and place. But whether it was or it wasn't, she could only follow the Project's protocols while history played itself out and pray that nothing she said or did would cause irreparable damage.

Reid returned some twenty minutes later carrying a burlap sack and a tray containing a porcelain pitcher and a huge breakfast. Sarah had gouged a shallow channel in the mahogany by then, a meager accomplishment considering all the energy she had expended. Reid looked pointedly at the bedpost and arched an eyebrow. She flushed, then raised her chin and gave him a defiant stare.

He set the tray on the bureau and dropped his sack on the floor. "And to think I'd decided to try to make friends with you. To attempt to win your cooperation. I was going to let you wash. Give you something to eat. Shackle your ankle instead of your wrist to give you greater freedom. But now . . ." He sighed heavily. "I can't reward rebellion, Sarah. I'm afraid that I'll have to punish you."

Although he sounded more rueful than angry, a shiver of fear snaked down Sarah's spine. In almost every way that mattered, he could do as he pleased with her. "But that's not fair," she said quickly. "You knew I would try to escape. If you planned to punish me for it, you should have warned me in advance."

He gave a pensive nod. "Hmm. An interesting viewpoint, Mrs. March. I wasn't aware that the rules of good sportsmanship extended to spies and traitors—''

''I'm neither of those things.''

''But if you say that they do, I'll think the matter over.'' He hesitated, then reached into his sack and took out a long length of chain. Shackles were attached to both ends. ''Very well, then. Stretch out your right leg and hike up your nightclothes. I'll lock this around your ankle and free your wrist. If you want any further concessions, you might try cooperating for a change.''

She extended her leg, grateful but also wary. The closer Reid came, the more uncomfortable she always grew. He glanced at her bare foot, then pushed her dressing gown a bit higher. She flinched, thinking about how vulnerable she was. She was naked under her nightclothes, and if Reid decided to remove them, not even her shield would be able to stop him.

Ty noticed her reaction at once, but then, it was hard *not* to notice when someone cringed and went stiff as a board. Sarah might as well have shouted it out the window—that she found him repugnant, that she feared he would molest her or even rape her if he got the chance. He'd done nothing to deserve such a reaction, and it bothered him more than he wanted to admit.

He snapped on the fetter, then yanked down her dressing gown and gave her an irked look. He was too damned attracted to her, that was the problem. True, his kindness was only a tactic, but he'd found that he liked being kind to Sarah March—and that was a dangerous weakness. The last suspect to affect him that way had been Peggy, and the affair had ended in disaster.

Sarah was looking blankly at the far wall, visibly afraid of him, obviously wishing he would move away. Nettled, he said flatly, ''I don't use that. Not ever. Relentless interrogation, yes, and also physical deprivation, but I don't look where I shouldn't look or touch what I shouldn't touch, and I've certainly never raped a woman. Do you understand that, Mrs. March?''

There was no mistaking the quiet vehemence in Reid's voice, and while Sarah was relieved by that, she was also very puzzled. Why would a man who worked for Baker and used the same odious tactics as his boss be so passionate about acts that all too often were barely considered crimes in this century?

She flushed and nodded. ''Yes. You, uh, you seem to have strong feelings on the subject, and I wondered—''

''Damned strong,'' he interrupted, ''and that's all I care to say about the matter. As for your escape attempt . . . I'll let it pass this time, but consider yourself warned. Unless you have a taste for stale crackers and foul water, don't try it again. Do you understand *that?*''

Sarah glanced at the tray, drawn by the aroma of bacon and biscuits. There were also pancakes, oysters, fried eggs, and pastries. Her mouth watered and her stomach rumbled. Her appetite had returned with a vengeance. The Willard was famous for its fine food.

She looked at Reid, who was standing beside the bed, holding the free end of the chain. His expression was stern but not harsh. Much to her relief, the way he talked and behaved indicated that he had little taste for brutality, at least in regard to her. He seemed to harbor a soft spot for her, or maybe he was gentler than she'd supposed. Either way, she'd been trained what to do with an opening like that.

Some of the tension left her body, but not all of it. The tempronaut had a confidence the woman lacked. ''I do, T.J., but I have to be honest. I'll still try to escape. It's only human nature to want one's freedom, you know. Just look at how the Negroes in the army distinguished themselves during the war.'' She managed a small smile. ''The smell of that breakfast is driving me mad. I'm absolutely starving. I know that I've caused you a vast amount of trouble, but if I promise to behave myself for the next twenty minutes, do you think you could forgive me and let me eat? Please?''

Ty walked to the bedpost, snapping the manacle in place with slightly more force than was necessary. Between Sarah's winsome smile and her dulcet voice, his groin had tightened and started to throb. His desire for her wasn't amusing anymore, just frustrating and very irritating. He'd never had to work to control himself with a woman and he didn't care to start. He didn't need that sort of distraction.

He reached into his boot and took out a key. ''Hold up your wrist, Sarah. And save the honey for your biscuits. You don't want me—the thought appalls you—so don't coo at me. Don't simper like a simple-minded schoolgirl. Both of us know that you're anything but.'' He unlocked the manacle around her wrist and let the handcuffs dangle from the bedpost, then tucked the key back in his boot. It would open the shackle around her ankle, too.

She scrambled off the bed and scurried to the window, but not before he saw the embarrassment on her face. Mollified, he set the pitcher of water on the bureau and carried the tray to the table. He called her name so gruffly that she jumped, turning and crossly demanding whether it was really necessary for him to bark at her that way. The complaint was accompanied by a glare of impressive authority, but she was also trembling slightly, and it ruined her fine display of outrage.

''I apologize,'' he said easily. ''You seem to have a talent for getting under my skin. Now come sit down and eat your breakfast before it gets cold.''

She walked to the table and sat stiffly in the wing chair nearest the bed, which was about a yard short of the farthest reach of her chain. He leaned against the bureau while she buttered a biscuit and wolfed it down.

"Do you have to stare?" she grumbled. "Don't you have anything better to do?"

Now that she mentioned it, he did. "Maybe. The way I see it, I've been extremely generous to you—"

"Minimally decent," Sarah said, thinking that she would have liked to recite the Geneva Conventions to the man.

"—but you haven't reciprocated," he continued without a missed beat. "It's time that you did."

She popped a fried oyster into her mouth. "God, these are good. Reciprocate how?"

"Maybe you haven't noticed, but one of your cubes is sitting in the middle of the floor, upside down. Could it still be operating? And if it is, what would happen if I picked it up? Would I be thrown away from it before I could press the button? Or trapped by an invisible wall?"

So she *had* turned on the cube. She wondered how he had gained access to it, but decided it was only prudent to assist him before she questioned him. It was a harmless bit of help.

She devoured another few oysters. "Don't pick it up, T.J. Every side but the bottom has to be at least two inches from any sizable surface or the cube won't work, so just slide your finger beneath it and touch the button. If it feels warm, the cube is on. To turn it off, press the button firmly." She sliced into her pancakes. "I'd offer to do it for you, but I doubt you would trust me not to turn it on again and trap you behind the barrier it would create."

He muttered that he probably shouldn't trust her instructions about the blasted cube in the first place, but crossed to it all the same, then hunkered down and gingerly slipped a finger beneath it. After turning it off, he regarded it as warily as a rattlesnake. Sarah attacked her eggs as he picked the cube up and set it flush against the baseboard. He pressed the button and felt the wall, then drew the cube back a few inches and pressed the button again, rapping on the now present barrier, mumbling something about the eerie silence. Finally, satisfied she had told him the truth, he switched the cube off and placed it beyond her reach, on the mantel above the fireplace, next to a Colt's revolver she assumed he owned.

He folded his arms across his chest. "Tell me what it is, Sarah. I want to know how it works."

Nothing but an understanding of quantum mechanics could have accomplished *that,* and the fundamentals were sixty years in the future. "It was invented by a Scotsman named James Clerk Maxwell." She gave him a lengthy spiel about Maxwell's work. "And then, last year, he showed that electricity and magnetism are different aspects of the same phenomenon. The cube contains magnets that act upon each other and generate what he calls an electromagnetic field."

Reid looked dubious. "I'm a friend of Dr. Joseph Henry, the Secretary of the Smithsonian Institution. He has a special interest in electricity and magnets, so we've discussed the subject often. And he's never mentioned anything like your field."

It was just her luck, Sarah thought, that Reid would be friends with a man who was destined to become a world-class physicist. "Henry is a fine scientist, but Maxwell is a genius," she said with a shrug. "His research is miles beyond anyone else's, so his colleagues have dismissed it as nonsense." She paused. "Think of the power of lightning, T.J. The pull of the earth's poles. Maxwell has harnessed them and used them to create his fields."

"He has, has he? And how did these unique gadgets of his happen to land in the hands of an obscure essayist?"

"They were given to me by Scottish friends of America to demonstrate to certain individuals here in

Washington. I'm not at liberty to tell you anything further.''

''Naturally not. I suppose I should be terrified of holding you here, given the powerful connections you seem to have.'' His expression said he hadn't believed a word she'd spoken. ''The material the cubes are made of . . . I've never felt anything like it. It's amazingly hard and smooth.''

''It's called plastic,'' Sarah said.

''Plastic,'' he repeated. ''Why haven't I heard of it?''

Because it wouldn't be invented until the twentieth century. ''Because it's very new, T.J. One of Maxwell's colleagues came up with it.''

''Ah. Another Scots genius, no doubt. And it's made of . . . ?''

''I don't know. Something they melt and pour into molds, like metal.''

Ty walked to the window, picked up the second cube, and set it on the mantel with its twin. Nothing Sarah had told him bore the slightest resemblance to anything in the journals he had read or the experiments he had witnessed. And it wasn't only the science in her story that flew in the face of logic; everything else did, too.

He continued to ask questions, grilling her about the cubes, the lamp, the barrier around her body, and how she had materialized here in the first place, and received glib answers that were delayed only by the fact that she kept scooping food into her mouth. She not only looked like she hadn't had a decent meal in a month; she ate the same way.

His patience ran out about the same time as her breakfast did. He sank into a wing chair and gave her an exasperated look. ''Enough, Sarah. I'm tired of listening to fairy tales. Your story doesn't hang together. The science you describe is preposterous. But you know what your biggest shortcoming is? You answer too fast. I know when I'm hearing someone who's been rehearsed, and you, my dear, have been rehearsed to a fare-thee-well. That's typical of spies."

Sarah set down her fork. Maybe a real tempronaut would have done better, but Reid was a damned sight tougher than any of the natives the others had faced. "If I sound rehearsed, it's because I'm speaking the truth. I don't have to think about what to say." She stretched languidly. "That was a wonderful breakfast, T.J. Thank you for bringing it up. Would you mind handing me my carpetbag? It's out of my reach, and I would like to wash my face and brush my teeth."

Ty pulled himself out of his chair. Not only did the woman's lies exasperate him; her intransigence damned near exhausted him. "Of course. After all, only a barbarian would refuse you. But as soon as you're finished, we're going to start all over, and we're not stopping until I have some answers. Honest answers."

He crossed to the carpetbag and picked it up, then stopped in his tracks. Sarah possessed a whole array of devices that weren't what they appeared to be, and there was a revolver in this bag. He set the bag down and fished out the gun. Sarah never moved, but a flicker of frustration crossed her face, and it was all he needed to see.

He sighed and shook his head. "Here we go again. Your gun is empty, but there's no ammunition in your baggage. So what does it fire, Sarah? Invisible bullets?"

So much for that little gambit, Sarah thought irritably. She should have realized Reid would check the chambers. God only knew what setting the gun was on. "It was fully loaded when I left San Francisco," she said, "but I ran into some trouble along the way."

"No doubt. It's a dangerous world. A skirmish here, an ambush there, and the next thing you know, you're completely out of bullets." He twirled the weapon, and Sarah winced. "If it's empty," he said, "why are you so nervous?"

"I'm not," she answered. "You should be more careful with guns, that's all."

Ty walked to the window and stuck his arm outside, pointing the revolver in the direction of the Avenue. He finally had her. It felt damned good.

He looked through the sights, pretending to aim the weapon, but before he could pull the trigger, she crumbled. "For God's sake, T.J., don't fire it. People could get badly hurt."

"Another obscure electromagnetic phenomenon, Sarah? Poisonous rays, perhaps?"

"It's not funny. I want you to turn the gun off. You see the colored designs on the cylinder? Line up the white one with the design on the right side of the barrel."

Ty did so, then set the revolver on the mantel. "I would have fired it straight up, by the way. So how does it work? What does it do?"

Sarah could have kicked herself for being so gullible, but even if she had suspected Reid was acting, she couldn't have taken a chance on being wrong. Having no choice, she gave him the response she'd rehearsed—that the gun fired harnessed lightning, and that depending on the setting, it could inflict anything from paralysis to excruciating pain.

He rolled his eyes at the lightning story, but instead of scolding her or asking more questions, he fetched her a bowl and some water, her soap and a towel, and her toothbrush and powder. Then, seemingly drawn by something down on the Avenue, he strolled to the window and stared outside.

In point of fact, however, the only thing on Ty's mind was what an idiot he was. It was possible that Sarah could penetrate the barrier around her at will and eat without turning it off, but the opposite was also possible. And like a dolt, he had never even thought to investigate.

Now she was washing her face, and the situation was likely the same. She might be causing the soap and water to pass through the barrier to her skin, but perhaps she'd been obliged to turn the barrier off. And if she had . . . What would happen if he touched her flesh? Would she be able to turn the barrier back on? Would it repulse him the way the invisible wall had repulsed his hatchet? Or would the barrier become useless to her?

He meant to find out.

Chapter 6

George Beecham was standing on the sidewalk at Pennsylvania Avenue near Twelfth Street, surrounded by a mob of screeching, gloating Yankees, watching the Grand Review with an ache in his gut and murder in his eyes. This smug and strutting army had sacked, torched, and slaughtered its way up the entire length of his beloved Shenandoah Valley. He had returned to his family farm near the village of Front Royal to find dead cattle, a burnt-out barn, charred fields, and a plundered house. The Garden of Eden had been turned into a facsimile of hell.

They called it total war. You didn't only kill the enemy's men; you destroyed his food, his railroads, and his cities, too. Still, the farm endured. George had resigned himself to picking up the threads of his former life. His brother Ned had sent him money with which to replant the fields. Rebuild the barn. Refurnish the house. Return the farm to life.

But people . . . People were something else. His sister Peggy had been the image of their late father and the light of their mother's life, and she was gone forever now. When George prayed at the family's church and visited Peggy's grave, he was consumed by hatred for the man who had killed her. And then he thought about the bastard's choice of a weapon, not a knife or a gun but his thrusting male member, and he grew even more enraged.

His mind drifted back to that awful January day when he and Ned had last visited Front Royal, summoned by a telegram from their mother to their encampment in Mississippi. They had found Peggy lying on her death-bed, bleeding helplessly. She was delirious from drugs and pain, but she had told them what they'd needed to know. Her abuser was a man she'd been ordered to spy on, a lobbyist and Yankee sympathizer named Thomas Jefferson Reid. He had raped her repeatedly, then trapped her into revealing herself as a Confederate patriot.

George had proposed an eye for an eye after Peggy's death, but Ned had balked, saying murder could get them hanged. They knew from Peggy that Reid had a relation in Ohio, a student at Oberlin College named Susannah Stone. Peggy had sneaked a look at her letters and deduced she was a half sister. Ned had suggested that Reid should be taught how it felt to have a loved one abused, and that the weapon he had used on Peggy should be severed from his body so it would never debase a female again.

And somehow, though Ned was the younger one, he had won. He always did. He didn't even have to argue very much. He just looked at you in a certain way, and you always gave in. Ned had gone to Ohio to see to Reid's sister, while George had stolen into Washington City to deal with Reid.

Neither attack had succeeded. Ned had been thwarted just short of success when the girl's moans of pleasure had turned to cries of protest, attracting the attention of some passing boys. He had escaped into the woods, then fled to California. As for George, he'd been snoop-ing around Willard's, asking questions about Reid, when someone had reported him to the authorities. They had thrown him into the Old Capitol, then learned he was a Confederate officer. He'd been released in one of the last prisoner exchanges and sneaked back to his regiment. With the war going so badly, he had expected to die in battle, his sister unavenged.

But fate had provided him with a second opportunity. He had been wounded in the leg, suffering a permanent limp, but he had survived. A year and a half ago he had failed, and it had eaten at him ever since. He wasn't going to fail again. He knew from the Washington papers that Reid was still at the Willard, still pimping for Yankee bankers. And now, with Ned almost a continent away, there was no one to stop him from taking vengeance.

It was only fitting, he decided, that a pig like Reid should die the way pigs lived, wallowing in the local filth. So he intended to hunt Reid down and slash him to within inches of his life, then douse him with miasmic muck from the Washington Canal. With any luck, he would survive the attack for days and suffer immensely before he died—exactly as Peggy had.

Sarah dried her face and sneaked a look at Reid. He appeared to be absorbed in the Grand Review. Deciding it was safe to brush her teeth, she poured some water into a glass and sprinkled powder onto her brush. The product was somewhat gritty, but the taste was a pleasant mint.

If you were rich enough, she reflected, 1865 wasn't a bad year to live in. Transportation and communications had been improving rapidly, so it was the little things she would have missed most, like jeans and wrap skirts, Coke and jicama chips, and modern hygiene products. Some cleverly disguised specimens of the latter were even packed inside her trunk, including a roll of dental floss in the form of a spool of sewing thread.

The gritty texture of the tooth powder made her long to request it, but that would have evoked a host of questions from Reid about what it was and where it was from.

She was almost finished brushing when, out of the corner of her eye, she noticed him move. Her reaction—to yank her toothbrush out of her mouth and jab at her cameo—was fast, but Reid was faster. Her lips were too wet for the shield to go on, and by the time she'd jerked a towel across them, it was too late. He had already struck.

He clapped a hand around her neck under her hair and pressed his fingers against the pulse point at the right side of her throat. His closeness alarmed her, but it didn't repel her. His touch was firm but gentle, and while she didn't like his politics, she had to admit there was nothing wrong with his looks. Quite the opposite, actually.

Her own hands were on top of the bureau by then, tensely gripping the edge. He covered the left one with his palm, no doubt because she had claimed that her wedding ring was the source of her shield. "Your heart is racing," he said. "What are you so nervous about? The fact that you can't turn your barrier back on if I'm touching you?"

She rinsed her mouth and straightened. "You said that you didn't molest women. That you didn't put your hands where they weren't invited. Kindly remove them, Mr. Reid."

"I'm not molesting you. I'm trying to prevent you from turning the barrier back on. You know that as well as I do." He ran his thumb casually back and forth along the ribbon at the back of her neck, and she flushed and stiffened. "Hmm. There's a chain beneath the velvet, but no visible clasp. It's in front, I suppose. Tell me, Sarah, if the barrier emanates from your ring, why did you press your cameo?"

The only way to escape Reid's grasp, Sarah thought, was to lure him off guard and attack. But he was stronger than she was and nobody's fool, so only one method of distraction occurred to her, sex, and she had tried that already and failed. Of course, her body was sending him a different message now. His touch had been exploratory, not sexual, but her reaction was female to the core. And as much as that appalled her, she also recognized that it might convince him her feelings had changed.

She told herself to go slowly for once, to employ a little guile and finesse. "You win, T.J. The shield does emanate from my cameo. I could activate it if I wanted to, even with you touching me, but I'd rather not. There would be"—she hesitated—"extremely intimate consequences."

"How fascinating." He pressed the cameo, but nothing happened. "Hmm. I didn't think so. But it was a nice try."

"It was the truth. It's just—I'm the only one who can operate it. It's programmed—I mean set—to respond to my fingerprint. The, uh, the Scots have discovered that each person's is different." She grimaced, thinking that she had lied to him so often that if she wanted him to believe her, she would have to show him how the cameo worked. She pressed it. "There. It's on. Take a step backward, but don't tighten your grip around my neck. You could hurt me."

He did as he was told—and took her along with him. She didn't resist, but even if she had, his size and strength would have decided the matter. The men in the world she came from wouldn't have used that sort of advantage to control a woman, either sexually or in any other way, but Reid obviously would, and without a qualm. As a rich white male of this era, he had been born at the top and assumed he belonged there. He'd done as he pleased as her jailer and would do the same in bed.

Of course, confidence could breed generosity as well as arrogance in a man, and for just a moment, she wondered which sort of lover he would be. Then, unnerved by the direction of her thoughts, she stabbed the cameo to switch the field back off. "You see? If someone is touching me when I turn it on, it locks us together. They say . . ." She reddened. "Supposedly, it's, uh, it's a property with some interesting—erotic ramifications."

It was true. Bound to Reid this way, Sarah felt a surge of sexual excitement stronger than any she'd ever experienced. Such raw physical attraction was nothing but biochemistry, of course, but that didn't make the sensation any less unsettling. For all her mixed feelings about Reid, her hormones weren't the least bit confused.

Neither were Ty's. The spice and lilac scent of Sarah's soap and the silky feel of her skin had made him hot and tumid from the first moment he'd touched her, and picturing the two of them naked and fused together, moving in a slow, sinuous rhythm, didn't help. He forced the image from his mind. Sarah didn't desire him. She couldn't have been any more uneasy if he had been Frankenstein's monster.

"Your opinion of me is obvious," he said, "so if you're trying to tempt me into forgetting why I'm here, you're wasting your breath. It won't work."

But Sarah wasn't so sure. She could feel the tension in Reid's body and hear the tightness in his voice. He was more vulnerable than he wanted to admit.

She lowered her voice to a purr. "You know something, T.J.? You talk a good game, but you're nicer than you pretend. You wouldn't have brought me breakfast if you weren't, or worried about my comfort. I don't much care for your questions and threats, or for the way you constantly bark, but I suppose that your duty comes first, and that I can't blame you for doing it.'' She paused, then added in a teasing tone, ''Besides, you're awfully pretty to look at—not that I'm the type to swoon at a man's feet, but if we'd met under other circumstances, I'm sure I would have liked you.''

He shifted his weight and said coldly, ''But as matters stand now, you *don't* like me. And unless you start telling me the truth, I'm going to have to do things that will make you like me even less.''

He pulled her left arm behind her back so that it was perilously close to a hammerlock, and whatever attraction she'd felt vanished abruptly. He wasn't hurting her, but the warning was all too clear, and it turned the breakfast she'd so recently enjoyed into lead inside her stomach.

She took a deep breath to steady her nerves and started to unbutton her robe. It was made of brocade, and unlike her nightgown, heavy and constricting. She wouldn't be able to attack him unless she had greater freedom of movement.

He stopped her after the first two buttons, stepping forward to trap her between his body and the bureau. She could feel his erection pressing against her buttocks, but she knew this wasn't about sex. The anger was all but steaming out of him.

She tried to wiggle away from his groin, but his hand tightened on her neck to keep her where she was. ''I said it won't work, Sarah. It annoys the hell out of me when you play at seduction, and believe me, you don't want me annoyed. So don't try to entice me with provocative comments, don't take off your clothing and flaunt your body at me, and don't squirm against me like a trollop. If I wanted a whore, I would buy one down the street.''

Her temper got the better of her. ''I wasn't squirming against you. I was trying to move into—into a less objectionable position. And I wasn't undressing for you, either.'' He was still too close. She gave a quick jerk backward, which only made him hold her tighter and press her harder against the bureau. She blanched at the intimate contact. If it hadn't been for the clothing between them . . . ''You're frightening me, all right? You're bigger and stronger than me, so it's obvious you can take what you want, and believe me, I can feel what you want. You can claim—''

Ty had heard enough. ''I'm not an animal, dammit.'' The woman had been married, for God's sake. She knew that a male couldn't control that particular reaction. ''What I want and what I take are two different things. How many times do I have to tell you that?''

''Right. You don't use rape as a threat. You only push your—your so-called manhood—against a half-naked woman and then claim that sex has nothing to do with it. And you have the gall to accuse me of provoking you!'' Sarah swallowed hard. ''I was hot and dizzy, so I was loosening my dressing gown. And that's *all* I was doing.''

But it wasn't all she was feeling. She was also intensely aware of Reid's sheer male power, from the muscles in his thighs to the heat in his groin to the calluses on his large, strong hands. Something inside her responded—her hormones again. But she was also intimidated, nervous, and confused—and furious with herself for not being braver.

She began to tremble. ''For God's sake, stop pressing against me that way. I'm about to faint or lose my breakfast or both.''

''Then tell me what I want to know.'' But he eased his grip and took a step backward. ''Why are you here? Who are you working for?''

She didn't reply, just finished unbuttoning her robe, and Reid erupted like a raging volcano. ''Bloody hell, Sarah, this isn't a blasted game! We're still under martial law in this city. If you object to the way I've treated you, that's too damned bad. You can call me a barbarian and accuse me of threatening you with rape, but both of us know that's nonsense. The fact is, I've controlled myself better than most men would. No judge here would quarrel with a single thing I've done.''

Given the time and the place, he was right, but her emotions were running so high that she could barely think, much less plan her next move. She took a slow, deep breath. She had to stay calm and focused.

''All right,'' she said. ''I'll talk to you. I'll even answer your questions. But let me turn around first. It's—it's dehumanizing, to have you standing behind me that way. It makes me feel like a slave—or a draft horse.''

''Or a prisoner, which is precisely what you are. Nonetheless . . .'' He slid his hand from her neck to her shoulder and carefully turned her around, maintaining a firm hold on her wrist as he eased it to her side. There was less contact once they were face-to-face, but the position was far more revealing. He could read what was in her eyes. He could see the contours of her body through the fine white silk of her nightgown.

He released her shoulder. ''I'm listening, Sarah.''

''I'm not what you think.'' She forced herself to meet his gaze. Maybe, just maybe, he would listen to reason, and this whole awful nightmare would end. ''I'm loyal to the Union. Nobody loves this country more than I do. I was sent to Washington on a mission. I had a duty to perform, just as you do, and that's all I can really say. I never wanted to cause any alarm here. Believe me, I was only trying to make things better, but I failed. All I want is to go home now—to my daughter and my friends and—and my state.'' And my time, she thought forlornly, and put a beseeching hand on his shoulder. ''Couldn't you just let me go?

Everything would be fine if you did. I swear that it would.''

It was such a pretty speech, and such a seemingly heartfelt one, that Ty almost believed it. But it was also irrelevant to the matter at hand. ''My orders come from the very top,'' he said quietly. ''I couldn't release you even if I wanted to. I would be thrown into the Old Capitol Prison, where I would be treated a lot less gently than you would ever be.''

He knew he should stop right there, but the pleading look in Sarah's eyes and the urgent way she was clutching his coat swayed him into wanting to help her. ''All right,'' he said with a sigh. ''I suppose I can do this much. If you tell me who sent you—their names, addresses, and positions—I'll wire them to check your story. If they're known to be loyal and trustworthy, and if they confirm what you've told me, I'll request permission to let you go.''

Sarah relaxed her grip on Reid's shoulder. She hadn't expected such a generous offer, not really, but there was a fundamental decency in the man that seemed to smack her between the eyes whenever his barbaric behavior had convinced her he was nothing but a thug. If the woman in her feared him and the tempronaut was scheming to escape, the historian felt a growing fascination. ''The very top'' could only mean Edwin Stanton, but by all accounts, Stanton had despised T.J. Reid. To learn that it had been a charade—that the lobbyist had actually been working for the war secretary—was incredible. A prize piece of scholarship.

Unfortunately, it also meant that Reid was as trapped as she was. He couldn't disobey a direct order from Stanton. And that put her back where she'd begun, trying to distract him into dropping his guard.

She was only too aware of her previous ineptness at the task, but still, she gave it another try. ''I can't give you names.'' She looked at him bleakly. ''If I could, I would have done it a long time ago. Couldn't you just trust me? Let me escape and tell your superiors that I slipped away?''

He shook his head. ''You know the answer to that as well as I do, Sarah.''

She lowered her eyes and said wretchedly, ''Then I don't know what to do or say. I've told you as much as I can, but I'm not a fool, T.J. I know you mean Stanton when you say 'the very top,' and I also know what a hard man he is. If he ordered you to break me, you'll have to break me—or at least you'll have to try. So what's to become of me?'' She shuddered. ''Am I to be starved? Or beaten? Or worse?''

Her terror wasn't entirely an act. Stanton wouldn't be patient forever, and if Reid lacked the stomach to make her talk, Stanton would have Baker do the job. She wouldn't be able to withstand the general's methods, and the truth would land her the Old Capitol or even the local insane asylum. If she couldn't get her shield back on, she could be stuck here forever.

She thought about Shelby, about the possibility of never seeing her again, and her eyes filled with tears. A small part of her was admiring her performance from a distance, thinking that crying was the perfect ploy, but most of her was overcome by anguish and dread. How had things gone so wrong? Lincoln was dead, Shelby was unreachable, and home was an eternity away. She knew what her next move should be—to act the distraught female and throw herself into Reid's arms, then strike while he was busy soothing her—but she couldn't do it. She wanted to be alone, to sob out her heart in private for a mission, and perhaps a life, in ruins.

Ty watched her for as long as he could bear it, then gave up. She was crying silently, the tears rolling slowly down her face, and he couldn't stop himself from wanting to comfort her. He told himself it was the big brother in him responding, wanting to offer solace to someone smaller and weaker, and then he attributed it to the veteran detective, who hoped that kindness would encourage her to talk. But deep down, he knew it was a man reacting to a woman he desired, and that providing solace and kindness was only a fraction of what he wanted to do. He also wanted to undress her and caress her all over. To kiss her with deep, hard passion. To haul her to his bed and make love to her until she melted beneath him and surrendered unconditionally.

At the moment, though, she was still his adversary, and her surrender was nowhere in sight. He moved warily, aware that desire could make a man careless, guarding against a possible attack as he took her in his arms. She resisted at first, holding herself stiffly away from him, but he persisted, keeping a firm hold on her to prevent her from engaging the barrier as he slowly drew her closer. In the end, she yielded very agreeably, putting her arms around his waist and sobbing against his chest while he massaged her nape and murmured words of comfort.

When her sobs had diminished to sporadic sniffles, he eased her away, holding her wrist with one hand and cupping her chin with the other. She avoided his eyes, focusing on his neck instead. Between her flushed cheeks and her grim expression, it was obvious she was appalled with herself.

"I don't want to see you hurt," he said, "but I can't help you unless you confide in me." He stroked her cheek. "Do that, sweetheart, and I'll protect you as much as I can. You have my word on it."

Sarah barely heard him. She was too busy cursing her own incompetence. No decent tempronaut would have fallen apart that way, but if she was mortified by her failure and ashamed of her tears, she was also more determined then ever to set things right. She took a step forward and met Reid's eyes. She felt the same alarming mixture of excitement, shock, and fear as she always did, but she ignored it for once. If she couldn't get past her crippling inhibitions, she would never get home.

She gave him a watery smile. "You know something, T.J.? You can be very sweet. You can't imagine how tempted I am to put myself in your hands, but I simply can't."

"Of course you can." He toyed with a lock of her hair, winding it around his fingers and brushing it against her cheek. "It's your only real choice, Sarah. I'm the only friend you have here."

"Is that what you are? My friend?" She turned her head and kissed his fingers, then snuggled against his chest and nuzzled his neck. "Can I really believe that?"

Her heart was beating wildly now, but from terror, not excitement. She was afraid she would bungle her last chance at escape and she was afraid of T.J. Reid. He was big and strong and dangerous, and if she failed, he would make her pay. She wanted this finished as soon as possible.

She put her arm around his waist and clung to him. He stiffened and sucked in his breath. He was heavily aroused now—breathing unevenly, perspiring slightly, fully erect. She trailed her mouth to his lips and awkwardly stroked them, preparing herself for the kiss that would surely follow—to accept it, to let him deepen it, to make him lose control of it. But it never happened.

Instead, still holding her right wrist, he stepped away from her and cupped her breast. The warmth of his hand seemed to burn through her sheer silk nightgown, making her anxious and a little queasy. She froze and looked at the floor, then felt his palm brushing her flesh, moving lightly back and forth over her nipple. Arousal entered the mix. He fondled and massaged her, toying with her nipple until it was erect and throbbing. She could feel the heat of her own excitement between her legs, but there was no pleasure in the sensation. Her body seemed to welcome his touch, but her mind fiercely rejected it.

"Sarah."

The firmness in his voice made her head snap up. His expression matched his tone. It wasn't harsh, only stern. He was caressing her other nipple now, stroking and rubbing it to full arousal, but his eyes remained fixed on her face.

Between his touch and his gaze, she had to force herself not to look away. His fingers made her hot all over, but his eyes chilled her to the bone. "Yes, T.J.?"

"You don't seem to be enjoying this. Do you want me to stop?"

Of course she did. She'd never expected this—to enjoy what should have repulsed her. It was tearing her in two. "No. It's just—it's so impersonal. The way you're touching me. The way you're watching me. I don't know what to think." She realized it was true.

He unbuttoned her nightgown from her neck to below her breasts. "Think that I'm damned wary. Think that I've lost count of the accusations you've hurled at my head, so when you suddenly start kissing me, I wonder why." A slow smile spread over his face. "And think that I'm telling myself that the only safe way to make love to you is probably to cuff your hands behind your back."

Given his smile, Sarah doubted he was serious. She knew what she should do next. Look at him coyly, offer him her wrists, invite him to go ahead—and then clobber him. But if it didn't work and he got the handcuffs on . . . She would be helpless, unable to attack him or shield herself. He would be able to touch her at will with that same cold skill, and God only knew how she would respond.

She abruptly shook her head, shaken by the pictures in her mind. "No. I don't want you to do that. But what could I really do to you? You're twice my size."

"I have no idea. You tell me." He fingered the cameo around her neck, then turned it over and fiddled with the clasp. But the only way to unlock it was to squeeze the chain beneath the ribbon in a predetermined sequence too complicated to discover by chance. "It's a shame I'm not a Scots genius, because if I were, I might be able to figure this out. But since I can't . . . I don't suppose you would be willing to take it off?"

"I would," Sarah said, "but I don't know how it works."

Ty had anticipated a refusal, but not a whopper so outrageous he almost laughed out loud. Smiling more broadly than ever, he said, "Of course you do, Sarah."

She didn't reply. Ty knew he should protect his hide and walk away, but her nipples were thrusting erotically against her nightdress, and whenever he touched her, she got an expression on her face that was halfway between heaven and hell. Unless he missed his guess, she was totally confused, physically drawn to him but furious with him for holding her captive. With a little patience on his part, she would stop fearing him, forget about fighting him, and start to enjoy him.

"I suppose you have a point about my physical superiority," he said, "and you *are* chained to the bed, so I'm probably safe." He hesitated, fighting a battle with his conscience that his conscience won. "I trust you remember the ground rules, Sarah. No matter how much I enjoy making love to you—and I expect I'll enjoy it very much—I can't let you go."

Her chin went up. "Who said I still wanted you to?"

"You mean you don't? I'm pleased that you've changed your mind." But she hadn't, he knew. She believed she would win him over in time, but she was wrong. "One more thing. In case you've got another gadget up your sleeve—'' He slid his hand under her nightdress, directly over her bare breast. She flinched but didn't withdraw, and he gently kneaded her flesh. ''—I aim to get you so hot and mindless, you'll forget to use it.'' He took her nipple between his thumb and forefinger and massaged it. ''That's a promise, sweetheart.''

In the world Sarah came from, a line like that would have had her rolling her eyes and asking incredulously if it had ever actually worked. But Reid was simply teasing her. His smile was a mile wide, his eyes were sparkling with warmth, and his fingers . . . His fingers were so seductive that her throat got tight, her palms began to burn, and the room started to tilt and spin.

He began by caressing her nipple in the same way as before, lightly and provocatively. But then his fingers grew rougher, offering an erotic little squeeze before gentling again, and she gasped. Visibly pleased, he kept repeating the sequence, and every time he did, a bolt of intense physical pleasure slashed through her. She was stunned by the sensations he was arousing, especially since they were entirely new to her. John's real wife and mistress had been physics. He had never done anything remotely like this.

She shivered and closed her eyes, and a flash of fear penetrated the fog of pleasure. She could feel her resistance draining away, and she knew just how dangerous that could be. But before she could tell Reid to stop, she felt his mouth on her bottom lip, nipping and sucking it, and all she could manage was a hoarse, ''Dear God, T.J., the things that you're doing . . .''

He stroked her lips with his tongue, and she parted them and hesitantly tasted him back. ''I'm glad you approve.'' His hand moved lower, making slow circles on her belly through the silk of her nightgown while he toyed with her lips. ''Lord, but you're sweet. But so shy and skittish . . . I'm not going too fast for you, am I, love?"

"No." John had gone too fast. Reid was perfection.

"Good. I don't want to frighten you." He kept caressing her, planting tender kisses around her mouth as his fingers crept slowly lower.

In a sensual daze, she moved against his hand and nuzzled him back, breathing hard, swamped by a dark, moist heat. She knew where his hand was headed and didn't care. She wanted his tongue in her mouth and wasn't ashamed. Who he was and what he had done didn't seem to matter.

A stranger. A cop. Her jailer. Her enemy. The words came crashing out of nowhere, exploding into her mind like thunderbolts. He was keeping her from Shelby. Playing the same game she was, only better. She was a fool. Foolish and easy and inept. Why had they sent her? She was botching the whole mission.

The magnitude of her blunders sent ice through her heart and drove her into a blind panic. What happened next was pure instinct, a product of months of training. Her knee shot up and slammed into Reid's testicles. At almost the same moment, she drew her hand up to her shoulder and swung her elbow against his face, driving it violently against his jaw. As he released her and staggered backward, she struck him again, hitting his knee with such a powerful smash of her foot that she knocked him to the floor. He wound up on his side, clutching his crotch and rubbing his jaw, retching and coughing, his eyes glazed with pain.

For a second or two, she was paralyzed by horror. She'd never actually hurt anyone before. But she quickly came to her senses and stabbed her cameo to turn on her shield.

She dropped to the floor. Reid's key was in his boot. She needed to get it before he recovered. But she was crouched on her haunches, and she couldn't reach him from that position. He was too far away, and the chain around her ankle stopped her from crawling closer. So she threw herself forward and stretched out on her stomach, and she was able to grab his boot.

But before she could get it off—before she could reach inside it—he yanked away his foot. He was shaking now, and panting when he wasn't coughing, but he managed to drag himself backward, only stopping when he was well beyond her reach.

She stood up, then slowly backed away. It was a long time before he finally looked at her, and when he did, she had to resist the impulse to cower. The expression on his face said he was coldly furious with her. Shielded or not, she was in worse trouble than ever.

Chapter 7

If Ty had ever doubted that Sarah March was a dangerous spy, he no longer did. He was a good fighter—he had learned the art from an expert, his friend Alex McClure—but Sarah had whipped him as if he were a rank amateur, and a weak one at that. If anyone had told him that a woman her size could pack the wallop of a bear, he wouldn't have believed it.

She had studied with a master, obviously, someone who had turned soft female flesh into sinew and muscle, then taught her exactly how to move and precisely where to hit. Ty couldn't imagine why anyone would train a woman in such skills, but one thing was abundantly clear to him. There could be no more leniency, no more indulgence.

As for touching her again, he wasn't going anywhere near her, not without a compelling reason. Aroused or not, he had never stopped anticipating a possible attack, and look what had happened. She had struck with such blinding speed that he'd never felt it coming, rendering him helpless with the first thrust of her knee. He winced at the state of his private parts. The creature had damned near unmanned him.

He examined his tender jaw, decided that nothing

was broken, and slowly sat up. His expression was stony. She had played him for a fool and beaten him almost senseless, and he hadn't cared for either experience.

She was standing by the window now, regarding him warily. If his mood had been less grim, he would have laughed at the absurdity of it. If anyone should be wary, it was he. With her barrier back on, he couldn't lay a finger on her, but the reverse was almost surely not the case.

He pulled himself to his feet, but felt so wobbly and nauseated that he had to grasp the mantel to steady himself. "Let's start at the beginning, Mrs. March. Who are you? Why did you come here?"

She hesitated, then replied, "I've told you who I am. I've told you why I came." Her expression grew earnest. "Look, T.J., I'm sorry I had to hurt you. You probably won't believe this, but I felt sick afterward, looking at what I'd done. I do like you, at least most of the time I do. And before, when we were—" She blushed and shook her head. "Never mind about that. The point is, I was only doing the same thing you would in my position and trying to escape. There's no moral high ground here. Both of us were working toward our own ends, you to seduce me into talking, and me to distract you into dropping your guard."

And she had won. Ty resisted the urge to cup his throbbing crotch, thinking irritably that if she had been any more effective, seduction was a pleasure he could never have enjoyed again. "No. There's a difference. I'm a patriot. You're a spy, and a skillful one at that—a glib liar, a superb actress, and an expert fighter. Who trained you? Who sent you?"

Her mouth tightened. "For God's sake, T.J., this is pointless. I've told you repeatedly, I can't answer those questions. Why waste your time and effort going over and over the same territory when there's only one way it can end?—in a stalemate.''

''I'm in no particular hurry to get anywhere. Are you?'' Feeling steadier now, he folded his arms across his chest. ''And it won't end in a stalemate. If I have to call in a partner, I will. We'll deny you even minimal privacy. We won't let you sleep, and the little food we allow you will be extremely unpalatable. As the hours and the days wear on, you'll grow more and more humiliated, hungry, and exhausted. In the end, you'll break. People always do.''

Sarah paled. It wasn't just the threats Reid had made, though the thought of a second jailer made her cringe. It was the cool look in his eyes and his casual tone of voice, which told her he would do precisely what he'd said, coldly and without compunction. Thanks to her attack, she had ceased being a person and turned into a fly to be swatted.

''No. Not always.'' She murmured the words, talking more to herself than to Reid. ''Sometimes they escape. And sometimes—sometimes they even die.''

''I'm not going to permit you to do either. Your choice isn't whether to talk or not; it's how much you suffer before you do.'' He paused. ''Unlike you, Mrs. March, I've tried to be reasonable in this matter. I made you an offer before. I'll repeat it a final time. If you tell me what I want to know, I'll help you as much as I can—and that's no small amount. Take it or leave it now, because later, when you're broken and begging for mercy, I won't be half as generous.''

Sarah didn't say a word, just turned on her heel and stared out the window. Her heart was pounding in her throat, making her feel faint and queasy, but if the raw power Reid wielded filled her with terror and robbed her of options, it also gave her an odd sort of peace. She was well fed and well rested, so the danger was far down the road. Only one course of action was possible, to resist for as long as she could and hope for a lucky break before she cracked.

Out on the Avenue, the mounted artillery was parading by, while directly behind her, Reid was dragging a chair across the room. He started questioning her again, but she paid no attention, focusing instead on the street below. For several minutes, the historian in her took over, watching spellbound as battery after battery of gleaming cannons, prancing horses, and smartly uniformed men passed by. And then the tempronaut intruded, thinking that if only she had attacked Reid sooner, the moment he had unchained her wrist, she might have knocked him cold and gotten his key. But at the time he had freed her, she'd been too frightened and hungry to think of it, and now it was too late.

She watched as more cavalry went by, and then the engineers, marching beside their boats and pontoon bridges. Reid kept drawling accusations and barking questions, his voice mingling with the cheers of the crowd, but she ignored him. She was riveted by the parade. She had read countless volumes about this army—had studied its artifacts in numerous museums—but to view the troops in person was one of the great thrills of her life.

She had just spotted some colorfully dressed Zouaves in the distance when a raft of gold coins came flying through the air, some of them bouncing harmlessly off the shield around her body and the rest slamming violently against the wall. She flinched, but that was her only response. In a voice dripping with irony, Reid asked if she was enjoying the Grand Review, and the question reached her in a way that none of the others had. Maybe if she could show him just how much, he would believe she was a loyal citizen.

She turned, regarding him with glowing eyes. He was sitting by the door, sprawled in one chair with his feet up on the second. "Oh, yes," she said softly. "It's wonderful, T.J. My home—it's so far away that I never thought I would see this. Everything this nation ever becomes, we'll owe to those men outside. It's enthralling to watch them."

His expression went from bland to cold. "And I'm an officer of that same nation's government. If you loved the Union as much as you claim to, you would cooperate rather than resist. As it is, your sight-seeing is interfering with my interrogation." He walked to the fireplace and removed her pistol from the mantel, then strolled to the foot of the bed. "I'll set it on yellow, I think. It should be amusing to watch a wide swath on the Avenue crumple to the ground."

Sarah slammed down the window before he could aim the gun, then closed the drapes. She didn't know if he was bluffing or not, only that she'd created enough mysteries in this time and place without adding a mass collapse into the brew. "Fine. I won't watch. But don't imagine that your threat will get me to talk. I would sooner let you shoot."

"I'll take your word for it—for the moment, anyway." He returned the gun to the mantel, then started badgering her again.

She positioned herself on the bed with her back to his chair and mused about the future. Suppose she escaped? How many days should she stay? Where should she go? But Reid's relentless insults to her motives and integrity kept breaking into her thoughts and distracting her.

Between her resentment about missing the parade and Reid's outrageous accusations, she was finally provoked into defending herself, but it was a waste of her breath. No matter what she said or how she said it, he kept pounding away in the same cynical tone, turning her earnestness to anger and then distress. Several hours went by, but he never seemed to tire and he never let up. When she couldn't stand it another minute, she curled up tight on the bed and wrapped her pillows around her ears to shut out his voice. It didn't work. She could still hear him.

He pulled away the pillows and tossed them aside, and she buried her head in her arms. "It's time for a short break, I think." She heard him ring for the bellman, then felt him sit on the bed. "I know, Sarah. It's been an endless couple of hours, and you've come to hate the sound of my voice. I'm going to order up a meal. Are you hungry?"

It had been a sarcastic Mrs. March all this time, but suddenly it was a kindly Sarah—and a gentle T.J. Reid. She sat up, glaring at him. He knew damned well she was hungry. "Why even ask? You're not going to let me eat."

"I would if you would answer my questions. You will eventually, so why make both of us suffer? I don't enjoy tormenting you any more than you enjoy being tormented, you know." Smiling at her, he fiddled with the sleeve of her robe. "I would rather make love to you. You're very beautiful. And when you're not thrashing me senseless, you're sweet and passionate and exciting."

Good cop, bad cop, Sarah thought, and pulled away her arm. "We've played this scene before. Besides, it's useless to talk to you. You refuse to listen to a word I say."

"I would listen if you would tell me the truth."

She wanted to throw something at him. "I *have* told you the truth—or as much of it as I can. Why won't you accept that?"

He shrugged and walked away. "Maybe later, Sarah."

A bellman arrived to take his order, delivering it some fifteen minutes later. He pulled a chair to the bed, sat down with the tray, and listed its contents: fried oysters, mixed bean soup, rockfish, quail in pastry, fillet of beef, blackberry pie, and charlotte russe. A feast, in short.

She refused to watch him eat, but she could smell the food, and it doubled her hunger. The man had a genius for torture. Not only did he extol each dish as he tasted it; he held out samples, daring her to shut off her barrier and take them off his fork. With luck, he said, she would be able to pop a morsel into her mouth and get her shield back on before he could touch her. She knew better than to try.

He set the tray on the bed when he was through, the enormous meal only half-eaten, mocking her by its very presence. The grilling he proceeded to inflict was more unbearable than ever, probably because she had less physical tolerance for it. She felt exactly as she had before the jump, weak and lethargic. She told herself it was the lack of food and the strain of psychological warfare, because the only other possibility, that the jump hadn't cured her, was too painful to contemplate. Besides, she still had the appetite of a horse. Surely that was a good sign.

Exhaustion overtook her. She needed to sleep, but she couldn't. When Reid wasn't talking, he was tapping, drumming, or singing with the crowd outside. The last was a torture all its own. He had a tin ear. An awful voice.

By late afternoon, when the first day's parade finally ended, she was reeling with fatigue and frustration. But Reid kept goading her, taunting her when he wasn't firing questions, and in the end, she couldn't take another word of it. She snapped and began to scream, using terms no lady of the period would have allowed to pass her lips. He grinned through the whole tirade, then complimented her on her knowledge of obscenities. He was winning this battle and he knew it.

Her screeching left her with a sore chest and throat and a pounding head. She grabbed her pillows, then lay on her back with her eyes closed, silently suffering. There was no pity in Reid, and no weakness, either. He continued to press her, turning his voice into a weapon, driving her so mad that her resolve finally faltered and she considered giving in. She was immediately disgusted with herself. It was nothing but tapping and prattling. It wouldn't kill her.

Her hunger got sharper, causing painful cramps by the time Reid ordered dinner. Even worse, she had to relieve herself again, but when she asked to do it in private, he refused. "After all," he said blandly, "you'll have to turn off your barrier first, and I can't be expected to pass up the chance to grab you and cuff you."

She rubbed her throbbing temples, feeling defeated and depressed. "And then what, T.J.? Will you slap me? Beat me? Hurt me until I talk?"

He frowned at her for several seconds, then abruptly turned away. "Fine. Use the damned chamber pot." He left the room, slamming the door behind him.

She yanked out the vessel and squatted above it, sure he was waiting in the hall. She was embarrassed that he could hear her and afraid he would burst through the door before she finished. It was a good ten minutes before he returned, however. Once again, he was carrying a tray laden with delicacies from the Willard's kitchen.

For the second time that day, she was compelled to smell his food and listen to him eat. The questions and accusations that followed were as forceful as ever, but her denials were less heated and her silences more despairing. She grew so tired that she repeatedly dozed off, but Reid kept up such a constant, nerve-shattering clatter that she never slept for long.

By nine o'clock, she was trembling with weariness and muddled from mental exhaustion. There was a knock on the door, and she fell asleep while he answered it. She awoke to the sound of him calling her name and saw a tray on the bed, filled with hot, fresh food. His earlier meals, the half-eaten ones, had vanished.

"Your dinner," he said, "but there is a price, Sarah. I have an errand to run, but I know better than to leave you alone. If there's a way to escape, you'll find it."

She found that hysterically funny. "You can't be serious. I'll be asleep within seconds."

"That's true, but you might wake up. To make sure that you don't, I've taken the precaution of lacing your food with laudanum." He strolled to the door and lazed against it. "Go on. Eat your dinner. You have my word that I'll stay right here, but even if I'm lying, you should be able to get your barrier back on before I can reach you."

Given how woozy she was, she wasn't so sure, but she would have done anything short of confess for the chance to eat and sleep. The mere thought of it—of having Reid gone for a while—pumped adrenaline into her system, and she pulled the tray onto her lap. She kept a wary eye on Reid as she ate, but he hadn't lied to her all day and he wasn't lying now. He watched her in motionless silence, looking almost as tired as she was.

Her sleepiness increased as her belly filled up, a combination of exhaustion, satiation, and the drug. Finally, unable to take another bite, she set aside the tray and turned on her shield. She yawned, and her eyes slowly closed. Just before she dozed off, she heard Reid approach the bed, but she didn't have the energy to look at him.

The room grew darker. She suddenly felt warmer. She felt herself begin to float. "Shelby?" she murmured, and fell asleep to the wrenching sound of silence.

* * *

Ty tucked the throw from Sarah's trunk around her body, then picked up his gun and quietly left the room. He had fought at Manassas, Antietam, and Fredericksburg, but none of those battles had exhausted him the way Sarah just had. The woman had a ferocious will, even for an accomplished spy.

Still, her victory was mostly his fault. In time, nature would have compelled her to use the chamber pot, and he could have stayed in the room while she did so. With her barrier off, he could have seized her and cuffed her. Strong-willed or not, she'd been sufficiently softened by then that the proper combination of threats and physical discomfort would have induced her to talk.

But it was one thing to kill or be killed and another to torture even a Rebel agent. Ty knew men who enjoyed that sort of thing, but he wasn't among them. As much as he loved the Union—and as willing as he was to fight, spy, and browbeat in the Union's defense—he drew the line at employing brutality. It negated a person's humanity.

Unfortunately, though, when you answered to a man who had hanged deserters without a qualm, scruples like that could be a treasonable offense. Success had usually kept him off Stanton's blacklist, but he was gloomy about his chances with Sarah. It wasn't only his scruples that kept getting in the way, but his feelings for her. Despite the thrashing she had inflicted, he couldn't stay angry with her, or even detached. It wasn't rational, but he liked her. He felt guilty when he abused her. He knew that she was a spy and a liar who should be forced to submit—but someone else would have to do the job.

He stopped into his suite to check for messages—there were none—then headed for Stanton's home. It was almost ten by then, but the streets were crowded with revelers, the heroes of the war and the people who had come to cheer them. All over the city, in its homes and hotels, in its taverns and brothels, the victors were celebrating wildly. The Stantons, a servant told him, were among the throng.

T.J. Reid, the ultimate opportunist, would have joined in the festivities, but Tyson Stone was too damned tired. Thanks to his friend Alex McClure, he could pick a lock with the best of them, so when he was turned away from the front, he slipped in through the back, sneaking up to Stanton's study and making himself comfortable with a book. Given the day's activities, he doubted Stanton would stay in his office that night, but if he did, his wife Ellen could send him a message fetching him home.

The wait was such a long one that Ty finally nodded off, only waking when the secretary discovered him and shook his shoulder. It was well past one o'clock. "Well, well. If it isn't Colonel Stone. Men have been arrested for far less than breaking into my house, you know."

Ty rubbed his eyes and got to his feet. The secretary was never cheerful, but his mood appeared benign. That was a good sign, because Ty needed all the charity he could get.

"Yes, sir. I hope you'll forgive me. I've come about Mrs. March. She's proving—extremely difficult. I wanted to explain the situation in person. To ask your—" Ty cut himself off. Stanton gave orders, not advice. "That is, to solicit further instructions, sir."

The secretary nodded, and Ty recounted the day's events. It was a humiliating exercise, but he never lied. It wasn't so much a matter of honor as that Stanton had an unfailing nose for deception.

As he'd anticipated, his superior was less than pleased. Ty stood at attention through an interminable tongue-lashing, the gist of which was that he was an incompetent fool who had the control of a satyr, the prowess of an invalid, and the toughness of a schoolgirl from the Georgetown Seminary. Sarah March was a dangerous spy with mysterious devices as valuable as they were powerful, and she needed to be crushed.

Ty conceded every word. He apologized abjectly. But when it came to doing what he had planned to and asking to be relieved, he thought about Sarah and held his tongue.

His likely replacement, Lafayette Baker, would shame her, malign her, and misuse her unmercifully, and with Stanton's blessing. The secretary was out for blood. But in Ty's opinion, anything beyond token punishment would be vengeance rather than justice. After all, Sarah could have wreaked havoc with her pistol and her barriers, but she hadn't. But how did he convince Stanton to let her go?

"Mrs. March is a formidable opponent," he said carefully, "but she's not invincible. If you could give me another day, sir, I'm sure—"

"Another day to do what, Colonel Stone?" Stanton's tone was withering. "Coddle her? Let her whip you like a dog? Make love to her, for God's sake? Didn't you learn anything from Peggy Moore?"

"Yes, sir. I won't repeat my mistakes." Ty marshaled his energy, then tried again. "By tomorrow evening, she'll have answered all my questions and sworn allegiance to the Union. I guarantee it. She hasn't broken any laws, much less used her devices to harm anyone, so surely we can allow her to leave."

Stanton looked at him as if he'd lost his mind. "Hasn't broken any laws? Good God, Stone, where did she kick you, in the groin or in the head? What about illegal entry? Robbing the Willard of payment? Conspiring against the Union? Assaulting a government agent?" He walked to the door and pulled it open. "You're to go back there, but only for one reason. For all your inadequacies, I can trust you to keep a secret, which is more than I can say for your colleagues. There are too many mysteries about the woman. I can't have the capital engulfed in gossip and panic.'' He waved a hand in dismissal. ''This time, you're to control your lust and do your job. That will be all, Colonel.''

Ty wearily saluted, then left. It was very late now, and the streets were finally quiet. The lights in most of the houses were out, and here and there, an exhausted reveler with no place to stay was sleeping on a bench or in an alley. He walked slowly, trying to unwind.

His thoughts returned to Sarah. Leniency could be cruel rather than kind, he mused, if it prolonged a prisoner's resistance, delayed her surrender, and thus increased her suffering. In this instance, then, harshness was the more compassionate choice.

Yawning, he turned down Fifteenth Street. The sooner he brought Sarah to heel, the happier Stanton would be, and the likelier to let her up easy. Mercy wasn't the secretary's strong suit, but Sarah could be irresistible when she set her mind to it. If he could arrange a meeting between the two, she might be able to sway him.

Ty was playing the scene in his mind, picturing a humble Sarah and a tolerant Stanton, when he sensed someone walking behind him. It wasn't the man's footfalls he noticed so much as his stench, which was as rank as the Washington Canal. The city had its share of thieves, but tonight of all nights, when there were soldiers all about and joy in every heart, Ty wasn't worried about being robbed. Probably a drunken vagrant, he thought absently. He decided to give the man some coins.

He turned, but he never made it all the way around. As he reached in his pocket and said hello, a bat crashed down on his head and knocked him to the ground. He lost consciousness, awaking to find someone attacking him with a knife. The man kept ranting about "Peggy," raving about "my sister." It could only be one of the Beecham brothers.

The world was shimmering and spinning insanely, but Ty managed to get his gun out of his coat and fire it. His attacker hurled the knife at him and fled down the street. Ty got off several rounds more, and judging by the way the man cursed and stumbled, he succeeded in hitting his mark.

The knife had tangled harmlessly into his clothing. He pulled it out, then touched his chest. His shirt was in shreds, and his flesh was full of cuts. And the smell. . . He gagged. He was reeking of filth.

Gagging, he staggered to his feet. Though disoriented, he knew he'd been incredibly lucky. He couldn't have passed out for more than a few seconds, because if he had, he would have been killed.

He continued on his way. He was reeling from fatigue and shock, but his mind wasn't so befogged that he had forgotten all the talk about Peggy. His attacker was one of her brothers, but which one?

Ty had only glimpsed him, but he was sure the fellow was taller than he was. According to Sukey, though, the man who had assaulted her, Ned, had been average in height at most. This must have been the other one, the soldier. George. He was still alive, then, and as twisted as ever, blaming Ty for Peggy's death when Ty had been eighty miles away at the time.

A gentleman passed him as he lurched toward the Willard, stepping into the street to avoid him. Others did the same. It was only when he reached the crowded sidewalk in front of the hotel that he was recognized by someone he knew. His friend, who was spectacularly drunk, gave an alarmed cry and offered to get help, then wove his way into the lobby.

The rest of the company gave him a wide but sympathetic berth, shielding their noses as they asked him what had happened. To Ty, both the people and their voices were a blur. He didn't reply. Standing beneath a streetlamp on the Avenue, he got a good look at himself and saw that he was soaked with blood and filth. He stumbled to the door, wincing with every step. His chest stung like fire, not just from the cuts, he supposed, but from the muck that had seeped inside them.

His friend came out with a bellman, who took him upstairs and helped him undress. One look at his wounds and the Negro offered to run down the block for Dr. Miller, but Ty refused. Miller was a good man, but Ty preferred the medicines he already had, a collection of Chinese potions sent to him from Hong Kong by his friend Melanie McClure.

The bellman insisted on bathing him, and he reluctantly gave in. Between shock, nausea, and exhaustion, he might have fainted and drowned without some help. Afterward, relieved of his own foul smell and soothed by the tepid water, he felt well enough to continue on his own. To his relief, he found that his wounds, though bloody and numerous, were rather shallow. They would require salve and bandages, but not stitches. For some reason, his attacker had slashed rather than stabbed.

Back in his room, he doctored himself, then pulled on a nightshirt and dressing gown. After tucking his gun and his keys into his pockets, he left his suite. He moved slowly and carefully in deference to his wounds, but in truth, his hazy state of mind permitted little else. Having spent so much time at Stanton's, he was anxious about Sarah, but she was sleeping heavily when he entered her room. Given the amount of laudanum he had dumped on her food, she would likely be out until well past dawn.

He stripped off his dressing gown and dropped it on the floor, then pulled the two wing chairs together. But his chest was so tender that he had trouble getting comfortable, and when he finally did, he didn't stay that way for long. The one thing that would have helped him, his laudanum, was gone now, expended on Sarah's food.

He finally sat up. At the rate he was going he would be useless by morning, and he couldn't afford that. Another day of failure and Stanton would have his head.

The wing chairs were hopeless. It was either the hard floor or the soft bed, and he chose the latter. Surely he would awaken before Sarah did, and besides, he was a wary sleeper who stirred at unusual movements or sounds. He was hot and sweaty, so he parted the drapes and opened the window, then unbuttoned his nightshirt and lay on his back atop the covers.

He tossed and turned, repeatedly going from sleep to wakefulness and back again. Once, dreaming about ice, he woke up shivering, and burrowed under the covers to get warm. Later, more asleep than awake and colder than ever, he stumbled around in the darkness, closing the window and drapes, then pulling his dressing gown back on. Toward morning, the searing heat came again. Though he moaned and threw off his covers, he didn't wake up.

Sarah was roused by someone's thrashes and moans. She blinked to clear her vision in the dim light of dawn, then squinted in astonishment. What was Reid doing in her bed? And what was he wearing around his chest?

She parted the drapes, then returned to the bed for a better look. The material on his chest was gauze, and it was spotted with blood. She gingerly parted his nightclothes. Here and there, above and below the gauze, the end of a scratch peeked out. She noticed the dampness next—the sweat stains on his clothes and the perspiration on his face.

Frowning, she switched off her shield and felt his forehead. He was burning with fever. He'd evidently come out on the losing end of a vicious fight, and even worse, seemed to be suffering from a virulent infection.

In 1865, that could kill you. Even a hundred years later, depending on the cause, the same had been true. But the world's scientists had finally triumphed over infectious disease, including the deadliest enemy of all, the retroviruses. Humans were still attacked and they still got sick, but only the young, the old, and the weak generally died. Like all tempronauts, Sarah carried weapons against historic ailments in her strongbox, a precaution in case a jump failed to confer the heightened immunity her colleagues had acquired in the past.

She glanced around the room. Her trunk was sitting beside the wardrobe, beyond the reach of her chain, but even if she could get to the drugs inside her strongbox, she wasn't sure she should use them. T.J. Reid was supposed to die tonight. Did it really matter whether he fell from a train or succumbed to infection? And even if it did, was she hard enough to cure him only to send him to his doom?

She couldn't answer those questions. She only knew that Reid was vulnerable now, and that his illness was the break she'd needed. But how was she going to take advantage of it? She was still in chains, and Reid was too delirious to respond to any threats she might make.

And then it struck her that he probably wouldn't have returned here without his gun, and if she found it, she could shoot through a link of the chain. But she didn't see the weapon on the mantel, or anywhere else, so where was it? In a drawer, perhaps? And what about the key to her fetters? Surely he had taken that up here, too.

An answer suddenly suggested itself—the items might be on his person—and she began to shake. Biting her lip, she checked the pockets of his dressing gown—and hit pay dirt. Within seconds, she had unlocked the band around her ankle and closed it around Reid's. He never even stirred.

Her first impulse was to throw on some clothes, grab whatever she could, and flee, but her training took over within seconds. Thanks to her neural pistol, she had all the time in the world.

She walked to the mantel, picked up the gun, and set it on orange. But as she raised it to fire, Reid opened his eyes and looked right at her.

"I was at Stanton's," he said in a slurred voice. "Pleading your case. Please don't shoot me, Sarah."

Maybe if he hadn't spoken . . . And maybe if she hadn't believed what he had said . . . But he had and she did, and she could see the pain in his eyes, and that settled the matter. She turned the setting down to yellow, then fired.

Chapter 8

November 10, 2096

After a week of living with the Fongs and trying not to cry, Shelby returned to school. It was better than being by herself all day, and anyway, the teachers didn't bother her when she got weepy. Like everyone else outside the Project, they thought her mother's health had taken a turn for the worse while she was back East, and that she was stuck in a local hospital getting stabilized. If Shelby was upset, they said, that was only to be expected.

By now, though, she wasn't only sad and scared, but seething. After the failed retrieval, every spare staffer had plopped in front of a screen and started reading, checking through copies of the *National Intelligencer* for the ad her mom was supposed to place if she got in trouble. But nothing had turned up, not in a whole year's worth of issues.

So they'd looked at the other Washington papers next, including some totally obscure ones. Now they were checking out other cities, starting with the ones closest to the capital. That was the protocol, and at the Wells Project, they always followed their protocols.

Shelby was sick of it. At the rate they were going, they would never find her mom.

A historian might have dug up some clues about where she was, but Sarah was the only such person on the Project. Nobody else had the knowledge to sort through thousands of facts and see what was missing or different. The Wellsians had read through the new version of history and learned what major changes had occurred, but that was *all* they'd been able to learn. It hadn't told them a thing.

Shelby was sitting in science class, fidgeting and brooding, when she realized that if clues were what she wanted, she should look in her mother's work. After all, her dad had proved that everything in the universe was connected in space and through time, so it only made sense that the changes were unique to Sarah—that a different tempronaut wouldn't have caused them. She must have let something slip or interfered in some way, without meaning to or even realizing it, and messed up history as a result.

Shelby didn't know how to discover what she'd done, but her mom's files seemed like the logical place to begin. Later that afternoon, she walked into her house and went directly to Sarah's study. She looked around at the file cabinets, bookshelves, and stacks of folders, and sighed. Nobody but her mom would have all this paper around. She loved the stuff. But luckily, most everything in print was also on disk.

She switched on the computer. She had no idea what she was searching for, so she began with Sarah's articles, which were stored in a directory called PUBS. The earliest one, written while her mom was at Cal, was about Noah Brooks, a reporter, and his friendship with Abraham Lincoln before the war. It was interesting enough, but there was nothing special about it. Nothing that struck Shelby as significant.

She went through two more articles from grad

school, then came to Sarah's dissertation. It was filed as THESIS, and it was one of the few documents in the directory that Shelby had read. Her mother had a thing about Tyson Stone. He'd been a great journalist, of course, but her mom's interest went far beyond his work, probably because she loved mysteries so much. She wondered about the missing years. She wondered why Stone had never married. She was always talking about finding the answers.

Shelby retrieved the document, then frowned in bewilderment. It wasn't about Tyson Stone and his influence on the civil rights movement of the early twentieth century. It wasn't about Stone at all. It was about Horace Greeley of the *New York Tribune* and his relationship with the Radical Republicans in Congress during Reconstruction.

She slowly got up. The date sounded right, June of '91, but maybe her mother had named the wrong file THESIS. Fortunately, it was easy to check. U.C. Press had published a paper version of the dissertation, and there were copies in Sarah's bookcase. Shelby fetched one down, a thin volume with dark blue binding, and looked at the title. It was the same as the one on the computer.

Shaking a little, she dropped back in her chair. She'd always thought time travel was creepy, what with the way it changed the past with almost no one knowing it, but this . . . This gave her the chills. In this new version of history, her mother hadn't written about Tyson Stone. Why not?

She exited Sarah's files, called up an encyclopedia she'd used for her schoolwork, and typed in STONE, TYSON. There was no entry for him. He wasn't important enough to include, not anymore. She would need a more detailed reference book. She nibbled on her lip. She couldn't recall the name, but there was a book on American journalists that listed just about everyone who'd edited a publication or written anything significant. Her mom had researched some of the entries for the latest edition.

She signed on to the net, accessed the database for general American history, and did a subject search. Something called *Fischer's Guide to American Print Journalists* rang a bell, so she retrieved it and entered Stone's name, and a brief bio appeared on the screen.

"Born March 3, 1836, in Philadelphia, PA," it read. "Parents: Mary (Barrett) Stone and Benjamin Stone, a bank clerk. Graduated from Central High School (Philadelphia) in 1852. 1852-1856, miner in CA. 1856-58, reporter, *Nevada* (in present-day Nevada City) *Sentinel,* in CA. 1858-1860, reporter, *Philadelphia North American.* 1860-61, pro-Union editor and publisher, *Nevada City Clarion.* Served in the Army of the Potomac (highest rank: colonel) as a Pennsylvania volunteer, 1861-1863; as an army regular (highest rank: lieutenant colonel) and a member of Lafayette Baker's secret service agency, the National Detective Bureau, using the alias T(homas) J(efferson) Reid, a lobbyist, in Washington, D.C., 1863-1865. Best known for his final essay, 'An Army Goes Home,' in the *Washington National Intelligencer,* May 30, 1865. Died June ?, 1865, en route to California."

Shelby stared at the screen in astonishment. In this new version of history, there *were* no "missing years." Stone had been in Washington, serving as an undercover agent. Maybe Sarah had met him there. Maybe she'd recognized him, blown his cover, and put him in danger. In any event, something she'd said or done had led to his death—to the loss of the man she'd admired more than any other, except, of course, for Lincoln. And as a result, the world Shelby had known had ceased to exist.

But was it possible? Could Stone have influenced history so much that his death had been close to disastrous? Maybe so, because Sarah said nobody had attacked racism and fanaticism more ferociously or championed justice and fairness more effectively. Without him, the wrong people might have flourished. The wrong people might have failed.

You didn't have to be a genius like Shelby's father to figure out how to reverse things: find Tyson Stone. The article he'd written had appeared in late May, but maybe he'd left the city by then. So first they had to track him to a specific time and place, and then they had to send someone back to protect him. If they'd had a second set of time travel equipment, it would have been easy.

Unfortunately, they didn't. They'd never had the money to build one. The only way to warn Stone would be to release the energy in the holding chamber, then run another mission. If they did that, though, they could never get Sarah back.

That left only one alternative, to find her first and warn Stone later. They could comb through historical records till they got a lead, then attempt another retrieval. Their budget would pay for two such efforts a year.

But what if there *were* no leads? They could skip through time, making random hits on Washington—the field had a retrieval radius of thirty kilometers—but she probably wasn't there. She would have put an ad in the *Intelligencer* if she were. But then, there was no ad in any other paper, either. It was like she'd vanished off the face of the earth. The odds of finding her sucked.

Shelby's eyes filled with tears. The world she'd known had died and gone to hell, but the new one was all that people remembered. Congress thought the Wells Project was a cosmology experiment, and a ridiculously expensive one at that. If they hadn't appropriated extra money before, they wouldn't do it now.

She put down her head and sobbed. She didn't think

she and her mother would see each other again. Not ever.

May 24, 1865

Ty saw a yellow glow in the air around his body, then felt a tingling weakness invade his muscles. Instinct prompted him to try to escape, but he couldn't. He was paralyzed except for his eyes, which he could focus, and his lids, which blinked of their own volition, and his breathing, which was normal but totally involuntary.

As for his heart, he assumed it was racing because of the fear rushing through his system and not the yellow light. Even in battle, he had never been this scared, but then, he had never felt this sick and helpless, either. And at least he had always known what he was dealing with.

Sarah set the gun on the mantel, walked toward the bed, and took a towel out of the washstand. She gazed at him for several seconds, then sat down beside him. "I need you to answer some questions, T.J. It will be a struggle to talk and swallow, but you can do it if you try. Don't panic and think that you can't, all right?"

She brushed the hair back from his forehead and patted his face with the towel. He was hot and sweaty, but he knew that the yellow light wasn't the cause. He could remember how he'd spent the night, alternating between ice and fire.

"I know the paralysis is uncomfortable," she added in a gentle voice, "but it won't harm you. And it won't last more than ten or fifteen minutes. It was a short discharge."

His fear subsided. Unless she was wholly evil, she wasn't trying to hurt him—and he didn't believe she was evil. The muscles in his face would move only a fraction, so he put what he felt into his eyes—bewilderment and a sense of betrayal.

He tried to speak, but nothing came out. He couldn't get his lips apart. So he cleared his throat and tried again, and this time he succeeded. "Why? I . . . told you. I tried . . . to help you." With his mouth almost closed, the words sounded like a rasp in a bizarre foreign accent.

"I believe you, and I'm grateful. But I have to escape, T.J. I have my orders. I need to leave Washington as soon as I can, but no matter what happens, I won't hurt anyone. That's a promise." She kept dabbing at his face with the towel. "I can see you were in a fight. It looks like you were attacked with a knife. Is that right?"

He whispered yes.

"Was there anything else? Did your assailant seem ill? Did he spit at you or lick you? Or smear your cuts with blood or human waste? Or put his hands on your wounds?" Her expression was very intent. "Or maybe you visited someone during the past few days who was sick, or who became sick."

Stanton's harangue to the contrary, there was nothing wrong with Ty's brain. He understood exactly what Sarah was getting at, and it terrified him. He felt ill enough already without ingesting the swill that passed for medicine in America. "No . . . drugs," he croaked. "No . . . doctors."

She smiled at that, but there was no meanness in the look. "T.J., the doctors where I come from are nothing like the doctors you're used to. They don't harm people; they cure them." A shadow passed over her face, then vanished. "Well, most of the time they do. You're burning with fever. You have a raging infection. If I don't know what caused it, I won't know how to treat it. Surely you can give me some clues."

If he could have, he would have shaken his head in

savage refusal. "No. No pills. I'll take . . . my chances."

"You could die if you do. I'm sorry, but I'm going to treat you whether you want me to or not." She paused, frowning deeply. "Did you walk through a field filled with mosquitoes? Or fall into the Washington Canal? Or come into contact with offal or garbage from some other source?" Her expression softened. "You have to tell me, T.J. All the things I mentioned can cause your symptoms, and where I come from, we can cure you. It's not like here."

"Where . . . you come from," he managed to repeat. She kept saying that. "And where . . . would that be? Not . . . California?"

She looked exasperated. "Don't you ever stop asking questions? Fine. I'll tell you. I was born in Fairbanks, Alaska. Now are you going to help me or aren't you?"

He had never heard of Fairbanks. "Alaska . . . is Russian," he said.

"Yes. So were my ancestors." Sighing, she took his hand and squeezed it reassuringly. "Please trust me and answer my questions. If you don't, I'll have to dose you with everything I have, and I'm sure you wouldn't want me to do that."

She was right there. "I don't . . . want your medicines. I won't . . . swallow them."

"You won't have to. I don't use pills or elixirs. My treatments are inoculations."

Like the one against smallpox, Ty thought. It was very effective. He began to reconsider, not that he had much choice. Paralyzed this way, he was incapable of resisting.

He thought about the devices she carried. They were far beyond anything he'd ever encountered, so maybe her medicines were equally advanced. "Will they really . . . cure me?"

"Absolutely."

"But why . . . help me? I'm . . . your enemy."

"No. My adversary. And the answer to your question is more complicated than you can imagine. Let's just say that it's possible I was meant to save you, and that—that when I looked into your eyes before I fired my gun, I found myself wanting to. Now about your fever . . ." She gave him a mischievous grin. "You *could* try cooperating for once and answer my questions."

Something inside him stirred—trust, hope, and unbidden affection—and he wished he could return her smile. "The attacker . . . he doused me . . . with filth. I smelled . . . like the canal."

"It *would* have to be that," she muttered. She crossed the room and picked up her pistol. "The canal is worse than a sewer. It's full of disease. You'll need a slew of different drugs, and they could make you somewhat ill. Nausea, intestinal discomfort, dizziness, that sort of thing. But I'm going to put you to sleep, and with luck, you'll doze through the whole cure and feel fine when you wake up. That will be late this afternoon, probably."

The sight of her gun was unpleasant enough, but the business about sleeping was worse. He hated losing control. He'd endured it after Chancellorsville, when he'd almost died, and he didn't care to repeat the experience. "No. Please, Sarah . . . no sleep. Let me . . . stay awake."

"I can't. You need the rest, and besides, I can't let you watch what I do." She smiled again, that same teasing smile as before. "Don't worry. You'll probably enjoy it. They say it causes wonderful dreams."

She changed the setting on her gun and raised it to fire. Ty tensed, forcing himself not to indulge in degrading pleading, but the light he expected never appeared. Instead, Sarah simply stood there, visibly struggling with something.

"One more thing," she finally murmured. "I've heard you need to travel to New York on business. Don't. Or if you must, stay off the cars. Do you understand me?"

"Yes." But he didn't really. "But why—"

"I can't answer that, T.J. But whatever you do, avoid the cars. And stay sober."

He was enveloped by a beautiful orange light, and then the need to sleep overwhelmed him.

Sarah put down her pistol. Her whole body was shaking. At the rate she was going, she was going to violate every rule in the book. Not only had she insisted on curing Reid's infection; she had told him about the train. She could justify the first—he hadn't been meant to die of disease—but the second was indefensible.

She'd known that even before she'd warned him, of course, but she hadn't been able to stop herself. She had no idea why. It wasn't as if his loss had damaged the nation in any way, and she had no personal feelings for him. It was simple humanity, then. She was too damned soft for this job.

She thought about reversing her mistake by not helping him, but neglect seemed immoral. If he hadn't gone to Stanton's to plead her case, he wouldn't have been outside in the first place. He wouldn't have been subject to attack. She'd caused the infection, so it was up to her to cure it.

She took out her strongbox, carried it to the washstand, and pressed the scanner to unlock it. The Washington Canal was a breeding ground for disease—staph, typhoid, cholera, and a host of other ailments. What the garbage and the human waste didn't carry, the mosquitoes and the rodents did. While Reid had taken sick very quickly, limiting what the immediate trigger could be, a host of other agents could be lurking in his system, poised to attack him.

There was no water in the room, so she washed her hands with gauze and disinfectant from her strongbox, then took out a scissor and cut through his nightclothes and bandages. He moaned as she eased him onto his side and pulled the putrid bandages from his body, but he didn't wake up. His wounds were swollen with fluid and oozing with pus and blood.

She'd read about the old infections, but that was different from seeing them. Retching, she dumped the gauze in the trash, then cleaned the wounds the same way she'd cleaned her hands. When she was done, she applied a topical germicide and sprayed on an antiseptic bandage.

He would need some instructions, so she scrawled them on a sheet from the notebook she'd brought along and left it on the night table. "T.J.—" it read. "Leave the bandage on. It will keep out disease and hasten healing. It will slowly dissolve of its own accord." A miracle, to be sure, but given the devices he'd already seen, a minor one.

She pulled out an assortment of cartridges next, a timed-release painkiller along with weapons against the many diseases to which he might have been exposed. She infused them, leaving a trail of tiny marks on his thighs, and then stripped him of his nightclothes to cool him down. Finally, she unlocked the fetter from around his ankle so he could move freely.

He had the body of an athlete, she noticed, lean but beautifully muscled. He'd been a banker in New York before becoming a lobbyist in the capital, but it was obvious from looking at him naked that he'd also been something more. There were large jagged scars on his left shoulder and right hip, suggesting that he'd either been wounded while working as an agent—or that he'd fought in the war.

She covered him with a sheet, then started packing.

As she worked, she kept checking him for a reaction to the drugs she'd infused, but there was none.

She hesitated before relocking her strongbox. Opening it had reminded her of something she'd temporarily forgotten, that she was supposed to draw some blood and run a series of tests on herself, but she decided to put them off. The sooner she left this room, the safer she would be, and besides, the tests had been delayed for so long already that another few hours could hardly hurt.

She put the strongbox in her carpetbag, added her weapons and her money, then squeezed in her toiletries, her jewelry, some undergarments, and her hand-sewn shoes. Her lamp would have to remain with the trunk—it was too large to take along—but of all her devices, it was the most impenetrable and the least revealing.

She checked Reid again. His fever was down and he was sleeping peacefully. Poking her head out the door, she glanced down the hall and then slipped outside. A minute later she was standing in the ladies' bathroom. She felt clammy and dirty and she was dying to wash her hair. Bathrooms this luxurious were such a scarce commodity in 1865 that she gave in to her longing to use the tub.

Back in her room, she applied deodorant that looked like perfume and put on a corset that appeared authentic but was constructed to be flexible and comfortable. The worst part of her outfit was the baggy open knickers she had to wear. She longed for a pair of panties, preferably silk bikini ones.

She dressed in her plainest gown, wearing too few crinolines to be in fashion, then pulled on her boots and pinned on a hat to conceal her face. Finally, after dragging her trunk and lamp into the hall and checking on Reid again, she picked up her cloak and carpetbag and left for good.

Down in the lobby, she approached a husky young

bellman and slipped him a gold coin, then described her possessions and asked him to convey them to the Kirkwood House Hotel when he had the time. Her next stop was the ladies' dining room on the second floor. She was very hungry, but it wasn't until one of the enormous meals of the period had been placed before her that she realized she was also very tired.

She was practical enough to know it could be an ominous sign. Adrenaline had surged through her when she'd first seen Reid, overriding any fatigue she might have felt, but now that the immediate danger was past, her illness might be catching up with her. In retrospect, she was glad she'd delayed the tests. What she didn't know couldn't distress her.

She lit into her breakfast, which was delicious, eating it so fixedly that she could have been the only one in the room. She wasn't sure when she felt someone watching her. She only knew that a chill ran down her spine, and that it was automatic to look for Reid, no matter how impossible his presence might be.

But there was only one man in the room besides the waiters, a middle-aged fellow who was staring straight at her. His face was familiar. She'd obviously seen his picture. She racked her brains for who he might be and finally came up with the answer—Joe Willard, one of the owners of this hotel.

He smiled at her, then started forward. It occurred to her that Willard might have been the one who'd discovered her that first night. If so, he might recognize her. He might wonder why Reid had released her.

She bolted from the table, flew out of the room and down the stairs, and fled the hotel through the ladies' entrance on Fourteenth Street. Then she ran to Pennsylvania Avenue, toward the crowd that had gathered for the second day's parade.

Chapter 9

Joe Willard peered up and down the Avenue, then cursed softly. Sarah March was nowhere in sight, and there would be no finding her, at least not today, when the streets were so choked with people. He returned to his hotel and headed for the stairs, giving short shrift to the customers who recognized and greeted him. The rest of his morning rounds would have to wait. If the woman had escaped, as her behavior indicated, God only knew what had happened to Reid.

Joe had just reached the third story landing when two bellmen descended from the next floor up, carrying a lamp and trunk he recognized as Mrs. March's. He asked what they were doing and learned they were about to dispatch the items to the Kirkwood Hotel, in line with the lady's instructions.

The Kirkwood was as full as the Willard, so Joe assumed she planned to retrieve them from someplace else. In any event, Reid—and Stanton—wouldn't want her to have the use of her possessions. "There's been a change in plans," he said. "Take them to Parlor Four and leave them in the sitting room."

The bellmen exchanged a hesitant look, then mumbled their agreement and continued down the stairs.

Joe was accustomed to crisp obedience, not reluctance. "Is there some problem?" he asked sharply.

The senior of the two shook his head. "No, sir. It's just—we hate to disturb him, what with him bein' so badly hurt and all. But we'll be extra quiet down there."

"Badly hurt?" Joe repeated. "What on earth are you talking about?"

The bellman poured out a story about how Reid had been attacked the night before. It was evidently the talk of the hotel, but Joe had been delayed when his wife had taken ill, so this was the first he had heard of it. If nothing else, it explained how Mrs. March could have escaped.

He accompanied the bellmen downstairs, dismissing them as soon as the trunk and lamp were deposited in Reid's suite. Then he let himself into the bedroom, hoping Reid would be lucid enough to confer with. But there was no one in the bed, delirious or otherwise. It had never been slept in.

Alarmed all over again, Joe hurried to the fifth floor. He didn't need his passkey to get inside the room; Mrs. March had left the door unlocked. When he first spotted Reid, lying motionless on the bed, he feared that the agent was dead, but then he noticed Reid's flushed color and deep, regular breathing, and he realized he was only asleep.

He felt Reid's forehead, which was warm but not hot, then shook Reid's shoulder to awaken him. Though the agent moaned softly, he was sleeping too deeply to rouse.

Joe looked around. Mrs. March's carpetbag and cubes were gone, but she had left a note on the night table. It was addressed in a familiar fashion to "T.J." and exhibited what sounded like concern. Whatever had gone on between these two, it hadn't been strictly hostile.

Frowning, Joe pulled down the sheet covering Reid's body and inspected his wounds. Not only was there no sign of the blood-soaked putrefaction he had expected from the bellman's description of the attack; he'd never seen a bandage like this in his life. It was a single unbroken expanse and gripped the skin at its edges with no apparent adhesive of any sort. Mrs. March's medical devices were as mysterious as everything else she carried.

Joe had seen a sufficient number of dying men in his time to know when a fellow would recover, and now that he was sure Reid would do so, the hotelkeeper in him took over. He was full to the rafters and needed all the space he could get, and there was a suite downstairs just waiting for its rightful owner. An hour later, Reid was sleeping peacefully in his own bed, carried there on a stretcher by two burly porters, and the fifth floor room had been cleaned and rerented.

Sarah plunged into the crowd at Fourteenth Street, then flung away her cloak and hat. She slumped over as she elbowed her way down the Avenue, trying to make herself as inconspicuous as possible. Unfortunately, that meant leaving her shield off, because anything it collided with bounced right off it. Given the sentries lining the streets, she couldn't afford startled stares, much less panicky questions.

Her training had taught her to prioritize, and now that she had finally escaped, her chief concern was her trunk and her lamp. If Willard saw them in the hall, recognized them, and learned where she had ordered them sent, he might follow them and try to trap her. She had to prevent that from happening, and not only because her freedom was at stake. Reid was puzzled enough by her devices without inspecting her clothing, too. At first glance, her garments looked ordinary enough, but a close enough examination would reveal otherwise. From the dyes to the stitching to the materials themselves, everything was a little too fine, a little too perfect, a little too—modern. The fewer mysteries he was able to study, the better.

With the sidewalk so packed and her carpetbag so heavy, she found it difficult to maneuver through the mob, and the task grew even harder when the first strains of the parade drifted through the air. The subsequent explosion of triumph and excitement was as physical as it was vocal, with people pushing and straining for a glimpse of the troops now leaving from in front of the Capitol. Sarah was jostled this way and that, so that it took every ounce of her strength just to make any progress at all.

It was the first time in her life that she'd been trapped in a frenzied crowd, and she was shaken and tired by the time she reached Twelfth Street and the Kirkwood Hotel. She took a minute to collect herself, then sought out the desk clerk. In return for a generous gratuity, he agreed to watch for her possessions and forward them to the Metropolitan after they arrived. Given the size of the throng, that would likely be at least another hour. If he was questioned about the matter, he would say he had never seen them.

Her business at the Kirkwood concluded, she looked cautiously around the lobby, but there was no sign of Joe Willard. She exited onto Twelfth Street and searched for him again, but he was nowhere to be found. Her shield was still off—given the congestion, it was impossible to avoid bumping into people—but she no longer felt worried about her safety.

The crowd was more boisterous than ever now. The first troops were passing by Tenth Street, a band was playing "Marching Through Georgia," and people were waving flags and throwing flowers. Sarah had read that William Tecumseh Sherman, the general who had marched his men from Atlanta to the sea and up the coast, loosing the hell of total war on a large slice of the South in the process, had been as popular with the people as Grant, and it was obviously true. The mob was roaring its approval and screaming his name.

He was less than a block away now. The historian in Sarah couldn't wait to see him. She was scaling the side of a building on Eleventh Street, carpetbag and all, seeking a better vantage point, when two men noticed her struggles and gave her a friendly push, propelling her onto the ledge of a first story window.

She spotted Sherman at once. He was riding at the head of his troops, tall and lean in the saddle of his prancing, flower-bedecked horse. He didn't seem jubilant, only alert and dignified—and visibly weary.

She lingered in the window, mesmerized by the spectacle beneath her. She had plenty of time, and besides, how did you turn away from a sight like "Sherman's bummers"? His army had foraged as it marched—or plundered, if you were from the South—and it was parading now as it had tramped through Georgia, followed by chickens, geese, and goats; a colorful variety of pets; mules laden with pots, pans, and other utensils; and newly freed slaves.

Journalists covering the review had reported that the men of the West had looked looser and freer than their Eastern brothers, and that was so. When it came to courage and toughness, however, the two were equals, but no braver than the men they had fought, so badly outnumbered, so daring and valiant. Sarah thought about the scars they all carried, both inside and out, both North and South. "This mighty scourge," Lincoln had called the war. Indeed.

In a somber mood, she climbed back down and made her way to E Street, where it was less crowded. Then she proceeded across to Sixth and doubled back to the Avenue. Her next stop was the Metropolitan Hotel. There were no clerks in the lobby—the help all seemed to be watching the Grand Review—but she finally ran a staffer to ground outside the building.

She repeated her actions at the Kirkwood, instructing the clerk to send her possessions to the National after they arrived at the Metropolitan. The two buildings were across Sixth Street from each other, but the area was so jammed that only a greased snake could have slithered between them. The trunk and lamp would have to be carried out the Metropolitan through the back door, then taken into the National the same way. That was how Sarah went, too.

She didn't know where she would spend the night yet, so her instructions at the National were less explicit. When she finally located a clerk, she handed him a silver bracelet as well as a bribe, then asked him to release her possessions when someone described the bracelet and requested its return.

That took care of the trunk and lamp, at least until she'd secured a place to sleep, so she proceeded to the next item on her list, altering her appearance. She knew it would take a fluke for Willard to spot her in this mob—historians had put the number of spectators as high as two hundred thousand—but she felt she should make some changes anyway, just to be as safe as possible.

The shops along the Avenue were open now, so she returned to Eighth Street and entered Harper and Mitchell's dry goods store. The salespeople, like the clerks at the hotels, were either peering through the windows or lining the streets, but a woman finally noticed her browsing and offered to help. Sarah emerged wearing a stylish shawl made of fine wool in shades of brown, taupe, and cream, and a cream straw hat with brown silk trim.

Her next stop was a few doors away, a hair and jewelry emporium whose proprietress was ignoring the review so staunchly that her sympathies had to be

Southern. Sarah purchased an auburn wig with curls like the ones Shelby had worn for the picture they'd posed for, then pulled it over her upswept hair and pinned her hat on top. It was the first time all morning that she'd thought of her daughter, and the image caused her throat to tighten with sadness.

She reached out hard with her mind, but it was the same as it always was. Only silence came back. Still, it was only what she'd learned to expect, and they would be together again soon, so it wasn't as distressing as before.

She would arrange for that reunion now, but she knew her colleagues. When things went wrong, their only goal was to retrieve a tempronaut as soon as they could. If she told them in tomorrow's *Intelligencer* that they should retrieve her next week, they would likely ignore her wishes and snatch her up at once. But if they couldn't confirm her presence in Washington until some future date, they would have to wait.

And she did want them to wait. She was safe now, and as much as she missed her daughter, her country had spent a fortune to provide her with what no other historian had ever enjoyed, the opportunity to see first-hand what she had studied all her life. Her original mission had called for her to remain in 1865 for twelve days, and while she couldn't bring herself to stay for so long a period of time, five or six days sounded manageable. She could witness a whole lifetime of research material before she left.

But when she reached the *Intelligencer*'s office at Seventh and D, she found a locked door with a sign reading "Back after the parade." That was an inconvenience, but not a major problem. She decided to watch the rest of the review, then return with her message. The parade had been over about three, the normal closing time in this era, but today, the staff obviously intended to stay open somewhat later.

She headed toward Fifth Street, hoping the Avenue would be less crowded away from the major hotels, thinking about what *was* a major problem, where she could spend the night. Reid was nothing if not thorough, so even if she could beg a bed in a hotel or a boardinghouse, he would probably have them all searched. There was always knocking on the doors of private homes, she supposed, and throwing herself on the mercy of strangers, but someone might report her. The war wasn't completely over yet, and there was still a paranoid atmosphere in this city.

She stopped for a minute, lost in thought. What she needed was a more personal connection, someone she could convince to take her in. She was supposed to be a journalist from San Francisco, so perhaps there was a native of California she could visit, claiming they shared a mutual friend. There had to be someone here she had studied, someone she could bluff successfully.

When a name finally occurred to her, she almost laughed out loud at who it was. Shelby would have loved it—the proper Sarah Maravich in Washington's most exotic brothel—but it was perfect. In 1863, a dispute with a local tong had driven a San Francisco madam named Ah Lan to the greener pastures of Washington, where she had opened up shop as "Asia Lane," offering a variety of stunning, mixed-raced women. Her sporting house, which was south of the Avenue in the notorious Marble Alley district, had attracted the most powerful men in the city. She didn't permit abuse, she kept the riffraff out, and her women were clean and healthy.

But from Sarah's point of view, the most important thing about Ah Lan was her relationship with Melanie Wyatt, the California mining heiress who'd been secretly part-Chinese. During her years in San Francisco, Melanie had devoted herself to social justice, especially to rescuing Chinese girls from prostitution. Ah Lan, understandably, had thought the trade acceptable, but she'd detested the coercion and violence that so often accompanied it. She and Melanie had become good friends, working to offer choices to the Chinese girls who were shipped to California as whores. Usually they preferred respectable positions, but sometimes they chose prostitution, and when they did, Ah Lan tried to place them in brothels where they wouldn't be beaten.

Melanie Wyatt, in turn, had been a close friend of Tyson Stone, which was why Sarah knew the details of her life. In 1861, Melanie had married a Hong Kong trader and detective named Alex McClure. She had moved to Asia, but she and Stone had remained good friends and faithful correspondents, as had she and Ah Lan. Many of those letters had survived. As an expert on Stone and his circle, Sarah had read them all.

She returned to the Avenue, thinking that Ah Lan was exactly the type she needed, discreet but unconventional. And then she caught sight of the troops again, and Ah Lan faded from her mind.

The next several hours left her exhausted but elated. She studied the parade, talked to her fellow spectators, and took page after page of notes. She only left before the end because she feared she would collapse if she didn't. If she could find Ah Lan, she decided, maybe she could beg a bed for a few hours, then return to the *Intelligencer* after she'd rested.

On a normal day, no decent woman would have ventured into the area south of the Avenue, but today, it was as mobbed as every place else. The crowd began to thin within a block or so, but there were people on all the roofs, and Sarah could sense them staring as she walked briskly to a house that resembled a Chinese temple. The feeling so unnerved her that she switched on her shield.

She knocked for a full minute before someone answered, a dignified-looking man with skin the color of mocha. He was startled to see a respectable lady at the door, but recovered quickly, asking if he could help her in an accent that hadn't changed in over two hundred years. Unless she missed her guess, he was from New Orleans.

"I apologize for my presence here," she said, "but frankly, I'm in a terrible jam." She gave him her most glowing smile, but suspected it was more wan than radiant. "I'm a journalist, you see, and we journalists will chance anything. The fact is, I arrived here this morning on the cars and I've got nowhere to stay. I'm a good friend of Melanie Wyatt McClure, who I know is a dear friend of Ah Lan's from San Francisco—but it's Asia Lane now, I'm told—so I thought, Well, why not give it a try? Maybe I can get myself a bed for the night, and even if I can't, it will be an adventure to visit a parlor house." She winked at him. "I'm always open to adventure. Is Ah Lan available?"

The man smiled politely and reached for her carpet-bag. "Let me take that for you, ma'am. Mrs. Lane is on the roof, watching the parade. I'll take you to her parlor, then find her for you."

Sarah switched off her shield and surrendered the bag, then followed him across a red and gold foyer to a wide staircase. Ah Lan's private quarters were up three flights, on the highest floor. Sarah was so tired by the time they reached the top that her knees were wobbling. She staggered across the parlor and dropped gratefully onto the sofa.

She removed her hat and shawl, then yawned and looked around. Ah Lan had done well for herself. The furnishings in this room were all Chinese, and utterly exquisite. Take them to 2096 and you would make a fortune.

Her eyelids drooped. She wanted nothing more than to sleep, even if it was only for a few minutes. She snuggled into a pillow. The room smelled wonderful, like jasmine and sandalwood. Give her this sofa for the night, and her life would be perfect. The sounds of the parade drifted in through the windows, but not even the music and cheering could keep her from falling asleep.

She awoke to find a delicate woman of thirty or thirty-five standing beside her, gently shaking her shoulder. "Ah. You are finally awake. Where I come from, we have a saying. The friend of my friend is also my friend." She spoke excellent but heavily accented English. "I am Ah Lan—Asia Lane to the people of this city. And you are . . . ?"

Sarah straightened. The room was whirling gently around her, but she wasn't so muddled that she didn't remember to select a new alias. If Reid sent men to search for her, they would ask about a blonde named Sarah March. "Rena Lamb. I'm sorry I fell asleep. Was I napping for very long?"

The woman made a dismissive gesture. "Half an hour, perhaps. It is nothing. You do not look well, Mrs. Lamb. You are very pale. I have ordered you a pot of tea. It will restore you."

Ah Lan poured out some tea for both of them, then sat down. "François tells me you know my friend Mi-Lan. He says you need a place to sleep. You may have this settee for as long as you wish. I would offer you one of the rooms downstairs, but a gentleman might enter with something other than conversation on his mind." She smiled coyly. "And, truly, my dear, you do not seem the type for such pleasures. You are obviously a *respectable* friend of Mi-Lan's, yes?"

Sarah smiled back and sipped her tea. It was some sort of herbal brew, and very refreshing. "Yes. Melanie—Mi-Lan—warned me about your sense of humor. You're outrageous, ma'am, but you're also exactly right. I am respectable, but I hope I'm not stuffy and boring."

''But how could you be? You are a friend of Mi-Lan's, are you not? From San Francisco, I assume?''

''Nevada City, actually.'' Ah Lan would know less about that town, and it would also explain why Melanie had never mentioned their friendship. ''We were all very close in those days—my husband John and I, Melanie, and her friend Tyson Stone and his sister. John was killed in the war in late '63, and I moved to San Francisco with our daughter.'' Ah Lan had left that year, so the two could never have crossed paths. Sarah stifled a yawn. ''Please excuse me. I'm still a little tired. Anyway, I make my living as a journalist now, and I came to Washington City to write some articles. I hope to sell them to a paper in California.''

''Articles about the end of the war and the new president, yes? But it is so busy this week! I am pleased that you thought of me—and that you had the courage to come here. We will be very discreet, to make sure your reputation does not suffer.'' Ah Lan's voice was teasing. ''You must tell me all about yourself, Mrs. Lamb, and about San Francisco, too. Everything there is silver now, is it not? The Comstock Lode?''

Sarah answered with a slightly altered version of the story she'd given Reid about herself, using her knowledge of history to discuss San Francisco. Ah Lan loved to talk, but Sarah welcomed every word. The woman was fascinating company. The two were soon chatting back and forth like old friends, discussing everything from Washington politics to Ah Lan's business interests. Then Sarah mentioned some of the places she hoped to visit, such as the White House, the Capitol, the Patent Office, and most of all, the trial of Booth's coconspirators, which was taking place at the Washington Penitentiary now, and Ah Lan said she had a great many friends and should be able to arrange it. A historian could have sold her soul to the devil and not received such help and information, so as weary as Sarah felt, her exhilaration kept her going.

Inevitably, though, her fatigue caught up with her, and she was forced to admit how tired she was. "It's been a long day," she explained, "and as you noticed, I've been feeling somewhat poorly lately. I suppose the trip from California took its toll. In any event, I have an errand I need to run before this evening, and if I could sleep a while longer, I'm sure it would revive me."

But she wouldn't have much time. The crowd had finally quieted, indicating that the last of the troops had passed by. When they reached the White House, the parade would be over and the *Intelligencer* would reopen for business, but perhaps for as little as an hour. "Could you wake me in half an hour?" she asked. "Then I could go."

Ah Lan looked at her sternly. "Rena, my friend, I refuse to hear of such a thing. You are exhausted, and it is all my fault. I have kept you talking for far too long. You will tell me what this errand of yours is, and if it is at all possible, I will send one of my men to do it for you. And then you will nap until dinnertime, and we will enjoy a fine meal together. Do you enjoy Cantonese food?"

Melanie Wyatt McClure, Sarah thought, had been fortunate in her choice of friends. Ah Lan wasn't only fascinating, but very kind. "I love Cantonese food," she answered. "I don't know how to thank you, Ah Lan. You're extremely generous. I want to place a message in the *Intelligencer,* a promise I made to my daughter. If you could give me a pen and some stationery, I'll write everything down and give you some money to pay for it."

"Of course. You will find what you need in my desk." Sarah crossed to the desk while Ah Lan disappeared into her bedroom. She emerged with a pillow and blanket, setting them on the sofa. Sarah handed her a sealed envelope and some coins, then settled gratefully down to sleep.

Ah Lan slipped out of the room, returning some ten minutes later. She assured herself that her guest was sleeping soundly, then picked up her carpetbag and carried it into the bedroom. A quick search of the woman's belongings confirmed what she had suspected. Her guest was not what she appeared. At best, she was a schemer; at worst, she was a swindler or a spy.

Ah Lan returned the carpetbag to the parlor, then went downstairs. Only one course of action was possible. She would have to notify the authorities.

Chapter 10

Ty awakened to the strains of "Marching Through Georgia." He'd been having a vibrant dream, something about Sarah, the Panama jungle, and a mine full of gems, and it took him a minute to pull himself back to reality. The Grand Review was still going on, he realized. The music was for General Sherman and the Army of the Mississippi. He looked across the room to check the time, but saw a wardrobe where a bureau should have stood. He was in his own room, not Sarah's. How the hell had she gotten him down here? Levitated him? He glanced at the clock on the mantel. It was almost three.

He noticed some sheets of paper on the night table and gingerly rolled over to grab them. He expected the movement to send waves of pain through his chest, but experienced only moderate discomfort. He recalled how he had spent the night, alternately drenched with sweat and icy with chills, but if he had a fever now, it was only a slight one.

There were two messages, the first from Joe Willard, who had seen Sarah flee and pursued her. He had lost her in the crowd on the Avenue, but intercepted some bellmen with her trunk and lamp. He had then returned

Ty to his suite. He promised to look in on him as often as he could.

The second letter, from Sarah, had him fingering the bandage on his chest with a mixture of amazement and anguish. It was true about Fairbanks, Alaska, then. The doctors there really *were* magicians, even more skillful than the sagest Celestials. Then he thought of Shiloh . . . Antietam . . . Gettysburg . . . The Wilderness . . . He wondered where those doctors had been when his comrades—and his adversaries—lay wounded or diseased. More than half a million of them were gone forever. How many men could her medicine have saved?

And why had she used it on *him*? She'd admitted she had a secret mission to carry out, so why not leave him to his fate and perform it? Why nurse him, then issue warnings and instructions that could endanger her own success? Her actions didn't make sense. Nothing about her made sense.

He walked slowly into the bathroom. He was able to stand and splash water on his face, but had to sit to relieve himself. While he felt a great deal less sick than he should have, he was still light-headed and nauseated, exactly as she had predicted he might be. Still, at the rate he was recovering, he would be back on his feet by morning.

He returned to bed, wishing she were here beside him. The thought that he might never see her again made him restless and irritable. And it was the damnedest thing, but the emotions had nothing to do with the questions he wanted answered or the reception he would receive from Stanton and everything to do with the look in her eyes when she'd warned him about the cars and the trembling in her body when he was making love to her.

Then he backed up a mental step, shaking his head at the enormity of his own stupidity. The way she had looked at him before she had shot him. The way she had trembled before she'd beaten him to a pulp. His flesh might be damaged, but his mind was as sound as ever, and it told him it was folly to think of anything but his duty, which was to recapture her and induce her to talk.

The only questions were, Would he get a chance to do so? And what did he do next?

By the time Joe appeared some twenty minutes later, Ty had reached only one conclusion. Tyson Stone would have to reemerge, because T.J. Reid had become a deadly liability. George Beecham was likely still alive, and determined to kill him. Sarah would turn on her barrier and run if Reid got anywhere near her. So Reid would have to die, and Joe was exactly the man to dispatch him and inform the press.

But removing him was a two-edged sword. Sarah might feel safe enough to remain in the city, but Beecham would surely leave. He might go after Sukey next. Ty had a Pinkerton in Ohio protecting her and a telegram would increase the man's vigilance, but he wasn't going to be able to rest until Sarah gave up, his sister was by his side, and George and Ned Beecham were either dead or in jail.

Within the hour, the doctor Joe had procured had certified Reid's demise, and the porter he had sent up had removed Reid's files for shipment to his employer in New York. Arthur, Ty's regular barber, soon arrived, and disposed of Reid's flowing blond curls. He was shaving off the last of Reid's beard when there was a knock on the parlor door. When Ty ignored the summons—after all, Reid was with the angels now—a female voice called insistently, "If you're in there, T.J., open the door. It's Ah Lan. I need to speak to you."

Ty directed Arthur to admit her, then invited her to take a seat. He and Ah Lan had known each other in

San Francisco through Melanie McClure, but he had managed to avoid her in Washington City until late '63. Something about him had struck a chord in her that night; she had an eye for the human face and form, no matter how well disguised. He had tried mightily to avoid a conversation, but she had trapped him and finally placed him.

There had been no keeping his work a secret from her after that, but far from betraying him, she had proved an invaluable ally. Men of power, influence, and position, both loyal and secretly Rebel, visited her brothel, drank too much champagne, and talked too freely during sex. Time and again, she had given him useful information, and in return, he'd seen to it that Baker, a self-righteous prig, had left her strictly alone.

When the barber withdrew, she removed her veiled hat and pecked him on the cheek. "Well, well. So T.J. Reid has vanished, and my friend Tyson Stone has reappeared." She touched the scar on his chin. "How nasty, Tyson. Is it a souvenir of the war?"

Ty nodded. "From the minié ball I took at Chancellorsville. As for Reid, he died about an hour ago, but why is a very long story, most of which I'm not at liberty to repeat." He smiled. "Tell me, my dear, did you come to see me because you heard I was murderously attacked last night?"

She looked startled. "Are you serious, Tyson?"

"Absolutely. It was an old enemy, Ah Lan. One of Peggy's brothers. He almost killed me."

"Hmm. I must say, you are looking very well for a man who almost died. I am surprised nobody told me. My sources are usually more prompt. It is all this to-do over the parade, I suppose." She removed an envelope from her embroidered silk bag. "I had a visitor, Tyson. She was unusual and very suspicious, if my nose for deceit has not failed me. She claimed to be a journalist, and a friend of Melanie's from Nevada City.

She said she knew you and Sukey as well, but Melanie has never mentioned her, and I thought that very strange. She wore a dark wig over what I suspect was blond hair, as if seeking to disguise herself. She said she wished to see the sights here, and to attend the trial of the conspirators. She fell asleep on my sofa after we spoke—her health seems rather poor—and I was able to search her carpetbag. It contained some odd-looking articles and a great deal of money. Also, I learned that the name she had given me, Rena Lamb, was not the name on the papers she carried, Sarah March." She handed him the envelope. "She wanted this message placed in the *Intelligencer*. I came here first, to learn if you truly do know her, and to obtain your approval before I carry out her instructions. I have invited her to be my guest for the next several days."

Ty took the envelope, staring at Ah Lan incredulously. "Good God. Do you mean to tell me that Sarah March is stashed away at your brothel?"

"Then you know her? She really is your friend?"

Sometimes, Ty thought, the fates truly smiled upon a man. "No. I have no idea where she got my real name. I only met her—or rather, Reid did—a few days ago. But that's another long story I can tell you only a part of."

He ripped open the envelope and read the sheet inside. "Please run this on Tuesday, May 30th," it said. The text followed: "Shelby, darling . . . I'm here in Washington, too late for L., but safe and sound and taking it all in. If I could have any wish in the world, it would be to join you tonight at eleven. Love, your mother."

Ty had come to believe that Sarah was innocent, or at least that she meant no harm, but Ah Lan's visit and the paper in his hands changed everything. Given Sarah's interest in the trial, he couldn't dismiss the possibility that she was indeed a spy, and that she had been sent to rescue the conspirators. This message might be intended for her cohorts, a coded request about where and when to meet her after the deed was done. L., he told himself, could only be President Lincoln, and the words "too late" were sickeningly evocative: not too late to interview him, as she had claimed, but too late to take part in the assassination.

He looked grimly at Ah Lan. "Sarah March was my prisoner. She escaped. I need to recapture her, but for reasons I can't explain, it's going to be extremely difficult. I could use your help in setting a trap."

She smiled at him. "Of course, Tyson. Did I mention that Baker came around on Monday, wanting to question my girls on which customers were disloyal and should not be pardoned?"

Quid pro quo, Ty thought, but he didn't mind at all. "I'll ask Stanton to get him off your back." He could have done ten such favors and not repaid Ah Lan sufficiently.

Sarah walked to the window and stared outside, seeing nothing. A few minutes before, Ah Lan's maid had brought in breakfast and a morning paper. She hadn't taken more than a few bites before she'd seen the headline about Reid: "Death of T.J. Reid; lobbyist attacked and murdered; assailant is unknown."

Her appetite had vanished. After all the medicine she'd pumped into Reid, how could he have died? Had she missed something vital? Done something wrong? Or was it the laws of the universe again, dictating that his life had ended and would always end, if not because of a drunken fall from a train, then as the result of something else. . . .

She blinked back tears. She knew it didn't make sense that the death of a dangerous adversary should distress her so much, but she couldn't help it. As resentful, angry, and frustrated as she'd often been, she knew in her heart that Reid and his job were two different things.

True, his methods had been barbaric, but only by the standards of 2096. In Washington in 1865, they were the norm. When it came to possible treason, even Lincoln had invoked his war powers, swallowed his distaste, and looked the other way, leaving the Bakers and Reids of the world to protect the Union.

She moved away from the window, remembering how Reid had held her when she'd sobbed against his chest. There had been tenderness along with the hardness, and no cruelty at all. She thought of the way he'd kissed her, and recalled the look in his eyes when he'd asked her not to shoot him, and knew there had been passion and vulnerability, as well. Most wrenching of all, he had tried to help her, and he'd died for it. She dropped onto the sofa, buried her head in her hands, and wept.

That was how Ah Lan found her, sitting and sobbing inconsolably. Ah Lan had ignored her customers the night before to spend the evening in the parlor with Sarah, and the two had discussed everything from their lives in California to the growth of Washington to their views on the great issues of the day. Between her knowledge of Ah Lan's past and their time together last night, Sarah felt as if she had known Ah Lan for years.

Ah Lan was disturbed to find her crying. She put a gentle arm around Sarah's shoulders and asked her what was wrong. As always, the best lies were as truthful as possible, so Sarah replied that she'd met T.J. Reid during a visit to New York and had found him to be kind and charming. It was terrible, she said, that someone so young and full of promise should be killed by random violence.

Ah Lan listened and sympathized, and if Sarah sensed a certain puzzlement at the intensity of her reaction, she knew that was only to be expected given how casual her tie to Reid was supposed to be. When Sarah finally contained herself, Ah Lan said she had some news that might lighten Sarah's mood. She had been working on Sarah's requests, especially her wish to attend the trial, and was making excellent progress. With luck, she would soon obtain everything Sarah had requested. In the meantime, why didn't Sarah take a walk, get some air, and see the sights? It would be good for her health.

Sarah agreed to do so, then forced herself to finish her breakfast. Later, assured of the first period of sustained privacy she'd enjoyed since her arrival, she carried her carpetbag into the bathroom and locked herself inside. After drawing a tube of her blood, she mixed a couple of drops with a number of different reagents, then studied the results.

She'd hoped for good news and steeled herself for the reverse, but she wasn't prepared for what she actually saw. The results were inconclusive. Her levels were substantially better, indicating that the jump had helped her, but there wasn't the immediate optimization the other tempronauts had enjoyed. Her numbers weren't even in the normal range. She could take another sample in a few days, but until then, she would have no way of knowing if her levels were rising, falling, or holding steady. And even if they were rising, she wouldn't be sure if the improvement was permanent or only temporary. In a way, the uncertainty was even more unsettling than bad news would have been.

Still, there was reason for optimism. If nothing else, the jump had probably bought her more time. The biology of her ailment was a mystery, but give the scientists another couple of years and maybe they would understand it—and find a cure.

Right now, though, she was probably dying, and that made her conscious all over again of how fleeting life could be. She had so little time and so much she wanted to do, especially in 1865, that it was foolish to sit and weep over a man she'd barely known. No matter how dearly she'd wanted to save him, he was dead now, while she was still alive.

Not for the world would she deliberately have bought her freedom at such a price, but facts were facts. Reid had been her most formidable opponent, and he was gone now. Joe Willard was still here, but he'd probably gotten only a few quick looks at her face and would be fooled by her wig, as would anyone else who was searching for a blond named Sarah March. She was probably safe now, but even if she weren't—even if she were somehow recaptured—she would be retrieved on Tuesday night. As long as she was in the Washington area, all the handcuffs in the universe couldn't prevent that.

She rose from the sofa. Ah Lan was right. Some activity would do her good.

She bathed and dressed, then slipped out of the house through the private door Ah Lan had told her to use. With so many soldiers and tourists in the city, the streets were reassuringly busy. Her first stop was the National Hotel, where she found the clerk she had bribed the day before and learned that her possessions had never arrived. She went across the street to the Metropolitan, and then to the Kirkwood, and heard the same story. What she had feared had come to pass. Willard must have spotted her trunk and lamp and cancelled her instructions. At worst, the field would retrieve them on Tuesday night, but the less time Willard and his cronies had them in their possession, the better. She didn't know how, but she had to get them back.

She strolled to the Center Market, her mind on bribery, extortion, and robbery. The market's dilapidated booths, piles of refuse, and pungent smells made it a civic embarrassment, but Sarah saw it through the eyes of a historian and was instantly enchanted. She stopped brooding about the felonies she would need to commit to recover her possessions and lost herself in the crowd. As she browsed, she tasted an occasional tidbit from the food stalls and purchased a number of garments from the dry goods shops.

After exiting onto Seventh Street, she headed toward the Mall, which was a few blocks to the south. The area was little more than a marshy field in 1865, and a haven for roving thieves, but between her shield, which could be engaged at a moment's notice, and her pistol, which was strapped into a holster above her knee, she felt reasonably secure.

Wrinkling her nose at the fetid smell, she crossed over the Washington Canal and continued past a collection of makeshift hospitals to the Smithsonian Castle. In January, a serious fire had destroyed many of the Institution's holdings and closed the building to visitors, but its red brick exterior, while charred, was poignantly familiar. She had visited this same building—and the many other museums and libraries that comprised the Smithsonian in her era—several times. Home was two centuries away, but for a few moments, standing before the Castle, Sarah felt as if the world she knew were directly in front of her.

The illusion quickly faded. At the end of the Mall stood the Washington Monument, but only the most imaginative soul in the world could have transformed the truncated stump Sarah saw into the graceful, 550-foot obelisk that would someday rise on that spot. She walked over for a closer look, a distance of several blocks.

Workmen had set the cornerstone of the monument in 1848, building it to its current height of about 150 feet by the middle fifties, when construction had been suspended. The wooden sheds at the base held memorial stones from assorted states and societies, but it would be sixteen years before work resumed and twenty before the monument was finished. That was typically American, Sarah thought. We don't always do things as quickly as we should, but at least we do them eventually.

She thought of Lincoln and gazed at the Potomac, at the tidal flats where the reflecting pool and memorial would one day be. It had taken over eighty years to honor Washington from the date this city was founded, and only a couple of decades less to honor Lincoln after his death. The flats had been filled and the project approved early in the twentieth century, but the memorial hadn't opened until 1923. She pictured it in her mind—that wonderful statue, those extraordinary words—and her eyes filled with tears. If only she could have talked to him . . . Saved him . . .

Shaking her head, she turned and walked away. For Lincoln, they'd been ready to break the rules. She'd had permission to tell him everything, a conversation she'd imagined with exquisite pleasure. "This is the judgment of history," she would say. "We place you above everyone, even Washington." And then, teasingly, "We thought you should know. We hope that you're pleased." And he would have been. He'd enjoyed a good triumph, and after all the suffering, insults, and vilification he'd been forced to endure, vindication would have been doubly sweet. But now, he would never hear those words.

Sarah walked slowly back to Seventh Street, wishing she could still say them, but to the millions who had come to cherish him. It might have provided them with some solace. But the Wells Project had its protocols, and they barred her from telling even his family and closest associates about the reverence he would come to inspire.

Somber and somewhat fatigued, she trudged back to the Avenue, then took a trolley toward the Capitol and returned to Ah Lan's. She had dozed for about an hour and was about to go back out when Ah Lan sailed in with a triumphant look on her face. Everything was arranged, she announced. Sarah could visit all the places she had named.

"And not only that, but I have brought you the most coveted commodity in our city." Ah Lan waved a piece of paper in the air. "This, my dear Rena, is a pass to the trial, compliments of General Hunter."

"Black" David Hunter, the abolitionist general whose nickname referred to the way he'd scorched the Shenandoah Valley, was serving as the president of the military commission judging the conspirators. Nobody could attend the trial without his written approval, but where most people gained admission by petitioning someone with good connections to the man, Ah Lan had gone straight to the top. Impressed, Sarah murmured, "My, but you have important friends. Is there anyone in this city whom you *don't* know?"

"Many people," Ah Lan replied with a laugh, "including the general, but important men usually have younger assistants, and many are my loyal customers. Indeed, at this very moment, if you will proceed to the west steps of the Capitol, you will find a young man waiting to give you a private tour of the building." She took a silk flower out of her bag. "I told him to look for a woman with a red rose in her hatband. He is a secretary to Senator Sumner"—she winked—"but not nearly so serious and moral. You will enjoy meeting him, I think. He is intelligent and amusing."

The senator, a Radical Republican, had been one of the great congressional leaders of the period. "I don't know how to thank you, Ah Lan. I can't wait to hear your friend's views and write about what he says."

Ah Lan handed her the pass and the rose, then said very seriously, "You may thank me by writing an article so brilliant that everyone will agree that all men, no matter what the color of their skin, are created equal. That *is* what you believe, is it not?''

''Not quite. It's all men and all *women,* Ah Lan.'' Sarah gave Ah Lan an impulsive hug, then floated out the door.

Ty had forgotten how much he loved being a journalist, but on Thursday he was reminded. He was reminded that if you were good at the job—and he was—men would tell you their private dreams as well as their public triumphs. He was reminded that if you were better than good—and he was—they would share their defeats, their nightmares, and even their darkest secrets. And he was reminded about the pleasures of sorting it all out, finding the deeper patterns and the larger truths, and writing about what you had learned. And at that, he was best of all.

Another day of interviewing soldiers, he thought, and he would be ready for those final steps. He even had a publisher lined up, Joseph Gales of the *National Intelligencer*. He had stopped at the paper that morning and described the article he wanted to write about the departing troops, and Gales had agreed to take a look. If he liked the material, he would run it.

He stretched out on the sofa, feeling tired but content. It had been a long day, but a successful one. It hadn't been easy to placate Stanton, much less to talk him into ensuring that the officers at the Old Capitol and the Washington Penitentiary would cooperate with his plans, but the secretary had finally issued the necessary orders. Ty had conferred with General Hunter next, briefing him over lunch, then stopped by Ah Lan's—she hadn't been in—with a letter containing his instructions. Everything was set now.

By tomorrow at ten, Sarah would be his. She could tell him the truth or wallow in misery. The choice would be hers. He felt a fierce satisfaction in finally trapping her, and no guilt at all. The woman was a traitor. And if he owed her a favor for saving his life, it would have to come later, after she confessed.

The daily papers were sitting on the table behind him, but he hadn't had time to read them. He picked one up—it was the *Chronicle*—but he didn't open it. His thoughts were still on Sarah. She was beauty and perfidy. Tenderness and deceit. He realized he looked forward to seeing her. To touching her. He cursed under his breath. She was Peggy all over again, but worse. He was a raging lunatic.

So much for contentment, he thought. With a sigh, he read about his untimely demise. It was an odd sensation.

He was thumbing through the rest of the issue when Ah Lan appeared, knocking on the door and demanding admission as she had the day before. His first thought was that something had gone wrong, but she assured him that everything was fine.

"Other than the fact that your suspect cannot possibly be a spy," she added, dropping gracefully into a wing chair. "I have spoken to her for hours, Tyson. She is a passionate abolitionist. She loves liberty. She loves the Union. And she worshiped the late president."

"She's a good actress," Ty answered. He had learned that the hard way.

Ah Lan shook her head. "No. After all, acting is my business—we pretend that men arouse us when they do not—so I have learned to recognize it when I see it. And I must tell you, when your suspect weaves stories about Melanie and San Francisco, she is lying. But when she speaks about her feelings and her beliefs, she is telling the truth. If she is a Rebel spy, my friend, she is a very peculiar one."

"You've got that part right," Ty muttered. He cleared his throat. "If that's all you came to tell me—"

"Is that a dismissal?" She grinned at him. "How

curt you are, Stone. Reid had better manners. And to think I abandoned my business and came all the way down here just to see how you were feeling!"

On the contrary, she'd fallen under Sarah's spell and had come here to plead Sarah's case. "I'm fine. I've made a remarkable recovery." He focused on the paper. "Thank you for your concern."

"You're welcome. God, but you're in a foul mood tonight." She rose from her chair and walked to his side. "Ah. You're reading the *Chronicle*. So was Sarah, early this morning. She saw the news of your death. I found her weeping forlornly."

Ty tried to ignore the statement, but it was impossible. He finally looked up. "You did? She was?"

"Yes." Ah Lan kissed him on the cheek. "But she recovered eventually. She was only a little in love with you. Good night, Tyson. Sleep well."

She sauntered to the door, then stopped and turned. "All women are not alike, and it is an insult when you men insist that we are. You might keep that in mind."

She breezed out of the room while he watched in silent disgruntlement. She was wrong, he thought. Sarah and Peggy were exactly alike. But when he closed his eyes, Sarah was asking him about his wounds with soft, concerned eyes. She was warning him about the cars in an urgent, troubled voice.

He wasn't going to enjoy tomorrow morning, after all.

Chapter 11

The Washington Penitentiary was on the grounds of the United States Arsenal, on a peninsula south of the city, where even in Sarah's time, a military installation still stood. She rode there in a hack driven by an African-American who owned the rig himself. The area she passed through was largely undeveloped; most of the streets were little more than trails, cattle roamed in the fields between, and the few existing structures were confined primarily to one side of the dusty and rutted main thoroughfare.

She arrived at a quarter past nine in the company of numerous other vehicles for a session that would start at ten. The penitentiary itself was an old brick building, three stories high, located in a pleasant, tree-dotted setting that belied the grim use to which its courtyard would shortly be put. On July 7, four of the eight defendants would hang there, and historians were still arguing about the culpability of two of them.

Soldiers were stationed at the main gate and the building's entrance, but nobody questioned her until she got inside. She was directed to a large room, where several officers sat at a table, receiving credentials. After a brief wait in a short queue, she gave her pass to an official who examined it and set it atop a mounting stack. An orderly soon appeared and took the stack away. Sarah knew from historical accounts that he would carry the credentials to the court on the top floor, where an officer would inspect each one, and, if he approved it, issue a card of admission.

About fifteen minutes later, pass and card now in hand, she climbed a narrow flight of stairs to a small room on the second floor, where another checkpoint had been set up. The atmosphere here was more casual; several orderlies lounged about, talking desultorily, while an officer examined visitors' papers. He was young, handsome, and something of a flirt, telling the woman ahead of her that her beauty would brighten the dreary courtroom, then smiling at Sarah and making a remark in the same vein.

"I haven't seen you here before," he continued. "Please prepare yourself, ma'am. The conspirators are sinister and grotesque." He set down her papers, taking her hand when she reached to retrieve them. "They glare at the spectators in the most evil way. I advise you to ignore them."

"I will. Thank you, Major." Sarah took back her hand, but before she could pick up her papers, she was seized from the rear by two men, each of whom captured one of her wrists and pulled it firmly behind her back.

She was twisting and kicking to get free, trying to extricate her hands to turn on her shield, when an officer strode up and barked impatiently, "Get those handcuffs on her *now*!" She looked at him and froze. That distinctive scar on his chin . . .

She gaped at him, oblivious to the manacles now restraining her wrists. The rank was right—a lieutenant colonel. His hat was pulled low on his head, but from what she could see of his face, his age and general appearance fit, too. It had to be. "My God," she whispered. "You're Tyson Stone."

He didn't say a word, just picked up her papers and took her by the arm. Too stunned to resist, she asked dazedly, "Where have you been for the past two years? What happened to you after Chancellorsville?"

Maintaining his silence, he led her out of the room and down the hall. She was pulled into a small, windowless chamber that was empty except for a desk and two chairs, one behind the desk and the other beside it. A set of irons sat ominously atop the desk.

He closed the door and released her. "Sit down, Sarah. And don't try to escape. Because I swear to you, if you so much as twitch the wrong way, I'll clap you in those fetters and chain you to your seat."

There was no mistaking that voice, especially the tone he used when he was exasperated with her. She stared at him, more shocked than ever. Now that she could see them, there was no mistaking those intense blue eyes, either.

"T.J.?" She gazed at him for several seconds longer. "My God, it really *is* you. I don't believe this. You're still alive." The thought filled her with relief and warmth. "I'm so glad. Your wounds—are they healing all right? You didn't fuss with the bandage I put on, did you?"

"No. Now sit." He hauled her to the chair beside the desk and all but pushed her into it. "No more questions, Sarah. You're here to answer them, not to ask them."

She barely heard him. "So Stone turned into Reid," she murmured. "He was in Washington all that time, working as an undercover agent. It's incredible." Still reeling with astonishment, she raised her voice. "When were you recruited? Shortly after Chancellorsville? And by whom? Baker? Stanton? How did you come to their attention? Why didn't anyone know where you were?"

Ty felt as if he had landed in a wizard's dreamworld. The capture had proceeded without a hitch, but he should have known it would never last—that something would quickly go wrong. After all, he was dealing with Sarah March, where nothing was ever logical or predictable. She should have been fearful and defiant, not pleased he was alive. Not worried about his health. Not bursting with questions that only a clairvoyant should have been able to ask.

He tossed his hat on the desk, grabbed the chair from underneath, and sat down beside her. Sarah—or the fictional Rena Lamb—had told Ah Lan she was a friend of Tyson Stone's, and it appeared to be true. She had known him on sight, related his history, even alluded to his disappearance. But how?

"You took one look at me and recognized me," he said. "Recognized Stone, that is. How?"

Sarah gazed into her lap, dazzled by her good fortune, repressing the urge to laugh in sheer delight. She probably should have chided herself for opening her mouth, but why bother? She was human, and this was Tyson Stone. There was no way on earth she could have stopped herself from voicing her astonishment—or from being excited to the point of intoxication at actually meeting him.

She looked at him again. God, he was handsome. Even better-looking without the beard and all that hair. And so utterly wonderful. An ethical and intellectual giant.

Her eyes shone with admiration. "I remembered you from Nevada City. I used to read your paper. You're an extraordinary journalist, Ty."

Ty had seen many different expressions on Sarah's face, but never rapt adoration. She was gazing at him as if he were a god from the stars, and it unnerved him. What was going on here? What sort of game was she playing?

He pulled himself together. If he had learned anything about Sarah March, it was the high price of letting her distract him. "Good, maybe, but not extraordinary," he said, "but thanks for the compliment. Now tell me how you know me. And forget the story about Nevada City. If we had met, I would remember you, and I don't."

A smile broke out on her face. "You never saw me, Ty. Let's just say—I worshiped you from afar."

Between the smile and the use of his Christian name, his heart began to pound and his groin started to ache. "From very far, obviously," he muttered. One look at her, and he would have invited her closer. And Jesus, her face . . . Worship was the word for it, all right. But she had never looked at *Reid* that way. Reid had frightened her, especially whenever he'd gained the upper hand, but she wasn't remotely afraid of Stone.

He wondered why not. With the handcuffs on, she was more helpless than ever, but she didn't seem concerned by that. Didn't she know how much trouble she was in?

And then he realized that her impotence was exactly the point. Whenever he trapped her, she managed to wriggle out. If he dropped his guard, she would do it again.

He rested his elbows on the arms of his chair, mostly because he was so tempted to do the opposite—to tuck his finger under her chin, or put his hand on her shoulder, or fiddle with the buttons on her coat. It was maddening.

"If you're looking at me that way in order to convince me to let you go," he said curtly, "it won't work. Let me be very clear, Sarah. You can answer my questions now, or you can sit in chains until you decide to talk. You can begin by telling me why you came to the trial. The mission you spoke of. . . Was it to free the conspirators?"

The pleasure drained from Sarah's body. There it was again—that icy annoyance—and it yanked her back to reality with a vengeance. He might be Tyson Stone, a man of decency and courage, but his greatness was all in the future. In 1865, he was a federal agent under Stanton's authority, and from the look of things, he was more determined than ever to learn who she was.

The full irony of the situation struck her. In the late seventies, Stone would write a long essay examining whether the wartime government had gone too far in suspending suspects' rights, but if he was worried about it now, it was solely in regard to himself. She knew firsthand that there were tactics he wouldn't employ, but when his colleagues had used those same methods, he'd silently gone along. She'd never dreamed he'd been right in the thick of things—that he'd written the essay from personal experience.

She thought about the question he'd just asked about freeing the conspirators. He still believed she was a Rebel spy, then. Given her resources, he had assumed she would attempt a rescue, and stationed himself at the trial to recapture her.

"If you check the pockets of my coat, you'll find a notebook and pencil, and nothing more," she said. "Regardless of why I was sent to Washington, I was never a spy, and I'm simply a journalist now. I came here to observe the trial and write about it."

"Since you've raised the issue of a search . . ." He stood, sliding the fetters off the desk. "I'm sorry I have to do this, but both of us know what sort of punishment your knees can dispense."

He crouched to put on the fetters. Sarah thought about kicking him in the head and running, but was afraid of inflicting a concussion. Besides, even if she knocked him unconscious, the place was swarming with soldiers. So she sat rigid in her chair, glaring at him as he bound her ankles. The display of outrage was intended to discourage him from being too thorough.

It didn't work. He pulled her to her feet, then yanked off her hat. A gentleman of this period would have confined his search of a lady to a visual one, but they were far from strangers, and he had learned by now how dangerous she could be. Her prospects, she thought glumly, were growing dimmer by the minute.

He checked inside the hat, then tossed it on the desk and pulled off her wig. His closeness made her pulses jump and her chest feel tight. She'd been attracted to Reid despite his politics, but with Stone, whom she so admired, it was ten times worse. He touched her, and her flesh began to burn.

She grimaced. It was damned unfair. Historians fell in love with their research subjects all the time. The penchant had always been a harmless one—until now.

He pulled the pins out of her hair, and it spilled onto her shoulders. She stared at his chest as he combed it with his fingers, flushing with arousal and uneasiness. He checked her pockets next, pulling out her pencil and notebook. He flipped through the pages of the latter, which contained her historical research, and set the items aside.

It was obvious he wasn't finished, but she gave it her best shot. "You see? I told you I was only a reporter. You have no right to detain me, much less to search me this way. I demand that you release me."

"If that's a formal objection, consider it noted and overruled." He unbuttoned the waist-length jacket she wore, taking his time, carelessly brushing her breasts as he parted the sides of the coat and checked underneath. Her stomach fluttered and her nipples tingled. He pushed the jacket off her shoulders and down her arms, then stepped closer and put his hands on her waist. She was breathing too quickly now, and it probably showed. Finally, his body almost touching her own, he slid his hands around to her back and trailed his fingers up and down, lightly and slowly.

She began to tremble. This wasn't a dispassionate inspection. It was an excuse to caress her. "That's enough," she said. "If you're going to search me, then do it, but I won't have you pawing me."

He pulled her coat back in place, then held it lightly by the lapels. They stared into each other's eyes. Electricity sparked back and forth.

He smiled in a way that could have heated a vacuum. "Why not, Sarah? After all, you think I'm extraordinary, remember? Anyway, I wasn't pawing you. I was making love to you. And you were enjoying it. You always do." He kissed her lightly on the mouth. "Almost as much as I do."

She turned her head, blushing harder than ever. He was right, but that didn't mean she condoned her own behavior. Stone had been a great man but also an incurable womanizer. The way she'd been raised, sex without love was as unethical as it was stupid. She expected fidelity. She wanted enduring devotion. A four-night stand was all there could ever be, and it didn't qualify.

"It's an unfortunate weakness I seem to have," she said. "God knows why. From what I've seen of you, you have the instincts of a Don Juan and the morals of an alley cat. Do what you have to do, Colonel Stone, but keep it impersonal."

Ty dropped his hands and backed up a step. He knew he had gone too far, but how was he supposed to help himself when Sarah gazed at him with such hunger in her eyes and responded so ardently? Now that he was Stone, she didn't only desire him; she admired him fervently, as well. Only a monk wouldn't have pressed the advantage.

Still, there was a time and a place for everything.

"My apologies, ma'am. I didn't realize your distaste was so profound. A natural mistake, given the glazed look on your face whenever I touch you, and the trembling and panting that invariably accompany it."

She rolled her eyes. "Conceited, too. I've already conceded that you're irresistible, although somehow I'll manage not to throw myself into your arms. Now, if you're finished—"

"Not quite." He hunkered down and slipped his hands under her skirt, then ran them lightly up her leg. The right one, first, because she was right-handed.

She flinched and stiffened. "I don't know what you think you're doing, but—"

"Looking for this." There was a holster strapped above her knee, and her pistol was tucked inside. He unbuckled the holster and slid it off, then got to his feet and dangled it under her nose. "Only a journalist, did you say?"

Sarah stared at the holster and sighed. She should have concealed it in her knickers, but then, he probably would have searched there, too, with mortifying consequences. "Be reasonable, Ty. You've seen what the pistol can do. If a rescue was what I'd had in mind, I wouldn't have waited for a pass. I would have come here right away. Freeing the prisoners would have been child's play. You know that as well as I do. The pistol was for my personal protection."

He set the holster on the desk. "Protection against what? Your barrier is impregnable. As long as it's engaged, nothing can harm you."

"That's true, but I can't leave it on. People are always touching me. You know how odd it feels—how objects bounce away from it. There would have been questions." She hesitated, then added, "Besides, it can't be used in a moving vehicle, and the area north of the penitentiary is very isolated. The pistol made me feel safer."

Ty remembered what had happened the first day, when he had moved Sarah's bed. If he had continued to pull, her head would eventually have collided with the headboard and the barrier around her body would have stopped the bed cold. The device was formidable, but it had its weaknesses. Maybe she was telling the truth.

He looked at the gun, with its brightly colored barrel, and her description of its powers slammed into his mind. Had she been honest about those, too? "Tell me something, Sarah. If I were to set your pistol on violet and fire it at you, how long would it take before you begged me to let you talk?"

She paled and backed away, bumping into her chair. She'd been honest, all right. She was quaking with terror.

"Not very long," she said hoarsely. "But you wouldn't do that to me." Not Tyson Stone, Sarah thought wildly. He was too humane. "I know you wouldn't. You're not that cruel."

Ty regarded her blandly. The thought of her in pain made him sick to his stomach, but he had a job to do, and he had failed thus far. "I don't want to hurt you, but the sooner this is over with, the better for both of us. After all, the ultimate outcome isn't in doubt. Only the timing."

Sarah knew why he thought so—he could have broken her the first day if not for his scruples—but the situation had changed since then. She'd acquitted herself poorly because things had gone so stunningly wrong, but now that she was assured of being rescued, her tolerance for pain and deprivation would be far greater.

But only for the torments of 1865. Nobody could withstand a neural lash, not when the pistol was on the highest setting. "The gun is dangerous," she said quickly. "It takes practice to use it correctly. A setting that causes pain can also cause permanent damage to—to your memory and your ability to think.''

He fixed her with an icy gaze that seemed to slice right through her. ''You're lying.''

''No. I'm not.'' But she was.

''I'm almost certain you are, but I won't use it on you if you don't want me to.'' He cupped her chin and stroked her cheek with his thumb, suddenly all warmth and gentleness. ''Listen to me, Sarah. . . . The only other alternative to talking is a filthy room, rancid food, and relentless interrogation, and I hate to put you through that. Is it really worth it? Is that what you want?''

''No. I want my freedom.'' She hated it when he went from threats to kindness and back again. The abrupt changes threw her off-balance. ''For God's sake, Ty, why can't you let me go? Deep down, you know I'm not a spy.''

He sighed heavily. ''One more time. Who are you? Where are you from? Who sent you? Why did you come here?''

She resigned herself to five days of hell. ''My name is Sarah March. I'm from California. Why I was sent no longer matters. My only goal is to observe and report.''

''Except when you're Rena Lamb from Nevada City, Melanie McClure's old friend, and mine and my sister's, too.''

Shock tore through her system. ''Where did you—I mean, I don't know what you're talking about.''

''Enough, Sarah. How do you think you got a pass to the trial? What do you think I'm doing here?'' He dropped his hand. ''Ah Lan came to see me. Unlike you, she *is* an old friend, and she knew who I really was. She gave me the message you wanted printed in the *Intelligencer,* so if you were counting on your masters to rescue you, they won't.'' He paused. ''Still not talking, hmm? All right. You win. I'll take you to the

Old Capitol. When you're ready to confess, ask for Superintendent Wood and tell him to send for me. In the meantime, I intend to retrieve your carpetbag from Ah Lan's and pay a call on Joseph Henry. Maybe *he* can figure out how your devices work."

A dozen different thoughts rocketed through Sarah's mind. Ah Lan and Tyson Stone—they'd known each other in San Francisco and still did. She'd gone straight to her adversary's old friend. She should have made the connection at once, but she'd been so stunned to actually meet him . . .

Oh, Jesus. He had intercepted her message. It would never be published. She would never be found. She would never get home.

The Old Capitol. Baker's Bastille. She'd wanted to see it, but not like this. Not as a prisoner, rotting there indefinitely.

And Joseph Henry . . . He couldn't examine her pistol and shields. He'd been a brilliant thinker, a pioneer in electromagnetism. They'd even named the unit of inductance after him. Suppose he understood too much, and the course of science changed? The atom bomb too soon, or in the wrong hands . . . Quantum shields and neural pistols as weapons of war . . .

Her face was a study in horror. "Please, Ty. . . I need a little time." Her mind went completely blank. There was so much to weigh that she couldn't even think. "Just—just a few more hours. Promise me you won't do anything until then. That you won't talk to anyone or show anyone my devices."

"So you want to mull things over, do you?" There was a calculating gleam in his eye. She'd handed him a trump card, and he meant to play it. "I might be willing to wait. It depends on what you give me in return." He fingered her cameo. "This would do."

"I've told you—I can't get it off."

"You've told me a lot of things. I've believed very

few of them. Give me the cameo, and you can have until five this evening to think things over."

She gave him a pleading look. "For God's sake, Ty, I saved your life. Haven't I earned your trust? Please, just let me go. It would be better for the country. Better for the world. I swear that it would."

"No." He folded his arms across his chest. "I've stated my terms, Sarah. Take them or leave them."

All the fight went out of her. Without more time, she couldn't make a reasoned decision, and this was the only way to gain it. "There are two bumps in the chain, under the velvet, below my ears. Find them and take them between your thumbs and forefingers. Press the right side four times, quickly and firmly; then the left side twice; the right, twice; and the left, once."

Fifteen seconds later the cameo was off and Sarah felt naked and defenseless. Ty collected her possessions and shoved them in his pockets, then hoisted her over his shoulder and carried her down the stairs. The soldiers hooted and joked; it was humiliating beyond words. She muttered insults—"bully" and "tyrant" were two of the milder ones—but he paid no attention.

Out in the yard, he dumped her onto the seat of a gig, then sat down beside her and drove away. Neither of them spoke for several blocks. Ty looked grim and unapproachable, while Sarah was uncomfortable and angry.

"You could have taken the chains off," she finally grumbled. "There's nothing here but open fields. Even if I escaped, where could I possibly run to?"

He snorted at that. "You mean after you'd whacked me on the head, kicked me in the crotch, and snatched back your cameo and pistol?"

Irritated or not, she had to smile. "What an imagination you have! It never even occurred to me."

"But it would have eventually."

"Hmm. I suppose you're right." She turned in her

seat. No matter how big a mess she was in, she was also alone with a man whom she'd studied for years, and it was stupid not to take advantage of it. "Why don't you stop scowling and tell me about yourself? Those scars on your shoulder and hip—"

"So you noticed those, did you?" He glanced at her, but only to cock a sardonic eyebrow. "I wondered who had undressed me. Did you like what you saw?"

"Like it?" She gave him an abandoned look, then breathed, "Oh, God, Ty, I didn't just like it. I was feverish and quivering." She wrinkled her nose and glowered. "After all, blood and pus are so intensely erotic."

His lips twitched. "It's a pity I was out cold."

"On the contrary, unconsciousness was your most appealing trait."

He burst out laughing, and she returned to her original subject. "Uh, Ty . . . You said that the wounds you suffered at Chancellorsville were minor, but they didn't look that way to me. What really happened?"

He frowned. "How do you know what I said?"

'I'm a friend of Melanie's, remember?" *You shouldn't,* Sarah thought—and then did. "I read the letter you wrote her after the battle. Tell me about the fighting, Ty. What was it like?"

"You ask too many questions."

"But you fascinate me. So does the war. I would enjoy hearing about your experiences."

"Not as much as I would enjoy hearing about *yours.*" He slowed his pace. They had reached South F Street now, a more developed area. "It's only a dozen blocks to the jail, Sarah. Are you sure you want to go there?"

"After all I've heard about the place? Of course I do. I'm dying of curiosity." But she felt the hard edge of panic in her throat. "Assuming I'll be left alone to think. That nobody will touch me or question me. You'll make sure of that, won't you?"

"I said you could have until five. Then we'll see."

Meaning, she supposed, that he might give her to Baker and Wood after that. The prospect, an unpleasant one, grew downright alarming when the jail came into view. The building was sprawling, ramshackle, and filthy. Armed sentries were stationed around the complex, guarding against possible escape. Ty took Sarah's fetters off and marched her inside, keeping his arm around her shoulders as they walked past clusters of lounging soldiers into the large chamber where the Senate had met after the War of 1812, while the burned Capitol was being repaired.

The room, a cellblock now, was lined with small, dirty berths in tiers of three. Rodent droppings were visible in the corners, roaches scurried atop the bedding, and the prisoners were pallid and unkempt. Sarah's stomach lurched at the pungent smell of garbage and human waste. This wasn't Andersonville, but it was bad enough. She was so appalled by the conditions in the place that she stopped and stared, tripping over her own feet when Ty hurried her along.

He caught her before she could fall and led her upstairs. She knew where they were going even before they got there—to the notorious Room 19, between the first and second stories, where suspects were always interrogated. She recognized the two men sitting there at once: General Lafayette Baker, with his dark hair and beard and his small, deep-set eyes; and Superintendent William Wood, a stocky, muscular colonel with blue-gray eyes and a florid complexion. The bad cop and the good cop.

Ty followed her into the room, remaining directly behind her after he'd closed the door. Baker regarded her with a contemptuous sneer, while Wood smiled pleasantly. As a historian, she had scores of questions she wanted to ask this pair, but she held her tongue. If she hadn't, they might have insisted on questioning her in return.

Ty saluted, introducing himself as Colonel Stone. If either man recognized him as the erstwhile T.J. Reid, it didn't show. "This is the prisoner Secretary Stanton referred to in his orders," he said. "With your permission, gentlemen, I'll show her the second floor before I take her to her room. She has a sweet little mouth, but regrettably, she refuses to open it for me. A good look at the cellblocks there might change her mind."

Baker leered at her, looking her up and down. It made her skin crawl. "If it's a confession you want, you should leave her here with us. Patience is a waste of your time."

Sarah backed up a step. Baker had enjoyed frightening people, especially people he'd considered enemies of the Union. He'd enjoyed abusing them, too. He would die in disgrace in 1868, convicted of false imprisonment. It was a fate he'd probably deserved.

Ty rested his hands on her shoulders and gently squeezed them. The gesture was so protective that she almost forgave him that obnoxious double entendre about her mouth. "For the moment, General, I'll have to follow the secretary's orders, but tomorrow is another day. If I could have the key . . . ?"

Wood handed it to him. "Here you are, Colonel Stone. Room 9, on the top floor." He smiled warmly at Sarah. "I would like you to be comfortable while you're here. I'll visit you later to see if there's anything I can bring you."

She smiled back. Wood's courtesy toward celebrated female prisoners was well-known. Unlike Baker, he had prospered after the war, becoming the first head of the new Secret Service. She was suddenly pleased by his coming success. "Thank you, Colonel Wood. That's very kind—"

"The secretary's instructions say solitary confinement," Ty interrupted. "No visitors. No favors. No comforts. And see that whoever delivers her meals keeps a healthy distance away from her. She might not look it, but she's extremely dangerous." He took her arm. "Come along, Sarah."

He pulled her out of the room and hauled her up the stairs. It was useless to object—he could do whatever he wished with her—but she was too annoyed to care. "That was totally unnecessary and very mean. It's not as if I could whip a whole prisonful of armed guards, and you didn't have to encourage them to abuse me. And stop dragging me around, damn you! I'm not a sack of grain."

He stopped dead, right in the middle of the stairwell. "I wasn't dragging you. I was leading you. And neglect isn't the same as abuse. You're a prisoner, for God's sake. Not an honored guest."

"And you think that gives you the right to treat me however you please."

"Treat you however I please?" he repeated in disbelief. "You've kicked the tar out of me—caused me more trouble than any woman I've ever known—but I've still handled you with kid gloves. They should make me a saint."

She scowled at him. "You were never a saint, but at least you were generous and honorable. I don't recognize you. You've changed, Tyson Stone. I want you to know that."

He scowled right back. "Recognize me from when? Changed from what? What in bloody hell are you talking about?"

"Nothing. Never mind."

"Never mind, she says." He cursed under his breath. "You would drive an ascetic to drink. Tell me something, Sarah. Has any man ever controlled you? Your husband? Your father? Anyone at all?"

She raised her chin. ''Don't be absurd. I would never permit a man to tell me what to do.''

He gave a long-suffering sigh. ''I should have known.''

Chapter 12

Room 9 was a small, dilapidated chamber containing a rectangular table, a rickety chair, and a single bunk fitted with grimy bedding and a board for a pillow. An assortment of insects scurried about in the filth, providing fodder for the spiders that seemed to lurk in every corner. The room was so hot and close that, within minutes, Sarah longed for a bath. If it hadn't been for the window—a barred one—the place would have been intolerable.

She removed her coat and tossed it over the chair, then gazed outside through the filthy glass. Soldiers were marching listlessly back and forth on First Street, while officials and petitioners loitered in front of the Capitol and strolled in and out through the east entrance. She absently watched them, weighing her options.

True, she was annoyed with Stone for behaving in a way he should have repudiated, but flawed or not, he was one of the giants of the nineteenth century. If she could trust anyone with the truth, she finally decided, it was Stone, and if Stone couldn't understand the complexities and the dangers involved, nobody could. So she would lay it all out, because the odds of minimizing the damage and getting home safely would be greater that way than if she refused to talk at all, and her story—and her devices—got spread all over the city.

She crossed to the door and pounded, calling to the guard who was patrolling outside. He entered the room with his pistol drawn, but she'd already retreated to the window. When Stone had uncuffed her wrists, he'd reminded her of how harshly Baker dealt with prisoners who tried to escape. She didn't want any trouble.

"Please ask Colonel Wood to send for Colonel Stone," she said. "I'll tell Colonel Stone what he wants to know—but he's the only one I'll speak to."

The guard said he would see to it, then locked her back inside. She expected to be released within the hour, but Stone never appeared. She wouldn't have minded if she'd been confined downstairs, where there were prisoners to interview and research to carry on, but stuck in this awful chamber, she was missing a unique opportunity. She was soon seething with resentment and frustration.

It was only when Wood arrived with a meal—some swill in dirty tin dishes—that she learned that Stone had gone out and couldn't be reached. "I left him a message at the Willard to retrieve you as soon as he returns," Wood added. "I'm sorry about the delay, Mrs. March—and about the food. I've brought you some extra bread. I wish I could do more, but you heard Mr. Stanton's orders."

Sarah said she understood and thanked him for his kindness. Nobody knew how many people had died in this loathsome prison, but the number, probably over a thousand, would have been even higher if not for the fresh bread Wood had insisted on providing to the inmates.

She sat down to eat. Other than the bread—six thick slices of it—the meal consisted of rancid butter, boiled beans, pieces of stringy, grayish meat in a thin sauce, and black coffee. It looked disgusting and smelled worse, but she would have tasted it just for the experience if she hadn't noticed a dead roach floating in the sauce. Repelled, she picked up the bread and walked to the window, then took a tentative bite. It wasn't a roll from the Willard, but it wasn't half-bad, either.

What she couldn't finish, she stored in the pockets of her coat, which were reasonably clean and offered protection from marauding insects. She was tired by then, but when she pulled back the thin, filthy blanket on the bed, she found a torn sheet sprinkled with animal droppings beneath, and she couldn't bring herself to lie down. The floor was equally repugnant, so she finally turned the table upside down, brushed away the dirt and cobwebs with the bottom of her skirt, and curled up inside.

She awoke to the feeling of something crawling on her scalp. She let out a yelp, frantically tossing her head as she combed through her hair with her fingers, and saw a spider drop out and scurry away. Even more revolting, her meal, now festering in the heat, was black with insects. She checked the bread in her pockets and shuddered. The bugs had found that, too. She flung the coat across the room and shook out the rest of her clothing, but she still had the feeling that insects were crawling on her skin.

The minutes dragged by. She stood at the window, thinking she had never been so bored, uncomfortable, and sweaty in her entire life. Then, around three, the workday ended and the Capitol emptied out, and there was even less to distract her than before.

She righted the table and sat down, resting her head on her folded arms on the top. After a minute or two she felt a bug in her hair, and languidly swatted it away. You could get used to anything, she supposed.

Stone, she decided, was doing it on purpose. Stalling in order to soften her up. Only one pleasure remained to her, to fantasize about the blistering lecture she would deliver, telling him about the moral icon he would become—and how short of that lofty standard he currently fell.

But when he finally arrived, he didn't look like a callous torturer. While he wasn't smiling, his sunny mood was impossible to miss, from the buoyancy in his step to the sparkle in his eyes. He closed the door. "So? Are you ready to talk?"

She smiled sweetly. "My, but we're chipper this afternoon. We must have had a lovely day." The smile turned into a scowl. "Some of us did, anyway. It's half past four. Where have you been? I sent for you this morning."

"Did you?" He removed a pair of handcuffs from his pocket. "Come over here, Sarah, and then turn around and put your hands behind your back. By the way, is your name really Sarah?"

"Yes." She stayed where she was, sitting at the table. "I said I'd sent for you. In case you didn't understand what that meant—"

"That you've decided to surrender. That you're abjectly sorry. That you'll make a full confession."

"I'm not sorry at all, but I will talk to you—as soon as I've had a decent meal and a hot bath." She raised her chin. "But you're not trussing me up. I'm not going to attack you or try to escape. What would be the use?"

"My groin and I have heard that one before." He turned to leave, but he was laughing now. "Maybe tomorrow, then."

"Dammit, Ty—"

"Yes?" He looked over his shoulder, still smiling.

"All right. Put the stupid handcuffs on." She rose from her chair, then turned on her heel. "So? What were you doing all day? Terrorizing *other* innocent women?"

"Talking to soldiers. It was glorious, Sarah." He

cuffed her and eased her around. The enthusiasm was all but bubbling out of him. "I'm writing about the lives they'll return to and the new attitudes they'll take with them. I've had some fascinating conversations. The war has changed us. We're not the same nation anymore. It's as if—as if a second American Revolution has taken place."

She was so startled—and so enchanted—that she forgot to stay annoyed. Years from now, historians would say the same thing, but nobody had known it so soon after the war. Stone was a marvel. "I don't remember that article," she muttered, "and I've read everything he's ever written. It must be new. This is incredible."

He looked puzzled. "I just told you—I'm still working on it. I spoke to Joseph Gales at the *Intelligencer*. Assuming he likes it, he'll run it next week."

"He will? How wonderful. I can't wait to read it." She beamed at him. He was so earnest and brilliant, so full of life and energy, that she couldn't help it. "You're a genius, Ty. You see things other people don't."

"Sarah." He put his hand on her shoulder. "Has a day in this place driven you mad, or are you only pretending that it has?"

"Neither, but we'll discuss it later. I've heard the walls here have ears." She scratched her head. "Can we leave now? If I don't bathe soon, I really will go mad."

"But you'll answer my questions as soon as we reach the Willard. We're agreed on that."

"After I wash and eat, and don't you dare object. We'll be talking for hours, and I'm not going to do it sweaty, stinking, and crawling with bugs. Anyway, if you'd come when I first sent for you, you would have had your answers by now, so it's your own damned fault if you have to wait."

Ty didn't argue. He preferred his women sweet and

clean and his rooms free of bugs, but even more important, he knew when someone had a mind to talk, and Sarah did. And not just talk, either, because there was a new openness about her and an ease in his presence that promised a great deal more.

He led her downstairs, helped her into a hack, and sat down beside her. Within moments, she was grilling him about his article, but he was happy to answer her questions. He enjoyed discussing his work, and she was proving a splendid collaborator. She professed a deep admiration for the men who had saved the Union, and for an ordinary citizen, knew an extraordinary amount about the war. Indeed, she was one of the smartest people he had ever met. As they spoke, the vague themes of his article came into sharper focus.

He removed her handcuffs as soon as they reached his suite. After visiting the bathroom, she scrutinized her belongings to make sure nothing was missing. He'd taken the precaution of locking her devices in his desk, and while he was willing to let her see them, he made her stand across the room as he held them up. Finally satisfied, she pulled out her toiletries and dressing gown, then helped herself to some towels.

"I'm off to bathe," she said cheerfully. "Assuming there isn't a wait, I'll be back within half an hour. In the meantime, could you order me up a meal? With some French wine, if possible. A Burgundy would be nice."

He rang for a bellman. If she thought he was letting her out of his sight, she was dreaming. "I'll have to track down Joe Willard—have him put an 'Out of Service' sign on one of the bathrooms so both of us can go inside."

Sarah clutched her belongings against her chest, momentarily speechless. Talking to Tyson Stone had been heaven, but her ecstasy had turned to anxiety in a heartbeat. "You can't come into the bathroom. You can't watch me bathe.'' She started forward. ''If you'll excuse me—''

''I'm afraid not.'' He crossed to the door and blocked her way. ''Credit me with some intelligence, Sarah. The tub rooms all have windows.''

''Which I have no intention of using. I told you before—''

''If you want a bath, you'll have to endure my presence. I know you by now. If I leave you alone, you'll be tempted to escape.'' He suddenly smiled. ''Would it help if I promise to keep my eyes on the floor?''

Her heart rate soared. The only thing that would have helped was if Stone were less appealing. *Him and his twenty-four-karat smiles,* she thought sourly. ''But you have all my things. If I wouldn't leave them this morning—''

''It's not open to discussion.'' He took a long, slow look, teasing her with his eyes. ''Besides, there's nothing I'm not familiar with.''

She made a face. ''How gallant of you to remind me.''

''I wasn't talking about Tuesday. The fact is, I searched you the very first night, and very thoroughly, too. I was looking for another cube, thinking it would turn off the barrier around your body, but I assure you I was honorable to a fault. I didn't remove your clothing. I just felt you through your nightdress.''

Her very *sheer* nightdress. She blushed fiercely, and to her horror, it wasn't because some stranger had violated her privacy. It was because she was so blasted scrawny, like a film star from back in the days when it had been fashionable to starve oneself. If someone other than Ty had done the touching. . . But he had, and she was hopelessly infatuated with him, and she wanted him to find her attractive.

She stood there, red with embarrassment, thinking she was so neurotic that even the psychomedics couldn't have cured her. If it was dangerous to want him, it was stupid beyond belief to want him to want *her*. When it came to women, he'd been pure heartbreak, and besides, he was only a fantasy. She would be home in a few days and he would be long dead.

He took a step forward and murmured her name, but whatever he'd planned to say was stopped by a knock on the door—a bellman responding to his ring. He disappeared into the hallway, returning a minute later. "Joe is in the dining room. I've sent him a message and ordered us something to eat. While we're waiting. . ." He crossed to his desk. "I was wondering. . . Would you look at my article and tell me what you think? I've written only a few pages so far, so it won't take long. They're in the back, after my notes."

Sarah was flattered to be asked, but Willard could arrive at any moment, and nothing had been settled. "I'd be glad to, but about my bath—"

"It's not negotiable. I know it will make you uncomfortable to have me in the room, but in view of what's happened in the past, I'd be a fool to trust you." He took a thick notebook out of his desk. "And about before. . . It's obvious I embarrassed you. I'm sorry." His voice was soft and regretful. "It's just—you're so good at putting me in my place that I forget how shy you really are, and I tease you more than I should. I won't forget again."

He held out the notebook, and she took it and sat down. John had never explained himself, and he'd never apologized, either, probably because he'd been sure he was always right. She wasn't used to a man who did both, and she found it appealing—very appealing. She probably could trust a man like that. And she certainly couldn't stay angry with him.

She began to read—page after page of research, quotes from the soldiers he'd interviewed along with his thoughts and observations. But what quotes! What observations! He exposed men's souls and saw into their hearts. He sensed what truly mattered, uncovered the deeper meanings, and discerned the larger consequences. It would be a brilliant article.

Someone knocked on the door, but she was too absorbed in his notes to care who it was. A moment later Ty handed her a glass of wine and a plate of food, and she absently thanked him. She ate and drank mechanically, so moved by what she was reading that she was constantly dabbing at her eyes.

She kept turning the pages, utterly mesmerized. And then Ty's hand came down on her shoulder, and she almost bolted up from the sofa. "Oh. You startled me. I was in another world." She gave him a smile full of awe and enchantment. "A world you sent me to. This is wonderful, Ty. Poetic, scholarly, insightful . . . It's vintage Tyson Stone, and you're not even thirty yet. It's just amazing. And I haven't even read the article. I'm still skimming the interviews."

Vintage Tyson Stone? Ty thought in bewilderment. What in hell was that supposed to mean? But then, when Sarah worshiped him with her eyes, and spoke of him as if he were Plato, Shakespeare, and Rousseau, all rolled into one, he didn't much care. It was all he could do not to lift her into his arms and carry her off to bed. He had expected to find it frustrating to watch her bathe, but looking at her now, he realized it would be pure torture.

Still, trusting her was out of the question. "We have to go," he said tightly. "Joe is standing guard in front of the bathroom, and he doesn't want it tied up any longer than necessary."

To his surprise, she didn't argue, just set down the notebook and collected what she needed for her bath. He ascribed her docility to a full belly, two glasses of wine, and her absorption in his work, which evidently enthralled her. Hoping to keep her submissive, he recounted some material that wasn't in his notes, and she listened raptly all the way down the hall.

She surprised him again when she saw Joe Willard. Far from fleeing in embarrassment, she was thrilled to meet him. It was fascinating to talk to him, she said. He knew so many important people through his hotel, and the story of his marriage was so romantic, especially the part about meeting Antonia when his commander had appropriated her father's house for his headquarters. Would he tell her about his life?

Afraid she would try to interview Joe on the spot, Ty took her by the arm and led her into the bathroom. "I'm glad you're more relaxed. If I'd known the effect a little wine would have, I would have provided it sooner."

Sarah shrugged and walked through a set of swinging doors into the tub room. It was all part of the training, she supposed. You accepted what you couldn't change and made the best of it. "You're right. Wine goes straight to my head." She scratched her neck. "But if you want the truth, I'm not so much relaxed as defeated. You're not going to leave me alone, and this itching is driving me crazy."

She set her things on the shelf behind the tub, then put in the stopper and turned on the water, which was piped up from boilers in the basement. But when it came to undressing, she couldn't seem to start. Instead, she walked to the double-hung window, pushed aside the curtains, and peered outside. The streets were quieter than yesterday. Now that the review was over, the city was emptying out.

She let the curtains drop. She would need to be more than tipsy to lose her inhibitions. She would need to be roaring drunk. "It's really very small," she murmured. "It would be an awfully tight squeeze."

"Not tight enough to stop you. You can either undress or we can leave, because I'm not changing my mind.'' His voice was husky and strained. ''Look, Sarah . . . There's nothing to be nervous about. I'm staying because I have to, not because I want to. You're simply a suspect. Your sex is irrelevant. I'm like a doctor with a patient. If you were a man, I would watch you in exactly the same way.''

A sensual chill ran down her spine. He was lying through his teeth. The arousal in his voice was unmistakable. A man wouldn't have affected him that way, but a woman he had an itch to sleep with was another story. He was going to watch her every move, and he was going to enjoy every moment.

Not that she blamed him for being careful, of course. He'd learned firsthand what a skillful fighter she was. She grimaced, thinking of herself at seventeen, when she'd first met John. She'd been so full and firm and ripe . . . If only she still were.

She returned to the tub and kicked off her shoes, then wrapped her dressing gown around her shoulders and fastened the first few buttons to keep it in place. The gown made an effective screen, but her heart still pounded violently as she removed her blouse and skirt and stepped out of her petticoats. By the time she got to her shift, her hands were so unsteady she was thinking about forgetting the whole business. But then a bug crawled out of her corset, and she flinched and yelped, and she couldn't get her clothes off fast enough. The sooner she got in the tub, the better.

Behind her, Ty was dying by inches, especially whenever another garment came off. He couldn't see a thing beyond the outlines of Sarah's body, but his imagination filled in the rest. The lush curve of a breast and the gentle flare of a hip . . . The long, graceful legs . . . The bones in her ribs and pelvis, all of them a bit too prominent . . . She was half-woman and half-waif, and he wanted to make love to her and take care of her, all at the same time. His body had never been this hard and hot, not even for Peggy, and his feelings had never been this tender.

When she shrieked, he almost dashed over to comfort her, but then he realized the cause and stayed where he was. "An insect?" he asked evenly.

Her shift flew across the room. "Yes." She pulled off her corset and threw it aside, visibly shaking. "Ugh. I may never forgive you for that prison." Her knickers came next, and he sucked in his breath. "The man who wrote the words I just read was ethical and compassionate. He would be ashamed of leaving me in that place. I hope you know that."

Watching her was making him sweat. He wiped his face with his sleeve. "I didn't want to, Sarah. I care for you, for God's sake. If you'd given me any choice . . ." His voice trailed off. Her foot was up on the tub now, and she was peeling off a stocking.

"Oh, right, Ty." A garter and stocking wafted through the air. "Blame *me* for your moral failings."

"Dammit, if you accuse me of being an unprincipled savage even one more time . . ."

She removed her other stocking. "Yes?"

"Never mind." She was naked under the gown now, and it was wreaking havoc with his respiration. He wanted to growl that he wouldn't have been here, swollen and throbbing, if she'd been reasonable from the beginning, but arguing was only making things worse. The desire in this room was so thick he was ready to strip off his clothes and join her in the tub.

She turned off the water, then glared at him over her shoulder. "Sit. I'm not giving you a bird's-eye view."

He did as he was told, and she climbed into the water with the gown outside the tub and lowered herself into the bath. He watched with reluctant admiration. It was a good technique. She only dropped the gown at the last possible moment, and since his eyes were level with the top of the tub, her head and her neck were all he could see.

But she'd made a grievous mistake. Her toiletries were behind her on the shelf, and she couldn't reach them without lifting herself out of the water and twisting around. So she sat there paralyzed, not knowing what to do, and he couldn't help grinning. Unfortunately, she chose exactly that moment to glance at him.

"It's not funny," she snapped. "Close your eyes."

He would have humored her if she'd looked embarrassed, but as far as he could tell, she was only aggravated by her own stupidity. His smile got broader. "I don't want to. I'd rather fetch your soap for you."

"So help me, Ty, if you move even an inch—"

But he was already on his feet. "Yes?"

She drew her knees up to her chest and wrapped her arms around them. "Patient and doctor, my foot. I knew you were lying. You're a satyr. Don't you dare come any closer."

"I'm sorry, but this is ridiculous, Sarah. All this fuss about a naked body . . . I'm going to look at you and get it over with." He walked to the edge of the tub and studied her. "You're lovely, all right? A bit thin, but beautiful all the same." He grabbed her soap and shampoo, then tossed a towel over her. "Here. That will preserve your modesty." He'd promised not to tease, but she was scowling so fiercely, he couldn't resist. "Can I scrub your back? Wash your hair?"

She held out her hand. "No to both. Give me my things. Then get back where you belong and *sit*."

He tossed the containers into the water and turned away, laughing. And then he realized what he had just seen, and did an astonished about-face. She was very fair, but a strip around her loins had been fairer than all the rest.

He was too late for a second look—the towel hid everything by now—but he was certain he wasn't mistaken. "Good God, Sarah. What sort of place do you come from? How can the men there permit the women under their authority to go out in the sun virtually naked?"

Sarah's lips twitched at the incredulity in Ty's voice. Now that the towel was firmly in place, she was more relaxed, and besides, she couldn't stay angry with a man who told her she was beautiful and obviously meant it. She glanced at him, and there was so much shock on his face—so much stern disapproval—that she dissolved into laughter. Life was bizarre. He'd realized that her home was utterly alien, and why? Not because of her pistol and shields, but because of her suntan, which she'd acquired in the privacy of her own backyard wearing the bottom of a modest bikini.

"The men don't have a thing to say about it," she answered blithely, "not that they object. Frankly, if anyone is shameless, it's men like you. You think I should cover myself with restrictive clothing in public, but in private, you try to remove it and get me into bed. It's not a concern about modesty that motivates you, but a desire for ownership. You want exclusive rights to touch and even to look."

He mulled it over, looking increasingly uncomfortable. "Maybe you're right. It reminds me of something my sister once said—that when it comes to women, we men want total control. We want to own a woman the way we own a house or a horse. But I've always denied I could be guilty of that."

"Then think again, because you are." But he would change. His sister Susannah would crusade for women's rights, and he would support her staunchly and eloquently. "If you have any interest in reforming, you can start by endeavoring to behave yourself." She pointed to the door. "Now go, Ty. And sit."

Ty retreated, pleased that the tension had finally eased. For all the trouble it caused him, he preferred

Sarah confident and feisty to hesitant and fearful. And if she was also more of a mystery than ever, he could live with that. His questions would be answered soon enough.

She began to wash, using the towel as armor, soaping, splashing, and sighing with contentment. Each glimpse of a bare limb made his desire surge higher, but it warmed rather than burned him. Obviously she wanted him. She had said so in every way that mattered. Now that she was on the verge of giving herself, waiting had its pleasures as well as its torments.

She opened her shampoo and lathered her hair, providing such an enticing view of her arms and shoulders that his loins tightened painfully. And then her towel slipped down, and before she could pull it back up, he caught a glimpse of a puckered nipple. He pictured it in his mouth, Sarah writhing and moaning while he nipped and suckled, and his manhood throbbed furiously. He wanted to arouse her until she opened herself completely, then lose himself in her hot, sweet body.

Groaning at the image, he forced his thoughts onto something more productive, the conclusion to his article. He cleared his throat and tried to sound detached. "Sarah . . . The change we discussed before, from an attachment to town and state to an identification with the Union . . . Some say it will last, while others believe it's a transient consequence of the war. Which do you think is correct?"

She looked up, smiling mysteriously. "That it will be permanent. The South will always be the South, but we'll never go back—" She cut herself off. "Let's leave it at that. I believe it will last."

"Tell me why you believe that. Is it the things you've read? The people you've spoken to?"

It took a little coaxing, but she finally elaborated. They traded ideas, she speaking broadly, he making inferences from his own experiences. The discussion was helpful, but it didn't distract him a whit. On the contrary, when their minds connected so strongly, the wanting grew even worse.

Finally, in a strangled voice, he informed her that they needed to be going—it was only fair to give Willard his bathroom back. She nodded, gazing at him blissfully. "It's all my fault. I could talk to you for hours. The time just flies. Let me rinse out my hair, and then we'll leave." She turned on the tap and stretched out her neck, closing her eyes as the water cascaded over her head.

Something inside him snapped. It wasn't the graceful arch of her body beneath the towel that did it so much as the way she'd looked at him and the words she had spoken. She was besotted with him, and he was besotted right back. He couldn't sit here like a statue, doing nothing. He walked to the tub, his body pounding savagely, and turned off the water.

Chapter 13

Sarah didn't sense Ty's presence until the water stopped flowing. Then she straightened and opened her eyes, but at first, she was so bewitched by the pleasure of talking to him, of learning from him, that she simply stared. The desire she saw on his face sent a stab of alarm tearing through her, and she tightened her towel protectively. "I don't know what you have in mind—"

"Of course you do." He lifted her out of the tub and set her on her feet, and she was so astonished by his audacity that she never even resisted.

He removed her wet towel and handed her a dry one, and she wrapped it around her body, under her arms, clutching it above her breasts so it couldn't fall. He was already toweling her hair by then, rubbing it briskly but gently. Coercion was foreign to his nature, she realized, but seduction was another matter entirely.

Her alarm quickly faded, but her common sense remained firmly in place. "All right—I do," she said. "You want to have sex, but I'm not interested. Let's go, Ty."

He dropped his towel, then stepped behind her and

curled his hands around her upper arms. "I'd rather stay."

He caressed her shoulders and nuzzled her neck, just as if she'd never objected. For all his gentleness, his kisses were so passionate and full of yearning they all but scorched her skin, and the experience was so erotic it made her reel. She'd seen things like this in holofilms, but she didn't know men actually did them. Certainly John never had.

He nipped her lobe, then kissed her ear, and she closed her eyes from the sheer pleasure of it. Given his technique, it was little wonder the women had stood in line. His intense emotion told her she beautiful, irresistible. And the raw physical excitement he made her feel . . . Her heart was beating so fast she could hardly breathe, and a deep sexual ache was suffusing her body.

She tried to edge away, but she was trapped between his body and the tub and couldn't move. A hard elbow or a sharp kick would have dislodged him, but she couldn't bring herself to attack him. He was playing by a different set of rules than she was, and besides, she was too crazy about him to deliberately hurt him again.

That left words, but men of his era tended to ignore them, so she used the most assertive tone she could muster. "I want you to stop, Ty. Right now. I mean it."

He did so, but only to pull her around to face him. "I heard you the first time." He twined a hand into her hair and cupped her buttocks, fitting her against his erection. "But you don't mean it at all." He nuzzled her jaw and moved lightly against her groin, teasing her with his body.

The thrusting arousal that had once so distressed her only inflamed her now. She was so charged with longing that she had to stop herself from arching closer and responding to his movements. "Where I come from," she said breathlessly, "no means no, and when a woman says it, a man stops immediately."

That, at least, got his attention. He didn't release her, but he finally stopped nuzzling her. "Even if a woman looks at a man the way you look at me? He still stops?"

"Yes."

He was openly dubious. "Even if she's burning with excitement, the way you are now? He lets her burn? He simply walks away?"

"Yes."

"Even though they're wild for each other," he muttered. "No matter how much they want each other."

"Yes." She straightened away from him. "Dammit, Ty, people should control themselves. We're not animals—"

"You're the one who talks as if we are." He glowered at her. " 'Have sex.' What a grotesque term. I adore you. I want to touch you. I want to give you pleasure. It doesn't have to include"—his tone was withering—"*having sex.*"

She'd had sex without pleasure more times than she could count, but never pleasure without sex. The notion was disturbingly tempting. "That's not the point," she insisted. "Where I come from—"

"Where you come from," he interrupted, "the men have stopped being men. They've lost their bloody senses."

She wanted to lecture him about the male behavior of his era and why it was unacceptable, but his mouth closed over hers to silence her. He kissed and nipped, and suddenly it wasn't an abstract male they were talking about but Tyson Stone, and what he was doing was pure magic. He began to taste her, coaxing her lips apart with his tongue, kissing his way from her jaw to her ear to her eyes, only returning to her lips when she moaned and sought him out. Then he slid his tongue into her mouth, edging his hand under her towel at the same time to explore the flesh beneath.

The kiss was slow, deep, and very thorough. It said

she was the only one in the world he wanted, the only one who existed, and she kissed him back the same way. When his fingers slid between her legs to stroke her inner thighs, she put her arms around his neck in a silent offer of truce. This wasn't about sex at all, she thought hazily. It was about *her,* and it was overwhelming.

Finally, after a kiss that seemed to last forever, he drew back a little and smiled at her, shakily but very warmly. "What, no more objections?" He pecked her on the nose. "Tell me something, sweetheart. Where you come from, would I be permitted to continue?"

She didn't know where she was, but it couldn't be earth. It was too perfect. Too blissful. "God, yes." She gazed at him through glazed eyes and smiled back dreamily. "Tyson Stone. I don't believe this. It can't be happening."

But it was. There was another shattering kiss, another intimate caress that began as light and teasing stroking, and when she groaned and responded to his rhythm, grew firmer and more insistent. She clung to him, hungry for more, then desperate for it, then flooded by the incredible pleasure of it. But just as she reached the edge, he drew back his hand and slipped a finger inside her, exploring her gently and provocatively, making her wait and burn and writhe before he finally returned and gave her what she craved.

She was hanging by a thread, only seconds from release, when he teasingly withdrew again, but this time, she dug her nails into his back and thrust her tongue into his mouth, demanding satisfaction for the first time in her life. He promptly provided it, in wave after ecstatic wave, each one so intense that she gasped out her pleasure in disjointed words and sharp little cries. Finally, sated and utterly drained, she slumped against his chest and buried her face in his neck. If that was a climax, she'd only had blips before.

He nuzzled her hair. "You're very vocal, my love. Joe probably thinks I was torturing you."

She blushed and pulled away. "When I was moaning 'Oh, Ty' and 'Don't stop'? I doubt it." She touched the scar on his chin, overwhelmed by emotion. "That was perfect. *You* were perfect. I'll remember it all my life." Her eyes slid away. "And, uh, I owe you one."

"You what?"

"I owe you one. If you want me to, that is." She blushed harder. "It's—it's sort of the custom where I come from. To return the favor."

"It is? Well, then, it's the first sensible one you've named." He sobered, regarding her with a troubled expression. "I don't want to alarm you, love, but before, when I was touching you . . ." He slipped a hand between her legs and ran his fingers over the inside of her right thigh. "I felt a lump, Sarah. Right here. You have such excellent doctors where you come from . . . I want you to consult one."

She finally looked him in the eye, quelling the urge to smile. He was truly worried about her, and she wouldn't have laughed at that for the world. "It isn't a tumor, Ty. It's a birth control device, implanted under my skin."

"Birth control?" he repeated. "What's that?"

"Something that stops me from getting pregnant unless I choose to try."

"And how does it do that?"

"If I press it, it emits high-frequency sound waves that incapacitate human sperm without damaging any other cells."

"Hmm. How remarkable." Looking thoughtful, he picked up her dressing gown and held it out for her. "Devices that can't possibly exist, but do. Facts you can't possibly know, but do. Matters almost too private to mention, yet you do it without compunction." She put on the gown, and he collected her things. "Tell me something, Sarah. Just how far in the future are you from?''

The question didn't surprise her. Assuming she wasn't from another planet, it was the only possible explanation, and Ty was too smart not to finally see it. ''Very far,'' she said with a sigh.

Ty and Sarah were sitting together in his parlor, talking and drinking wine. She had told him what year she was from, 2096, and what place, Virginia City, Nevada, and he didn't know which had astonished him more—the notion of traveling in time, or the fact that Virginia City was much the same in 2096 as it was right now.

''Of course, the mines were played out a long time ago,'' she was saying. ''The merchants wanted to attract sightseers and vacationers, so they restored it to look like it did in its heyday in the 1870s. We chose it—''

''In the 1870s?'' he interrupted. ''Then the biggest silver strikes are still in the future?''

''Yes, but actually, it wasn't so much the strikes themselves that led to the boom as the speculation in mining stocks.'' She grinned at him. ''I'm sure it's occurred to you that with the knowledge I have, I could make you a wealthy man. What do you think, Ty? Should I do it?''

There was a mischievous gleam in her eyes that told him she wasn't serious. ''Money isn't important to me,'' he drawled, ''but if you want to give me a list of the best mines to invest in, I'll gladly accept it. Of course, random changes in history could have undesirable consequences. I assume you've been instructed to avoid them at all costs.''

''You're right,'' she admitted. ''My colleagues at the Wells Project—the top secret time travel project I work for—they would be horrified I'd even mentioned the boom in the seventies. We're not allowed to change the past in any way without the president's explicit approval, or even to talk to the people we meet about what will happen in the future. Getting back to Virginia City, we chose it because it's close enough to Berkeley—'' She cut herself off. ''Berkeley is across the bay from San Francisco. The college there is part of the University of California. It was the successor to the school that's in Oakland now, and the first U.C. campus of what will become twelve. The physics of time travel was discovered there. Anyway, we chose Virginia City because it was close enough to Berkeley for our project personnel to travel back and forth in a few hours, but isolated enough to preserve secrecy.''

There was so much information in that casual little speech that Ty scarcely knew what to ask first. ''There are twelve colleges in California? My God, how many people live there in your time? How do they travel from Berkeley to Virginia City so quickly? By train? And who was Wells? The scientist who invented time travel? How does it work?''

''There are over a hundred colleges in California,'' she answered, ''but only twelve are part of the U.C. system. The population is about sixty million, around fifteen percent of the U.S. total. California isn't the largest state in the Union—Alaska is—but it is the most populous. As far as—''

''Wait a minute.'' His head was spinning. ''When will we acquire Alaska? When will it become a state? Were you really born there?''

''Umm. I told you—in Fairbanks.'' She sipped her wine. ''It's in the central part of the state. The city was founded around 1900, after gold was discovered in the region. My parents were professors at the Fairbanks campus of the University of Alaska. Secretary Seward—''

''Your parents?'' The startling revelations never seemed to end. ''Do you mean your mother as well as your father? *Both* of them were professors at the university?''

She nodded. ''Women do everything men do in my time, from voting to running corporations to constructing buildings. In fact, the current president is a woman. Most American women don't even take their husbands' names anymore. They use their mothers' names, keep them after they marry, and pass them on to their daughters. My real last name is Maravich, but I used March here because Maravich sounded too foreign. So my daughter is Shelby Maravich. The 'Shelby' is for my late husband, John Shelby.''

Ty could see the logic of the custom, but found it cumbersome and offensive. ''And the men of your time don't object? They aren't insulted that their wives and daughters refuse to take their names?''

She looked amused. ''Only if they're extremely backward. Getting back to my parents, my mother was a physicist and my father was a conductor and composer. I'm a historian—nineteenth century American, especially the postwar West. My doctorate is from Berkeley, where I met John. As for Alaska, Secretary Seward bought it from Russia in 1867 for about seven million dollars. People said it was an icy wasteland—they called it Seward's Folly—but they were wrong. Vast oil and mineral deposits were eventually discovered there. It became a state in 1959, the forty-ninth of what's now fifty-two.''

Fifty-two! Ty shook his head, amazed and thrilled. ''Then Lincoln truly did save us. We'll grow and progress. Will you tell me the names of all the states? Show me their locations on a map?''

''Sure.'' Sarah frowned in concentration. ''What else did you ask? Oh, yes. Why we call it the Wells Project. It was a whimsical choice. It refers to an English writer, H.G. Wells. He was born in the 1860s and wrote a famous story called *The Time Machine* around the turn of the century—not that I literally traveled here in a machine. The nature of the universe is such that all time and all space simply *are,* simply exist, all at once. And just as there's a path from the sun to the North Star, there's a path from 2096 to 1865. If you can seize material from the past and pull it into the present, the past will compensate by pulling an equivalent amount of material right back. You simply have to ensure that the past removes precisely what you want to send there—in this case, me."

Ty had only the vaguest notion of what she was talking about. "By what process do you accomplish the transfer? What is the nature of the paths you just spoke of?"

She shrugged. "I'm not a physicist, so my understanding of the science involved is very limited. All I know is, with enough energy, you can rip apart the normal fabric of space-time and open whatever pathway you need."

Which explained exactly nothing, Ty thought. She might as well have been speaking ancient Greek. "And the cubes? The cameo? How do those work?"

"It has to do with the fundamental nature of matter. The particles that make up matter don't so much exist as have the potential to exist. The operation of the shields hinges on our ability to coax particles into existence—to make them adopt the tangible form of matter—just where and when we choose. In practice, they flicker back and forth between the two states, so the shield is a little porous. It can stop solids and liquids, but not gases."

That made no sense either, so Ty turned to something he *would* understand, the transportation of her era. He was repeating his question about travel to Virginia City when something far more important occurred to him, and his heart leapt with excitement. "The transcontinental railroad . . . The whole country yearns for it, especially those who are farthest from their families. Will it ever be built?"

She smiled so knowingly he realized she must have studied the subject at length. "It will be finished in May of '69. Historians are still writing about what a momentous accomplishment it was. We still use various kinds of trains, but the commonest types of transport are ground-level vehicles called cars and flying ones called planes." She described them in detail, then explained their operation. "We've traveled into space, too, but only as far as Mars. There's a colony of a few hundred there."

Ty nodded dumbly, so overwhelmed that he'd finally run out of questions. Fifty-two states. Four hundred million people. Women who did the work of men, and even a female president. A universe that could be changed repeatedly and matter that wasn't there at all. Machines that propelled themselves over the land and through the air with energy stored in small boxes, and a settlement on another world. How was he supposed to comprehend such things?

"My time—this place—must seem very primitive to you." He grimaced, thinking about how educated she was, about how far her level of understanding surpassed his own. "*I* must seem very primitive. You're a doctor of philosophy. I never even made it to college."

She set aside her wineglass, stroked his cheek, and gazed into his eyes. To his bemusement, the adoring look was back on her face. "You didn't have to, Ty. You were so gifted that formal education was irrelevant. You were one of the greatest men of the nineteenth century. A brilliant thinker, an uncompromising humanitarian, and an absolutely remarkable journalist. I wrote my dissertation on your work. As you've already pointed out, by telling you who I am and why I came, I could change history in ways we can't predict. But you're so extraordinary that I'm breaking all the rules for you.''

He understood her earlier silence now, and also her knowledge of his past. She had studied his life. She had read his writings—his personal correspondence as well as his articles. He wasn't so much shocked by all that as uneasy. How could a man live up to praise like hers?

She was walking a fine line, he knew, trying to satisfy his curiosity without affecting history, but he couldn't help fishing for information. ''You wrote about my work? But why? What will be so special about it?''

''Let's just say . . . You fought all the right fights, Ty, for justice, liberty, and equality—and very effectively, too. When it came to ethics and morality, you were a giant.'' She smiled sheepishly. ''Which is why I get so annoyed whenever you bully or threaten me. I know how extraordinary you were, and I expect you to live up to your reputation.''

He scowled. He had been this, he had done that . . . It was damned unsettling. ''Sarah . . . Do you think you could stop talking about me as if I've been dead for hundreds of years?''

Ty looked so comically vexed that Sarah smiled. ''I'm sorry. I forget that it's not very pleasant in this era to be reminded of your own mortality, but if it's any comfort, our experiments indicate that the soul endures to the same extent the universe does. Of course, that's only logical given the fact that the universe is a continuum—all space and all time at once.''

Ty shook his head at the arrogance of that statement. ''Your experiments indicate . . . Good Lord, Sarah, is there nothing you don't investigate? What comes next? Why we exist?''

''Our scientists seek, but they don't always find,'' she replied matter-of-factly. ''The evidence points to numerous possible fates after death—joining the cosmic whole, bliss or pain, resting or seeking, coming back in a different form . . . One's beliefs might influence one's destiny, or the life one has led might determine it. We really don't know. The direct knowledge of God and the ultimate purpose of the universe remain beyond the reach of science.''

''I'm gratified *something* does,'' Ty grumbled, and added wryly, ''Given my future greatness, I believe I deserve rest at the very least, if not eternal bliss.'' He slid his arms around her waist from behind and pulled her against his chest. ''I would like to visit your time. Study its technology. Learn about your society.''

''We don't have the capacity to bring you forward, but even if we did, the president would never approve it. The results would be totally unpredictable. I'll answer your questions as best I can to the extent I think I should, but you have to promise that whatever I say will go no farther.'' She gave him an anxious look. ''I've already changed the future just by coming here, Ty. That article you're working on about the troops—in the world I come from, you never published it.''

So that was what she'd meant about the article's being totally new, Ty thought. ''Which I surely would have, if I'd written it. But I couldn't have, because in the original version of history, I almost certainly left Washington Wednesday evening— That is, Reid left. I had—personal business to attend to. Stanton knew how impatient I was to depart, so he accepted my resignation effective at the end of the review. And then you arrived, and I was ordered to stay here and investigate.'' He remembered the plan Stanton had suggested for his disappearance, and a fierce satisfaction surged through him. ''That's why you warned me about the cars, isn't it? Because according to history, Reid died Wednesday night in an accident. You knew that, and you couldn't bear to let it happen.''

''It was an illogical impulse, nothing more,'' she said

uneasily, then switched to her cool historian's tone. ''Nobody knew your death was faked—that Reid was really Stone. No letters came down to us—''

''An illogical impulse, eh? Do you know what I think, my love? I think you adored me even then, despite all the insults you hurled at my head.'' He nuzzled her neck, highly pleased by the thought. It wasn't just some future icon she had wanted, but him. ''After all, you cried when you read I had died. Ah Lan told me so.''

Sarah wasn't sure how she'd felt about Reid—or whether she loved Stone—but it really didn't matter. She would be leaving soon, and knowing Ty as she did, that would suit him very well. He would enjoy her company while she was here, just as he had enjoyed so many others', but after she had gone, he would find someone else to amuse himself with.

''No matter what you called yourself, you tried to be kind and decent,'' she said, ''so yes, I did mourn you a little. But why all the mystery, Ty? I've read every letter you ever wrote— Excuse me. Every letter you'll ever write, at least the ones that will survive, and there's nothing from the past two years. Why not?''

''Personal considerations.'' His brusque tone warned her not to pursue the topic. ''And you? What was your mission? Why were you—'' He went tense and still. ''Oh, God. It was Lincoln, wasn't it? That's what you meant in your ad—that you had arrived too late to save him. You use old newspapers to communicate, and the notice was a message to your colleagues in the future. You came here to prevent the assassination, but something went wrong, and you were trying to contact them, to tell them where you were.''

''Yes,'' Sarah said softly. ''I would have given my life to succeed, but I never even got to try.''

Ty was shaking now. ''Was Lincoln that important, then? Was his death that devastating to the nation?''

Sarah explained in detail, and Ty found it wrenching. He was stricken by renewed grief to discover that the loss was even greater than he had imagined—that Reconstruction would go so horribly wrong, that so much suffering would result, that over two centuries later, despite an amount of racial progress that astonished him, America would still be paying the price.

They talked quietly, trading stories about Lincoln, finding comfort in the feelings they shared. Finally, looking thoughtful, Ty asked slowly, "Is it possible that you can't change the past, at least not who lives and who dies? That what was, must always be? Is that why things went wrong?"

"But you can. We know that for a fact." Sarah related the history of the Wells Project—how they had sent back inanimate objects first, then animals, then people. "But rearranging the past—that was never our intention. We only planned to observe. We hoped to unravel history's mysteries. And then—then our director's little daughter drowned in a swimming pool accident."

"A swimming pool?"

"A man-made pool we build for exercise and pleasure. This one was in the director's backyard. And, of course, it was only a small step from observing his grief to wondering if we could negate it. So we ran an experiment."

"You sent a time traveler back to save the child."

"Yes. We call them tempronauts. He went to the director's house an hour before the accident and stopped the child from falling in. When he returned, the director told us he remembered both versions of the past. But his wife didn't, Ty. It was eerie. We learned that unless a person is present at a jump—jumping is what we call traveling to another time—unless you actually see a tempronaut depart, you remember only the new past, not the original one."

"So if you had saved Lincoln, with all the benefits you hoped would result—"

"Not just hoped." She told him about the government's history computers and the predictions they had made.

He looked skeptical. "I wouldn't trust machines to do my thinking for me, no matter how complex they were, but let's assume they were correct. If your mission had succeeded, then only the people who saw you depart would have known about the president's assassination? Countless details of history might have changed—your friends and neighbors might even be different people—but nobody else would have realized it?"

"That's right. But remember, souls are as eternal as the universe, so we weren't really depriving anyone of life, not in the larger sense. Given the events of the past two and a half centuries, we thought we were justified."

His expression said he didn't agree. "Humph. That's damned unnerving, Sarah. Men—and women—aren't gods, and they shouldn't try to be. Maybe that's why you failed."

"Maybe, but the director's little girl died four years ago, and she's still here." She regarded him soberly. "I've thought about it, of course. Asked myself why I landed in the wrong month when a technical error was impossible. But we know that the universe can behave like a living, sentient organism. Sometimes it prohibits us from doing things, and this might have been one of those cases. For example, you can't converse with an earlier version of yourself. We've tried, and something always prevents it. You can't kill a parent to prevent your own birth. A tempronaut went berserk once and tried it, because of the way his father had abused his older sisters before he was born, and a revolver in perfect working order just wouldn't fire. And once a jump occurs—once you tear the fabric of space-time—that jump will always occur. Three years ago, one of our tempronauts was attacked within minutes of his arrival, and all we got back was a dead body. So we decided to transport someone to the day before the jump to abort it, but our machinery refused to function."

"So you lost him forever."

"No. We went back a month and instituted the practice of arming our tempronauts with shields. And then, because his mission had proved so dangerous, we retrieved him only seconds after he'd arrived in the past. But we learned that jumping takes a toll on a living creature—the deep sleep that follows seems to be the body's way of repairing itself—and two jumps in so short a period of time put him into a coma. He had brain damage when he came out of it. He's still in therapy, still working to recover."

What Sarah ascribed to the universe, Ty attributed to God, but he wasn't about to argue theology. "So you think the universe wouldn't let you save Lincoln? But why not?"

"I don't know, but maybe time is like a great and powerful river. You can diverge from the flow in minor ways, but the basic current always sweeps you along in the same general direction, again and again, no matter what you do. And saving Lincoln was just too big a change."

Ty sat there for a long minute, saying nothing, then grasped Sarah's hand and fingered her ring. She knew what he was thinking without being told. "You're wondering how John died," she murmured, "and whether we sent someone back to save him." She waited for his nod, then continued, "It was suicide and we did, but his mind was made up."

"Because he was ill? Suffering intensely?"

"In a way. He was a genius, Ty. The father of time travel. Jumps are enormously expensive, and they never would have spent the money on anyone less important and revered. But the great breakthroughs in physics usually come from the young, and the creative part of John's research was done before he was thirty. It was just detail and elaboration after that. After the first few jumps by humans, when his work on the project was finished, he realized he would never have another brilliant insight, and he couldn't go on. Our tempronaut was what we call a psychomedic, a physician who uses medicine and conversation to help people in emotional distress. He and John spoke for hours, but John was in great mental pain, and ready for whatever might come next. It was a rational decision."

Ty couldn't accept that. He didn't understand how John Shelby could have left his family, or how Sarah could discuss the loss so calmly. "You're very dispassionate about it. Didn't you love him? Haven't you missed him?"

Sarah heard the disapproval in Ty's voice and felt tired and a little depressed. He didn't know it, but love was the last thing he wanted. He'd rejected it again and again, while she had yearned for it with all her heart—and never found it.

"It wasn't—an easy marriage," she said. "I was little more than a child when I met John, only seventeen. My parents had died in an earthquake when I was nine, but they'd mentioned him all the time, because they'd all gone to school together at Berkeley. He was famous before my parents even left, so naturally they had followed his career. It was only much later that I put things together and realized that he'd been in love with my mother. It must have galled him—that my mother, a fellow scientist, could have preferred a musician to the greatest physicist of our century."

"So you were curious to meet him, and when you became a student at Berkeley, you went to see him. And he took one look at you, and he saw your mother, and he wanted you."

Ty was very perceptive, Sarah thought, but then, he always would be. ''Exactly. Naturally I was flattered. He'd won the Nobel Prize already, the most important honor a scientist can receive in my time, and he was only forty. He was handsome and dynamic, and I was very attracted to him. Idolized him, really. I think I was looking for a father as much as a lover. So I married him and had Shelby, but I suppose genius by its nature is selfish. His work was what mattered most, and I couldn't share it with him. My role was to make his life run smoothly and to limit his contacts with what he called the fools all around him. And given who he was, how could I object? How could I not feel honored? I had my work, which was important and satisfying, and I had Shelby, whom I love dearly, so I was reasonably happy. But my marriage . . .'' She hesitated. ''I've never told this to another soul, but I think I was lonelier before John died than afterward.''

''I see.'' For a genius, Ty thought, John Shelby had been a singular fool. He'd had everything a man could want—fulfilling work and a loving family—and he had walked away from it.

He pulled Sarah onto his lap, cupped her chin, and kissed her deep and hard. She shuddered, responding with the same unbridled passion and fierce emotion as she always did. She didn't seem to know it, but she loved him, and God knew he loved her back.

Unlike John Shelby, he wasn't going to walk away. And he'd be damned if he was going to let her do it, either.

Chapter 14

The first time Ty had made love to Sarah, in the tub room, the twisting fear he had felt upon discovering a lump under her skin had driven all the need from his body, leaving only a desire to hold her and give her pleasure. But now, as he drank in the torrid sweetness of her mouth, as he massaged her nipples through the fabric of her gown and felt her arch eagerly against his fingers, his frustration and yearning exploded like volatile gases in a stoppered bottle. He was gripped by a hunger so violent that it pushed him beyond rational thought, almost beyond physical control. It was too much to bear—the knowledge that no precautions would be necessary when he took her, that he could excite her with his unsheathed manhood, that when he slid in and out of her tight, moist body, every sensitive fold of her skin would lie open to his hot, hard flesh.

He stood, taking her with him, and strode into the bedroom. As he tumbled her atop the crisply made bed, he told himself to cool off, to slow down, but he couldn't stop kissing her. He wound up on his knees, straddling her hips in a way that left his groin exposed and defenseless, fumbling impatiently with the buttons on her gown. He was only half-finished when he felt her fingers stroking his member through his clothing. He sucked in his breath. He couldn't let her touch him. At the rate he was going, he would go off like a Spencer repeating rifle within seconds of burying himself inside her.

And then she was unbuttoning his trousers and drawers, and freeing his member, and he was so eager for the feel of her hand on his bare skin that he couldn't make himself stop her. He only tore away his mouth when she ran her fingers lightly up and down his turgid shaft. "My God, Sarah . . . If you keep doing that . . ."

She regarded him with mock sternness. "I want you on your back, Colonel Stone. Right now. That's an order."

There was no question of disobeying. He could barely speak, much less argue. Besides, if she wanted to be on top and control his movements while they made love, he was more than willing. He did as he was told, finding her playful arrogance wildly exciting, wondering where her earlier shyness had gone.

She eased down his clothing, then cupped his testicles and teasingly kneaded them. His manhood was piercing the air like a quivering arrow now, and every inch of it was desperate to be inside her. He sat and reached out his hands, intending to pull her astride him, but she grabbed his wrists before he could touch her and pushed them toward his sides. He pushed the other way, easily defeating her, and yanked his wrists from her grasp.

They stared at each other. He was consumed by fire, determined to have her at once, but her face was such a study in feminine reproval that he cooled a bit. "I thought I told you to lie down," she said with a frown.

She was visibly annoyed, but she was also very aroused, so he stayed where he was. So did she, permitting him to cup her breasts and stroke her nipples with his thumbs, shivering when he offered the erotic little pinches she so enjoyed. She murmured a token protest, but he ignored it. She wasn't even retreating, much less resisting. It wasn't that she didn't want to, only that she'd had some specific scheme in mind, and he had overridden it.

He prevented further objections with a hard kiss, and she parted her lips, met his probing tongue, and sucked it deep into her mouth. He loved the way she responded. She was nothing like Peggy, who, for all her fiery passion, had been calculating and controlled. Sarah was all helpless, guileless desire.

Wanting her still hotter, he bent his head to her nipple and rummaged beneath the folds of her gown. To his surprise and amusement, she swatted away his hand, then twined her fingers into his hair to pull his mouth from her breast.

"That's enough. You're impossible." Her voice was exasperated but husky, scolding and seducing him at the same time. "For once in your life, you're going to do as you're told. I have plans for you, Tyson Stone, and they start with you flat on your back. Now stop distracting me and allow me to make you happy."

He bit gently but sharply on her nipple, evoking a startled gasp of enjoyment, then removed his hands. "Whatever you say, my love." Her plans sounded highly erotic. He had the feeling she meant to kill him with pleasure, and only a fool would have resisted *that.*

She pushed against his shoulders, and he lay back down with a cheeky grin. "Do your best, sweetheart. I'm entirely at your mercy."

"Good. See that you stay that way." She straddled him, poising her womanhood above his thighs, then stroked his member. Her fingers felt exquisite. His grin faded and his eyes closed. The next thing he knew, she was raking him so provocatively with her nails that he had to seize the bedclothes to stop himself from grabbing her again.

She explored him very delicately after that, lightly rubbing the tip of his shaft, then stopping. Clawing along its length with beguiling tenderness, then stopping. It wasn't long before he was writhing beneath her fingers and clutching the covers for dear life.

He finally groaned in frustration. "That's enough, Sarah. No more teasing. Either touch me harder and finish me off, or I swear to you, I'll part your lovely thighs and climax deep inside you."

"My, but we're bossy." She withdrew her hands. "And so impatient, too."

He looked at her and saw she was smiling. She lowered her head and explored him with her tongue, curling it around his width and running it down his length. "You didn't mention my mouth, darling. Is it an acceptable option?" Her lips repeated the process, nuzzling and sucking. "Or perhaps I should stop. Perhaps you find this offensive."

"God, no," he gasped. There wasn't a man on earth who wouldn't love what she was doing, but you didn't expect such pleasures from a lady like Sarah. Except that Sarah was from the distant future, and customs could change. Obviously *had* changed, he thought hazily.

He closed his eyes, burning with excitement and anticipation. In response, she began to nibble him, but only the tip of him. That was inflaming enough, but when she drew him in deeper and suckled him vigorously, he thought he would go mad from sheer delight. He was torn between hanging on to prolong the ecstasy and letting himself experience the ultimate pleasure, but waiting won. After all, he didn't want to be accused of impatience again. Then she took him still deeper, and his control slipped badly. On the other hand, how much could a man be expected to endure?

When she slowly withdrew, he had his answer. She had pushed him beyond his limit. He grasped her head and drove himself back in her mouth, then held her to his groin. In the end he was thrusting wildly, panting so hard his chest burned, exploding like fireworks on the Fourth of July.

By the time he regained his wits and opened his eyes, she was lounging against the headboard, casually rebuttoning her gown. He pulled his clothing back in place, then joined her. "You have the hands and mouth of an expensive courtesan, my love." He slipped his arm around her shoulders, grinning at her. He couldn't believe how lucky he was. "Your customs have a lot to commend them. Do all the women of your time possess such skills?"

She stared into her lap. "I really don't know. My husband taught me to do that. But I'm glad you liked it."

Her tone was subdued and her face was flushed. A wave of guilt washed through him. "Sarah, darling— Believe me, it was meant as a compliment. Nobody has ever given me pleasure like that. It wasn't only your skill. It was the emotions both of us felt. You know I adore you."

She finally looked up, and there was a wistfulness in her eyes that made his blood run cold. Something was very wrong here. "Then I hope you'll think of me now and then. That you'll remember me fondly." She paused, then continued softly, "John wasn't anything like you. He took, but he didn't give back. Genius has its privileges, I guess. What I did just now—it was mostly just a duty with him. I never imagined I could enjoy it so much. Thank you for showing me, Ty. I'll never forget you." Her eyes slid away. "Not ever. You're everything I dreamed you would be."

If he was supposed to be pleased by that, he was anything but. The only emotion he felt besides anger was an icy fear. "And that's the end of it? You think you can return a sexual favor, tell me we've even, and stroll out of my life?" He grasped her chin and turned her to face him. "Maybe in 2096, Sarah, but not in 1865. You gave yourself too passionately to walk away. We belong to each other now, and I refuse to let you go. I'm not some fantasy you can dally with and then dismiss."

Sarah twisted her hands together in her lap. It was the last thing she had ever expected—to feel such wrenching anguish. If she'd had even an inkling, she wouldn't have let Ty touch her in the first place, much less pleasured him with such abandon. But how could she have guessed what a powerful force it could be, this business of making love? How could she have known that giving herself so freely could bind her to a man so strongly? Nothing in her life with John had prepared her for the emotions she'd experienced with Ty.

There was only one saving grace, she thought unhappily, and it was that the hurt and anger he seemed to feel would fade very quickly after she'd gone. She removed his hand from her chin and nestled against his chest, her back to his front. After a few seconds, he put his arms around her waist in what she interpreted as forgiveness.

"You'll probably be annoyed with me for reminding you," she said quietly, "but remember, I know about the life you're going to lead, and you don't. At least a dozen women will fall hopelessly in love with you, and while you'll be kind to them, and honest about your intentions, you won't love a single one back. When you were younger, in Nevada City, you wanted a wife and family—or you said that you did—but something inside you changed. You'll never marry. You'll never even consider it seriously. As for me . . . I'm a novelty, an oddity from the future who worships your work, discusses it with you like a professor, and makes love to you like a whore, and what man wouldn't enjoy all that? You're just infatuated with me, Ty. Whatever I mean to you—whatever you think you feel—it can't possibly last."

Ty neither moved nor spoke, but only because he was so good at controlling himself. In truth, he wanted to scream down the walls until Sarah was quaking and repentant. He was tired of dancing to her tune. Of feeling ignorant and inadequate. And most of all, he was tired of being told what he thought, how he felt, and what he would do with the rest of his life. Only hours before, he had denied the urge to own a woman, but if owning Sarah meant giving her orders and being obeyed for once, he decided he rather liked the idea.

He forced himself not to answer until he could do so without raising his voice. "If I never married or fell in love—" He stopped and glared. "Hell. You've even got *me* doing it now. The point is, you might know everything about my life except for the past two years, but the past two years are what changed me. I did fall in love, and I learned that love isn't enough. Not for me, anyway. She didn't share my views the way you do. She didn't love the Union the way you do. You've given me a sense of what my life's work will be, and she would never have admired it and encouraged me, much less discussed it with me the way you have. If I never married in the past you grew up with, it's because I was looking for all those things, and I failed to find them." All the anger suddenly drained out of him. "It's because I never met *you*. Surely you can see that."

But Sarah couldn't, not really. She was only a woman, not a goddess. Ty must have met others just like her over the years—just as bright, far more beautiful. If he'd truly wanted to settle down, he would have done so.

Still, if his life was like a giant puzzle with a key

piece missing, that piece had finally dropped into her lap. There had been a love affair, and it had ended badly. It had taught him to want more than his lover had given, more than most men of his era would have thought to seek. So he had gone from woman to woman, always measuring them against some impossible standard, taking whatever pleasures they offered but never finding the perfection he demanded. Listening to him now, she suspected he had been deeply lonely.

She wondered what had happened during the past two years, what had changed him so completely. "Tell me about it," she said. "Tell me about *her*."

He cursed under his breath, looking disgruntled. "I know that voice. It's the historian talking. That's who wants to know, not the woman who just made love to me."

He was more right than wrong, but Sarah hedged. "You can't blame me for asking questions. I want to understand you. Who was she? How did you meet her? And when?"

"I don't enjoy talking about it," he said.

That was obvious. "Yes, I can tell. Do you feel guilty about it? Did you leave her because of the things she couldn't give you?"

He didn't reply for several seconds, but finally sighed in resignation. "I made mistakes. She died in the end. Maybe it was my doing. I've never really known, but her family certainly thinks so. The man who attacked me the other night—it was one of her brothers."

Sarah heard the anguish in Ty's voice and ached for him. She of all people knew how ethical he tried to be. His principles had almost cost him his life, so he wouldn't have hurt the woman he'd loved—at least, not deliberately.

She turned in his arms to face him. "Then he's insane, Ty. Her family is wrong. You don't have even an ounce of malice in your body. Whatever happened, it wasn't your fault. It couldn't have been."

Ty didn't think so either, but deep down, he'd always felt a gnawing uncertainty about the matter. He wasn't sure why he decided to tell Sarah everything, but maybe it was because there was no other way to gain her understanding. And maybe it was because, as a historian, she might remember some crucial fact from the past that would enable him to lay his demons to rest.

He began with his service in the Army of the Potomac, describing his experiences as a scout. He'd been good at reconnoitering—it required a journalist's skills—and what he had seen and heard had convinced him that the Rebel forces were far weaker and fewer than General McClellan and his personal spy, Allan Pinkerton, had insisted. He'd told McClellan as much, but the general hadn't listened to such reports, either from Ty or from anyone else. Time and again, he had refused to fight.

Sarah nodded. "You were right, Ty. Right about everything." Given the Union's numerical and technological superiority, she confirmed, if McClellan and his successors had fought the way Grant had later, if they had pursued the enemy aggressively and pressed him at every turn, the war would have been over far sooner.

Ty continued with his story. Ignored by McClellan, he had gone higher, writing to an officer in the War Department whom he knew from his days in Philadelphia. It was an act of insubordination that could have gotten him punished severely, but nothing had come of it, with one exception. Everything he wrote to his friend was passed along to Stanton, who could no more light a fire under McClellan than anyone else could. Lincoln, of course, had ultimately replaced the general, in late 1862.

Then Ty was wounded at Chancellorsville and sent to a hospital in Washington City to recuperate, putting him in direct contact with his old friend. He was no sooner back on his feet than Stanton sent for him. The war secretary took his measure and liked what he saw. He asked Ty to resign from his volunteer regiment, accept a commission in the regular army, and remain in the capital, nominally as one of Lafayette Baker's social spies.

The job entailed adopting a new identity, that of the amoral and prosperous lobbyist, T.J. Reid, and frequenting Washington's drawing rooms to learn who was loyal—and who only pretended to be. But Stanton had a deeper aim, to place an agent inside the National Detective Bureau to keep a secret eye on the volatile Baker. Spying wasn't to Ty's liking—he would have preferred to return to the field—but he was a patriot and couldn't say no, especially after the president himself mentioned that he had as keen an interest in the matter as the war secretary did.

And that, he said, was how he had met Peggy Beecham Moore—at the imposing home of one of Washington's grandest officials, the secretary of the treasury, Salmon P. Chase. "But nobody knew her sympathies were with the Rebels," Ty explained. "She was the widow of a Union officer who had died during the first battle of Bull Run. She applied for work at the Treasury Department soon afterward, to help support her elderly in-laws. She claimed she was all they had. They lived in Baltimore."

A city rife with its own Rebel plots, Sarah knew, including one to assassinate Lincoln before he took office. Had he been a less skillful politician, Maryland might well have joined the Confederacy. "Were they loyal to the Union?"

"As far as we know, they were. Peggy's own family lived in Front Royal—they still own a farm there—but she was frank about their political views. They were secesh, and so were her grandparents in Kentucky. Both her brothers had signed on with Forrest's cavalry there.''

Divided families had been common during the war. Indeed, some of Lincoln's own in-laws had fought for the South. ''So you didn't suspect her?''

Ty smiled wanly. ''I didn't say that. She was from Virginia, after all. Only a fool wouldn't have kept up his guard.'' He stared at the wall. ''She was beautiful and very intelligent, and she had a certain way about her . . . aloof and seductive at the same time. She was always surrounded by men, and she could torment them just by the way she looked at them. She'd been a widow for over a year by then, and people said she was restless for a man, but nobody seemed to interest her. And then I came along.''

''And she pursued you?''

''Oh, yes.'' He laughed harshly. ''The way only Peggy could. She flirted with me. Teased me. Flattered me. We saw each other several times a week, and if I was in a room, no other man seemed to exist for her. I took to escorting her home, but it was a month before she invited me inside. She led me up to her room that night, put her arms around my neck, and let me kiss her and touch her until I was desperate to have her—and then she laughed and pushed me away. After a few weeks of nights like that, I asked her to marry me. I was in love with her, and I assumed marriage was what she wanted. But she said she needed more time, that she'd gone from her father's home to her husband's and was enjoying her freedom. And then she suggested a private dinner in my suite, saying it was time we got. . .better acquainted.''

Sarah felt a suffocating tightness in her throat. It was crazy, but she was jealous of Peggy Beecham Moore—jealous of a manipulative little tease who had been dead for almost two and a half centuries. ''And?''

''We ate. We drank. We talked. I was permitted the

usual kisses, then pushed away, but I'd taken as much as I could stand. I picked her up, but between lust and too much wine, I couldn't even make it to the bed. I didn't even undress her—just tossed up her skirts and took her on the floor. Or rather, we took each other. She wound up on top of me—'' He stopped abruptly, looking embarrassed. ''Well, you get the idea. Making me take command seemed to be her whole aim. I felt dizzy and faint after we finished, but Peggy was just getting started.'' His lips twitched. ''She had a voracious appetite, and a very varied one. It was quite an education.''

Not only a tease, Sarah thought with a scowl, but an insatiable sexual athlete. ''In other words, she taught you everything you know about making love.'' And from the nostalgic look on Ty's face, he had enjoyed every lesson.

For the first time since he had begun this tale, he broke into a grin. ''Not quite everything. I wasn't a total oaf. Anyway, I hung on long enough that night to acquit myself reasonably well, then passed out.''

''From what?'' Sarah asked with a sniff. ''Ecstasy or exhaustion?''

''Neither. She had drugged my wine.''

Her jealousy turned to astonishment. ''Good Lord! How long were you out? What was she after?''

''It was only about twenty minutes, but she must have assumed it would be longer, because when I came around, she was rummaging through my papers. It was no secret that I used my suite as an office as well as a residence. I kept the most confidential material locked in my desk, but my filing cabinet contained information about the Union's finances, troops, industries, and transportation. Reid was a powerful lobbyist, and it was his business to know such things. I pretended I was still unconscious and watched her. She finally slipped away, leaving me on the floor.''

"So she only pursued you to get to your records." And to utilize him as her private stallion. On second thought, he must not have enjoyed it at all. He had loved Peggy Moore, and she had used him very badly. "I suppose you reported her to Stanton." He would have had no choice. "Was she thrown into the Old Capitol? Is that where she died?"

"No." Ty wound a lock of Sarah's hair around his finger, looking somber now. "I came to understand that in Peggy's view, what I did was far worse. Stanton wanted me to use her to deceive the enemy, and I never even argued. We used to come here every few evenings to dine and make love, but she wasn't like you. She wanted the pretense of being seduced, and I willingly supplied it. All I cared about was having her when the war was over, and Stanton agreed that I could." He paused. "I set a trap for her—placed erroneous information inside my desk about troop strength, provisions, battle plans, and so on, and made it easy for her to pick the locks. About once a week, she would drug my wine and search my files, but I always drank less of it than she thought. Unfortunately, it wasn't the sort of game I could play indefinitely. She eventually got word that the information she was passing along was incorrect. She burst through my door in a rage one evening, cursing everyone from me to Stanton to Lincoln to the whole Union."

"Because she'd realized you were using her right back."

But Ty shook his head. As much as he had disagreed with Peggy's views, he had never faulted her for spying. On the contrary, he had respected her loyalty to her state and admired her courage. He had even understood her anger toward the Union and its army, which she blamed for her husband's death.

But angry or not, she had gone eagerly to Ty's bed that evening, and he had inferred, as a man of his era naturally would, that a lady who displayed such undeniable passion for a gentleman must love him very much. "And since she loved me, I expected her to defer to my greater wisdom and bow to my wishes," he continued wryly. "I told her she had two choices. She could take the oath of allegiance and marry me, or she could sit in the Old Capitol until the war was over. It never occurred to me that she wouldn't do the first. Other women had—Joe Willard's wife, for one. But she refused to do either. She demanded to be paroled to the farm in Front Royal, and I agreed to try to arrange it. I believed that once she'd had a chance to think things over, she would accept the inevitability of a Union victory and marry me."

"So you went to see Stanton? He agreed to let her leave?"

The sardonic look on Ty's face said Sarah surely knew better. "Of course not. He wanted her thrown in jail. He said I could have her after the war, just as we had agreed. He was angry enough to string me up when I argued, but he finally said we could marry if I kept her in Baltimore. She'd promised to wait in my suite for his answer, so I returned to give her the news." He sighed. "I've learned a thing or two since then. I should have cuffed her to the bedpost."

"What did she do? Steal out of Washington and sneak over to Front Royal?"

"Exactly. Stanton was so enraged he tossed me into the Old Capitol to punish me, but Lincoln ordered me released. I decided to wait a couple of weeks before I requested leave to go see her. Stanton needed time to calm down, and so did Peggy." Ty grimaced. "She was well-known in Washington, Sarah. One week everyone was talking about her spying and her escape, and the next, they were gossiping about her death. She'd fallen ill shortly after returning home—a massive infection, they said."

Sarah couldn't make sense of that. "But then why did her family blame you? You had nothing to do with her illness."

He shrugged, looking weary and bewildered. "I have no idea. She was angry with me, so perhaps she claimed I'd hurt her in some way. The rigors of the trip might have weakened her and made her more susceptible to illness, or maybe she injured herself along the way. All I know is, within days of her death, her brother George—the one who just attacked me—he checked into the Willard. He began handing out money to the staff, asking them about my habits. But I'd always made a point of tipping generously, and within hours, three different bellmen told me what he was up to. I reported the matter to Baker, who took him to the Old Capitol for questioning. I listened from the next room. Beecham admitted to being a Rebel officer, then ranted that I was a rapist and a murderer. He was released in one of the last prisoner exchanges. And the second brother, Ned . . ."

Ty's voice had softened to an anguished rasp. He grew ashen, then began to shake. Sarah put her arms around him and held him tight. "What, Ty? What about Ned Beecham?"

"He—he went after Sukey. My little sister. She's twenty now. I've taken care of her since she was eleven. She's an excellent student, Sarah. She's in college—" He closed his eyes for a moment. "I keep forgetting. You've read my letters. You must know all about her."

"Yes. I know your father died when you were sixteen and your mother four years later. I know Sukey attends Oberlin College. And I know you're very proud of her. But there was nothing about Ned Beecham in anything I read. I've told you—there are no letters at all from the past two years."

"Because of what happened to Sukey. Her letters to

Reid were stored in my desk. Peggy found them and read them. After that, we learned to destroy anything to or from T.J. Reid. The Beechams weren't his only enemies. There were others, and I couldn't have them striking at the people I loved."

"Then Peggy told Ned about Sukey before she died? She realized Sukey was a relation?"

"The different last names . . . The Beechams assumed she was my half sister. Ned went to Ohio to find her. It was during the winter vacation, and she was helping a family over in Elyria with their new baby. Ned gave her a false name and claimed he was my friend from Washington. He won her confidence and admiration. He's intelligent, charming, and very handsome. One evening, after he'd taken her to dinner with the family's permission, he convinced her to go for a walk in the woods. She let him kiss her and touch her . . . lay her on the ground and press himself against her. She says she doesn't know what came over her, that the world seemed to blur and she couldn't control herself. When she finally came to her senses and told him to stop, he started to force her. She fought him as hard as she could, but he was too big for her, too strong. Some boys from the town—some neighbors—they were out in the same area that night, and they heard her screams and yelled back to her. Ned fled when he heard them coming, and they were content to let him go. He hadn't been able to—to finish what he had started. Stanton's agents have been looking for him for over a year. Sukey is a good artist, and she drew them a likeness. As far as we know, he's in Colorado now."

Sarah had never read of this incident, undoubtedly because any letters about it had been destroyed. "You mean they let him escape? He was never arrested? No charges were ever filed?" Cold disapproval replaced the bewilderment in her voice. "Oh. I see. They wanted to spare your sister the awful shame of a trial."

Ty stiffened. "If you think it would have been better to subject her to prying eyes and filthy speculation—"

"No. I'm sorry." She looked at him with soft regret in her eyes. "It's just that we handle such attacks differently now. The woman is the victim. She shouldn't be treated as if she had invited her own assault—blamed for it, or denigrated for it, or looked upon as somehow ruined."

"I agree," Ty said curtly, and she realized he was coldly angry with her. "Unfortunately, we're not so enlightened in 1865 as you gods from the future are. My sister was anguished enough from the assault without—" The tirade ended abruptly. Ty stared at her in sudden torment. "Will she ever recover? Will she ever marry?"

Sarah hesitated. He was already in agony over this incident. The answer would only pain him further. "I'm not supposed to talk about what will happen. You know that."

"Tell me, Sarah. Will she?"

She winced and said nothing. He looked at her bleakly. "In other words, no."

"Ty . . ." She took his hand. "Marriage isn't everything. She'll be a teacher and a writer. A leader in the fight for women's rights. She'll inspire thousands of young women to pursue their dreams. From everything I've read, she'll lead a productive, fulfilling life. Isn't that enough?"

"No." He grasped Sarah by the shoulders. "I want it changed. I want it to be different. Talk to her, Sarah. Tell her how it is in the future. Convince her she shouldn't feel dirty and ashamed. Convince her that she shouldn't be afraid of every man she meets."

Sarah almost said a flat no. The rules had been drummed into her, month after month and year after year. Follow the protocols. Don't talk about the future. Don't alter the past without permission. If it had been anyone but Ty . . . If he hadn't felt such guilt . . .

"Your sister was a force for social progress," she finally answered, "just as you were. Will be. I can't have that changed. It's almost impossible in your time for a woman to combine the brilliant career Sukey's supposed to have with marriage and a family. I think we should leave the past alone."

"But she's my sister, Sarah, and if I can do it, so can she." He looked at her grimly. "And I'm damned well going to do it. Don't think I'm not."

He meant with her, but it was impossible. She suddenly felt like weeping. "I can't stay here, Ty. I have a daughter in 2096, and I love her more than life itself. I would never leave her."

"Then put a message in the paper. Tell her to join you."

"To a world where women are raped and feel ashamed? To a world where only a handful of colleges will even admit us? Where we can't even vote, much less serve in Congress or try a case before the Supreme Court?" She slowly shook her head. "Shelby is brilliant, beautiful, and talented. She's not even twelve yet, but she's already more knowledgeable than the most educated adult in your world. She's accustomed to a level of freedom and physical luxury you can't begin to comprehend. She would hate it here. It wouldn't be fair to her. I have to go home."

Ty understood what Sarah was saying. He grasped the logic of her arguments. He saw the lack of any alternative to her position. Even if she loved him, she loved her daughter more, so she was going to leave him. And there wasn't a damned thing he could do about it.

The thought of it almost killed him. He suddenly

needed to get out of this room—into the cool night air to walk until he was exhausted, or down to the bar to drink himself into a stupor. Anywhere but here, where he had to look at what he could never have.

Chapter 15

Ty mumbled something about going downstairs to work on his article, then grabbed his notebook and coat and strode out of the suite. For all her apparent sadness, Sarah had been maddeningly composed. He wasn't about to rant, bawl, or admit to the need to get drunk when she could sit there so calmly, talking about her departure. She expected him to become a literary giant, so he could bloody well behave like one—or at least pretend to. And if lying was the act of a weakling, he had been stung so badly that he simply couldn't help it.

But as he was belting back the first of what threatened to be countless whiskeys of the night, some journalists he had known as Reid arrived in the Willard's bar, the favorite hangout of the Fourth Estate. Seeing a new face, they began questioning him about who he was and why he was in the capital. Perhaps he craved some human companionship, because he welcomed the distraction. He found himself talking about his background—Tyson Stone's background—and then telling them about his current project.

They were interested, then impressed, then fascinated. Their admiration was balm to his wounded ego.

There were many kinds of escapes, he supposed, and losing himself in work was more constructive than drowning his sorrows in whiskey. Less maudlin and less painful, too.

He remained in the bar for about an hour, then excused himself. Some new ideas had occurred to him, and he wanted to get them on paper. He wound up sitting in the dining room, thinking and writing.

He was absorbed in his work, oblivious to the comings and goings all around him, when someone tapped him on the shoulder. He looked up to find Joseph Gales of the *Intelligencer* smiling down at him. "I've got myself a bargain, I hear. They're talking about you in the bar. Here you are, they say, a small-town journalist who arrived in Washington from out of nowhere, and you're going to show them all up with the best damned essay on the peace that anyone's written. You should have asked me for more money." He nodded at Ty's notebook. "You're working on it now, I take it. Do you mind if I have a look?"

Ty handed it over. "This is the first half—maybe a bit more. It's running somewhat long, I'm afraid."

Gales sat down to read, and Ty watched anxiously. He knew the article was as fine as Sarah had said when Gales brushed at his eyes with the back of his hand. There wasn't much sentiment in the publisher, but he was clearly moved.

He finished what Ty had written, then gave the notebook back. "Don't cut it, Stone. Say what you think should be said. Get it to me by Monday, and I'll run it on Tuesday and offer it to other papers." He paused. "They were right. You're good. If you're planning to remain in Washington, I'd like you to join my staff."

Ty said he would think the matter over. Deep down, he wanted to return to California, but he wasn't sure that he should. He wondered if he actually had. He decided to consult Sarah about it.

"Well, let me know once you've made up your mind. Either way, I'm sure I'll be reading you in the future." Gales got to his feet. "I think I'll whet my subscribers' appetites. Run a story in Monday's paper that you've been in town for the past few days, talking to our soldiers. Promise you'll enlighten them and touch their hearts if they buy my next edition."

Ty said he would do his best, then returned to work.

Sarah knew what the rules required her to do—depart from this time and place as soon as she could, before she could mess up the past any further. But the rules couldn't feel the pain she had caused Ty by divulging that his work as Reid had triggered a blow from which his sister would never recover. The rules didn't understand that when you loved a man—and she did love Ty, though she knew it wasn't the man so much as the future icon she adored—it tore you to pieces to watch him suffer. So what was she supposed to do? If she followed the rules, nothing would improve, but nothing would deteriorate, either. And if she broke them, if she spoke to Sukey and changed her life, Ty's guilt would be eased, but the effect on the future would be totally unpredictable.

The day had been so traumatic and exhausting that she couldn't think clearly for long, and she soon fell into a sound sleep. When she awoke a few hours later, Ty was still gone and the room felt terribly empty. She went into the bathroom to wash and brush her teeth, and caught sight of herself in the mirror. She looked pallid. Haunted. Maybe it was only anguish, but she knew it could be something worse.

She hadn't checked her immune levels in over thirty-six hours and wasn't eager to do so now, but all tempronauts were required to be scientists at times, and running the tests was part of her job. She fetched her medical kit.

Once again, she thought she was prepared for the outcome, but her levels had dropped so markedly that she trembled. At the rate she was regressing, she would be back where she'd started within weeks—a month at the most. A part of her wanted to put a message in the paper that read "Still in Washington, and still ill. Don't retrieve me until you can cure me," but it was out of the question. She was only one small person, one minor life. They couldn't use the chamber again until she returned, but it could take years before they found a cure. In the meantime, the Project had to go on, and that would mean retrieving her exactly as scheduled, to 2096.

But if she was a realist, she was also very human, and staring death in the face changed everything. It wouldn't matter to Shelby if she stayed a while longer—she would return on the same date in 2096 that the schedule had always called for. Once there, she wouldn't live any longer, but she wouldn't die any sooner, either.

But staying would give her some happiness before she died. She would enjoy a little love and physical pleasure. She would need to tell Ty about her health, of course, but she thought it would provide some comfort. He would mourn with her for the time she wouldn't have, but he would also know that he wasn't giving up a whole lifetime with her, only a year or two.

Her heart leapt. Only a year or two. Surely she could ask Shelby to join her in the past for that length of time. And then it sank just as quickly, because the plan contained a fatal flaw. In order to send Shelby back, the Wellsians would have to empty the holding chamber of the energy they had exchanged for Sarah. Once they did that, she could never be retrieved. But miracles could happen. A cure could suddenly be found. If Shelby returned after her death and learned that Sarah could have been saved after all, she would grieve for the rest of her life. Sarah couldn't take that risk.

So she would stay for a few weeks longer, then depart. And as to whether she would meddle with the past—again!—she simply didn't know. She changed into her nightgown and slipped into bed, trying to decide.

Ty trudged up the stairs, thinking that Sarah was surely asleep by now. The evening hadn't been wasted—he had made good progress on his article—but leaving had been the act of a fool. Their time together was bitterly short, and the hours he had lost could never be reclaimed.

It wasn't until he reached his door that he thought about Peggy and wondered if he should have cuffed Sarah to the bedpost, but then, if he had to keep her here by force, he didn't want to keep her at all. Still, when he entered the parlor and saw her belongings still scattered about, relief rushed through him. The bedroom door was ajar, and a light was on inside. He crossed into the room and found her sitting up in bed, wide-awake. Her nightdress was unbuttoned to her waist, giving him a splendid view of the inner curves of her breasts. His throat tightened.

He walked to the bed and ran his finger down the center of her chest. "Does this mean what I think it means?"

"If you think I'm inviting you to make love, then yes." She sighed. "But we have to talk first. You were so upset before . . . I don't want you to misinterpret my feelings. I don't want any misunderstandings between us."

In other words, she was still going to leave him. "You're returning home. I've accepted it. If that's what you wanted to talk about—"

"Only in part." She patted the bed. "Sit down. Tell

me how you spent the evening. I slept, mostly. It's been a long day.''

It was typical of women, Ty thought, that they needed to chitchat before they could get to the point. He quashed his impatience and joined her, explaining about the men he had met in the bar and his encounter with Joseph Gales. She was very pleased for him, especially about the publicity and wider distribution Gales intended to give him.

''The essay deserves it,'' she said. ''As far as remaining in Washington goes . . . Originally, your career was in California—San Francisco, mostly. But that doesn't mean it still has to be. We've already changed the past, so you might as well do what you want.''

''Then I'll return to California.'' He shrugged out of his coat and tossed it over a chair. ''I've been thinking, Sarah . . . You've contributed so much to my article . . . I want to credit you as my coauthor.''

Her eyes got misty, and she gave him an adoring smile. ''You *would*, Ty. You're just incredible. But people would wonder who I was. They would be baffled when I was never heard from again. I think you should leave me out of it.''

''If that's what you want.'' He looked away. He found it hard to sit so close to her and not touch her, especially when she smiled at him as if he were a god. ''I'll be back in a minute. I need to wash away the cigar smoke and whiskey.''

''Whiskey? You're not drunk, are you?''

''I get drunk whenever I look at you, sweetheart.''

''Then stop looking. We haven't finished yet.''

''I was afraid of that.'' He walked into the bathroom, hoping to persuade her that talking could wait.

When he emerged ten minutes later, he was well scrubbed, freshly shaved, and, after much internal debate, dressed in nothing but a towel around his waist. Sarah stared at him, but to his chagrin, she wasn't gazing hungrily at the erection poking flagrantly against the towel. She was studying his chest like a physician.

"As you can see, I'm healing very well." He fingered the bandage she had applied, which was slowly disintegrating as his knife wounds mended. "It's remarkable stuff. What is it made of?"

"Various chemicals. It's a synthetic—that is, an artificial sort of skin." She lifted the covers in silent invitation. "Like real skin, it allows in air to promote healing but keeps out germs."

He got into bed beside her, leaving some space between them to reduce temptation. "Germs? What do you mean?"

"Sorry. The word has an additional meaning in my time—a microscopic organism that causes disease. Cholera, yellow fever, pneumonia, typhoid . . . Most of the ailments that puzzle your doctors are caused by tiny organisms, usually a different one for each disease. Tempronauts carry agents against all of them, some cures, others preventatives. After I put you to sleep, I injected you with almost everything I had, just to be on the safe side. Because of that, there are many ailments you're now immune to. It's similar to being inoculated against smallpox. I'll give you a list before I go, so you'll know which diseases you can't catch."

It was a hell of a statement, Ty thought. You'll have the health of Methuselah, and by the way, good-bye forever. He pictured that final parting and stared somberly into space. "Before you go? And when will that be?"

She put a gentle hand on his shoulder, drawing back his gaze. "Three or four weeks. That's what I wanted to talk to you about. If you still want me to, I'll travel to Ohio and speak to your sister. It would be breaking all the rules . . ." She shrugged, looking resigned. "But that's nothing new, is it?"

"No. I appreciate it, Sarah." He took her hand and

pressed a kiss into her palm. Those three or four weeks were a glorious reprieve, but he would still lose her in the end, and the thought tore a hole in his gut. If anyone had told him he could be so deeply saddened, yet so hotly aroused, he wouldn't have believed it. "Are we finished talking yet?"

Sarah wanted to throw herself into Ty's arms, but edged away from him instead. She felt the same way he did, and it shook her to the core. Her sadness was overwhelming, almost as painful as the thought of being parted from Shelby forever, but her arousal was equally intense, a shattering mixture of lust and emotional yearning.

She took a deep breath, fighting both tears and desire. "Not quite. There are a few things more. It would ease my mind if you could assure me that the causes your sister embraced lie deep in her heart. I know you can't promise she'll be the same sort of leader if she marries and has children, but I hope you can tell me she'll try."

Ty didn't answer for several moments. Then he said slowly, "What she is now isn't what she'll become, Sarah. Remember, she's only twenty. She must have struggled and grown over the years. So tell her what she accomplished. Explain why she was important. She's an intelligent girl who feels things deeply. I can promise you at least this much. She'll listen and she'll try to understand."

Sarah nodded. Another man might have told her what she wanted to hear regardless of whether or not it was true, to convince her to talk to his sister or to get her into bed a little faster, but not Ty. "Then I'll try my best and hope things work out."

She had just one more issue to discuss, but it was the most sensitive subject of all. "Just now, while I was waiting for you to come back, I was thinking that you'll never have any peace until you understand what happened with Peggy. How she died. Why her family blames you. Why Ned assaulted Sukey. If it was an eye for an eye—you killed his sister, so he was going to kill yours—then why try to seduce her? Why not just murder her?''

''I told you before—I don't know.'' Ty's tone was clipped. ''You're the historian. I was hoping you could shed some light on the subject, but obviously you can't. I'll probably never learn the truth. I have to accept that.''

In Sarah's opinion, learning the truth was critical to any future action. ''And what about Sukey? She was attacked by a man she liked and trusted, and she has no idea why, except that he was striking back at you. It's irrational, but on some level, she undoubtedly blames herself. She thinks it was all her fault. If only she'd been smarter, more cautious, less provocative . . . The only way to help her is to convince her that nothing she could have been expected to do would have made the slightest bit of difference in what occurred.''

Ty regarded her coolly. ''And how do you propose I do that?''

''By giving her the facts. By going to Front Royal and talking to Peggy's mother and perhaps her friends.''

Ty swallowed back the blistering reply he longed to make—that visiting would be a waste of his time, that he wasn't going to change the plans he had made over a year before, and that none of it was Sarah's business in the first place. Instead, he said evenly, ''Stanton knows I want to bring the Beechams to justice, and he's finally given me permission to resign from the army and try. So if it's the truth Sukey needs, I'll get it from Peggy's brothers—even if I have to beat it out of them.''

Sarah raised her eyebrows. ''Beat them, Ty? Heavens, even Reid wasn't that barbaric. Tell me, how else do you plan to violate your own principles and take the law into your own hands? By maiming them? By killing them?"

"If they give me an opening—if I can do it in self-defense and get away with it—you're damned right I will. This is 1865, not 2096. We're uncivilized savages, remember?"

He expected Sarah to be shocked, but she merely looked at him in the same ironic way as before. "Not you. You're rational and ethical. Obviously you came to your senses and did neither of those things, because if you had, you would have written about it, either in personal letters from 1865 or in an essay later in your life, and you never did."

Ty was ready to tear out his hair. "Will you stop telling me what I am and what I'm not? What I did and didn't do? This is between me and the Beechams. You have nothing to do with it. There's nothing more to discuss."

"You involved me when you asked me to talk to Sukey. I can't do that blindly. I'll need some information first." She folded her arms across her chest, the picture of feminine recalcitrance. "I refuse to obtain it by resorting to vigilantism. I assume George left Washington after he read of Reid's death, and if he did, he might have returned to Front Royal. If you find him there, you have nothing to lose by questioning him. By all means have him arrested after that, but I don't approve of torture. I won't sanction violence against him."

"I'm not sure he's even alive—I got off several rounds during the attack—but if he is, what makes you think he would confess to Tyson Stone? What makes you think his mother would, either?" Ty's lips twisted into a grim smile. "Hell, they'll probably spot me for a Yankee the minute they see me coming and shoot me like a rabid dog. You're a historian, for God's sake.

You know what happened in the Shenandoah Valley last fall. They hate us Yankees with a passion."

Sarah mulled over Ty's words, then admitted his point was well taken. "I'd forgotten about Sheridan's ferocity—and about Virginia's suffering and bitterness. You're probably right. They won't cooperate." She thought for a moment longer. "Still, you're such a skilled interrogator that you might be able to extract the facts we need. But there's the problem of your safety to consider."

There was another lengthy pause. Ty had the feeling she was struggling with some inner demon. And then she smiled in the same dark way that he just had. "Of course, you can't kill someone who's wearing a shield. Not with bullets, anyway. Would you like to borrow my cameo? There's a pin on the back. You can wear it inside your lapel or cuff."

Ty was astonished by the suggestion. "But nobody but you can operate it. It responds to your fingerprint. I saw that for myself on Tuesday."

"It can be reset. Reprogrammed, we call it. It takes under a minute if you know the proper code—and I do." She leaned forward a little. "The shields were developed for self-protection. The future can be a dangerous place. There are kidnappings, assassinations, and random shootings, but a half billion or so will buy you some extra protection."

"Half a billion *dollars*? That's what a cameo costs?"

"Miracles don't come cheap," Sarah drawled. "I brought one along for the same reason every tempronaut does, to protect me while I was sleeping, but unlike my colleagues, I wasn't going to bring it home. My orders were to leave it with Lincoln, to convince him to use it. We knew that saving him from Booth might not be enough. There were other plots, and if we didn't protect him permanently, one of them might succeed."

Ty was more dumbfounded than ever. "But the way a barrier feels when you touch it . . . The way objects bounce away from it . . . You were horrified at the thought of Joseph Henry's tinkering with your devices and learning too much of your science, so surely you were concerned that something similar might happen if you left a cameo with Lincoln."

"Of course we were, but if you're smart about when you engage it, people will never know you have it on. And nobody was smarter than Lincoln."

"You can't conceal deflected bullets, Sarah."

She gave him a pained smile. "It was Lincoln, Ty. He could have managed an explanation. And even if he couldn't, saving him was worth the risk. Whatever the potential liabilities were, the benefits outweighed them."

Ty couldn't disagree. The intense admiration he and Sarah shared for the late president was such a powerful bond between them that his earlier irritation faded. Maybe a trip to Front Royal wasn't so pointless, after all. "You're willing to give me the shield to wear in Front Royal, despite the risks. You think that my sister will never recover unless she understands the past."

"Exactly. But give her all the facts, and with luck, she'll grow stronger and more sure of herself. Her doubts and guilts will begin to diminish."

"Perhaps," Ty murmured.

Sarah trailed her fingers up and down his arm, coaxingly and seductively. "You have questions, too. This is your best opportunity to get them answered. Surely the prospect is tempting."

"Yes." He slipped his arm around her shoulders and pulled her close. His questions faded from his mind when she touched him that way. "But not as tempting as you are." He nuzzled her lips, then trailed his mouth to her ear. "Right now, I'd rather have you turn off the lamp, come into my arms, and let me hold you."

"What a lovely idea." Sarah glanced at the clock and yawned. It was twenty of two. "Lord, it's late." She reached for the lamp. "Before, while you were working downstairs . . . I was thinking you could let Sukey skip the summer term. Take her to California and give her as much love and attention as you can. I think it might help."

"I agree. I was already planning that." Ty slid downward, and Sarah turned off the lamp and settled into his arms. The window was shaded but not draped, admitting just enough light to reveal the vague outlines of his body. He kissed her and stroked her, taking things slowly, making love to her with a heartstopping tenderness that left her dreamy with contentment. "I thought I'd pick her up at school. Take the stage to California."

Sarah sighed at the sheer romance of it. "God. The Overland Stage and Mail. I would love to make that trip. See the country when it was still young. The virgin forests and the endless prairie . . . The mountains before the highways went through . . . Virginia City when the mines were still producing and San Francisco before the earth—" She grimaced at the slip. She was far too comfortable around Tyson Stone.

He tensed and stopped caressing her. "San Francisco before what, Sarah?"

She pulled the towel from his waist, trailed her fingers to his groin, and curled her hand around his shaft. "Nothing, darling." She rubbed the tip with her thumb.

He groaned softly and pulled away her hand. "Stop trying to distract me. You said earth. Was that earth as in earthquake?"

"I shouldn't have mentioned it. I have a big mouth."

"You have a lovely mouth. A very clever mouth." He gave her a gentle, lingering kiss, but when she parted her lips and tasted him with her tongue, he turned his head away. "Tell me about it, Sarah."

He was naked and flat on his back, which suggested a means of shutting him up. She slid on top of him and moved against his erection, teasing him with the silk-covered feel of her womanhood, then lifting her hips to end the contact. "You know what I think, Tyson Stone?" She repeated the motion, slowly and provocatively. "That you only love me for my knowledge of the future."

His hands drifted to her buttocks and his breathing quickened. "Not true." He pressed her close, proffering slow, erotic thrusts that made her wish her nightgown weren't in the way. "It must have been catastrophic. You wouldn't have mentioned it otherwise."

She wrinkled her nose at his persistence. "You and your damned questions. . . . You're infuriating, do you know that?"

"I'm a good journalist, that's all." He eased her onto her back and slid her nightgown off her shoulders. "How bad was it, Sarah? Was the city completely destroyed?"

She gave up the fight. It was either that or get badgered indefinitely. "All right, but remember, you're to keep this to yourself. The earthquake was very severe, but most of the buildings survived and could have been repaired if the pipes that brought water into the city hadn't ruptured. Gas lines broke, electric lines fell, chimneys collapsed, and stoves tumbled over, so fires kept breaking out, and without sufficient water to fight them, the heart of the city went up in flames. The fires lasted three days. The damage was immense. Three thousand dead. A quarter of a million left homeless. Five hundred blocks devastated."

Ty sat motionless by her thighs, her nightgown only half-removed, visibly stunned. "My God. We're accustomed to fires in California, but such massive destruction . . . When will it happen? Does the city even exist in your time?"

"Many years from now," Sarah replied, "but I won't give you the date. You'll write a brilliant article about it—the chaos and suffering, the selfishness and opportunism, the altruism and heroism. It's one of your best." She wriggled out of her gown and tossed it on the floor. "But don't mourn for San Francisco, Ty. The city still exists, and it's more beautiful than ever. They keep having earthquakes, but the people always rebuild. You'll live to see it rise from the ashes, and for a long time afterward." She reached over to stroke him and found him fully aroused. "How impressive. It's not every man who can grill a woman so ruthlessly and remain in such a majestic state of readiness." She kneaded him very lightly. "You might as well put it to use, darling, because I've said as much as I'm going to say."

He bent his head to her breasts and stroked a nipple with his tongue, and it hardened instantly. "I doubt that. I remember this afternoon." He stretched out on his side and gently nibbled her, and she arched against his mouth and caressed him harder. "But given the lateness of the hour, I trust you'll manage to contain your verbal outbursts. We wouldn't want the neighbors to complain."

Sarah swatted his buttocks and he yelped and laughed. Then she fondled him with her nails in the way he most liked, and she felt his response in his raspy breathing and thrusting hips. But he was setting her body on fire at the same time, suckling and nibbling her breasts with a mixture of forceful passion and exquisite gentleness, and she couldn't help whimpering from the pleasure he was giving her. It wasn't long before she wanted his mouth so badly that she twined her fingers into his hair and tugged at his head.

He looked up, then eased her onto her back. He covered her with his body at an angle, and she put her arms around his neck. His chest was flush against her breasts, but there was no other intimate contact. John would have been long finished by now, she thought, but Ty was taking his time.

He cupped her chin and kissed her—her nose, her cheeks, her eyes, and her ears—and she told herself he was the sweetest man who had ever lived. She could feel the intense emotion in his lovemaking, which warmed her heart even as it scalded her body, and it created a need to get as close to him as she could. Panting now, dizzy with wanting, she stroked him wherever she could reach—on his shoulders, his arms, his back, and his hips—learning the contours of his muscled flesh, enjoying the slick, hot feel of his skin.

He finally took her mouth, sucking on her parted lips, meeting her searching tongue, and then, when she thought she would go mad with longing, kissing her with deep, scorching dominance. The kiss went on and on, and it was wonderful, but she ached for more, and he wasn't providing it. And then she realized what he was doing. He was very confident, very much in command despite the slight tremor in his body, and it made her feel deliciously submissive. But the submission was an illusion, because he never made a move until she silently asked him to.

She clutched at him, needing him fully on top of her, and he broke the kiss and did as she wished, supporting himself on his elbows. The feel of his erection was so wildly exciting that she lifted her hips to press herself closer. "Please, Ty. I want you inside me."

"You're sure it's safe," he murmured. "That you can't conceive a child. Because if there's any question—"

"There isn't. Don't worry."

"Then I'm blessed, my love." He pecked her on the nose, then kissed her again. A hard thigh was wedged between her legs to part them. She writhed against him, matching his teasing movements, and then, when he slid lower and began to enter her, she pulled up her legs and wrapped them around his buttocks.

He grunted with pleasure. "God, yes. I adore you. You're so sweet and passionate . . . Stop me if I go too fast." He shuddered and kissed her savagely.

But once again, he seemed determined to follow her lead, easing himself only a little way inside her and limiting himself to shallow thrusts. Then he returned to the swollen nub of flesh at her core and stroked her into a state of helpless arousal. By the time he entered her and probed her more possessively, she was clinging fiercely and moaning deep in her throat. It went on like that for several minutes longer, the teasing and the slow penetration, until she dug her nails into his back and drove herself violently against him.

Her movement took him as deep as he could go. He stilled, raising himself onto his elbows. "Are you all right? I know it's been a long time . . . Was there any pain?"

She was half out of her mind with wanting, but the question made her laugh. "Of course not. I'm a mother, remember?" She put her hands on his cheeks, wishing she could see him clearly enough to read the expression on his face. "But thank you for caring enough to worry. You make me feel precious and cherished."

"Because you are. I love you, Sarah." He began to move slowly in and out of her. "And what about hot, sweetheart?" He pulled almost all the way out of her. "Do I make you feel that, too?"

"You know that you do." She put her hands on his buttocks to keep him where he was. "I wouldn't leave if I were you. I'm frustrated enough to claw you to ribbons."

"Are you? How flattering. I'm sure I would enjoy it."

She brought his mouth down to hers, giggling. Somewhere in the distance, a clock chimed twice. "Next time, darling."

He entered her hard and kissed her the same way. Slid his hand between her legs to caress her. Increased his pace and took her along. She deliberately held back, and thought she would shatter from the raw pleasure of denying herself.

Mom? *Mom, are you here*? Astonishment, then amusement. *Good grief, what are you doing*? Laughter. *Well, actually, I know what you're doing, but I'm not quite sure I believe it. Talk about bad timing . . .*

Shelby? Sarah was stunned into total paralysis. *My God, where are you*?

The fifth floor of the Willard Hotel. Teasing coyness. *And I'll bet I know where* **you** *are. Parlor Suite 4 on the second floor.*

Ty pulled away his mouth, but he couldn't stop moving his hips. "Sarah, darling? Is something the matter?"

Darling, huh? Another giggle. *God, the man sounds frazzled. It* **is** *Tyson Stone, right? I mean, you wouldn't be doing it with anyone else, would you?*

Sarah was so shocked she could barely respond. *You* **heard** *him? How could you do that*?

"Sarah, please. Talk to me. Tell me what's wrong."

It's a new talent I have. I can pick up other people if they're strong enough—and wow, does Stone ever emit. He has almost as much vestigial telepathic ability as you do. It's going to be fun to clue him in. You want to listen?

Shelby, it would be better if—

But Sarah was too late. Ty was caressing her hair, trying to calm her so she would tell him what was troubling her, when a voice slammed into his brain. *Hi, Colonel Stone. I'm Sarah's daughter, Shelby. I'm what we call a telepath. I can talk and hear with my mind. Listen, I'm sorry about the interruption, but I've missed my mom like crazy, and I really want to see her.* Amusement. *I'm right upstairs. How about if I give you ten minutes to finish? Given the state you guys are in, that should be long enough. Don't worry, I won't listen in. I'll get out of your minds now. See you at a quarter past two. Have fun*!

Ty turned scarlet. His member was still buried in Sarah's body, and he felt it go limp. "Your twelve-year-old daughter can listen with her mind? She could hear us making love?" He closed his eyes, totally mortified. "Dear God."

But Sarah only smiled and hugged him hard. She didn't know what Shelby was doing in Washington, but her presence meant they had built a second chamber. It meant she could remain here with Ty, and that Shelby could stay with her until the end. If she hadn't been grinning like a hyena, she would have been weeping with joy. "I don't think she's twelve anymore," she said.

Chapter 16

Ty pulled out of Sarah's body and rolled onto his back. "Not still twelve? You mean she might have left from a time later than 2096? What makes you think that?"

"The way she talks, and the fact that they wouldn't have left me in 1865." Sarah explained how energy from the past was trapped and held, then used to precipitate a tempronaut's return. Ty couldn't visualize the equipment used or the processes involved, but he understood the implications well enough. If the Wellsians intended to retrieve her, they couldn't have sent her daughter into the past via their original time machine. They would have had to build another, something that would have taken them years to achieve.

Sarah turned on the light and checked the time. "I'm sure Shelby will explain things when she comes downstairs, but in the meantime . . ." Smiling coyly, she stroked his manhood. Her touch gave him pleasure, but his member failed to stir. "We've got eight minutes, darling. I don't know about you, but I could finish in under two. I'm ready to explode." She fondled his testicles, which usually drove him to pounding madness, but his male apparatus remained inert and useless. "Ty?

Do you want me to turn off the light? Would it be better if I aroused you with my mouth?''

He was about to decline when she bent her head to his groin. The first brush of her lips made him throb in anticipation, but he caught her by her hair as she was taking him in her mouth and pulled her away. ''Don't, Sarah.''

She straightened, gazing at his growing erection in bewilderment. ''I don't understand. You obviously want—'' She stopped and grinned. ''Oh. It's Shelby. You're afraid she's going to hear us.''

He swung his legs over the side of the bed. ''She's right upstairs. However old she is, she's only a child, and she all but ordered us to— Well, you know. You realized we had eight minutes left, so obviously you heard what she said. What she thought. I don't want to offend you, but your daughter is a hoyden. She eavesdrops without a qualm. She could listen to every— Hell, I don't know. Every moan. Every movement. Every thought. And we wouldn't even know.'' He ran an agitated hand through his hair. ''It's unnerving. I know you love the girl dearly, but how can you accept such intrusions? How can you ignore her constant presence?''

Sarah cuddled up behind him and put her arms around his chest. He didn't respond, but sat stiff, silent, and shaken. He knew he had been too frank about his feelings but was unable to take back his words. The girl had appalled him. Her closeness—her very existence—made his skin crawl.

''I first heard Shelby's mind when she was in my womb,'' Sarah said quietly, ''so I've had twelve years to get used to her presence. I don't even think about it anymore. But to be confronted with it so suddenly, when your emotions were so exposed . . . Obviously you're shocked. I don't blame you.''

There was no point replying. He had spoken of how he felt, and Sarah had understood. He simply shrugged.

Releasing him, she walked to the wardrobe and took out her dressing gown. "The problem is, you've expressed so many groundless fears and wild misconceptions that I hardly know which to correct first." As she slipped on the gown, he crossed to the chest to pull out some clean clothing. "The eavesdropping, I suppose. She doesn't, Ty. Not ever. She started training herself not to as soon as she understood that we were two different people. Unlike you, I can hear her whenever she listens in, and by the time she was seven or eight, she knew when I was reaching for her with my mind, and she knew when I was simply thinking, and she respected the difference. There *are* no intrusions."

"No?" Ty pulled on a pair of drawers. "You could have fooled me, Sarah."

"That's not fair. She just landed here. To Shelby, years have gone by, and she's missed me terribly. She was impatient to find me, so she reached out hard enough with her mind to wake me if I were asleep, and she heard everything we were doing and feeling. She couldn't help it. And of course, it was screamingly obvious what she'd interrupted."

Ty tugged on his trousers and buttoned them. "That's exactly the point. It was obvious to *her*, but no unmarried girl should comprehend such emotions, much less comment on—on—" He grabbed a shirt, reddening again. "Dammit, Sarah, she was laughing at me. Making sport of how aroused I was. She was impudent and disrespectful. I'm sorry to have to say this, but you've been much too indulgent a mother. And whoever's been rearing her since you left—your friends, your relations—they've done a bloody poor job of it."

Sarah might have been annoyed by Ty's presumption if she hadn't been so amused by how convenient his memory had become. "Is that so? Am I talking to the same man whose sister went off with an actor when she was sixteen? Who had to trek all over the foothills to run her to ground? Who lost a brand-new gig and team when she ran out of money and sold them from under his nose?"

Ty scowled at the dry irony in Sarah's tone. He had recounted the incident in a letter to his relations in Pennsylvania, so naturally she had read of it. It was damned irritating, this business of arguing with someone who knew every detail of his life.

"It was a girlhood lapse," he muttered. "Anyway, her intentions were completely selfless. She only left because she thought it would free me to serve in the war. She was simply—young and a bit too spirited."

"Just as Shelby is, but times have changed." Sarah fetched her brush from the bathroom and began pulling it through her hair. "In the years to come, the country will alternate between periods of sexual propriety, like now, and great sexual license, like in the 1980s and 1990s. By the time I was born, we'd had almost eighty years of fatal diseases that were transmitted primarily by sexual relations. People had grown very cautious, and rightly so. Millions eventually died, including my husband's parents. But the diseases were finally conquered when Shelby was eight, and it was like opening Pandora's box. In our books, our plays, and the lifelike moving pictures we watch in our homes and theaters, sex is utterly pervasive. There are depictions of nudity and people making love. Both our humor and our dramas often revolve around sexual themes. And our behavior echoes all that. By the time I left, fidelity in marriage was suffering and most unmarried people were taking lovers. That includes girls in their teens, Ty, and nobody calls them whores for it. They're held to the same standards males are. I assume the trend has continued. It's rather like the whole country is adopting the morals and customs of Ah Lan's brothel. That's what Shelby comes from, so you can hardly expect her to behave like a nineteenth century schoolgirl."

"No. I don't suppose I can." Ty had read widely, so he was aware of times and places when carnal activity had run rampant. He knew it wasn't fair to judge someone from 2096 by the standards of 1865.

But theory was one thing, practice another. The notion of confronting a living example of such attitudes in the person of his lover's daughter filled him with horror. Sarah's world, he thought, was a cesspool. Even worse, though Sarah claimed the girl kept her mind out of other people's heads, only Sarah could feel such intrusions, and only against herself. He had no way of knowing if her daughter would show him the same respect.

Still, he loved Sarah passionately, and their time together was short. He assumed Shelby would depart very soon, leaving them to enjoy each other in peace, and in the meantime, the least he could do was welcome her. Sarah, after all, had responded with great patience to remarks that were blunt to the point of cruelty.

He tucked his shirt into his trousers, then walked into the parlor. Sarah followed, her brow furrowed in a way that told him she was distressed. He knew she was waiting for him to unbend a little.

He turned on a light. He wanted to say he looked forward to meeting the girl, but he couldn't force the words out of his mouth. Finally, unwilling to lie, he gave her the only assurance he could. "I'm finding it hard to deal with all this, but I'll try to be open-minded."

Sarah looked at him with real hurt in her eyes, but before he could think of a way to assuage it, she broke into a smile. A second later, the door opened and Shelby Maravich strode into the room. Several inches taller than Sarah, with identical green eyes and flowing auburn hair, she was wearing trousers that resembled a miner's Levi's except that they were extremely tight, and a black shirt similar to a chemise but far more clinging. She looked about Sukey's age, and God knew her attire revealed every womanly curve. His eyes bugged out at the sheer wantonness of her appearance.

She and Sarah ran joyfully into each other's arms and hugged fiercely. In the meantime, the bellman who had unlocked the door deposited a valise and a carpet-bag inside the room, looked straight at Ty without appearing to see him, and departed, closing the door behind him. Ty wondered what had possessed the man to unlock his door without permission, especially for a female dressed the way Shelby was.

She and Sarah were still touching, looking at each other with glistening eyes and glowing smiles, not speaking a single word. Ty watched them from across the room. Their silence gave him the creeps.

Several minutes passed. He finally grew annoyed enough to correct them. "Didn't anyone ever tell you two that it's impolite to talk to each other in a language that a third person present can't understand?"

They looked at him, startled, and then sheepishly apologized. They had been exchanging endearments and basic information, Sarah explained—what had happened to her in the past and how Shelby had coped in her absence.

The girl walked over to him, stopping a few feet away, and inspected him so thoroughly he stiffened. She was as bold as one of Ah Lan's whores, he thought. A real beauty, too, but the paint on her face was as heavy as a trollop's.

"So you're Tyson Stone," she drawled. "God, Mom, no wonder you stuck around. He's a total babe." She grinned at him. "If you have a younger brother, do you think you could introduce me?"

He glowered at the sheer indignity of it. "I'm

twenty-nine, young lady, which is hardly a child, and—''

He was interrupted by Sarah's gurgle of laughter. ''It was a compliment, Ty. A babe is—it's a very virile, very handsome man.'' She strolled to Shelby and took her arm. ''You know perfectly well that his only sibling is a sister. Don't tease him. He's very unnerved by all this.''

''Yeah, I heard.'' She sobered. ''Don't get any madder, Colonel Stone, but—''

Why do you keep calling him ''colonel''? Because of his rank as a volunteer?

Because I know he's in the U.S. Regulars. I'll explain in a minute, Mom.

Ty realized at once what was causing the unnatural silence. The two of them were at it again, talking to each other with their minds. More annoyed than ever, he said sharply, ''Don't get any madder about what, young lady?''

''That I listened to your thoughts. I didn't do it on purpose. It's just that they're almost as clear as my mom's, which is totally incredible, and they keep whipping into my mind before I can stop them. I know Mom tried to talk to you just now, to explain about me and my talents, but obviously she didn't succeed. Maybe I can do better.''

She detached herself from Sarah and sprawled onto the sofa. ''I'm seventeen, and my clothes and makeup are fairly modest for my time. I didn't bother changing into a costume because I can make people do whatever I want, especially simple things like unlocking a door, or not seeing what's right in front of them, or forgetting they ever met me. Besides, the clothes in your era are stupid. The women are idiots to put up with wearing them. And by the way, if looking you over makes me a whore, then your morals are as dumb as your clothing.'' She paused and frowned. ''Also, I don't know what a trollop is, but if it's the same as a whore, I'm not one of those, either. In fact, I'm one of the last virgins in the senior class. Is there anything else you want to know?''

Ty felt much as he had when Beecham had smacked him on the head with a bat. Befuddled. Reeling. The girl had the powers of a witch and the mouth of a slattern.

''Excuse *me*, Colonel Stone,'' she said with a toss of her hair, ''but there's nothing supernatural about telepathy. It's a scientifically explicable phenomenon, and so is witchcraft, by the way. And I don't know what a slattern is, either, but if it's another one of your insults, it's not very nice of you to call me that.''

He glared at her. ''Get out of my blasted mind, young lady. You weren't invited there.''

''Then stop radiating like a pulsar! And don't keep calling me 'young lady.' My name is Shelby. Or Ms. Maravich.''

Ty closed his eyes for a moment in intense frustration. ''What's a pulsar?'' he asked Sarah.

''A star that emits periodic bursts of intense electromagnetic radiation.''

''I see.'' But he didn't at all, and his impatience suddenly spiraled out of control. ''For God's sake, Sarah, how could you let her talk to me that way? You're her mother. You should teach her some bloody manners!''

''But your thoughts were full of insults, Ty. Surely she had the right to defend herself. In fact, if she hadn't done it so well, I would have taken on the job myself.''

Not only wasn't Sarah taking his side, Ty thought grimly, but she had the gall to look amused. ''I'm not used to censoring what's in my own brain. Besides, you assured me she wouldn't listen.''

''Your mind is both powerful and telepathically active, darling. She's having trouble shutting you out.''

"And believe me, I'm doing my best." Shelby looked at her mother. "I take it he's not always this judgmental and offensive. I mean, I know he's a world-class hunk and all, but you're a total prude, so fun can't be your only reason for sleeping with him, right? He obviously has hidden depths." She made a face. "*Well* hidden depths."

Sarah rolled her eyes. "That's enough, Shelby. Stop provoking him." *You know what a genius he is. You know how much I admire him. I couldn't resist him.*

"Your mother is not a prude," Ty said, and reexperienced a quick, hot flash of the pleasure they had shared. "She's a lady. You could learn something from her."

Shelby looked meaningfully at his groin, then giggled. "Yeah, I'll just bet I could."

Ty groaned and dropped into a chair. His face, he knew, must be crimson. The girl was shameless, Sarah refused to curb her, and thoughts that should have been private were his own worst enemy. In other words, his position was hopeless. As an experienced soldier, he knew it was time to retreat. "And I thought Sukey was a handful," he muttered.

Shelby was still smiling. "Ice it, Colonel Stone. I've got a lock on you now. I'll be able to cancel you out."

"Translated into English, I take it that means you've discovered how to shut out my thoughts. But how do I know you won't continue to listen?"

"Because I say so, and I always keep my word. Anyway, I never wanted your stupid thoughts chasing around in my head in the first place."

"Really! And here I thought you were enjoying yourself immensely at my expense."

Admit it, Sarah thought, *and tell him you're sorry.*

"You're right," Shelby said promptly. "I'm sorry, Colonel Stone."

Ty looked at each of them in turn and saw bland innocence. "An extracted apology if I ever heard one, but I accept it, Shelby." He felt a twinge of guilt. "And, uh, I know my thoughts were sometimes unwarranted. *I'm* sorry, as well. For your mother's sake if nothing else, I hope we can stop arguing."

"Yeah, okay. But just for the record, I'm not a brat or a bimbo. A lot of what I said—it served you right. And if you're as honest as history says you were, you'll admit it."

"Fine. I shouldn't have judged you by the standards of 1865, but let's have a little honesty from your end, too. Women may be equal to men in your time, and sexual standards may be more permissive, but I can't believe that girls your age—or boys—are in the habit of speaking to their elders the way you addressed me."

Shelby shrugged. "Maybe I went a little too far."

Sarah walked to the sofa and put her arm around Shelby's shoulders, thinking she'd been naive to expect Ty and her daughter to take to each other on sight. Like any man of his era, especially a high-ranking officer, Ty was accustomed to courtesy and deference. Like any teenager, Shelby relished being provocative. Add in a huge cultural difference and her ability to read his mind, and fireworks were almost inevitable. But if Ty was still uncomfortable and disapproving, and Shelby still resented his hostility, at least the two of them had finally shut up.

She ran her fingers through her daughter's hair. "You're not yawning. Aren't you sleepy yet?"

"Nope. We've got better stimulants now. I've got another hour, maybe longer."

"Oh. Good." She paused. "So you're seventeen now! I can hardly believe it." She began to French-braid Shelby's hair, just as she had years ago. Days ago. "Then it took five whole years to build a second chamber?"

"Not exactly, Mom. The first thing you need to know is, you messed up the past in a major way." Shelby elaborated, explaining how much worse things had grown. Listening, Sarah grew sick with horror and guilt. "I brought back a bookfile with hundreds of sources loaded into it," Shelby continued, "so you can learn what went wrong. But I can tell you this much. You never contacted us, and we checked through thousands of newspapers. We searched for a mention of you in the history books, but there wasn't one. I know you wouldn't have stayed here on purpose, not for very long, so you must have died before you were ready to send us a message."

She looked at Ty. "You died, too, sometime in June, but there's no exact date. What few facts we have come from a letter to Melanie McClure in Hong Kong from her father in San Francisco. You and your sister were crossing the continent on the Overland Stage when you were killed by Native Americans. The authorities must have learned where you were from, because they sent the bodies to Nevada City. That's where you're buried. Your death was obviously a terrible loss to the country, but whether it accounts for all of the changes that occurred, we just don't know."

Shelby explained that, with so few people aware that history had changed, or even of what the Wells Project really was, no sentiment had existed for spending tens of billions of dollars on what had appeared to be an obscure physics experiment. But as that first long year had dragged on, Shelby's telepathic powers had grown, until she was able to push Congress into doing what she wanted. The Wellsians had inaugurated the second chamber when Shelby was fifteen and had used it regularly ever since.

Sarah gave her a quizzical look. "Then why the two-year wait? Did it take you that long to push them into letting you be the one who searched for me?"

Shelby shook her head, then burst into tears. Sarah held her, deeply alarmed, wishing Shelby would say or think something to explain her distress. But even Sarah's strongest mental pleas couldn't evoke a response.

Finally, sobbing, Shelby blurted, "I told you—I wasn't going to let you die. I made them wait." She shivered and sniffled. "Wait till they found a cure. I brought it along. It's in my carpetbag."

Sarah went dead white. She tried not to weep—tried not to tremble—but it was impossible. She buried her face against Shelby's shoulder and clung to her. "Oh, my God. I can't believe that I'm going to live. That I'll see you finish college. Continue with my work. Maybe even hold a grandchild in my arms. What did I ever do to deserve you?"

Ty stared at them, his heart pounding wildly. He couldn't believe what he'd heard, but then he thought about how thin Sarah was, and how her energy often flagged, and he knew it was true. "You're ill," he said hoarsely. "You're dying."

You didn't tell him?

Sarah straightened a little. *No. Not yet. But I was going to very soon.*

Shelby held Sarah as protectively as a lioness guarding her cub. "She had a year or two left, Colonel Stone. Traveling in time boosts the human immune system. Helps you fight disease. We thought that jumping might cure her, but we were wrong. There would have been an improvement, but only a temporary one." She focused on Sarah. "It's an infectious disease, Mom. The virus inserts itself into the mitochondria and literally saps the life out of you. But it mimics human DNA so perfectly that they only started to guess what was going on when some spouses of the original victims got sick. There's a long latency period—up to fifteen years. They figure you got infected after I was born. They told me you needed a transfusion."

"Yes." A stab of terror slashed through Sarah's

heart. She had breast-fed Shelby. "Dear God. Were you—"

"No. I didn't catch it."

Sarah's head snapped around. She stared at Ty. Her stomach began churning so badly she almost gagged.

Shelby hugged her reassuringly. "Don't worry. It's not very contagious, which is another reason it took them so long to realize it was infectious. You probably didn't transmit it, but I brought an extra dose along, just in case. He'll be fine."

"You did? But how did you even know I was with him, much less that he and I— That the two of us— You know. That we'd gotten together."

"First of all, in the new version of history, the past two years of his life aren't a mystery. I know about T.J. Reid. It's in his biography in *Fischer's*. It also mentions the article he wrote for the *Intelligencer* about the soldiers and how the attitudes they brought back from the war will affect the country." She turned to Ty. "I read that essay. I don't care how brilliant you are, or how latently psychic, you couldn't have predicted the future—not so accurately. You obviously had help, and there was only one place it could have come from. Which meant my mom broke the rules and told you what would happen after the war. We could hardly believe she had done it, but there was no other explanation."

Sarah regarded her daughter with awe. "So it was all you. Nobody at the Wells Project knew enough about Ty to wonder how his life might have changed, much less to realize that the article in the *Intelligencer* was completely new."

Shelby told them how she'd skimmed Sarah's writings, found that her thesis was now on Horace Greeley, and realized that Ty might be the key to what had gone wrong. After that, it was a simple matter of learning as much as she could about his life and drawing the right conclusions. ''You were obviously spending a lot of time with my mom,'' she told him, ''and you'd had a ton of mistresses during your life. Your first life, I mean. So I figured you'd try to get her into bed, but frankly, knowing how conservative she is, I didn't think she would do it. But I've seen your picture—it was taken when you were fifty—and you were handsome even then. She was bound to be physically attracted to you, and she's always been totally fascinated by you. She knew she was dying, and she'd been told she wasn't contagious. If she was going to sleep with anyone she wasn't married to, I knew it would be you.''

Shelby added that there had never been any question about who would go back to find her mother. They'd known Ty was in Washington on the twenty-seventh and twenty-eighth because an article in Monday's paper would say so, and they'd figured Sarah would still be with him, but they couldn't be sure. Since of all the Wellsians, only Shelby had the capacity to jump to 1865 and find Sarah instantly no matter where she was, she was the logical person to send.

Listening to Shelby's explanation, Sarah knew exactly what she would be required to do, and it broke her heart. ''Now that you've found me—now that you know the date I landed—you're going to leave. You'll bring me back as soon as it's safe to, when I first wake up here. The Sarah who returns to 2102 will never experience this. Never meet Ty.'' Never work with him. Never love him. Her eyes welled with tears. She would live, but there would be no wonderful year with Ty and Shelby, not anymore.

Wrong again, Mom. Not even close. Don't be unhappy. It will all work out.

Sarah's eyes cleared instantly. She blinked in confusion. ''How? What have you got planned?''

''Dammit, Shelby,'' Ty grumbled, ''if you're going

to think something at your mother, would you think it at me, too? I hate being left in the dark.''

Shelby smiled slyly. ''I thought you didn't want me to mess with your head, Colonel Stone.''

He cursed under his breath. ''Your daughter is a minx, Sarah.''

''What's a minx, Mom? Did he insult me again?''

''Not really. He meant that you drive him crazy. Go on, honey. What's our next step?''

''The thing is, Mom, if we snatch you up at the beginning of your mission, nothing is going to get worse, but nothing is going to improve, either. When you spoke to Colonel Stone—when you helped him with his essay—you were on the right track. The essay was influential. It got people thinking about this country and what it should become. It got us headed in a better direction. But then he died, and everything fell apart. So we need to learn what else you changed, and how it made things worse. We have to figure out what would have happened if I'd never come here—what *did* happen the second time around, including when Ty and his sister died. And then we can make things better.''

''We?'' Ty repeated with a frown. ''You mean you're staying for as long as your mother does?''

Shelby looked at him so resentfully that he assumed she was poking around in his head again. Irate, he gave her a violent mental blast: *Get out of my bloody mind, you little snoop*!

She flinched and glared. *Don't scream at me, damn you. I was never inside it.* ''Obviously you don't want me here,'' she said, ''but the future of the whole country is at stake, so maybe you should stop thinking about how often you'll be able to screw my mom and concentrate on what you can do to improve millions of lives. And while you're at it, you should consider something else. I'm a telepath. I can't hear most people think without working really hard, much less hear them as clearly as I hear you, but intense bursts of thought and strong emotions are much louder. Emotions like hate, fury, and resentment. If I were you, and I knew I was about to be killed, I would want someone like me around.''

Ty grimaced and looked away. Not only had he misjudged the girl badly; his remark about her staying had been singularly ungracious. Sarah loved her dearly and was overjoyed to have her here—indeed, if not for Shelby, Sarah would have died—so the least he could do was accept her.

He glanced at her, saw her watching him through narrowed eyes, and sighed. He didn't take kindly to being lectured by a child, but he had earned every cutting word. The nation was all that mattered, and if she could help to protect it, she needed to stay. He had acted like a prize fool.

He was about to apologize when she yawned and continued, ''Anyway, my mom is crazy about you. She always has been. I wanted to give her more time with you. I wanted her to be able to remember you after we left.'' She yawned again. ''And this was the only way I could think to do it.''

In other words, Ty thought, she had pushed people into taking a course of action that would make Sarah happy, and the fact that it was also best for the country was merely a bonus. No wonder Sarah adored her.

''Look—I'm sorry,'' he said. ''I've behaved like an ass, but try to understand—''

But there was no use going on. The apology came too late for the girl to hear it. She looked at Sarah blankly, then keeled over and fell into an exhausted sleep.

Chapter 17

Ty pulled out the spare bedding that was stored in his chest and carried it out to Sarah, returning to the bedroom to undress while she settled Shelby on the sofa. As he stripped off his trousers, his manhood began to swell, causing him to glance at the organ in wonderment. True, Shelby was dead to the world thanks to the jump, and would remain so for more than a day, but still, it was startling how quickly his passions had revived once he was assured of a little privacy.

He didn't bother with a nightshirt, but slipped under the covers naked. Sarah entered the room some five minutes later, closing the door behind her. She was carrying an object the size and shape of a book, fashioned of a sleek, white substance he recognized as plastic. Still wearing her dressing gown, she got into bed and opened the device up. Instead of paper, he saw a flat dark surface on each side, with rows of square buttons beneath. Some were stamped with words, others with numbers or symbols.

"It's like a small library," she said. "We call it a bookfile. I'll show you how it works."

He unfastened the top few buttons of her dressing gown. "Show me later, sweetheart."

Frowning, she removed his hand. "Stop it, Ty. I have reading to do."

She pressed a button marked POWER, and the surfaces lit up like lamps. The word CONTENTS appeared in black letters on the left one. Beneath it was a list of titles that continued onto the other side.

"Fascinating," he mumbled, and indeed it was. But his interest lay elsewhere at the moment. He reached under her dressing gown, cupped a breast, and rubbed the nipple with his palm. He was gratified by how quickly it peaked. "Look at your body, darling. Your reading can obviously wait."

She wiggled away from him, still holding the bookfile. "No, Ty. I'm not in the mood."

That's when he realized she was angry with him, and he knew that he fully deserved it. He had been selfish and provincial just now, and was still deeply ashamed of himself. "Sarah . . . I know I didn't cover myself with glory out there, and I'm sorry. No matter how shocked I was, I shouldn't have allowed your daughter to provoke me. I promised to be open-minded, but I persisted in drawing the worst possible conclusions. I'll apologize to Shelby when she wakes, but until then, there's nothing I can do, except to say that she's beautiful and very clever, and that I appreciate the love and devotion you share. She saved your life, and there are no words to express my gratitude for that." He stroked her hair. "Come, sweetheart. I know I'm a backward, uncivilized wretch, but surely I've proved myself willing to be enlightened. Can't you can manage to forgive me?"

Sarah touched the screen on her bookfile, calling up a history of the postwar period through the end of the century. Ty had a knack for making speeches, she thought, but the prettiest apology in the world couldn't negate his narrowness, his arrogance, or the fact that he wanted Shelby gone. "No. I love my daughter dearly, and you don't even like her. You can barely even tolerate her presence."

"But that's not fair. I hardly know the girl. Besides, given how—how unique she is, don't I deserve some time to adjust? I admit my initial reaction was harsh, but—"

"Yes. It was." Sarah made the mistake of looking up, saw desire as well as regret on Ty's face, and lost whatever charity remained. "That's exactly the point. The Tyson Stone I worshiped wouldn't have reacted that way. He would have listened and learned. He would have seen how special she is and welcomed her into his heart. He would have behaved like an adult, for God's sake, and ignored the teasing of a child."

"The Tyson Stone you worshiped . . ." He repeated the phrase with a weary sigh. "You know something, Sarah? I'm sick of the man. I can't compete with some saintly version of myself who existed only on paper. I'm a human being, not a damned icon."

Sarah stabbed a series of buttons with unnecessary vigor, and an index appeared on her screen. "You were happy enough to be an icon when it got you into my panties. I mean, my knickers."

"You mean your hot, sweet body, and I'm aching to come back there." He massaged her neck, sending an insidious coil of warmth spiraling downward. Irked by her own response, she pretended to concentrate on the index. "Besides, you wanted me when I was Reid," he added. "Be honest, my love. It wasn't the icon who seduced you. It was the human male."

"Well, he's not going to seduce me again." She pulled away from him. "Either leave me alone, or I'll read outside in the parlor."

Ty figured he could have her if he insisted—her flushed cheeks and husky voice told him she was physically aroused—but after it was over, no matter how much she enjoyed it, she would be crosser than ever. At him, for seducing her against her wishes, and at herself, for being unable to resist him. Resigned to being punished, he pecked her on the cheek, told her how much he loved her, and apologized for his myriad faults. She stared at her bookfile, coolly ignoring him until he gave up and buried his head in his pillow.

Sarah was scanning the index for Ty's name, but she couldn't really concentrate until his deep, regular breathing assured her he was asleep. Annoyed or not, she was relieved he had settled down. He'd had a long, full day, and with his wounds still healing, he needed a good night's rest.

She was soon lost in her work. She'd studied with the professor who had written this book, so she remembered the original contents and was able to compare the two versions. It was only when her eyes were burning from exhaustion that she finally stopped reading, but she'd gotten an astonishing lead by then.

Tyson Stone was mentioned only once, for his essay in next week's *Intelligencer*. His sister wasn't included at all. But Ned Beecham appeared again and again. Totally unknown in the first version of history, he would become a fiery, charismatic leader who would unify and strengthen one of the most infamous outgrowths of the Civil War—the Ku Klux Klan.

Ty awakened at twenty past ten with a pounding erection and a racking anxiety. He had dreamed of losing Sarah, not in a month, but today, and not to the lures of the future, but to the anger and disappointment she felt right now. He gazed at her for several moments. She had changed into her nightdress and was sleeping near the edge of the bed, as far from him as she could get, but at least she hadn't left him.

Frustration lashed at him, and then a possessiveness akin to madness. She was going to leave him, and it ate at his innards like acid. He refused to be ignored. He refused to be dismissed. And he refused to be forgotten.

He threw back the covers, placed a pillow beside her hips, and lifted her on top of it. Then he unbuttoned the bodice of her nightdress and eased the skirt up her body, bunching it around her waist. She stirred a little when he massaged her nipples to life, but she didn't rouse. So he caressed the soft, blond curls between her legs, and parted her thighs, and ran his fingers along the tender flesh inside. She squirmed and moaned softly. Asleep, she enjoyed his touch. He hoped she wouldn't awaken until he had aroused her past the point of wanting to refuse him.

He gently opened her womanhood, then bent his head to the sensitive bud inside and explored it with his tongue. As he tasted and stroked her, her breathing quickened and she began moving in time with his erotic ministrations. And then she woke up. He knew the exact moment it happened, because she jerked wildly, then went rigid.

No verbal protest followed, but she tried to twist away. He grasped her hips, ordered her to keep still, and went right on teasing her with his tongue. But she wasn't like Peggy, whose refusals had been meant to provoke. If she insisted, she would mean it. He would have to stop.

But Sarah was in no fit state to make such a demand. She had awakened befogged by arousal, on fire from the magic of Ty's mouth. She'd only withdrawn when she'd remembered the night before—how annoyed she had been, and how agreeing to make love would have seemed like a personal defeat.

Far from offending her, his persistence only excited her more feverishly. Instead of objecting, she found herself submitting. And trembling. And opening herself wider, then pressing herself to his mouth. When he pleasured her so sweetly, she wondered why she had refused him last night. After all, you couldn't expect a man to be perfect, not even Ty. How could she have forgotten how giving he was? How tender and passionate?

The stroking took on an arrogant sensual insistence, and she groaned his name. "Ty . . . Dear God . . . I can't bear this . . ." The sensations tearing through her were splintering her into pieces. She dug her nails into his back, and then, afraid she would lose control and hurt him, grabbed at the the bars of the headboard instead.

He raised his head. "You can't? Then I'll stop."

She shook her head convulsively from side to side. "No. Please. I don't want you to."

But his mouth moved to her breast and suckled her hard, and his fingers slipped between her legs, sliding in and out of her, touching her everywhere but where she most wanted him to, driving her into a frenzy. Panting now, she opened her eyes and clutched his shoulders. "Stop teasing me, damn you. I don't like it."

He eased himself upward, looked her in the eye, and entered her with a gentle but determined thrust. "No. Last night I took the orders. This morning I mean to give them. I'm going to take my time with you, and you're going to like it very much." He drove himself as deep as he could go. "And if that's teasing you, madam, then prepare yourself to be teased to death."

The words inflamed her. So did the hard, full feel of him. She shuddered violently and twined her legs around his thighs. "Yes. All right. Whatever you want."

"What I want"—he rocked provocatively inside her—"is to make you explode with pleasure. You can leave me, Sarah, but you won't ever forget me. You won't ever forget *this*. I swear to God you won't."

He was as good as his word. There was always a fiery intensity with Ty, a sense that no one else existed for him, but it was joined by a searing mastery to which she yielded completely. She was relaxed and utterly trusting, without fear or inhibition.

He took her right to the edge, then slowly cooled her down, and all she could do was moan endearments, plead incoherently, and savor every spectacular moment. Then he aroused her again, and when she was desperate and clinging, murmured, "Should I make you wait? Do you want it again?" And she whispered yes and wondered if you could die from too much excitement.

By the fourth time, she was drained and dazed. He didn't stop. He didn't ask questions. He didn't keep teasing. He simply drove her higher and higher, muffling her cries with his mouth, until both of them shattered. Then he rolled onto his back and pulled her against his chest, massaging her neck and shoulders while she caught her breath.

She lay in his arms afterward, languid and content, marveling at an intimacy so deep that embarrassment became impossible, wanting to thank him for showing her the stars. But somehow, all that came out was a husky, "Good grief, Ty."

"Ah! So you liked it as much as I said you would."

She smiled at the male preening in his tone. "No. It was odious and boring. Frankly, it needs work. You'll have to practice till you get it right." She yawned. "I'm still angry with you, you know."

Ty chuckled. At that moment, he was happier than he had thought was possible. Sarah had given herself as completely as a woman could, she was soft and loving in his arms, and he was sure they had set a record for erotic bliss. "Yes," he said. "I can tell."

"I mean it, Ty." She snuggled into the crook of his neck, planting sleepy kisses along the way. "Umm. I love the way you taste. The way you feel. But I expect you to redeem yourself this morning. With Shelby, that is."

"Yes, ma'am. As soon as she awakens. Will I be forgiven once I have?"

"I believe you just were. Would you order me up some breakfast? I think I'll doze a while longer. Savor the afterglow." She smiled in the most peculiar way. "But put on a dressing gown before you go into the parlor, all right?"

He blanched. "Are you telling me—"

"Yes."

He rose from the bed. "So soon?"

Sarah put her nightgown to rights, then burrowed under the covers. "She's healthy. I wasn't. Seven or eight hours is the norm." She yawned again. "I can't seem to stay awake. You exhausted me, darling."

"How long has she been—"

"I'm really not sure." Sarah sighed contentedly and closed her eyes. "I felt her toward the end, but believe me, I was too far gone to care."

Or even to muffle her cries of pleasure, Ty thought with a groan. No pirate's prisoner had ever walked the plank with more terror than he felt when he opened the parlor door, but his only other choice was to hide in the bedroom like a coward.

Shelby was propped up on the sofa, bundled under her blanket, reading a magazine. She turned and grinned, giving him a look that made him feel like a stallion on the auction block. "That was some performance, Colonel Stone. You have impressive staying power, I'll give you that. You're sure you don't have a younger brother?"

He flushed so hard that his ears burned. "Quite sure." He yanked the bellpull. "All right, Shelby. Let's get it over with. What did you hear? How much did you—sense?" He closed his eyes for a moment, wishing he could dive under the carpet. "How mortified do I have to be?"

She giggled. "Listen, Ty—can I call you Ty?—where I come from, if a woman moaned and thrashed that way, a guy wouldn't be embarrassed. He'd want to film the whole thing—make a moving picture of it—and show it to all his friends."

"We're talking about your mother, Shelby. Doesn't it bother you? Embarrass you? Are discretion and privacy extinct in your era? And you didn't answer my questions. But yes, you can call me Ty."

Her answer slammed into his mind. *Gee, I kind of like that. Verbal shorthand. It's almost as efficient as thinking things back and forth.*

"Dammit, you know how much it unnerves me—"

"Yup. It's just that it amazes me—how well I can pick you up. Send you my thoughts. It's fun to experiment." She winked at him. "It must be the intensity of your life force, Colonel."

He regarded her suspiciously. "If you're making sport of my—my male appetites again—"

"Only a little." She tossed aside her magazine. "The thing is, it's not just the latent telepathy. You have a powerful personality, too. I've heard your type before, but only from a distance, so the vibes were weaker. And the time period might add to it. The violent, primitive past and all that." She wrinkled her nose. "Speaking of which, is there a bathroom here? I'm in desperate need of one, and if there isn't, I'll need a robe so I can walk down the hall."

"It's off the bedroom," he said, "but why—"

Because I can only control two or three minds at a

time. She uncurled herself from the sofa and stood. *Four, tops, if they're especially pliant.*

You promised not to— ''Bloody hell, Shelby. I want you to stop doing that, do you hear me?''

She strolled past him with blithe unconcern. *Loud and clear, Ty.*

He rolled his eyes, then conceded defeat. *And you haven't answered my questions yet, minx.*

Shelby picked up her pace once she left the parlor, pulling down her jeans and panties as she dashed past her sleeping mother into the bathroom. She wasn't sure why, but whenever Ty was around, she wanted to act really cool, really outrageous. Maybe his hostility had something to do with it, except that he wasn't hostile or even disapproving anymore, only incredibly uptight, and she was still at it. But he didn't know what to make of her, and when he wasn't shocked or bewildered, he was exasperated, and it was fun to make him lose it completely, and start stammering, blushing, and even cursing.

She used the toilet—thank God the Willard contained whatever amenities this pit of a burg offered—then washed and left the room. Her mom was sprawled on her side now, looking impossibly content. Shelby scowled at the sight. It should have been her daughter who had made her feel that way, not some nineteenth century sexual magician.

She returned to the parlor and dropped onto the sofa. Ty was talking to a bellman, ordering breakfast. The guy did a startled double take when he saw her, so she made him forget. It was easy in cases like that, when people doubted their own eyes or thoughts.

Ty dismissed him and closed the door. ''He stopped seeing you, didn't he?''

''Yeah. And then he forgot.''

''An amazing talent. You were right last night. I'm

lucky you came." He paused. "You'll like the food here, I think. Your mother certainly does. She was starving when she first woke up. Is that typical of jumping?"

"Yes." Shelby tucked her feet under her body, thinking it wouldn't kill her to answer Ty's questions. After all, he was keeping his promise to her mother and trying to be nicer. Sarah would want her to meet him halfway.

She gazed at him. "So you want to know how it felt to listen, huh? Then I'll tell you. It was funny at first. Unbelievable. I'd never heard stuff like that from my mom, not even when I was a kid and she was with my dad. And you—" She felt her face grow hot, and stared at her lap in chagrin. "I've only had one boyfriend, and I couldn't read him too well, so I had no idea that men could feel so—so totally wild. But it was over in seconds last night, and this morning . . . Believe me, I wasn't listening with my mind. I'd heard enough. But all that thumping and moaning—it woke me up. I would have left—I brought a costume along—but I figured you'd be done by the time I could dress. So I waited—and waited—and it was—"

She grimaced at the memory of how she'd felt. "Listen, Ty, I'm not a baby. I've seen actors do it in holofilms a hundred times. But this was different." She looked up, struggling for the right words. "It was my *mom*, for God's sake—Sarah the prude—and she was so turned on, she couldn't control herself. And now . . . She's sleeping in there with this grin on her face, and it's nice that you made her so happy, but I hate you for taking advantage of her."

Ty joined Shelby on the sofa, then gave her the warmest, gentlest smile she had ever seen. She had no idea what it meant, only that she suddenly felt better. Special, somehow. It was her first real inkling of why her mom was so crazy about the man, other than the sex, of course. He could smile at a person and light up their world.

"What?" she demanded irritably.

"Just that I never expected such honesty. I had no idea how sweet and innocent you were." A teasing gleam entered his eyes. "I was misled by your colorful language and provocative behavior, as I suppose I was meant to be. Still, I'm told I should have known better. I'm a future icon, you know. Your mother expects moral perfection from me. I hope you'll be less exacting. I wonder, Shelby . . . If I promise to stop being judgmental and offensive, do you think you could tolerate me for the next several weeks?"

So he could be charming too, Shelby thought. She didn't know why, but she didn't want to be charmed. "Maybe. I guess you're a decent enough guy, except for one thing. Unlike me, my mom really *is* sweet and innocent, and she never had a chance against someone like you. You should have left her alone. But me—I've been on my own for the past five years, pushing people to save her, and I've had to be hard and manipulative. And realistic, too. You need me here, but you wish you didn't."

"I suppose so, but then, your mother wants me here, and you wish she didn't." He leaned back on the sofa. "The truth is, we're jealous of each other. It's only natural, because we love the same woman. But I'll have her in my life for only a few weeks longer, and then she'll return to the world you both come from. Believe me, Shelby, I'm no threat to you." He looked away. "No threat at all."

Shelby was trying to block out Ty's mind, to screen out the emotions he was emitting, but it was impossible. His tone had been calm and reasoned, but his feelings were flooding the room. Poignant longing washed through her, then aching sadness. "Jesus, Ty." Her stomach clenched and her eyes welled with tears. She brushed them away, but she couldn't erase the nausea and pain she felt. "The stuff in your mind . . . It's like a physical attack. Do you love her that much? Really?"

He shrugged. "I'm sorry, Shelby. I'll try to control myself better. You shouldn't have to listen to such thoughts."

He actually meant it. He regretted upsetting her. "But what about my mom? Does she feel the same way?"

"No." He smiled slightly, but there was a terrible pain behind the look, and Shelby felt it keenly. "She loves what I'll become. What I am now—I seem to have a talent for disappointing her. But both of us know how infatuated she is, and uh, what a powerful force making love can be. From what you said before, I suspect you've figured out that . . . that physical pleasure is a new experience for her."

Shelby bit her lip. "Yeah, you're right. Like I told you, I may be a virgin, but I'm not naive. I realized it last night—that when it came to sex, my father was probably a nonstarter. I mean, lousy at making love."

"I took your meaning. I almost always do." His mood lightened a fraction. "I can't believe we're having this conversation, but God knows the slang you use isn't the problem."

"Right. My age is. And the fact that I'm the daughter of—whatever she is. Your girlfriend. Your mistress. But like she said last night, times have changed."

"Yes." He stared at the wall. *She's my lover, Shelby. My soul mate. I wanted her to share my life, but one of us was born in the wrong time, so it can't happen. Let's talk about something else, shall we?*

Shelby knew why Ty had thought her the words. If he'd tried to speak them, he would have broken down. His pain—his unshed tears—made her bleed inside. Pitying him, she reached out her hand, hesitated, and then placed it on his arm. "Ty . . . When this is over—when we've fixed things and we have to leave—I could make you forget her."

He moved closer and put his arm around her shoulders. His mind was full of tenderness and gratitude now. She was startled, then deeply shaken. She'd been feeling people for years—their closed minds, their stubbornness, their self-righteousness—and she knew how rigid they usually were. But Ty was different. He really listened.

"That's sweet and very generous," he said quietly, "but no. I don't want to forget her."

"Then how about forgetting how much you love her? I'm not sure I could do it—that I could separate things out in your brain that way—but I could try."

"Not that, either, Shel. I want to remember the joy, even if it means living with the pain. But thank you for the offer."

There was a knock on the door, and Ty got to his feet. Shelby only prayed it was breakfast, and not really because she was so starving. After five long years without her mother, she wasn't accustomed to such intense emotions. She needed some relief from the double telepathic barrage.

But instead of a porter with a tray, she saw a middle-aged man in a black suit carrying an envelope in his hand. As he entered the parlor, he spotted her on the sofa, and, in a response that was beginning to annoy her, blinked and gaped. Ty's face was politely bland, but she couldn't help sensing the amusement he felt—at the man's shock and at her own reaction to it.

"My God," the man said, "that's the girl in the picture. Or her older sister."

Ty nodded. "Uh, yes. It was an old photograph, Joe. Her name is Shelby. She arrived last night. Shelby, this is Mr. Willard. He and his brother own this hotel." *He saw your mother arrive. He saw her shields. He thinks she's a spy. God knows how I'm going to explain you two away.*

Shelby beamed at him. "Hi, Mr. Willard. You have a fabulous place here." *No offense, Ty, but it's a total hole.* "So beautiful and luxurious." *Yeah, right. No showers, no central heat or air, no elevators, no netlink, no electricity, no holoscreen . . .*

"Uh, thanks," Joe said, still staring at her.

I'll look forward to learning what you're talking about, Shelby. Ty looked meaningfully at the envelope Joe was holding. "Is that for me?"

"Yes." He lowered his voice to a near-whisper as he handed it over. "From the secretary. I assume he wants to see you. About Sarah's daughter . . . What is she doing here? And what on earth is she wearing?"

"It's a long story," Ty murmured back. "I'll explain later. Thanks for bringing up the letter." He took Stanton's message, then hustled Joe out of the parlor.

He ripped the envelope open and pulled out the paper inside. "Lt. Colonel Stone," it read. "You are to report to me in my office at one o'clock this afternoon with your prisoner. I will expect a signed confession from her at that time. If you have been unable to obtain one, both you and she will be turned over to General Baker for questioning. E. M. Stanton, Secretary of War."

He stared at the letter in dismay, wondering how he was going to extricate himself from the mess he was in. He couldn't tell Stanton the truth. Sarah would never approve it, and besides, the secretary was distrustful and temperamental. Even if he let Sarah go, he would want to analyze her devices, and they couldn't allow that. And now, to top it all off, there was Shelby to protect.

He was still frowning at the letter when Shelby strolled over and removed it from his hand. He was a journalist, not a novelist, he thought grimly. He didn't have the talent to invent a story that could explain a series of miracles. Only one alternative occurred to him. Flight.

Chapter 18

Nebraska Territory, on board the Overland Stage

Ned Beecham awoke with a start and looked out the window of the Concord coach in which he was riding. The first light of dawn was creeping over the plains. It would be hours before they stopped to dine, so he settled back in his seat and tried to go back to sleep.

It was impossible. His brain was galloping even faster than the Overland's horses. He couldn't stop thinking about the two telegrams that had changed his life.

The first, from his brother George, had reached him late Wednesday night, at his boardinghouse in Denver. Like his family's letters, it had been addressed to Sam Potts, the name he had adopted after he had fled Ohio. "Found Peggy's murderer," it had read. "Success uncertain. Am severely wounded. Return home now. G."

Ned had assumed "severely" meant fatally, or close to it. Why else would his brother have sent for him? It wasn't the most convenient time for him to leave—he'd had an appointment on Thursday afternoon, to make an inspection of the Lucky Eight Mine in Central City before deciding whether to invest—but his family came first. The next morning, he had boarded the stage to Atchison, Kansas.

He was carrying only a single piece of baggage, a small trunk, but then, he'd had little besides money to pack. Fine possessions would have attracted attention, and when a Yankee soldier kept sniffing around with your portrait, asking if anyone had seen you, that was the last thing you wanted to do. Ned had told only one other person, his broker, about the wealth he had accumulated speculating in mining stocks; he had also changed his appearance, growing a luxuriant beard and using henna to turn his blond hair chestnut.

His caution had paid off. So far as he knew, nobody had recognized him. As Sam Potts, he had been able to devote himself to stirring up trouble among the Indians and increasing his bank balance, using both his subversion and his money to further the Southern cause.

But the war was over now, and the Confederacy was dead. He should have felt crushed by that, but oddly, as defeat became inevitable, he had gained a renewed purpose in life. Everything that had transpired was part of some grand design, he'd realized, and it was time to carry that design out. Only one thing stood in his way, the continued survival of Peggy's abuser, T.J. Reid, who was bound to seek revenge for his own sister's disgrace.

Ned sighed deeply. Reid had friends in high places who wouldn't stop aiding him until he was six feet under, so if George hadn't killed him, *he* would have to do it. There was no getting around it. As for Reid's tease of a sister, she had met him willingly and given herself freely, until well past the point where a man could be expected to stop.

And if, deep down, he'd had doubts about the matter, the second telegram had removed them. It had been a routine one conveying the Denver-area news to Julesburg, the first major station on the stage line east, and he had seen it on Friday when they had stopped to dine. ''Central City, May 25. Lucky Eight Mine cave-in kills Supt. Dimity, six others,'' one item had read. If George's message hadn't arrived when it had, summoning him home, it would have been seven others.

From boyhood, Ned had felt he was special. He spoke and people listened. He acted and they followed. For a time, he had even heard voices, but he hadn't liked that, so he had made them go away. After that, he had known he could master anything.

The older he had grown, the surer he'd become that he was destined for great things. When the war had broken out, he had expected to win glory on the battlefield, but Reid and his sister had robbed him of that possibility and forced him to use spying and money to gain the respect and influence he deserved. His cause was lost now, and his patrons dead or in hiding, but the South endured. She would never die, not as long as men of passion and goodwill united to save her.

Ned meant to lead those men. That was why fate had spared him, he felt it in his bones. God had chosen him to deliver his beloved land from the villains who were trying to destroy her, and he was ready to get on with the job.

Washington City, the Willard Hotel

Hey! Stone!

Ty looked up, then turned around. Shelby was back on the sofa, waving Stanton's letter at him. Her mental interjections no longer bothered him, but he needed to concentrate, and he couldn't do that if her thoughts were bouncing around in his brain. ''Not now, Shel. I have to think. We've got problems. Big problems.''

Maybe. Maybe not.

He blinked, then shook his head in bewilderment.

One minute the girl was sitting on the sofa, and the next, she had vanished, as if she had popped back into the future. Stanton's letter, meanwhile, was wafting gently toward his feet. It was the damnedest thing he had ever witnessed, even more astonishing than Sarah's devices were.

Baffled, he picked up the letter and glanced around the room, but she was nowhere in sight. He was reaching out his hand to feel where she had just been sitting when she giggled into his mind. *Good thinking, soldier. You're right. I haven't moved.* And the next instant, she reappeared.

"A neat trick," he said. "How do you do that? Control what people see, think, and even remember?"

"To be honest, I don't know, but it's the same as any other sense. I touch and I feel. I listen and I hear. I look and I see. And if I focus very hard on what I want to happen, it does, and I can feel it in my mind. It should work on Willard and Stanton—and on anyone else who knows about my mother." She paused, then added thoughtfully, "I wonder if that's what got you into trouble the last time. Running away, I mean."

"Oh?" He raised his eyebrows in a mock rebuke. "Then you listened to me just now? Without my intending it?"

"I couldn't help it, Ty. You were so upset, I began to worry. I mean, I had to know what was wrong before I could take care of it for you, right?"

He didn't know whether to feel pleased or humiliated. "Humph. Some soldier I am. Instead of protecting the women I love, I have to rely upon—"

What did you just say?

The mental caterwaul brought him up short. "Listen here, Shelby, men and women may be equal in your time, but in 1865—" He cut himself off, suddenly understanding her astonishment. "Oh. That. God knows why, given how gleefully you torment me, but I'm growing oddly fond of you. Men of my era are raised to protect women and children, so I feel I should take care of you, not the reverse. I don't mind telling you, it doesn't sit well—to be rescued by a seventeen-year-old girl."

Sarah opened the door, yawning and rubbing her eyes. "I knew you would like her if you gave her half a chance." She beamed at him. "And you were an excellent soldier, darling, but remember, she's no ordinary seventeen-year-old."

"So I've learned," he said.

Ninety minutes later, Ty and Shelby strolled out of the hotel and headed north, to keep Ty's appointment with Stanton. Shelby would deal with the secretary first, the group had decided over breakfast, then visit Baker and Wood before taking on Joe Willard. As for the others Sarah had encountered, the contacts had been brief and harmless. They would be left alone.

Sarah, meanwhile, was reading up in the suite—and being cured of the disease that almost had killed her. Shelby had inserted a needle into her arm, then connected it via a tube to a bag filled with liquid. A tiny bit of medicine was tucked into each molecule, she had explained to Ty, so that when the nourishment was absorbed by the cells of the body, the antidote was taken up as well. The therapy would take six hours to administer and three to five days to assimilate. It was somewhat fatiguing, so Ty would be treated later, after he had completed his essay for Joseph Gales.

They were no sooner out the door than Shelby sniffed the air and wrinkled her nose in distaste. "God, this city stinks. It's totally revolting—the way you use the canal for a sewer. I can't believe how clueless you people were, not to realize how much disease it spread."

"We've noticed the connection," Ty replied, "but

we lack the science to investigate the subject properly.'' He didn't bother to add that the canal was less fetid than usual that day, or that he could barely smell it. Shelby was in a mood to complain, and if it hadn't been the canal, it would have been something else. The nineteenth century didn't suit the girl, not for a moment.

She had hated taking a bath rather than a shower, hated waiting in line for the tub room, and even hated the texture of the towels. She had grumbled about the clothes she was compelled to wear, though everything from her boots to her corset was more comfortable than its authentic counterpart. She had claimed she lacked the necessary appurtenances to fix her hair correctly, though Ty thought it looked charming in the braid Sarah had fashioned, not that much of it showed outside her hat. And she'd pouted when Sarah refused to let her use any of the makeup she'd brought along. Only the food found any favor with her, probably because she was so hungry from the jump.

Half a block later, she was slapping her cheek and scowling. ''Ugh. Mosquitoes. I'd probably die of malaria if I hadn't gotten a shot for it.'' She coughed. ''And the streets . . . How can you stand all this dust? I can't believe you haven't developed decent paving yet.''

Ty's patience was wearing thin, but losing his temper would only make things worse. ''We're inventing as fast as we can,'' he said calmly.

They were almost at G Street now. Directly ahead of them, Ty noticed, a white man was berating a young Negro who had remained outside a shop with some packages while his employer went inside. The Negro's position, it seemed, had forced the white man to detour as he exited in order to avoid getting too close to the fellow, and he was irate. Ty winced when he delivered a hard blow to the Negro's head with his cane. The Negro stumbled and backed away, apologizing.

Ty was dressed in his military uniform, which gave him an air of authority. He was striding over to avert further violence when a clap of mental fury from Shelby stopped him in his tracks. The attacker suddenly clutched his head and dropped to his knees, moaning in agony.

"I'm sorry," he finally shrieked. "I won't do it again. Yes. I will. But please, Lord—stop punishing me." With a sob, he crawled to the astounded Negro and kissed his tattered shoe, then dragged himself up and staggered away.

The incident left Ty shaken. He hadn't realized what power Shelby could wield. Not only could she alter what you saw and remembered; she could make you behave in a manner that utterly humiliated you. But she was also an adolescent, and having raised a sister, he knew that lecturing her was the surest way to alienate her. So he asked evenly, "Would you care to explain that?"

"I made him hurt, that's all. He was a vicious racist bastard." Her eyes narrowed. "Stupid and weak, too. I told him I was the voice of God, and he believed me and took my orders. He deserved what he got."

"Perhaps, but your mother wouldn't agree. She disapproves of torture." Ty gestured casually toward the left. "This way, my dear. I'm all for speaking up, but inflicting excruciating pain is another matter entirely. Brutality can turn you into the very thing you're fighting. A savage and a tyrant. Besides, if you were to respond that way to every such incident that occurred, you would be doing it constantly, and I worry about the emotional price you would pay. Men like that are much too common, I'm afraid."

"Maybe in your world," she snapped. "Not in mine."

Ty knew otherwise—Sarah had said the future still had problems in that regard—but he held his tongue. To his relief, there were no further outbursts, though Shelby's stunning beauty and uncommon height caused more than one male head to swivel around as they walked down the street. Still, Ty felt a stab of anxiety as they entered the War Department. As long as Stanton ran this place, an air of acute suspicion would prevail here.

He handed Stanton's summons to a young officer, who quickly read it. He obviously assumed Shelby was the prisoner Stanton had mentioned, because he gave her a lecherous, contemptuous look that visually undressed her.

She smiled seductively. The officer gaped. Grew beet red. Broke into a sweat and began to pant and squirm.

Ty noticed the man's swollen crotch and stifled a groan. *I don't know what you're doing, Shelby, but—*

He's a pig. Most of the men here are. I'm sick of the way they leer and condescend.

The soldier turned chalky white. Visibily shaken, he backed up a step, returned Stanton's summons with a trembling hand, and clumsily saluted. "Uh, go right upstairs, sir."

"Thank you, Captain." Ty took Shelby's arm. *All right. Let's have it. What did you do to him?*

He was easy. Suggestible. I made him think I was giving him a blow job, and right in the middle, I sliced off his dick with a knife. Bitter amusement. *If you need a translation—*

No. Your meaning is clear enough. Ty didn't know which shocked him most, the girl's language, her thirst for revenge, or her sexual worldliness. *He shouldn't have looked at you the way he did, but I wish you had ignored it.* He thought about the secretary and felt a rush of apprehension. *As I told you, Stanton can be—extremely difficult. Please, don't let him provoke you.*

Stick to the plan we agreed on. And above all, control your temper, because if you don't, Stanton can have a dozen men in his office in a flash, and not even you can handle so many minds at once.

Anger sliced through him, making him stiffen in pain, but it was followed almost at once by profound remorse. "God, Ty, I'm really sorry," Shelby said softly. "I forget how well you can hear me. It's just—the way the people here think and act—I can't get used to it, and I react too fast. But don't worry. I won't screw up. I promise."

And, in fact, she didn't. Within moments of meeting her, Stanton blinked in confusion and forgot his icy anger about Sarah's absence. He listened with increasing attentiveness to the story Ty spun: that Shelby was his cousin from Pennsylvania; that he had stopped by Stanton's office to introduce her to the greatest man in Washington before returning her to her family; that once he had brought the Beechams to justice, he planned to retrieve his sister in Ohio and proceed to California. The secretary was visibly taken with the girl, but unlike his underling, his feelings were fatherly and respectful. After some final pleasantries, Ty thanked him for his help, and he delivered himself of a rare smile and offered Ty a pass to expedite his travels around the country. Among other things, the note would gain Ty access to military trains where the passenger cars weren't running. Quite clearly, the secretary had forgotten that Sarah existed.

Their second destination of the day, Lafayette Baker's office at the National Detective Bureau, was a few blocks away. The general was in Georgetown on business, they learned, but was expected about four that afternoon. Ty said they would return, then headed toward the Old Capitol Prison and Colonel William Wood.

Within a block, Shelby was grumbling about the fit

of her new boots, saying her feet were killing her, so they took the trolley rather than walk, resulting in complaints about the dust, the bumpy ride over the Avenue's broken cobblestones, and the pungent smell of the horses, instead. But once again, when the time came to perform, she set aside her grievances and executed their plans to perfection. By the time they left Wood's office, all traces of Sarah had been erased from the superintendent's mind.

Their next call was on Ah Lan. She was a good friend with little incriminating knowledge and the discretion of a rock, so there was no need to alter her memories. Ty simply wanted to tell her she had been right, that Sarah wasn't a spy at all, and to ask her to hold her tongue about anything connected to Sarah's presence. Given Ah Lan's occupation, he had remarked during breakfast, it would be highly improper for Shelby to attend.

But of all the things to see in the capital, visiting a genuine brothel was at the top of Shelby's list. No such establishment existed in her time. Women—and men—still sold their bodies, but arrangements were made privately, over a worldwide communications system called the net. She had protested vehemently at being excluded.

Ty had hesitated, then held fast. But far from backing down, Shelby had thrust up her chin and reminded him that she could make him change his mind, and if she did, he would never even know it.

It was the ultimate blackmail. Do what I want, or I'll *make* it what you want. Sarah had regarded her daughter sternly. "But *I* would know, and I wouldn't like it. You're to leave his mind alone."

The order hadn't sat well. After five long years, Shelby was accustomed to doing as she pleased. Still, faced with the sharp disapproval of the person she loved most, she had quickly given way. Then she'd begged and wheedled until Ty reversed himself, saying it might be best to satisfy her curiosity, thinking of how sulky she'd been, and of how cross she would be if he denied her. Besides, he'd added aloud, it wasn't as if the place could shock or corrupt her.

He introduced her to Ah Lan as Sarah's daughter from Virginia City, explaining that she was as unconventional as their friend Melanie and wanted to see the house and meet the girls. Ah Lan summoned François to give her a tour, then took Ty off to talk. To his chagrin, she guessed his feelings for Sarah at once and cornered him into admitting that his suit had been refused. But she insisted that Sarah did love him, and that things would work out, and since he couldn't very well tell her that Sarah was from the future and planned to return there, he could only smile weakly and respond that he hoped she was right.

When his business with Ah Lan was concluded, he collected Shelby and left, steeling himself for the outrageous speech about whores and copulation that was sure to follow. But she was oddly subdued as he escorted her back to the Avenue, not saying a word about what she had seen.

His first reaction was surprise, his second relief. She wasn't embarrassing him, thank God, and she wasn't complaining again, either. And then she reached for him with her mind, a vulnerable and anguished cry, and a wave of distress surged through him.

He put his arm around her, puzzled and deeply concerned. "What's wrong, my dear? Did something happen at Ah Lan's to upset you?"

You're kind. It was a mental whisper, so soft he almost missed it. He felt her gratitude, her sudden affection, and his heart turned over. For all her worldliness, she was still a child, and she was terribly troubled.

"I shouldn't have allowed you to come," he said guiltily. "Their attitudes and their activities . . . I shouldn't have exposed you to such debauchery, no matter how much knowledge you seem to have. I'm sorry, Shelby."

She replied in a low, hoarse voice. "Don't be. I wasn't shocked. It's just—the women there—they say they like what they do. That it gives them independence. That the work is easy and the pay is good. But deep inside . . ." She regarded him through haunted eyes. "Most of them feel so small, Ty. So worthless and dirty. No matter how nice the men are, the women are still objects that are bought and used. And for some . . . They let men have them and pretend to enjoy it, but it's like rape to them, every single time." She hugged herself, trembling a little. "Females don't matter in your world—I knew that before I came—but when I met those women at Ah Lan's, when I felt their minds, I understood the full truth of it. And their sisters on the outside, the ones who are supposedly respectable—we're little better off than the whores are. We're patronized. Trivialized. Oppressed. Abused. It's horrible. I don't know how your sister stands it."

Ty didn't miss the change in pronoun from "they" to "we." When Shelby listened that deeply, when she felt her subjects' emotions so strongly, she began to share them, and in this instance, it had been intensely painful for her.

To deny her charges would have been to insult her intelligence, but 1865 wasn't as uncivilized as she believed. Like most journalists, Ty had a bit of the teacher in him, so he tried to give her some perspective, speaking of the progress the country had made toward the goal of accepting women as equals and explaining how their work during the war had demonstrated their talents and advanced their cause. But Shelby was looking backward from much too far ahead, and nothing he said could sway her. She looked at the men of his time and saw villains. She looked at the women and saw victims. And she was heartsick.

The trolley arrived, and he helped her climb aboard. *You're tired*, he thought with gentle intensity. *Perhaps we should return to the hotel. Baker and Willard can wait until tomorrow if you like.*

She didn't respond, just stared blankly into space. He touched her arm, knowing better than to tell her what to do. The girl made her own decisions about the use of her gifts. "Shelby? What do you think about that?"

She turned around. "What do I think about what, Ty?"

"What I just said. I mean, what I just thought."

"Oh. I'm sorry. I didn't hear you." She rested her head on his shoulder and shut her eyes.

A brotherly protectiveness welled within him. He put his arm around her and drew her closer. "You didn't, my dear?"

"No," she murmured. "Sometimes, when I'm tired or upset, I can't. I guess I'm both right now. Wood was easy, but Stanton was really hard. His mind was so strong that it wore me out." She hesitated. "To be honest, I guess I was tired to begin with, from the others. And then the visit to Ah Lan's . . . Well, you know. About Baker and Willard . . . Would it be a problem if we left them till tomorrow?"

So she wasn't invincible. Her talents could fail her. It was a sobering thought. Baker had a fierce will, and Willard had seen almost everything. What if she couldn't erase their memories of Sarah?

"No problem at all," he said.

Chapter 19

"Baker was tough," Shelby said to her mother the following afternoon. "It was like the connections in his brain were wired all wrong, and it was a bitch just to untangle them. But I'll say one thing for him. He didn't want to—" She glanced at Ty, then cleaned up her language. "To sleep with me. It never hurts when a man lets his hormones do his thinking, but Baker was suspicious the whole time. It made him a pain to adjust."

Sarah nodded and yawned. She was so fatigued from her therapy that she'd done little lately besides read and sleep. In fact, she'd left the suite only once in the past twenty-four hours, to bathe this morning.

Ty and Shelby, meanwhile, had paid a visit to Baker's church, intercepting him after the service in what had appeared to be a chance encounter. Twenty minutes of intense exertion had followed, draining Shelby so greatly that Ty had suggested leaving Willard till later. But in what truly *was* a chance encounter, they had run across Joe and Antonia while strolling back home, and Shelby had tested the waters.

Fortunately, Joe had been an easy mark. The arrival of Sarah and Shelby had disturbed his orderly existence so violently that, deep down, he wished he had never seen them. He believed Shelby to be Ty's cousin now, and Sarah to be his journalist friend from California.

"Baker might have been a raging paranoid," Sarah replied, "but he was never a sexist. He had female agents, and if it had been up to him, women suspects would have been treated just as harshly as men were. Believe me, he didn't shed a tear when they strung up—" She stopped and sighed. "Well, damn. I wish I would stop doing that."

Ty cocked an eyebrow at her. "When they strung up whom, Sarah? Mary Surratt, perhaps?"

Shelby rolled her eyes. "So much for our crack training program."

"Then Mrs. Surratt is going to hang?" Ty persisted. "They're really going to execute a female?"

Sarah confirmed it, remarking that historians were still arguing about whether or not she was guilty. "Some say yes, others that she hadn't a clue about Booth's plot, or that she knew but wasn't directly involved."

"And me? What did *I* think about it?"

"Years later, you wrote that the trial was a travesty, and that Johnson should have commuted her sentence."

At the moment, Ty found it hard to be so charitable. He didn't believe in executing women, but he mourned Lincoln too deeply not to have a secret thirst for revenge. "I see," he said. The topic pained him, so he changed it. "So how was your morning, Sarah? Productive?"

"Very. I think I know what happened." She walked to the bellpull and gave it a tug. She was hungry all the time now. "Let's order some lunch. There's just one more thing I need you to tell me before we talk about what to do next. Originally, before I came here, what were your plans for the next several weeks?"

Ty had expected this question. After all, Sarah had

spent almost every waking hour with her bookfile lately, searching for what had gone wrong. He wondered if she would be less distracted now that she had developed a theory—if sharing a bed tonight would disturb her. They had abstained last night—she might have infected him yesterday morning, and if she had, he could infect her right back—but holding her without making love had left him restless and tense, and he wanted her to feel the same way.

As soon as he finished his treatment, he decided, he was going to rent Shelby a room and pleasure Sarah all night, and to hell with being embarrassed. He hoped Sarah would find happiness after they parted, but he also wanted to be the great love of her life. God knew she was the great love of his.

He forced his attention back to her question, answering with a calmness that belied the turmoil he felt. "I would have drunk heavily—or appeared to—during the trip to New York on Wednesday night. As we approached the bridge over the Delaware, I would have slipped away, then changed my clothing, shaved my beard, and cut my hair. Afterward, as Tyson Stone, I would have raised an alarm about a man falling overboard into the water. When I reached New York, I would have met with Peter Vandenhoevel, Stanton's banker friend—the one who hired me as a lobbyist and persuaded his colleagues to do the same. I really did work for the man, more effectively than I preferred to at times, and I owed him a final report. I planned to go to Front Royal after that, to see if either of the Beechams was there."

Sarah returned to the sofa and sat down beside him. "So far, so good. Now tell me this. Suppose you'd arrived to find the Beechams' farm destroyed and their house draped in mourning for Ned? Suppose George's only concern was to restore the farm and go on? Remember, he would have read about Reid's accident by then and assumed his enemy was dead. What would you have done?''

Ty reviewed what Sarah had told him yesterday evening. According to her books, Ned Beecham had roamed the West after fleeing Ohio, made a tidy stake as a miner, and turned it into a fortune by speculating in mining stocks. He had used some of those funds to aid the South, bribing Indians to attack settlers in order to divert Union soldiers from the war into the protection of civilians, and contributing money to Richmond for the care of the Rebel wounded. His efforts, once revealed, had made him a hero in the former Confederacy, and he had soon joined his one-time commander, Nathan Bedford Forrest, in a movement to restore ''the Southern way of life''—a movement that had quickly begun to tyrannize and oppress Negroes. Originally, he had been a total unknown, but in this revised version of history, he had become a famous and powerful leader. Sarah believed that his rise had been even more damaging than Ty's death.

''Then you have evidence that Ned died originally?'' Ty asked.

''Maybe,'' Sarah said. ''How would you have reacted if he had?''

Ty's compassion was at war with his anger. Sukey deserved avenging, but you couldn't punish a dead man. If Sarah never had come, George would have failed to stab him on Tuesday night. The farm would still have been in ruins, and from what Sarah had just indicated, Mrs. Beecham would have lost Ned as well as her husband and daughter. Under those circumstances, further vengeance would have been savagery. Ty would have left things alone. *Had* left things alone, according to what Sarah had previously told him.

He reluctantly admitted as much, then grumbled, ''So speaks the moral icon, Sarah. I hope that you're pleased.''

She looked amused. "Of course I am. I wouldn't want to think I'd worshiped a saint with feet of clay all this time."

"Me? A saint?" He scowled at her. "If you were a telepath like your daughter, you would know that the things I want to do to you—with you—aren't remotely saintly."

Shelby broke into a grin. "Hmm. Some girls have all the luck. He has an incredibly fertile mind, Mom."

Ty reddened but refused to retreat. The girl was only baiting him. She no longer listened to his thoughts. "Given what I've heard about your popular entertainment, my dear, you probably know more than I do. But do me a favor. If you have any suggestions, make them to your mother."

Shelby's laughter was interrupted by a knock on the door. Ty answered it, ordered a meal from the bellman, and returned to the sofa. "So what happened to Ned Beecham, Sarah? What have you learned?"

Sarah began by explaining that mining had played a vital role in the growth of the West, and since she was a specialist in the postwar history of the region, she had studied the various rushes in some detail. "I was reviewing the history of Colorado in the spring of 1865, since Ned was living in Denver at the time, and I came across an account of a famous cave-in. It occurred at the Lucky Eight mine in Central City on May 25, which was last Thursday. William Dimity, the superintendent, was leading a group of potential investors on an underground tour when a tunnel collapsed, trapping and killing the whole party." She paused. "In the history I remember, that party was called 'The Unlucky Eight,' a pun on the name of the mine. Otherwise I wouldn't have recalled how many had died. But in the history I just finished, only seven men were killed."

Ty gaped at her. Until now, this talk of alternate histories hadn't seemed entirely real, but if Ned had lived instead of died because of Sarah's arrival . . . "Good God. Then Ned was originally the eighth?"

"Apparently so. After all, he was a successful speculator who was living in Colorado, so he would have been a likely investor. He also had a direct tie to you—you wounded his brother George and might even have killed him. My guess is, someone sent Ned a telegram that reached him in Denver on Wednesday and made him cancel his trip to the mine. It could have been George himself, if he was still alive, or someone in Washington, informing him of George's death."

"Then George isn't mentioned in your histories," Ty said. "You don't know his ultimate fate."

"No, but that only proves he wasn't important enough to write about, not that he died young."

"And then what?" Shelby asked. "Did Ned return to Front Royal when he got the message? Or did he stay in Colorado?"

Sarah replied that she could place Ned in Virginia in late July but had no information about his previous whereabouts. "But remember, Ty, you and Sukey were killed by Native Americans—Indians—while traveling to California on the stage, and Ned had contacts among the tribes. Suppose he spotted Sukey by chance in Denver and recognized her? And suppose he had plans for a future in the public eye? He might have decided to make sure his attempted rape could never come back to haunt him by having the two of you murdered." Sarah pursed her lips in frustration, wishing she could offer definitive answers. "On the other hand, the attack might have been random. The Indians were unusually active in the spring of 1865, and my memory isn't good enough to remember every incident and recall if one of them didn't occur originally."

"Then to be on the safe side," Ty said, "we should alter the actions we took after we fled Washington. That way, if Ned saw Sukey by chance, he no longer will.

And if the attack was random, we'll be in a different party of travelers.''

Sarah nodded. The problem was, in this current version of history, Ty had no sooner received Stanton's summons and decided to flee Washington than Shelby had intervened. ''So what do you think we originally did?'' she asked.

He answered without hesitation. ''Traveled to Front Royal to look for George, to Ohio to pick up Sukey, and to Colorado to search for Ned. All I cared about was seeing the Beechams punished, having you talk to Sukey, and keeping you by my side for as long as I could. After you left, had I lived, I would have returned to Washington and told Stanton the truth, although I doubt he would have believed me.''

''And what would the timing have been? When would we have reached Atchison? Left on the stage?''

''Hmm. Let me think . . . I must have finished my article for Gales on Saturday morning, then left immediately. Stanton would have sent someone to find and arrest me when I didn't respond to his summons, so I would have wanted to move as quickly as possible.'' Frowning, he began to calculate. ''Assuming we couldn't get access to a train, it's almost two days to the Beechams' farm, then another few hours to Winchester. With luck, we'd have reached Wheeling on Monday, and Oberlin on Tuesday or Wednesday. We would have had to remain there for several days, to pack Sukey up and get permission for her to miss the summer term. Then it's two or three days to St. Joe and down to the ferry into Atchison, depending on what connections you make.'' He paused. ''Probably Monday or Tuesday morning, but now, with Stanton off our tail, we can afford to slow our pace. I still owe Vandenhoevel a report, so why don't I make a brief trip to New York while you remain here with Shelby and regain your strength? You can shop and sightsee. Catch up on each other's lives."

Sarah agreed, grateful for some private time with Shelby yet saddened that Ty would be leaving. It was the first time in her life she had experienced such a conflict.

Ty trudged out of the Baltimore & Ohio station, wearily hailed a hack, and climbed inside. After taking his therapy Sunday evening, he had awakened the next morning so fatigued that he'd been forced to ask a porter to deliver his essay to the *Intelligencer*. Still, he had dragged himself onto the cars that night, arriving in New York around dawn and spending the next two days there.

Now, after a tedious trip south, he was back home. It had been an exhausting four days. An interminable four days. He felt as if he had been away from Sarah forever and couldn't wait to see her, to touch her. But it had been only *four* days. Not five.

A man of control and good sense would have waited twenty-four hours for his pleasures, but Ty was pitifully lovesick. While he understood that the exchange of bodily fluids could be dangerous, he hoped less intimate activities might be allowed. If they were, he was ready to beg for whatever form of lovemaking he and Sarah could safely share.

Tired or not, he entered the lobby of the Willard ready to dash upstairs and take her in his arms, but he was stopped by the sound of singing. He took a few steps forward. A large group was gathered around the performer, so he couldn't see her, but her voice was exquisite, sweet and rich and strong, and every word she sang was remarkably clear.

The ballad she was performing, "When This Cruel War Is Over," was about fighting for liberty and the Union despite the constant threat of death. Memories of his fallen comrades swamped his mind as she sang the final verse, and his throat tightened painfully.

She proceeded to the chorus, and everyone joined in. He continued forward, wanting to see what manner of face went with the extraordinary voice, but he was intercepted within a couple of yards by Joe Willard. "Ty! Welcome home! Why didn't you mention the way your cousin could sing?"

"My cousin?" Several moments passed before Ty remembered their conversation on Sunday and realized Joe meant Shelby. "Oh. Of course. I, uh, I confess I'm completely amazed. She's always hated performing in public."

Joe laughed. "Then she's changed her mind. She sat herself in front of the fireplace on Tuesday and started singing, and it's turned into a nightly performance. The crowd's been bigger each evening. Very profitable for my bar, Ty. I send out waiters with trays of champagne, and it's purchased in no time flat."

"Then I deserve a finder's fee. A discount on my suite will do." Ty grinned at him, set down his valise, and elbowed his way through the mob. Shelby was sitting on the floor, holding a guitar, dressed in an emerald satin gown with short sleeves, a daring neckline, and an abundance of fringe. While it wasn't indecent, it displayed her charms to rather staggering effect.

She was bantering with a handsome male spectator, telling him she had learned a new song for him, when she spotted Ty and smiled. "Here's my cousin, everyone, the famous author of 'An Army Goes Home.' Isn't he brilliant?"

To Ty's astonishment, the group erupted in applause. He stared at the girl as he shook people's hands and accepted their congratulations. *Tell me something. Do you really sing that well, or do you only make us think that you do?*

I really do. I love to entertain. But I admit, I seem

to reach people's emotions when I sing, so there's probably a form of telepathic connection involved. Sly laughter. *Go on upstairs. Mom is dying to see you. I'll be at least another hour—longer if you want.*

An hour will be sufficient. Flushing at her frankness, Ty left. As he crossed the lobby, she began singing something about California and the New York island, and since he had never heard the tune before, he suspected it was newer than her admirer could possibly imagine.

Up in the suite, Sarah ran into his arms as he closed the door, and they hugged fiercely. For several moments after they separated, they could do nothing more than smile besottedly at the wonderful sight of each other. Finally, still holding Sarah in his arms, Ty managed to ask her about the song, repeating the lyrics Shelby had sung.

Sarah's eyes widened. "And she says *I* have a big mouth! That song won't be written for almost a hundred years." She sighed. "She shouldn't be singing it, but it's so appropriate for 1865 that I guess she couldn't resist. It's about this country and how it belongs to all of us."

Ty slid his hands to her waist and nuzzled her neck. "The country will survive the insult to cause and effect, although if the song catches on, I pity the poor composer." He nibbled her earlobe and felt her tremble. "It must have earned him a goodly sum. It's a splendid piece." He cupped her breast, fondling the nipple through the fabric of her dressing gown. "But not as splendid as you, my love. Do you have any idea how much I've missed you?"

Sarah had an excellent idea, because she'd missed him just as much. If her longing was this intense *now*, when she'd had five years of Shelby's life to discuss and all of Washington to explore, she couldn't imagine what it would be like later, after she'd returned to her own time. To preserve her sanity, she'd become an expert at not thinking about the future.

She put her arms around Ty's waist and pressed herself against his erection, and he cupped her buttocks and moved slowly and heatedly against her. He was breathing unevenly and shaking with desire, but no more so than she was. In retrospect, it was laughable that she'd planned to wait until tomorrow even to touch him. A single look, a brief caress, and she'd been aroused past the point of stopping. A minute or two more of *this*, and she would explode.

Still, when he grasped her chin to take her mouth, she quickly turned away. He was so passionate—all that nipping and deep, torrid kissing. "We can't," she said. "The chance of transmission is infinitesimal, but it still exists."

He grunted in frustration and put some space between them. "Then what, Sarah? Can we undress each other? Touch each other? Because if we can't, I'm not going to get a moment's sleep tonight."

She unbuttoned his waistcoat and unknotted his necktie. "You could always lock yourself in the bathroom," she teased. "Relieve your own suffering."

Ty turned as red as the carpet. God knows the thought had occurred to him—he was only human—but was there nothing these people from the future didn't speak of? "You've been spending too much time with your daughter," he mumbled, avoiding Sarah's eyes.

She laughed. "You're probably right. I've talked more about sex and relationships in the past four days than in my whole life. I have no inhibitions anymore. Shelby has chattered them out of me."

She pulled his shirt out of his trousers and ran her fingers up his chest, examining the scars from his wounds. Her touch, while light and impersonal, made his nipples tighten and his manhood throb. If she had done that twenty-four hours from now, he would have tumbled her onto the floor, driven himself deep inside her, and brought them both to a swift, hard climax.

Intimacies like that were out of the question now, so he took a quick, stoic breath and endured the inspection. "As you can see, I'm almost completely healed. Do you think you could get your mind off medicine and back onto lovemaking?" He blushed again. "Assuming we *can* make love—in, uh, some fashion or other."

She gave him the most lascivious smile he had ever seen. "I believe it can be arranged. Why don't you go to the bedroom, strip down to your drawers, and get into bed?"

He remembered the last time she had issued such an order, and the subsequent cleverness of her fingers and mouth. "And then?" he asked unsteadily.

She stroked his groin, tracing his male contours with playful fingers. "I thought I'd give you a little show. Get you nice and hot before we start."

He pulled away her hand. "Heating is the last thing I need." When she tortured him that way, he wanted to seize control—to tease her until she begged for mercy—but he walked meekly into the bedroom instead. When the reward was Paradise, a man with any sense didn't resist.

He was soon waiting as instructed, swollen with desire and anticipation. But her actual appearance was unlike anything he could have envisioned. She was entirely naked except for the cameo around her neck and two black wisps of silk and lace. The first girded her chest, molding and lifting her breasts in the most provocative way imaginable, and the second covered her womanhood and the flesh where she was whitest—and not a whit more.

He was so shocked he all but choked out his next few words. "Is that what you take the sun in? In public?"

"No, but you're close." She did a seductive pirouette. "We wear these under our clothes. A bra and panties. Shelby brought them back, just for fun. Do you like them?"

"God, yes." He stared at her, utterly transfixed. Her body had filled out during the past few days, giving her a softness that made her more beautiful than ever in his eyes. "They sell those in your shops? Right in the open?"

Sarah strolled to the bed, enjoying Ty's stunned disbelief and pure male lust. "Not only that . . . they're advertised in catalogs and magazines, with photographs of women wearing them." She joined him under the covers. "You can take off the top if you want. You see this tiny closing? You just . . ." Her voice trailed off as he twisted and pulled, then stripped off her bra. It seemed to be programmed into the male genes, this facility for removing female clothing.

He bent his head and kissed her breasts, and she shivered with pleasure and desire. "So, darling? Do you want to be on top or on bottom?"

"You're going to turn on the cameo? Lock us together?"

"Ah. So you noticed I was wearing it."

"It was hard to miss, given how little else you have on." He straightened, sliding his hands under her panties to open her to his touch, then stroking her deftly with his thumbs. "Can I take these off? Remove my drawers? If I promise not to come inside you?"

Burning now, she teased him the same way he was teasing her, tracing gentle circles on the hot, moist tip of him with her finger. "I don't think so, Ty. It's too tempting. Too dangerous."

With great reluctance, he admitted she was right. He was much too desperate for what he knew he couldn't have, especially when she caressed him that way.

Without another word, he rolled onto his back and pulled her atop him, gripping her hips under her panties to fit her against his groin. Then he began to move; he couldn't help himself. She tucked her hands under his back, twined her legs around his thighs, and buried her head against his neck, rocking sensuously, matching his rhythm.

Half out of his mind with wanting, he pressed his member against the passage to her womb and pushed. He found it impossible not to. But his drawers, unlike her panties, were a formidable barrier, and he still had wits enough not to unbutton them.

She clutched him hard. "Should I turn on—"

"Yes. Now."

The next moment, they were locked together so tightly there was almost no room to maneuver. He couldn't lift her and bring her back; the sweetly seductive friction they had enjoyed only seconds before became impossible. He was wild to kiss her, to plunge himself inside her, even to thrust himself against her, but he could do none of those things. It was the most frustrating experience of his life—and the most intimate and erotic.

Sarah, meanwhile, couldn't decide whether she was being pleasured or tortured. Ty was grasping her hips, controlling her body, and the tension kept building and building, but release hovered tauntingly out of reach. And she knew from his breathless movements and hoarse grunts that he was suffering just as acutely. Finally, unable to bear it, she gasped that she would turn the cameo off.

He actually laughed. "Don't you dare."

So she didn't, and he somehow managed to ease his hand between them, to slide his finger between her legs, and she whimpered deep in her throat and lost all sense of herself. There was only her need, and his gentle pressure, and then wave after wave of pleasure. She was still reeling when he stiffened, cried out her name, and climaxed violently.

Panting, she turned off the cameo and nestled into his arms. ''Sweet Jesus,'' he whispered. ''No wonder people will pay half a billion dollars for that thing.''

''I told you, it's for protection—''

''Don't try to claim that people don't want them for lovemaking, too, because I won't believe you. That was astonishing.'' He chuckled. ''I can't wait to try it naked.''

''Satyr,'' she said, but she was thinking the same thing.

Then, as their blood slowly cooled, they cuddled and talked, telling each other how they had spent the past few days. The conversation soon turned to Shelby, who was settling in well, Sarah reported. She'd enjoyed touring the capital, especially the buildings she remembered from a childhood trip, and was learning to control her reaction to the prejudices of the inhabitants, although her anger and revulsion were as strong as ever.

''She's even getting used to the clothing,'' Sarah remarked. ''She says she thinks of it as dressing for a role on the stage. We went on a shopping spree on Tuesday. That's when I bought her the guitar and the music. She loves to entertain. She's been performing professionally for a couple of years now, in local theaters and clubs. She'll be going to Juilliard next fall. That's a top college for actors and musicians in New York City.''

Ty hated being reminded of a life he could never share, but he tried not to show it. ''The entertainers of your time . . . Is there a stigma attached to female performers?''

''That they're looser than other women?'' She laughed. ''That would be hard, considering the prevailing morals of my era, but no. If you're famous enough, you're written and gossiped about, but you also make millions of dollars.''

"She *will* be famous," Ty murmured. "Her talent is extraordinary."

"Yes." Looking at Shelby, learning about her life, watching her perform, Sarah found it intensely painful that she'd lost so many years of her daughter's childhood, but she was also bursting with maternal pride. She needed Ty to understand that.

"A lot of her behavior—the complaints and provocation—it was just fear, Ty. She felt my emotions, sensed my feelings for you, and she was afraid I would decide to stay. I know you told her it wasn't so, but she didn't quite believe you. But we've done a lot of talking over the past four days, and she finally understands that my first commitment will always be to her, no matter how much I care for you."

"I see," Ty said evenly, just as if his gut weren't twisting in pain. "Then she's been cheerful these past few days? There were no further outbursts?"

"Nothing major. You raised your sister, so you know that any girl in her teens is going to be moody at times, and Shelby has the added burden of learning to cope with the enormous powers she has." Sarah stroked Ty's cheek, very tenderly, then kissed him lightly on the mouth. "Don't worry about her. She'll control herself. Let's just concentrate on repairing the damage we've done and try to enjoy whatever time we have left."

"I plan to do exactly that," Ty answered, but there was a clipped edge to his tone that told Sarah he was picturing all the tomorrows they would never share. An awful agony rose in her chest, but she fought it down. It would be weeks before she had to leave. It was stupid to think about it.

Chapter 20

Shelby was frowning deeply as she stepped off the train in Front Royal—their fourth stop of the day, and all for a lousy eighty miles. After packing till late the previous night, they'd left for the station at dawn, only to wait around for hours before a military supply train pulled out on the old Orange & Alexandria tracks. They'd barely gotten going when they'd stopped at Fairfax Court House, sitting there for no apparent reason. They'd debarked at Manassas Junction and cooled their heels forever. Some cars had finally rolled in on the Manassas Gap tracks, but the second train had been even slower and bumpier than the first, and it had stopped and done nothing for even longer, at a dot on the map called Salem.

All in all, the trip had made her muscles cramp, her head throb, and her stomach churn, and it was all Ty's fault. She wouldn't have been stuck in this godforsaken era if not for him. If he had left her mother alone, history would have done what it was supposed to.

He went to retrieve their trunks, and she made a face at his retreating back. Him and his brilliance, she thought irritably. Him and his stupid charm. And bravery. And compassion. And world-class sex appeal. He'd made himself so attractive that her mom couldn't resist him, and even worse, she was clueless about her own feelings. She thought it was lust. Or infatuation. Or hero-worship.

But Shelby had felt those emotions hundreds of times, and she'd felt true devotion only a few, and she'd learned the difference. Her mother was wildly in love with Tyson Stone, and sooner or later she was going to wake up and see it, and then the thought of leaving him would hurt her even worse than it already did. Shelby hadn't rescued her to watch her suffer, but she knew her mom. Sarah would want the memories. She wouldn't let Shelby remove them. So the least she could do was to give her mother another couple of months here, but 1865 was so primitive and narrow that all she could think about was going home.

Sarah got off the train and walked over to Main Street, and Shelby absently followed. Downtown Front Royal was a nice little place, several blocks square, situated near the South Fork of the Shenandoah River on the east edge of the valley. Relatively little damage had been done here, and the streets were lined with well-kept houses and shops. There was even a respectable courthouse in view. If they had to be stuck in the middle of nowhere, she thought, Front Royal was probably as good a spot as any.

Sarah obviously agreed. She was gazing around in awe, as if the streets were made of gold rather than dirt, but then, if it was historical, her mom ate it up. "If this isn't the cutest place!" Shelby drawled, choosing an accent to match her frilly costume. "It makes my blood boil, to think of Yankee soldiers marchin' all over this valley, bossin' our folks around."

"I agree, but we lost, and there's nothing we can do but bear it," Sarah replied in her normal voice, then asked silently, *Did you study antique celluloids in school*? Gone with the Wind, *maybe*?

Yeah, in my History of Film class. I was doing a Scarlett, Mom. She had the coolest accent.

Unfortunately, she was from Georgia, sweetie. You're from Maryland. You'll have to tone it down.

The two were posing as sisters from Baltimore by way of Georgetown, with Ty playing the role of Sarah's Virginian husband. *Humph. And just when I was beginning to enjoy myself.* Shelby nodded at a hotel about a block down the street, a three-story building that was as grand as this town seemed to get. *Don't tell me. We'll be spending the night there, but there's no indoor plumbing. No room service. No heat or air. And the mattresses are probably hard and lumpy.*

Maybe, but you like camping, and it can't be any worse than that. Now that we're finally here, I expect you to stop grumbling and focus on the work you need to do, or I'll parrot back your speech to Ty about how he should stop being so selfish and think about what he can do to improve millions of lives.

Shelby smiled despite herself. She'd learned something over the past few days. Telepathy was like performing; the biggest challenges were the most satisfying. And the Beechams promised to be the hugest challenge of her life.

Their starting point had been Ty's old girlfriend, Peggy Beecham Moore, who seemed to be at the root of the changes in history, and whose death had triggered such terrible violence against Ty and his sister. According to Sarah, Ty and Sukey were obsessed with the past, and unless they could find out how Peggy had died and why her brothers hated Ty so much, they always would be. If there were a justification for the family's attitude, Ty needed to hear it, but nobody thought any of the Beechams would come right out with the answers. That meant Shelby would have to pull out specific thoughts, which was the weakest of her telepathic skills.

Then there was the survival of Peggy's brother Ned, the future Klansman, to contend with. If he was here in town, Shelby was supposed to probe his mind, separate out the hatred that had made him so dangerous, and remove it. Given how complicated and delicate the task was, she would have had her hands full even with a normal person, but with Ned, who was strong-willed and possibly sociopathic, she would be tested to the limit.

She sighed theatrically. *Okay, Mom. I'll behave. I mean, I wouldn't want to have to listen to some lecture from Ty about how I talk a good game, but when it comes to actually helping—*

A savage burst of emotion exploded in her mind, and she gasped and doubled over, burying her face in her hands in a futile attempt to shut it out. "Oh, my God. Mommy . . ."

Sarah tried to run to her, but she couldn't even talk, much less move. She was too queasy. Then the feeling eased, and she shot to Shelby's side and put her arm around her shoulders. "What's wrong, honey? What happened?"

Shelby straightened, slowly lowering her hands. Her face was ashen and her eyes were wide and glazed. "It was—fury and anguish," she said in a near-whisper. "From outside. Something awful just happened, and I heard him react. He's—very strong. Very close."

Ty, meanwhile, had sensed Shelby's distress, glanced at her in alarm, and hurried over to help. Now, hearing her words, he shook his head in confusion. "But even at Ah Lan's brothel . . . I've seen you upset when you feel the emotions of others, but never like this. Was the man unusually twisted? Or suffering unbearably?"

But Sarah knew that no ordinary person could have seared Shelby's mind that way. "It wasn't just a man," she said in soft, cold horror. "It was another telepath. Wasn't it, Shel?"

And Shelby shuddered and nodded.

* * *

She was still pale and shaken as they settled into their rooms at the hotel. She wanted her mother and nobody else, so Ty left Sarah to comfort her in private. In truth, he welcomed the respite, because he wanted to search out Peggy's grave, and he preferred to do it on his own.

As he had expected, she was buried in the local Methodist churchyard, as were several other late Beechams, none of them named George. Someone had visited here recently, he noticed; the spray of lilacs sitting on the grave was barely wilted.

He stared solemnly at the flowers, picturing Peggy flirting and laughing, remembering the passion they had once shared. A vibrant light had gone out of the world, and its loss still saddened him deeply, but standing here now, thinking about her death, he realized he felt it more in his head than in his heart.

He read the inscription on her tombstone: "Margaret Beecham Moore, 1838–1864. Beloved daughter and sister. She gave her life for her country."

It was a stretch, he thought, since Peggy never would have become ill if she had remained in Washington, but then, the bereaved were entitled to whatever comfort they could derive. In any event, he was no longer among the mourners. This tombstone belonged to another life, a different world. The Ty who hadn't known Sarah might never have gotten over Peggy, but he was no longer that man. He had come to love a woman who was his equal in every way, who shared his opinions and convictions, and who gave herself without reservation. He had once spent a lifetime seeking her, but he had failed to find her. Now he finally had found her, but he was destined to lose her. The thought made him furious with his Maker, then profoundly despondent.

He turned away, walking down Main Street to Luray Avenue. He supposed he must have enjoyed that original life, at least some of the time—all those women!—but he knew that would no longer be true. Not without Sarah. But if he survived, he promised himself, he would make as great a difference as she expected him to. He would devote himself to improving the future of this great land. If he mentioned her in his letters, she would read them two and a half centuries from now, and she would know how much she had inspired him. The thought gave him comfort.

Depression gave way to somber acceptance, and he finally returned to the hotel, entering the front parlor to the strains of the Southern anthem "Dixie." Shelby was performing again, singing in the dining room next door. He paused to listen, remembering how a great crowd had gathered at the White House the day after Lee's surrender, and how the president had called down to the celebration from an upstairs window. He had announced that he had a great fondness for the tune, adding that since the Union had rightfully captured it, he wanted the band to play it. And so they had.

Ty was humming the song and thinking of one of Lincoln's favorite yarns when a pair of arms came around his waist from behind. "Is there any musical talent in your family," Sarah asked, "or do they all sing as badly as you do?"

He smiled to himself. "Ah. An insult. I'll look forward to making you pay for it."

"Not by more singing, I hope. It was the worst thing about being your prisoner. A weaker woman would have cracked on the spot."

"You're still in my custody, you know. I've never officially released you." He turned around and pecked her on the nose. "And, as your captor, I hereby order you to tell me the best thing about being my prisoner."

"Discussing your work," she said promptly.

He knew that, but managed to look surprised. "Really? I was sure you would say the way I made love to you. The incredible pleasure I gave you.''

''Oh? Was it enjoyable? It's been so long, I've forgotten how it felt.'' She grinned at him, then whispered in his ear, ''How *you* felt, lying naked between my legs, sliding deep inside me, moving slowly—''

''That's enough, Sarah.'' Ty shifted uncomfortably. ''I promise you, I'll remind you tonight, and very thoroughly, assuming Shelby doesn't still need you. Which I trust she won't, since she's recovered enough to sing in public. Were there any further—intrusions?''

''Yes. Another few flashes of emotion. In retrospect, you felt one too, back at the train.'' Sarah took Ty's arm and led him to a quiet corner of the parlor. She and Shelby had discussed the episode at length, reaching some troubling conclusions. ''Think about it, Ty. You were busy with a porter, yet you suddenly got alarmed. As for me, before I even realized how upset Shelby was, I felt a wave of queasiness. Our emotions came from the telepath. We're both latent sensitives, and he was strong enough to affect us. Shelby reached out to him, to ask him who and where he was, but he didn't reply. Absolutely nothing came back.''

''Could he have left the area?'' Ty asked. ''Failed to have heard her? Ignored her?''

Sarah shook her head. ''Even if he's gone, it wouldn't make a difference. He'd have to be thousands of miles away to be out of Shelby's reach. That means he blocked her out, but a telepath needs extensive training to shut out a direct question from another telepath. There's always a reaction otherwise, even if it's only annoyance or mental retreat. He must be strong-willed and very powerful, to do the things he's done. Shelby claims she can handle him, that he's not malevolent, but I can't help worrying. Even without training, his range could be hundreds of miles.''

''Then the sooner she's out of his reach, the better.

We'll buy ourselves a rig and leave at first light, although from what you've said, it could be days before she's rid of the fellow. Still, she knows her own talents, Sarah. If she says she can block him, she can." Ty turned toward the desk. "In the meantime, why don't we make some inquiries about the Beechams? The more we know, the quicker we'll be done at their farm, and the sooner we can get on our way."

Sarah nodded and followed him. They would need whatever edge they could get, so while they waited for the clerk, she contacted Shelby. *How are things going, honey? Have you heard anything more?*

Nope, but I've got a partial block up. Not even a whisper has come through. I told you before—

Why only partial? Sarah interrupted. *Couldn't that give him an opening?*

Not enough of one to harm me, Mom. Believe me, I don't take chances. She was plainly impatient. *The problem is, I don't like to block myself when I'm singing. It ruins my feel for the audience. But the partial is more than enough. He won't be a problem. I've been very well trained.* A pause. *So you need some help, huh? What with?*

Shelby was too damned good, Sarah thought. She picked up thoughts even when Sarah was trying to suppress them. Still, Sarah had sensed confidence and prudence in the girl's mind, which reassured her. *We're asking around about the Beechams. Could you keep an ear open while you're singing? And then, if anyone needs a push—*

No problem. I'll jump right in. I'll see you guys later. And stop worrying. I'll be fine.

*Mothers **always** worry,* Sarah replied, and turned her attention to the clerk. He was new in town and unacquainted with the Beechams, he said, but thought that his boss, Mr. Tucker, would know the family. After all, Tucker had grown up here, and his dining room was both a local favorite and a fount of the latest gossip. Ty and Sarah could stop in at his office if they wished. He always enjoyed visiting with his guests.

They were directed to a room down the hall, where a plump, middle-aged man was poring over a ledger. Ty shook his left hand because he didn't have a right one. The war again, he thought somberly, introducing himself as Thomas Johnston, saying that he, his wife, and his sister-in-law, Miss March—the singer in the dining room—were passing through on their way to California. His wife had worked with Peggy Beecham Moore at the Treasury Department, and like Peggy, he confided, had secretly favored the South. Since they were in the area, she hoped to pay her respects to Peggy's mother. Could Tucker tell them how Mrs. Beecham was getting along? And how her family was doing?

"Yes, but I'm afraid the news isn't good," Tucker said. "Please, have a seat." He rang for a waiter and ordered some refreshments, then gave Sarah a gentle smile. "So the little beauty with the big voice is your sister! I can see the resemblance, ma'am. I'm honored to have you all as my guests. About your friend Mrs. Moore . . . I'm sorry for your loss. She was a lovely girl. I was in Pennsylvania when she died"—he looked ruefully at his truncated right arm—"but they tell me the town was just sick about it. She was so young, and it was so sudden." He sighed and shook his head. "And now this terrible business with her brother . . ."

"Her brother?" Ty repeated. "Would that be Ned or George, sir? Obviously we hadn't heard."

"George. It happened the week before last. Ned was still in Denver at the time." Tucker settled back in his chair. "Life takes some peculiar turns, Mr. Johnston. Just imagine, a man survives the whole war in one piece, then goes to Washington City to visit a friend, and what happens? He's attacked on the street by a madman. The lunatic didn't even rob him, just doused him with filth from the canal and unloaded a revolver into his leg."

Sarah gasped and fanned herself—the way a gently bred female in this society would be expected to react. "Oh, Thomas! I can't bear it. Why should one poor family suffer so much tragedy? Please, Mr. Tucker, tell us he survived."

"The good Lord willing." Tucker hesitated, then announced he would wait for the refreshments before he continued, so Sarah could rest and restore herself. Only after he had served her some lemonade and cake did he reveal that George had staggered back to his friend's boardinghouse and collapsed. "The landlady did some nursing during the war, so she knew how to take out bullets. They bathed him and patched him up, but he was in such awful shape, he expected to die. He even wrote out a message to Ned that night, calling him home to help on the farm, and his friend sent it off to Denver by wire."

But far from dying, George had improved dramatically, returning to Front Royal within days. "He was feeling so well, he wired Ned at the stage office in Atchison and told him he could go back to Denver if he liked. But Ned ignored that second message and it's a good thing he did, because by late last night, when he finally got home, George's fever was up and his leg was hurting him something fierce. Ned drove him to town early this morning. He's in the hospital up in Oakley, near Main and Luray. It's the big brick house on the hill. My cousin is one of the surgeons there. Ned was pleading with him all day, begging him to save George's leg. Lord knows he tried his best, but maybe he shouldn't have, because the longer they waited—"

Sarah sucked in her breath, prompting Tucker to gaze at her as if he feared she would collapse in shock if he continued. She was shocked, all right, but not because of a weak stomach. She leaned forward and finished his sentence. "The worse George grew. Your cousin had to remove it in the end." *Are you following this, Shel*?

Yes. The anguish we heard at the station . . . It was Ned. He's our telepath.

Tucker nodded. "I'm afraid so, ma'am, not three hours ago. Mrs. Beecham took it well, but Ned howled like a moon-crazed wolf, he was so torn up about it. He blames himself, you see. He says he should have stopped George from going to Washington, that *he* should have made the trip, but nobody knows what he means. After all, he was still in Denver at the time, and George had a hankering to visit his friend."

Ty was slower than Sarah and Shelby, but not by much. Hearing about Ned's behavior, he was so stunned that several seconds passed before he had the wit to respond. "Ned's grief . . . It must have made him irrational, Mr. Tucker. Can you tell us how George is doing?"

"He's in a deep sleep. Delirious and often highly agitated, I'm afraid. But he has a strong constitution, so he might pull through." But Tucker looked doubtful. "Ned and Mrs. Beecham are keeping a vigil at his bedside."

In other words, Ty thought, he would never know the answers to his questions, not unless Shelby could glean them from a distance. Sarah might object to giving up, but one couldn't intrude on a deathwatch, and they would learn nothing new if they tried. He would have to come to terms with the past and unravel the changes in history by some other means.

He touched Sarah's arm, then said in a tone meant to head off arguments, "We'll have to be on our way tomorrow, my dear. It would be best if you wrote your sentiments in a letter and sent it to Mrs. Beecham at the hospital."

"I'm sure my cousin would be happy to drop it off," Tucker said. "Let's just hope the poor woman will find some comfort in it." He frowned, then stared blindly into space. "Hmm. Comfort," he said slowly. "Now there's an interesting notion." After several seconds of silence, he finally returned to earth. "Uh, tell me, Mr. Johnston, did you fight in the war?"

"Yes, sir." The Beechams never would have spoken with a shirker, so Ty had prepared a likely history. "With Jeb Stuart, until Gettysburg. I was captured there and sent to Camp Douglas in Illinois."

Tucker looked impressed. "Ah, you're a horseman, then. You had a great leader."

"One of our finest, may God rest his soul. I would have followed him for a lifetime." Ty regarded Sarah fondly. "Fortunately, I had a woman who was willing to wait for me. We were married only last week."

"I'm glad you've found some happiness in these troubled times. My best wishes to both of you." Tucker chewed distractedly on his bottom lip. "Getting back to my original subject, sir . . . Perhaps, like me, you witnessed the comforting power of music on our sick and wounded during your years in the army. And I was thinking just now . . . Since Miss March has such a splendid voice, perhaps she could sing for poor George. Some mellow ballads and soft lullabies might calm him and better his chances."

Ty was startled, then impressed. A suggestion like that just couldn't be blind luck. *Shelby? Have you been listening all this time? Did you manipulate Tucker's mind?*

What do **you** *think? He wasn't going to get there on his own, you know.*

But won't it endanger you? To be so near to Ned?

A mile or a hundred miles . . . It's all the same thing.

"Why don't you call on them after dinner?" Tucker continued. "That way, you could enlist the support of my cousin. He dines here each evening at seven. I would be honored to have you join us." He winked at Sarah. "The least I can do is treat you to a glass of champagne. Offer a toast to your new marriage."

Ty said they would look forward to the meal, then escorted Sarah from the room, going directly upstairs to the privacy of their own quarters. He closed the door, still a little stunned. "Ned Beecham. My God, Sarah."

"Yes. It scares me, Ty. Ned is a grown man, and Shelby is only a child."

Shelby directed her answer to both of them. *Even if he's older, I understand my talents in a way he doesn't. I've been trained to use them and he hasn't. I keep telling you, Mom, he's an amateur compared to me. I can handle him just fine.*

"Can you?" Sarah asked. "We've seen what he can do. What he *will* do, if he isn't stopped. Remember, he had to be extraordinarily powerful to exert the sort of influence he did. It's one thing to block out Ned's emotions or even to sense him passively, but to enter his mind and manipulate it . . . He could lash back and hurt you. Affect your brain."

Not if I'm prepared for an attack. Which I will be, I guarantee it. And tonight is the perfect time to take his measure. To discover his strengths and weaknesses. And then I can decide how to proceed.

Ty was as concerned as Sarah now. Shelby might be skilled in the use of her talents, but she was also very young, and the young always thought themselves invincible. "Your mother is right, Shelby. You can study him tonight if you're careful, and I'll welcome whatever information you can provide, but I won't have you trying to adjust him. It's dangerous and pointless. He can't be permitted to survive. He did too much damage.

But believe me, I have very few scruples about killing the man who tried to rape my sister."

"If anyone's going to kill him, I am," Sarah said. "I'm leaving this era and you're not. I'll keep you unconscious with my pistol if I have to, but I won't permit you to commit a murder and risk being hanged. We need you alive and writing."

Ty didn't argue, but only because he'd decided to wait for Ned to attack and then kill him in self-defense, since that was the only way to satisfy Sarah's requirements. She might be his equal in every way, but in 1865, a man didn't hide behind a woman's skirts.

Forget it, Stone. My mom is right. You're too important for us to risk. Whether you like it or not, you're going to do things our way. I'll make sure of that.

"Then your way had better become *my* way," Ty said, glaring at Sarah, furious at both her and Shelby for treating him like a dimwit and a coward. Sarah glared right back at him, but Shelby only laughed.

Ty was still seething some two hours later, as he stood by George's bed, shaking hands with the handsomest bastard it had ever been his misfortune to meet, Ned Beecham. While Ty's face wore a mask of grave sympathy, his fingers itched to choke the life out of the villain, and his dark mood only intensified the feeling. Sarah, he thought sourly, would be vastly disappointed in him. A moral icon would have hated Ned for the poison he would one day spread, but Ty saw only the would-be rapist, and he wanted vengeance.

As for the would-be murderer, he was tossing and moaning in his sleep, critically ill but holding his own. His mother Caroline was sitting at his bedside, murmuring words of encouragement. Perhaps they comforted George, but they did nothing for Ned. A sense of acid despair filled the ward—the product of Ned's mind, according to Shelby.

Dr. Tucker, a compassionate fellow, explained their connection to Peggy and the reason for their visit, then gently suggested to Mrs. Beecham that she relinquish her place to Shelby. Sarah had finally agreed that she could use her mind as well as her voice to create a calmer, more trusting atmosphere, but only if she was extremely cautious. She sat down with her guitar, sang a tune by Stephen Foster, and flooded the room with serenity, and the despair began to lift.

Ned and Ty discussed the war and their plans for the future while Sarah told Caroline about her friendship with Peggy. Shelby eavesdropped on both conversations, ready to push when she thought it would help. She was prepared to take on Ned if she had to, but she quickly realized that Caroline was the likelier to open up. She was pliable and vulnerable where Ned was rigid and wary, and besides, Sarah was making better progress. When Ned wasn't bragging about his triumphs, he was mocking his enemies or damning the Union, and Ty, while secretly enraged, could only agree. But Caroline yearned to bring Peggy back, if only for a little while, so the more Sarah talked about Peggy's life in Washington, the more accessible Caroline became.

"You should have seen her that night at Mr. Chase's," Sarah was saying with a smile. "She was so beautiful and full of life, there wasn't a man there who didn't want her. If I hadn't been promised to Mr. Johnston, I confess I would have been jealous. But then she met Mr. Reid, and the moment they set eyes on each other . . ."

A towering rage filled the room. Sarah's voice trailed off. Shelby winced and stopped singing. Caroline paled and Ty frowned. Even George reacted, opening his eyes and staring blankly into space. The ward was full of people, both patients and visitors, and every last one of them looked Ned's way.

He stalked to Sarah's side and began to thunder. "You will never mention that name again, madam! Not in my presence!"

Shelby quaked. For the first time in her life, she was afraid of another mind. There was so much bitterness inside, so much raw, undisciplined power. But she couldn't pass up the chance to get some answers, and she knew if she was very careful, he would respond without knowing he'd heard her.

Why, Ned? She whispered the question directly to his unconscious. *Why do you hate Reid—*

He struck back blindly, mentally attacking what he must have sensed as a formless and threatening intrusion. Shelby's world rocked crazily. There was no pain, only a split second of pure, wild horror. Logic disappeared and madness took its place, and it was awful.

She paled and shivered, and Ty bolted over and put his hand on her shoulder. *Are you all right*?

Yes. Just—surprised. It was an outright lie. She was reeling. Ned hadn't known what he'd felt. He didn't even know what he'd done. His response had been pure instinct—immediate, insensate, overpowering. She'd underestimated the man, but she wouldn't make that mistake again.

Sarah looked at him with cold, hard anger in her eyes. Like Shelby, she was badly shaken, but she was also savagely protective. *Don't, Mom*, Shelby begged, but Sarah ignored her. "Where I come from, Mr. Beecham—"

"Let it go, Sarah," Ty said firmly. "We'll be leaving now. Mr. Beecham doesn't want us here."

"—a gentleman doesn't address a lady in such a fashion. I was simply telling your mother about the man your sister loved—"

"She didn't love him," Ned snarled. "She hated him. He raped her. Killed her. Tried to kill my brother." He loomed over Sarah, glowering at her.

"Your husband is right. You aren't wanted here. Get out."

Caroline was visibly distressed. "But, Ned, dear—"

"She's upsetting George, Mother. I won't have it."

It was true, Shelby thought. George had looked blankly at each of them in turn, sightless but creepily alert, and then focused on Ty. She probed his mind, but felt only disorganized spurts of emotion.

She got her mental defenses in place, steeled herself, and took another shot at Ned. *How did Reid kill Peg—*

But he lashed back violently, slashing through the barrier she'd erected and stopping her before she could finish. She instinctively struck back, attacking him as fiercely as she could, and saw him stagger to the bed and collapse. Then the room went black. Every muscle in her body froze. Time seemed to stop. The outside world disappeared, and a nameless, irrational dread took its place.

Ty was holding her in his arms when the nightmare ended and sanity returned. She didn't remember being lifted up. She felt muzzy, disoriented.

He started out of the ward, and Sarah followed with Shelby's guitar. Panicking, she looked over his shoulder at the Beechams. Ned was sitting on the bed, visibly dazed. George was staring blindly into space. And Caroline was looking from one son to the other in deep concern.

This was her last chance, Shelby thought wildly. If she didn't do something now, they would never get any answers.

With a power that bordered on cruelty, she screamed into Caroline's conscious mind, in a way no human could ignore. *Reid loved your daughter. He knew she was a spy, but he still wanted to marry her. She might have refused, but she loved having sex with him. She wanted him all the time. He didn't rape her or kill her. He had no reason to. Why does Ned say that he did?*

A host of jumbled emotions and images came back the other way. Guilt. Confusion. Anger. Pain. Peggy laughing. Peggy surrounded by admiring men. Peggy naked and seductive. And then she was lying in bed, wan and almost lifeless, and the sheet beneath her was soaked with her blood. It was running from between her legs. In Caroline's mind, a shapeless lump of tissue came out, then turned into a tiny baby. She smothered it, then threw it in the trash.

Shelby retched. Women didn't get pregnant in her world unless they wanted to, but she'd read about this. She knew what it was and why it had been done. And she knew women hemorrhaged and died from it.

And finally, suddenly, another voice from another source filled her mind. It was a silent wail, so piercing no trained telepath could have failed to receive every word, even Shelby, who so often had trouble hearing. *He's alive, Ned. That was Reid. That man—the one who just left here—he was REID*!

Chapter 21

Shelby was propped up in bed next to Sarah, thinking that even if challenge was a good thing, she'd had a little too much of it lately. Ty was sprawled in a wing chair a few feet away, his feet propped up on a trunk, trying not to think at all. Sarah's pistol was on his lap, not that he would need it. Cameos protected Sarah and Shelby, and shields secured the door and window. Nobody could enter this room and harm them, at least not physically.

Mentally was another story, though. If Ned opened his mind, he might hear George's thoughts. If George regained consciousness, he might communicate those thoughts aloud. But so far, neither event had occurred, because if it had—if Ned had learned that Thomas Johnston and T.J. Reid were the same man—his howl of mental outrage would have penetrated even the dense mental barrier Shelby had erected. Or some thread of it—some wisp of it—surely would have. But from the time they had left the hospital, she'd heard nothing from Ned at all.

That was over two hours ago. They'd been huddled here ever since, talking within the safety of this shielded room. Ty had his answers about the past now, and Sarah had a theory about the timing of Ty's death, but Shelby . . . Shelby had only fear and confusion. She had rescued the mother she adored, but the perfect life she'd envisioned for the two of them would never come to pass. The love she felt was making conflicting demands on her, and the duty imposed by her talents was doing the same thing. The world was more complicated than she had ever imagined.

She was totally drained now, but she couldn't wind down. She was far too troubled, far too frightened. It was hard work when she was this tired, to block another telepath while still keeping a mental ear on her mom and Ty . . .

"Do you think Ned is still at the hospital?" she finally asked Sarah. "I mean, he wouldn't wait there all night, would he?"

"Probably not. Caroline mentioned they were staying with friends on Chester Street, so I imagine they've left to get some sleep. We should do the same." Sarah looked at Ty, adding softly, "You're still blaming yourself. I can tell. But believe me, it wasn't your fault."

Shelby saw the tender expression on Sarah's face and her heart ached—not with jealousy of Tyson Stone, but with pity for him. All that guilt and pain . . . He grumbled about the moral perfection her mother expected, but the truth was, he held himself to an even higher standard than Sarah did. It was ridiculous.

"On the contrary," he replied, "it was precisely my fault. Peggy was troubled and unstable. I should have seen it from the start, but I wanted her too much to look. And the worst part is, I walked away whole, while Peggy died as a result of my stupidity and self-indulgence. And Sukey . . ." His voice caught, and he stared at his lap. "Sukey was never the same, and it was all my doing."

That was their first priority, to get to Ohio and speak to Ty's sister, though Ty had guiltily suggested that

Ned should come first. But Sarah had pointed out that Ned hadn't figured in history until late July, and could wait. Besides, the delay would give them some time to develop a safe and effective plan.

"Maybe the first time around," Sarah said, "but I'll talk to her, and so will Shelby, and we'll change what happened. She'll be fine, Ty, I promise."

Ty muttered his thanks, thinking that if she was, he was luckier than he deserved. He had made mistakes, more of them than Sarah knew, and he was paying the price. All he cared about now was ensuring that the whole country wouldn't have to do the same thing.

Shelby frowned at him. "What mistakes, Ty?"

"It's none of your business. You shouldn't be listening to my thoughts. Anyway, you need to concentrate on blocking out Ned." But he wasn't really angry with her. He didn't have the energy.

"With you or Mom, I can do both at once. Besides, somebody has to talk some sense into you, and I can't do that unless I know what's going on in that convoluted brain of yours. So what mistakes are you supposed to have made?"

Ty didn't answer aloud, but he couldn't control his thoughts, and Shelby picked them up. His guilt was over her mother, and the pain she would feel when she left him. He believed that if he had left Sarah alone—turned her over to Stanton and departed for New York on schedule, as Reid—Shelby still would have rescued her and she never would have had to suffer. And in all likelihood, history would have remained unchanged.

"Oh. So that's it." Shelby made a face, wondering how a man as smart and decent as Ty could be such a total dope, conveniently forgetting that not seven hours before, she'd told herself the exact same thing. "God, you're obtuse. They never would have agreed to build a second chamber if history hadn't gone so wrong, no matter how hard I pushed them, so if you'd left Mom with Stanton, I couldn't have come back to find her. Sooner or later, they would have given up looking for her and scheduled another mission, and she would have been stuck here forever. She probably would have died in Baker's pit of a prison."

"More likely, she would have bribed a guard to place an ad in the *Intelligencer,* Shelby. She would have been rescued within days."

"Fine. Have it your way. She would have been retrieved, then died of her illness in a year or two. This way was better, Ty. Mom got cured, and by the time we leave, history will be better than ever."

He didn't reply, just sat there looking grim. Shelby was torn between empathy and frustration. "And about Peggy, Ty . . . She knew exactly how she felt and exactly what she wanted—your body and your files—and she got them. She might have been self-delusional, but she wasn't irrational. She understood the risks, and she willingly took them. You weren't responsible for her death. She was. She could have married you, but she ran away. She could have told the truth about the baby, but she accused you of rape. If you ask me, she was nothing but a manipulative liar."

Ty thought of his sister at seventeen and told himself it was an age when children believed they knew everything. "An amazing analysis of Peggy's character, my dear, considering that you never met her."

A damned good analysis, Sarah thought to Shelby, *but a little harsh by the standards of 1865.*

Then she looked at Ty and said aloud, "Shelby is accustomed to a world where women control their own lives and their own bodies. We're free to be honest and assertive, and no stigma is attached to sex or pregnancy out of wedlock, so it's hard for her to understand Peggy's behavior. But she's right about at least one thing. You expect too much from yourself. Peggy pursued you, and you allowed yourself to be caught. Only a saint or a mind reader would have turned her down, and the last I heard, you were neither.''

''Not a saint?'' He smiled slightly. ''I thought you believed that I was. I'm pleased that we're making progress.''

Sarah was about to retort that she had never expected saintliness, only the high morality he had so consistently displayed, when Shelby silently told her to drop the subject. Her analysis of Peggy, she explained, came straight from Ty's own mind, but he was hurting too much to listen to what Sarah said, much less to analyze what was stored in his own brain.

She probed his emotions, wanting to lessen the pain and slip in some peace, but the depth of his remorse, and her own profound response to it, left her trembling and helpless. He wasn't only beyond her logic; he was beyond her ability to adjust him. But no one knew better than a telepath that a warm body and a loving touch could sometimes be as healing as mental manipulation was.

''You're exhausted,'' she said aloud. ''If you're going to drive us to Winchester tomorrow, you'll need a decent night's sleep, and you're not going to get it in that chair.'' She sat up, then added gently, ''You take the bed. I'll take the chair. You need my mom a lot more than I do right now.''

Ty was so touched by Shelby's generosity that his mood lightened a little. ''On the contrary, Ned might lash out at you again, and if he does, I want you rested enough to block him. So we'll stay where we are, but there's no need to worry that I'll lose my concentration and land us in a ditch. When I was in the army, I learned to sleep just about anywhere.'' *But thank you for the offer. It was very kind.* His tone turned teasing. *It must be a real curse at times—to hear people's emotions so well. No matter what wretches they are, you doubtless feel obliged to sympathize.*

Shelby's sympathy had been freely given, but she followed Ty's lead and teased him right back. *Yeah, Stone, especially when it comes to you, so why don't you give me a break and start acting like a jerk again? Then I can crash you without feeling guilty.*

He was amused. *You can do what?*

He'd understood her slang, of course. He almost always did, they were so in tune. *Erase you from my mind, but I wouldn't ever do that. I really like you, you know? I really care.*

Ty felt a burst of affection explode in his brain. *Yes. I know. The feeling is mutual.* But ultimately painful, he thought, for the bond was destined to be broken. Shelby obviously heard him, because a wave of sadness came back the other way. *If you keep listening to me, you'll only feel worse, my dear. It would be best if you shut me out and went to sleep.*

To his relief, she agreed, and he turned off the lamp beside his chair and closed his eyes. But earlier, she had relayed the images from Caroline's brain, and they kept flashing through his mind, keeping him awake.

He knew now that Peggy had considered her passion for him to be a terrible weakness. Having an affair with him would only be acceptable if she was spying for her country—if her duty as a patriot required her to sacrifice her body to his lust. It didn't matter how eager she had been in the end; in her mind, his lovemaking was always rape and their child was the result of violence.

And Ty was left with one overriding, damning fact. Night after night, week after week, Peggy had teased him to the edge of madness, and he had never asked why. He had never refused to go along. He had wanted her, and she had needed to be swept away, and nothing else had mattered. And in the end, his blindness and selfishness had killed her.

* * *

In the beginning, when Ned was still a child, he hadn't known when a voice was about to intrude. One moment he would feel normal and safe, and the next, disjointed thoughts would start bouncing around in his head, coming at him from out of nowhere. He had hated the sensation and feared what it implied—that he was a lunatic suffering from bizarre delusions. So somehow, he had learned to make the voices go away, usually within seconds of when they first arrived.

And then, in time, he had noticed there was a tiny warning initially, a mental tingling, and he had taught himself to vanquish a voice before it could even break through. To his relief, it was only a short step from that skill to the next one—eliminating the tingling. Preventing even the smallest alien sensation from intruding. For the past five or six years, nothing had been able to graze him. He had felt sane and secure.

Until last night at the hospital. The awful tingling had come back, and it was ten times stronger than ever, so strong he had wanted to clap his hands over his ears and howl down the building in dread. He had flung it out of his mind, but not forcefully enough, because it had returned. So the second time, he had attacked it with all his might.

To his horror, it had fought back hard. He had almost fainted. But in the end, he had defeated it for good.

Still, the incident had shaken him. He was the tougher brother, after all, the smarter one. He could have returned to the East at any time and disposed of Reid himself, but he had remained out West, leaving the injured George to do the job. And now he was paying the price. In the wildness of his guilt and grief, the dark side of his mind was turning on him again, dragging him back toward madness.

In truth, had any man but George been lying in the hospital where the tingling had taken place, nothing could have induced him to return. But return he did, at half past eight the next morning, because his brother was fighting for his life, and you didn't turn your back on family, not even at the risk of madness. He and his mother entered the ward to learn that George had spent a fitful night. He was still restless and feverish, so Caroline sat at his bedside while Ned visited with some other patients.

Dr. Tucker arrived an hour later, performed an examination, and pronounced George slightly more responsive. Thrilled, Caroline took Ned's arm and begged him to try to break through. ''Talk to him. Pray with him. I know you're the younger one, but he always listens to you. Everyone does. You have a special way about you.''

Ned knew he had talents that others lacked, but he had prayed with his brother yesterday, with little or no success. Still, he dropped into the chair and took George's hand. This time, he decided, he would be fervent and very insistent, because it meant so much to his mother.

You have to send him back to us, Lord, he thought. *Mother will be needing him on the farm. And me—I know you saved me for a special purpose, and I mean to carry it out, but I want him here to help me. He's my big brother, and I want him to share my life.*

George squeezed Ned's hand, then began to mumble. Ned leaned forward, his pulses racing, to try to make out George's words. He couldn't, but he had the oddest sense George wanted to tell him something important. Somehow he had to pull out what it was.

He bent closer. ''Now listen to me, George,'' he said sternly. ''You have to wake up. You have to get better.'' He was concentrating so hard, he felt as if he were reaching into George's mind, dragging him back to awareness by the sheer force of his will. ''You made it through the war alive, so you can't let that bastard Reid be the end of you. You and I have work to do.''

George opened his eyes, staring at Ned in the same eerie way as he had last night. "Reid," he said hoarsely.

A chill ran down Ned's spine. Behind him, Caroline gasped. According to Dr. Tucker, George wasn't really awake, yet he had replied directly to Ned's words, or so it seemed. Maybe it was only a fluke, but Ned wanted to think it was deliberate.

"Yes," he said in a soft, fierce voice. "Reid. But you killed him, George. He's dead. And you're going to live."

"No," George said, peering sightlessly into space.

Ned straightened. "You damned well are. Now wake up. We can't let him win."

But instead of rousing, George closed his eyes and went limp. It was no use, Ned thought. His brother was only muttering incoherently. He felt a wave of despair, then a strong tingling, and his alarm was such that several seconds passed before he could marshal himself to attack it.

He wasn't fast enough. A voice broke through. *He's alive. That man—the one from before—he was REID, Ned.*

Ned turned deathly pale. This wasn't like the voices from his childhood. It had known his name. It was strong and lucid, and what it had said made sense. And, God help him, it had sounded like George. He couldn't say how, since there was never any sound when a voice intruded, but he had recognized the essence of his brother.

The voice had spoken straight into his mind, so it was only logical to respond in the same fashion. *George?* he asked silently. *Were you talking to me just now?*

Then Ned did something he had never done before. It was terrifying, but he forced himself to open his mind to an answer. It came almost at once.

Reid—he's alive, Ned. The voice—George's voice—was very agitated now, and his hand had grown rigid within Ned's. *That man with the girl who was singing—I saw him. I knew him. He was Reid.*

Ned wondered if it could possibly be true. He had never seen T.J. Reid, but George had described him in a letter. He was over six feet tall and solidly built, and would be about thirty years of age now. He had blue eyes and blond hair—long hair where Johnston's was neatly trimmed, and a full beard where Johnston was cleanly shaven—but nobody knew better than Ned how easily such details could be changed.

I suppose he might have looked like Reid, but—

No. Those eyes. That voice. George was on the edge of hysteria. *It was Reid, Ned. You have to kill him.*

Ned didn't want to upset his brother still further. *I believe you, and I won't let him live. I promise.*

"Good," George muttered. *Revenge me,* he thought weakly.

Ned sensed his brother was fading. Afraid of losing him completely, he asked urgently, "Who were the two females with him? Do you know?"

But George didn't reply. He didn't even stir. Ned tried yelling the question into his mind, but it didn't work. Only silence came back. George was utterly immobile now, and his hand had slackened within Ned's grasp.

Knowing it was hopeless, Ned released him and stood. The conversation had exhausted him. Caroline, he noticed, was gazing at him in the strangest way. "Is something the matter?" he asked.

She shook her head, but in confusion rather than denial. "The air around you—it felt all charged up. Other people must have sensed it, too, because a few of them looked our way." She lowered her voice. "It's like I said, Neddy. You have a special way about you.

Look at your brother. He's so peaceful now. Whatever you did, it must have helped.''

She was right. George was sleeping quietly, as if their talk had calmed him. Ned felt his brother's forehead, and found that his fever had gone down. Maybe he had turned the corner.

The implications were as frightening as they were astonishing. Ned muttered that he would be back in a little while, and then, desperately in need of some air, fled the building.

All this time, he thought as he walked blindly down Main Street, he had assumed that the voices were delusions, ghosts that hovered at the edge of a dark and awful pit, seeking to drag him in. But George's words, though few, had dovetailed with George's thoughts. The conversation, whether verbal or mental, had been all of a piece, and entirely rational.

The conclusion was inescapable. The voices were no illusion. They were real, the contents of other people's minds, and Ned had overheard them. If he chose to, he could answer them back. He was special, all right, and in a way he had never dreamed possible.

It was no coincidence, he decided, that just when three strangers had entered his presence, the invasions he had kept at bay for so long had erupted again, opening the mental door he had so arduously closed. After all, if George had been the source of last night's tingling, he would have had that effect before, and he never had. So one of their visitors had been the culprit.

The logical suspect was T.J. Reid—or Thomas Johnston, or whoever he really was. The man had thrived during the war, believing in nothing, playing one side against the other to perfection in a city where neutrality was all but impossible. He had destroyed Peggy, a brave and determined woman, and defeated George twice. Clearly, he had a powerful will—powerful enough to have penetrated Ned's defenses. Powerful enough to have made Ned reel. Indeed, Reid had even induced his protectors to persecute Ned over that incident with his tease of a sister.

Ned stopped in his tracks. In his grief over George, he had forgotten about Susannah Stone, but he suddenly realized that Reid could have come to Front Royal for only one reason, to exact vengeance for her ruin. Ned touched his right pocket, reassured by the hard feel of the pistol inside, then strode into Tucker's Hotel. The sooner he killed the villain, the better, and given the circumstances, a demand that they meet on the field of honor would have to be accepted at once. Fortunately, he was a crack shot.

But when he questioned the clerk, he learned that "Johnston" had left over three hours before, driving his party to Winchester in a newly purchased rig made heavy by trunks and bags. He had mentioned moving to California, the clerk added, and Ned remembered the same being said the night before, and decided it was likely the truth. For one thing, there was all that baggage, and for another, Winchester was where one boarded a train to Harper's Ferry and the West. A train to Oberlin, Ohio, too. Maybe he planned to pick up his sister, then travel to Atchison for the Overland Stage.

In any event, the man had fled instead of issuing a challenge. He only attacked women and cripples, it seemed, not vigorous men. When it came right down to it, he had proved himself a coward as well as a murderer.

Ned walked slowly out of the hotel. He longed to run Reid to ground and kill him, but his mother would want him to stay here with George. She believed he was helping his brother mend. Maybe she was right.

But it was a big country. If he didn't follow Reid at once, it would be hell to track him down. Even worse, Reid might adopt yet another identity, and Ned might never be able to find him. So what did he do next?

* * *

Two telepaths, even modestly gifted ones, could communicate across hundreds of miles. Increase the talent and training, and the range increased to thousands. And for a select few like Shelby, the ones who were gifted enough to be labeled Class A, there was no known limit at all.

In 2102, Shelby thought, Ned Beecham would have been categorized as a Class A. Though completely untrained, he was astonishingly powerful. He was evidently too ignorant of his own nature to mount a willful attack, but rage or pain made him strike out fiercely and blindly. After three such assaults, she was wary of a fourth, so she kept her defenses at their maximum height as they started toward Winchester.

But they were riding in the only vehicle they'd been able to buy, a battered wagon pulled by the sorriest pair of horses she had ever seen, and it was crammed so full of baggage that a trot was their top rate of speed. As the miles dragged by, her guard began to drop from discomfort and resentment. She didn't know how the people here stood it—the endless dust, the rutted roads, the excruciating heat and humidity that had invaded from out of nowhere. By comparison, the trains here were luxury mag-cars. And the countryside was totally depressing—dead fields, scorched hills, charred woods, and ravaged buildings. Only the mountains were still beautiful.

Even worse, Ty and Sarah never noticed how awful it was. They were so busy yammering about Reconstruction that nobody else existed. And when they weren't drooling over each other's minds, they were panting over each other's bodies. You didn't have to be a telepath to know what they were thinking. They couldn't wait to be alone so they could do it.

Shelby wrinkled her nose at the thought. That might be days from now, since the trains were so screwed up.

So they would get more and more mushy, and she would feel it in her mind—feel her mother and some historical character who'd been dead for almost two centuries oozing all over each other like slugs.

Scowling, she reached into Ty's pocket for his watch, and he was so wrapped up in her mom, he never even noticed her check the time. It wasn't even ten yet, but she was already sticky with sweat from the long, stupid dress she'd been forced to wear. She closed her eyes to meditate, hoping it would put her to sleep.

She'd gone through five fruitless minutes of a Tibetan chant when the first filaments of emotion invaded her mind—pleading or praying, then anger. She recognized the source at once. It was Ned. The filaments were faint enough that she wouldn't have sensed them if her mental barriers hadn't dropped, so in a delicate balancing act, she kept them low enough to maintain contact but high enough to provide some additional protection.

It came in handy. The despair that rolled through her mind a minute later made her stiffen and sway. It was followed by such a strong burst of alarm that the world dimmed for a moment, and she grabbed Ty's arm for support.

Ty reined in the horses, stopping by the side of the road. He'd felt an instant of dizziness as Shelby took his arm. "Is it Ned, Shelby? What did you hear?"

She gave him a distracted glance. "Yes. He's in turmoil. I'll try to give you a play-by-play . . . There's confusion, but . . ." Her voice trailed off. Unless she was mistaken . . . "My God. He's talking to George now, mostly with his mind. He's picking up George's thoughts. He—George—he's repeating what he was thinking last night. That he recognized you, Ty. But Ned doesn't understand his own powers. What his mind can do. George's thoughts—he can't quite believe they're real."

She hesitated for a few seconds, then continued, "He's fading. There's some fatigue, but . . . Oh, Jesus, Ty. It just hit him—what happened between him and George, and what it implies about what he is. He's really spooked about it, too."

But as Shelby continued to listen, Ned began to calm. He seemed to be sorting things out and starting to accept them. "Wait a minute. I'm getting something stronger. It's about Reid. Ned thinks you're the one who attacked him last night. Mentally, I mean. There's something about Peggy and George . . . I'm getting hatred. Anger. Toward you, Ty." The intensity of it made her queasy. "He wants to kill you."

"That's hardly a new development," Ty drawled.

He could joke about it all he liked, but Shelby was more frightened for him than she wanted him to know. "But it's different now. He's so icy about it. So controlled. It will make him harder to defeat."

Ned is too damn intelligent, she added to Sarah. *He recognizes the nature of his powers now, and he could learn to use them at will, especially against* **me,** *once he realizes I'm the same thing he is. But we can't let Ty know that, because he'll kill Ned to protect me and wind up with his neck in a noose.*

Sarah was even more terrified than Shelby was. The two people she loved most were in deadly peril. *How strong do you think he is? Will you be able to block him out? To protect yourself without the risk of a mental shutdown?*

Of course, but protection isn't the issue, Mom. I need to defeat him, not just to fend him off.

For God's sake, Shelby, have you forgotten what happened last night? The way you collapsed?

No, Mother. Have you? I was almost unconscious, and I still almost sent him to the floor. If I ever hit him with everything I've got—

He'll hit you right back, and you'll both pass out. I

want you to keep your tentacles out of his brain, Shelby, do you hear me? It's too damn dangerous.

Only if I know I can't destroy him, Shelby replied grimly, *in which case, you're welcome to shoot him.*

Ty cocked an eyebrow at her. "You've been awfully quiet for the last minute. You wouldn't be conversing with your mother, would you?"

She made a face at him. "Would you please just be quiet? How am I supposed to listen with you yammering at me that way?"

"Listen?" Ty gave a dubious snort. "More likely, the pair of you were scheming behind my back."

Shelby ignored him and focused on Ned's mind. Several minutes passed without a whisper, and then she picked up extreme ambivalence. "He's confused again. In torment. He can't decide what to do. But what he's so unhinged about . . ." She frowned, struggling to pull out his thoughts. And then she understood. "He knows we've left town. He can't decide whether to stay with George or chase us."

"Unlike the last time," Sarah said. "This supports my hypothesis. If George recognized Ty last night, when he was almost comatose, he must have recognized him originally, too."

Sarah was referring to the previous version of history, when Ty and Sarah had fled Washington. She believed they had arrived at the Beechams' farm while George was still improving, and while Ned was en route from Denver. In the current version of history, George had wired Ned in Atchison, saying he could return to Denver if he liked, but in that previous version, the telegram must have contained the news that Reid was still alive and headed to California. Sarah thought Ned had lingered in Atchison, arranging for the attack that had taken the lives of Ty and Sukey—and probably her own, as well.

Shelby continued to listen, hoping that Ned would

decide on a course of action. But it was only hours later, when they reached the outskirts of Winchester, that she heard anything further from his mind. It was a grief so terrible, a rage so overpowering, that she cringed.

George Beecham was dead, and Ned was consumed by a lust for vengeance. Reid had taken both his sister and his brother, and he meant to kill Reid and everyone close to him in retaliation. But if he had decided when and where he would strike, the information remained beyond the reach of Shelby's mind.

Chapter 22

In Winchester, Ty resumed the use of his real name, and learned he was something of a celebrity. The town, once the northernmost outpost of the Confederacy, had been both a commercial center and a strategic prize. As such, it had witnessed almost continual fighting during the war, changing hands over seventy times. Most there had favored the South, and they had paid a heavy price for it.

Hundreds of structures had been torched, demolished, or appropriated by the Union army. An explosion had destroyed the station, so the North had repaired the torn-up train tracks only as far as Stephenson's Depot, five miles up the road. Union occupiers had closed the newspapers and smashed the presses, looted the shops, and cannibalized the buildings, causing such widespread damage that almost every structure still standing needed substantial repairs.

Ty shook his head at the wanton destruction as he drove down Main Street. Most in the South, though saddened by Lee's surrender, had accepted the outcome as inevitable. They were relieved the killing was over and prepared to get on with their lives. But would the residents of Winchester, who had suffered so greatly, be as stoic in the face of defeat?

The topic, he decided, would make a fine one for his next article, so he interviewed the people he met as he went about his business in the town. Some were ordinary residents, like the petitioners at the provost marshal's office, where he presented Stanton's pass and learned that the next train north wasn't until Monday, and others were local leaders, like the liveryman with whom he quartered their rig and the owner of the tavern where they took their lunch. Far from being hostile toward a Yankee, they seemed eager to tell him their views. They had followed the nation's affairs in the newspapers dispatched from other cities, and were very well informed.

In general, they were resigned in the wake of defeat, bitter toward the Union army, apprehensive about the fate of Virginia, and interested in what form the reconstructed Union would take. None of that surprised him. What did was how often "An Army Goes Home" was mentioned.

The locals had read it in the *Intelligencer* or the *Baltimore Sun,* which had reprinted it a day later. The moment Ty gave his name, he was praised so lavishly that his head threatened to swell out of his hat. Everyone wanted his opinions and predictions. Indeed, the manager at the Taylor Hotel, after glancing at the register and inquiring if he was *that* Tyson Stone, even asked him to address the Winchester Masons that evening.

He hesitated before replying. His only plans were to eat and rest, since they were driving to Martinsburg in the morning rather than waiting for Monday's train. The town was closer than Harper's Ferry and farther west along the B & O. So time wasn't a problem, but Ned Beecham *was.* Though Shelby had heard nothing since their arrival and believed he had remained in

Front Royal to bury his brother, she wasn't certain. He could still show up here.

If he did, Ty wanted Sarah and Shelby within sight. He wasn't afraid they would be physically harmed, since their cameos would protect them from attack, but that they would ignore his wishes about Ned. A showdown was inevitable, of course, but Ty meant to be the one who provoked it. If there was killing to be done, he would do it himself.

He finally agreed to speak, but only if his companions came along. They were posing as a journalist and her younger sister, friends of Ty's whom he was escorting back to California. The manager all but gaped in astonishment. Females, he sputtered, couldn't possibly be permitted to invade the sanctity of a fraternal meeting. But Ty had been to many such gatherings, and he knew that the usual activities—performing rituals, exchanging gossip, discussing politics and business—were neither sacred nor exclusively male. And maybe that was the real point, he thought. Excluding women denied them access to information and influence, which in turn limited their power in society.

I suppose it's different in your day, he thought to Shelby. *These all-male clubs no longer exist.*

Not if they hold political and economic power—it's illegal—and nobody is all that interested in the social ones. Tell him you'll speak at a lecture open to everyone, and I'll see that he goes along.

With Shelby pushing, the manager decided that a public forum was a fine idea, and sent out a porter to spread the word around town. Some four hours later, Ty found himself standing before a large crowd in the main parlor of the hotel, talking about his research and pleading for tolerance and reconciliation. According to Sarah, he had given many such speeches during his original life, but this was the first of them in *this* life, and he was anxious about how he was doing.

Sarah noticed, and reassured Ty with nods and smiles. She didn't know whether he was changing any minds in this room, but she was sure he was prying a few of them wider open. She hoped his success here tonight would hearten him—divert him from his agony over Peggy and remind him of how vital he was to the nation's future.

Still, the most incredible moment of the evening wasn't during the lecture, but afterward. Shelby had agreed to sing, to provide a break before the question-and-answer session. She had finished "Dixie" and was performing a Negro spiritual when three African-Americans slipped into the room and stood quietly at the back to listen.

No other people of color were present. Socially if not legally, this was a segregated community and would remain so for many years, despite periodic black protests. So if the trio had decided to enter, it could only be because Shelby had sensed them outside and started to push.

Sarah waited for someone to abuse them, but no one said a word. To her astonishment, several people even smiled at the men in welcome. Shelby could handle up to four minds at a time, but dozens here must have had objections. Sarah was stymied as to how Shelby was controlling them.

She didn't want to disrupt the girl with telepathic questions, so she waited until later that night, when they were sequestered in Ty's room, to raise the matter. How had Shelby kept the whole audience in line? Did she have talents she hadn't told them about?

Shelby was sitting by her side at a table while Ty lounged on the bed. She cocked her head, looking pensive and a little puzzled. "I've always known there's a form of telepathic connection when I perform, but all this time, I assumed it related to my singing. That unconsciously, I was pushing people to like my performance. But it might be more than that. My singing might make them more receptive. Easier to adjust."

"Might?" Ty repeated. "Hasn't the subject been studied in regard to other telepathic artists?"

"There haven't been any," Shelby replied. "In the first place, telepathy is really rare. Lots of people have flashes of it now and then—you and Mom more than most—but only about one in twenty million has a consistent talent for it. Of those, maybe a dozen are as powerful as I am—or rather, as powerful as I'll become, once I'm fully mature. Class A telepaths, we're called. We're expected to devote ourselves to humanity—to cure people the psychomedics can't help, or reach people who are comatose or traumatized. We calm and instruct them during disasters, which saves lives, and we find them when they're lost. We help in hostage situations and kidnappings. The list goes on and on and on." She slumped lower in her chair. "We're always on call, to anywhere in the world we're needed."

To Ty's surprise, Shelby looked as if she resented the role. "But I've seen the way you listen and sympathize. Helping is second nature to you"—he smiled gently—"except when you lose your temper. So what's the problem?"

Shelby grimaced. It was hard to explain her feelings to Ty, especially after watching him lecture. He was so damn moral and caring. "That it's your whole life. Believe me, they'll train all the temper out of me. But I'm a singer. My emotions, even the bad ones, are a part of who I am and what I do. Besides, I want to be something besides a professional do-gooder. Pretty selfish, huh?"

In 2096, when Sarah had last seen Shelby, her future hadn't been an issue. It was unusual for the telepath in a mother-child link to develop wider abilities, so it was only on the day before her jump that Sarah had gotten an inkling of what Shelby might become. "No Class

A telepath has ever had your musical talent before,'' she pointed out. ''If your father had been a world-class violinist instead of a gifted amateur, nobody would have thought he was selfish to choose music over physics.''

Shelby had expected her mom to support her—she always had—but Ty was another story. She was steeling herself to ask his opinion when she realized he was miles away, like her dad during one of his brainstorms.

She snapped her fingers to bring him back to earth. ''Hey, Stone. Are you going to tell me what's up, or do I have to pull it out of your neurons?''

He was startled, then amused. ''I don't believe it. She's actually asking my permission.''

''Not really. It's just that I worked so hard tonight, I don't have the energy to snoop. So what's on your mind?''

''You,'' Ty said, knowing Shelby could have plucked out his thoughts in an instant, pleased that she hadn't done so. ''The way you affected the audience tonight . . . Can you tell us what happened? Give us a play-by-play, as you put it?''

Shelby nodded, explaining that she'd sensed the trio outside and had wanted them to come in. She'd expected objections, so she'd sung the song about how awful slavery was, assuming the racists in the audience would be cynical and hostile, intending to adjust them toward greater tolerance. But when she'd opened her mind to listen, she was amazed by what had come back.

''Nobody was angry or cold,'' she continued. ''They were receptive and sympathetic. I figured I had your lecture to thank for that. To make sure they stayed that way, I decided to mellow them a bit more. It's easy and fast when people are that pliant. So I chose a group at random, and I made them placid and accepting, and suddenly the whole audience went along. They were like a row of dominoes lined up on their ends. I pushed a few, and they all fell over. Most were at least neutral when the men came in, and a few were even approving. There must be something about the dynamics of a group . . . When I sing to people—move them—they enter a sort of collective trance and absorb my mood.''

''And you never sensed that before because you never pushed people so deliberately before,'' Ty said.

''Right. It was always unconscious.'' She frowned in concentration. ''But now that I think about it, the bigger the audience is, the better things always go. It's as if—as if, once I start affecting people, a chain reaction begins, and they all start affecting each other. So if there's a hundred people in a room, all influencing each other, the effect is greater than when there's only ten.''

''Like the behavior of a mob. It feeds on itself.''

''Yeah, except tonight, it was good instead of bad.''

Sarah could see where Ty was heading now. ''But it won't always be good. You think that if a telepath who sings like an angel can sway a crowd that way, then a telepath who was one of the great orators of his day could, too. That's why Ned did so much damage. He reached his listeners in a uniquely visceral way.''

''Visceral and lasting. I believe he converted them. Unconsciously adjusted them.'' Ty turned to Shelby. ''Is it possible? Could the changes you induced be permanent?''

She thought for a moment. ''If you picture a continuum with altering people's memories at one end and affecting their current emotions on the other, what happened tonight was in the middle. But don't forget, Ned was much more intense than I am.''

''So his listeners might have absorbed his attitudes to a deeper, more lasting degree?''

''Right.''

Sarah gazed at Ty in amazement. ''The connections you make . . . I used to admire that about your writing, but to actually watch it unfold . . . It's fascinating, Ty.''

She broke into a smile. "This whole night was fascinating. I know I keep saying this, but you were brilliant. Winchester will be talking about you for weeks."

Ty's interest in Ned Beecham and the mechanics of telepathy diminished rapidly. Sarah was giving him the sort of adoring look she reserved for the literary icon, the kind that aroused him, exasperated him, and made him want to prove that he was human to the core. But with Shelby here, no gentleman would have shown it. "You can say it as often as you like. I'd rather be called brilliant and incredible than barbaric, narrow, and arrogant."

She laughed. "You've improved since then, but don't you start believing you're perfect. You had an appealing humility the first time around. It was part of what made you so effective."

"Thereby adding to my perfection," he drawled, but the warmth in his eyes said Sarah was the one who was perfect.

She reddened and gave a tiny shake of her head. Not now, it meant. Not tonight. But she didn't make a move to leave, and Ty didn't suggest that she go. Smiling now, he continued to watch her. He could see how much it heated her blood, and the sight pleased him.

Shelby glanced from one to the other, then stood and stretched. There was no doubt about it—hormones that raging should have been illegal in people their age—but for once, she really didn't mind. The feelings in this room were too special for that, too true and pure.

It was sweet, really, the devotion and admiration they shared. Only a brat wouldn't have been happy for them. And touched. And guilty, dammit, because she was the only thing keeping them from happily ever after.

She touched her mother's arm. "I'm out of here, Mom. Call me when you're ready to leave. I'll make sure nobody sees you."

Sarah jumped to her feet. "But I'm not going to stay—"

"Why not? I haven't heard a word from Ned, but I'll turn on my cameo and shield the door, just in case. I'll be fine." She hesitated, then added softly, "I can't give you a lifetime, but I can give you tonight. Next week. Next month. So take it."

Sarah's eyes got misty. *Thanks, sweetie.*

Then you understand? You know why it's pointless for me to stay?

Of course I do.

And you're caught in the middle. I'm sorry, Mom. I know how much it hurts you to have to choose. She walked over to Ty. In a single week, despite a rocky start, he'd exhibited more interest and caring than her father had in ten years. In some small way, she wanted to pay him back.

"I wish we could bring you forward," she said. "We could use you in 2102. Your decency and energy and hope. You were awesome tonight." *So awesome, she finally knows that she loves you.* ***You,*** *not some character out of a history book.* She heard his shock, and then his joy and gratitude, and pecked him on the cheek. "You're welcome. Good night. And Mom—don't forget to shield the door after I leave."

Shelby walked out, and Sarah closed the door and turned on the field. If anyone but her daughter had claimed to understand the torment in her heart, she would have said it was impossible, but Shelby really did. "I wish she couldn't hear me so well. She knows how torn I am, and it's killing her. She would offer to stay, but she knows it wouldn't work. That I couldn't be happy, knowing *she* wasn't happy." She sat down on the bed, and two tears rolled down her cheeks. "I don't want to leave you. I don't want to leave *her*. I wish I could split myself in half."

Ty's whole body went rigid. Surely that was better

than choosing—two Sarahs, each with a person she loved . . . "So why don't you? If they retrieved you from May 23—"

"Then everything that followed would instantly change. A new past would come into being. You wouldn't be in Winchester on June 3, sitting here with me. I would be gone, and you would be someplace else, with different memories."

"Of course. I'd forgotten." Because he'd yearned so desperately for the rules to be different. He pulled her into his arms, and she nestled against his chest. "Please, Sarah . . . Leave things the way they are. I can live through losing you, but never to have met you—"

"We wouldn't know. We wouldn't have any memories of each other after the moment I disappeared." She stroked his cheek. "Maybe it would be better that way."

A sense of icy horror suffused him. He hated the idea. "No. I'll be more useful to the nation, knowing what I do about the future. I want to remember our time together. Picture you reading my words and watching me live my life. Promise me I can have that."

Sarah didn't want Ty to suffer, but with so much at stake for the country, she had no real choice. "I promise," she said, and sniffled. "But how can I go? No matter what century I'm in . . ." Her emotions overwhelmed her, and she started to cry. "It's not fair. I can't leave Shelby, but I love you so much. I don't want to forget you, either. I'll never want anyone else. I watched you tonight, and I thought you were the finest, kindest, smartest, bravest . . ." She bit her lip, then buried her face against Ty's neck and sobbed, a rasping, choking sound that tore at his heart.

He held her and stroked her hair, his own eyes glistening with tears. So Shelby—as usual—had been right. He had what he'd wanted so fiercely—he was the great love of Sarah's life—but it pained him as much as it thrilled him. Whether she stayed or left, nobody would be truly happy.

Sarah finally looked up, saw the anguish in Ty's eyes, and ached to relieve it. So she nuzzled his lips, and then, when he opened his mouth to deepen the kiss, drew back a little and nibbled him playfully. He tasted her lip with his tongue, and her own tongue danced to meet him, but she still wouldn't let him enter. Her hand, meanwhile, had drifted to his groin to explore him. He was hot and fully erect.

She caressed him very lightly, and he grunted and sucked in his breath. It aroused him to be teased that way, but it also frustrated him unmercifully. Deliberately provoking him, she unfastened his trousers, burrowed beneath his drawers, and cupped him, refusing to stroke him even when he writhed against her palm.

It was more than he could take. He slid his fingers into her hair and eased away her head. "Look at me, Sarah."

"Yes, darling?" She gave him a wicked smile. The pain in his eyes was gone, replaced by smoldering passion. Without another word, he rolled her onto her back, pushed up her skirts, and parted her thighs. A moment later he was kneeling between her legs . . . freeing his sex . . . pulling her forward and raising her up to meet him. He grasped her hips and rubbed himself against her, and she twined her legs around his back and followed his lead.

And then he was pushing himself inside her, driving himself as deep as he could go, then staying immobile while he caressed her with his thumb. She moaned and closed her eyes, twisting against him as her excitement grew, and he finally began to thrust, hard and fast and very, very wildly. She wanted him to take her in his arms and kiss her, but she was too aroused to ask him to stop. Her climax came almost at once, and his while she was still convulsing.

He pulled out of her before she was finished, and she gave him a reproachful look. "That was nice, Ty, but a little rushed. Were you going for a world speed record, or do you have another appointment to get to?"

"Neither. I've wanted to do that for weeks. Make us both lose control. See how fast and hot it could be. Leave us hungry for more." He grinned at her, then started to undress her. "It makes the second time so much nicer, my love. Slow and easy and very, very sweet."

He was right. It was all those things and more. Sarah had always assumed the most intense moments of her life would be shared with Shelby, because they could bypass words and go straight to feelings, but Ty said as much with his body as Shelby did with her mind. He was passionate, generous, and tender, not to mention spectacularly thorough, and after it was over, she knew she should be grateful for however long they had. Few people ever experienced such deep love—or such shattering pleasure. Not even once. But she was greedy. She wanted eternity.

Chapter 23

Ty, Sarah, and Shelby arrived in Oberlin late Tuesday evening, having traveled by rig, ferry, and train in order to get there. Though Shelby didn't complain, the primitive transportation took its toll. She'd spent three solid days guarding against an explosion by Ned Beecham while remaining open enough to sense his thoughts, and between that and the travel, she was beat. To her utter disgust, she'd heard nothing after Sunday, when she'd picked up a short burst of surprise, then a longer one of anger. Either she was hopeless at listening or out of Ned's range. Or maybe he'd kept himself on such an even emotional keel that nothing had broken through.

If it was the last, that was more than *she'd* been able to do. She would lie in bed at night, asking God to make her enjoy this era so she would want to stay, but the next morning, all she would see was isolation, bigotry, ignorance, and physical discomfort. Every moment of the day was an agony of stress and guilt.

Their first stop in Oberlin was at the Palmer House on Main Street, a few blocks north of the depot. The hotel was the best in town, and right on the edge of the campus, so Ty always stayed there when he visited.

The manager greeted him by name, giving him rooms on two different floors. Later, laughing, Ty said the fellow was probably guarding against sin. The hotel was owned by the college, and no drinking, smoking, cursing, or reveling was allowed. Oberlin wasn't only the most integrated community in America; it was also the most religious. They would have to respect that.

After washing and changing, the trio walked through the campus to Professor Drive. Some five hundred females attended the school, a fifth of them local, but the Ladies' Hall could house only sixty. The rest boarded with nearby families, including Sukey, who lived with the Reverend James Fairchild, a renowned professor and abolitionist and the devoted father of six. After the attack, Ty had arranged for a Pinkerton named Endover to join the household, nominally as its butler.

Ty greeted Endover warmly as the agent opened the door. The man had done an excellent job in a tedious assignment. "I assume things have been quiet here, because they've been the opposite in Washington and Virginia, where we've just come from. I've crossed swords with the Beechams again."

Endover glanced at Sarah and Shelby but said nothing. "Discreet as ever, I see," Ty teased, then explained that the women knew everything and could be trusted. "George is dead now, but Ned is still alive, and even more dangerous than we supposed. It's possible he'll show up here."

Ty was about to elaborate when Fairchild strode into the hall. He would be Oberlin's next president, according to Sarah, and was as amiable as he was distinguished. He welcomed the trio to Oberlin, then congratulated Ty on his "brilliant article," which he had read in the *Cleveland Herald*. "Susannah showed me your letter. I was pleased to learn that T.J.—" He looked at Sarah and Shelby and checked himself. "That is, that you had taken up journalism again. I had no idea you were such an original thinker. Would you be able to deliver a lecture about your work? Tomorrow evening, perhaps?''

Ty said he would be honored and Fairchild beamed. ''Wonderful. You and the ladies will stay for dinner, I trust. I know you'll enjoy our other guests. My wife's cousin, Caleb Washburne of the *Herald,* is visiting, and Professor Allen of our history program will be joining us.'' He put his hand on Ty's shoulder. ''I know how much your sister has missed you, so why don't you go up and visit? Dinner will be at six.''

The trio climbed to the second floor. Ty knocked on Sukey's door, then opened it and poked his head around the edge. His sister and her roommate were absorbed in their lessons, but Sukey's eyes lit up the moment she saw him, and she ran into his arms for a hug.

As he released her, he thought bleakly that she was still too thin and dourer than ever. After Ned's attack, she had taken to wearing dark, loose clothing, pulling her hair into a tight bun atop her head, and wearing round little spectacles that made her resemble a myopic barn owl. It was pointless to beg her to eat; she said she wasn't hungry. He had stopped sending her pretty dresses, because she never wore them. Life, once a lark and an adventure to the girl, had become a deadly serious business.

Ty introduced Sarah and Shelby, then made small talk about the rigors of travel and the girls' progress in school. Sukey had never blamed him for Ned's attack, but every time he saw her, his guilt intensified, especially since she adored him so unreservedly. There was only one cause for hope: every now and then, when he was intolerably dictatorial or teased her too much, she would retaliate with a flash of the high spirits and sharp wit he remembered from her girlhood. He had once torn out his hair over those qualities, but now he longed for their return.

Her roommate excused herself, and he leaned against the door and pondered where to begin. "I have a great deal to explain," he finally said, "but I'll start with this. Shelby isn't Sarah's sister. She's Sarah's daughter."

Sukey's eyes widened. "Goodness, Mrs. March, you must have been terribly young—"

"Eighteen," Sarah said, "but we're only thirteen years apart now. Try to be patient, Sukey. It's a long, complicated story, but Ty will tell you everything."

"Their surname is Maravich, not March," he continued, "and Sarah isn't a journalist, but a historian and scientist. It's *Dr.* Sarah Maravich. She arrived in Washington two weeks ago, and Shelby came five days later. They live in Virginia City, Nevada, but not in the year 1865—"

But Sukey was suddenly racing forward, ignoring him. "Shelby March! I don't believe it!" She threw her arms around the girl, a look of amazed delight on her face. "It's so good to see you! Good heavens, do you remember all the mischief we got up to in Elyria? How are your parents? How was Paris?"

Then, just as suddenly, her smile vanished and her cheeks turned scarlet. "I don't— I thought— Please excuse me, Miss March. I mean, Miss Maravich. I know we've never met. I can't imagine what made me think otherwise—what came over me just now."

"What came over you was me," Shelby informed her. "I'm what's called a telepath, and that was a demonstration. I can talk directly to your mind, without your even knowing it if I choose to, and I can make you believe whatever I want you to. You met someone just like me once, Ned Beecham. Unlike me, he doesn't understand the nature of his powers, but that hasn't stopped him from using them damn well, and—"

"Watch your language," Sarah murmured. "Remember, Oberlin is a religious institution, and Mr. Fairchild is extremely pious.''

''Whoops. Sorry, Mom.'' But Shelby looked more amused than sheepish. ''Anyway, Suke, Ned controls people with his mind, instinctively and very effectively. I met him on Friday. He's a handsome son of a— Uh, man, isn't he? When you add his looks to how powerful his mind is, it's amazing you told him to stop. Very few women could have. Like me, he can make you do things you normally wouldn't.''

Sukey dropped onto the bed, looking dazed. ''I don't understand. Who are you? What are you? How do you know about—about me and Ned? What did you do to me just now?''

I'm from the future. I was born in 2085. People like me and Ned are as rare there as they are here, but in the world I come from, we're identified when we're young and trained to use our abilities. My mother was sent here from 2096 to prevent Lincoln's assassination, but something went wrong, and she landed over a month too late. Then she was spotted arriving, and they thought she was a spy. And from the vantage point of 2096, history got worse instead of better. Shelby sent a small wave of amusement through Sukey's mind. *Actually, it was all Ty's fault. Stanton told him to get her to talk, but he was more interested in taking her to bed. Which he did, and they're madly in love now.* She sobered abruptly. *Which is wonderful and terrible at the same time, because they're total soul mates, but she's not supposed to stay here. Anyway, we didn't know where Mom was, so I came here to find her and fix up history, but not until five years later, in 2102.*

Ty rolled his eyes at the prolonged silence. When he added that to the glazed expression on his sister's face . . . ''Shelby, if I've told you once, I've told you a dozen times: if you're going to talk to one of us, then talk to all of us, so we can hear what you say. And for

Pete's sake, use a little discretion from now on. The girl is in shock.''

Shelby grinned at him. ''Ice it, Stone. I was filling her in, that's all. She's fine. I mean, she hasn't even flown into orbit and started calling me nasty names.'' She gave a haughty sniff. ''Unlike *some* people I could name.''

''It was a reasonable reaction, given the things you said and the appalling way you were dressed,'' he retorted.

''Yeah, well, your nineteenth century priggishness didn't stop you from liking that sexy little outfit Mom was parading around in.''

Ty reddened and said sternly, ''Remember where you are, Shelby.''

She giggled. ''Sorry, but you're so easy to embarrass, it's hard to resist. Anyway, it was just a guess. She didn't say anything. Frankly, your sister is handling this telepathy stuff a lot better than you did. *She* doesn't think it's creepy or disgusting.''

''Because you aren't listening to her thoughts, much less examining her like prize horseflesh or rating her performance—'' He flushed and cut himself off.

In bed, Suke, Shelby finished silently, letting all of them hear her. *Your brother is a genius in that department.*

''That's enough, young lady.'' Ty glared at Shelby ferociously. ''You'll corrupt the girl.''

Sarah glanced at Ty's sister. She looked astonished and fascinated, but certainly not shocked. Choking back laughter, she drawled, ''I doubt it, darling. Sukey is finding this extremely enlightening, and education is never a bad thing. Besides, it's only the truth.''

''I'm gratified you think so, but your opinion isn't particularly helpful just now. We're talking about a girl who was bold enough to dabble in witchcraft, so the last thing she needs is any encouragement to—''

"Actually, it's not just *my* opinion," Sarah interrupted, and winked at Sukey, who was smiling now. "It's your brother's opinion, too. He's told me so a dozen times."

Sukey's eyes twinkled. "I can't say I'm surprised. He does have a pompous streak. Tell me, Dr. Maravich, have you made any progress in reforming him?"

"It's Sarah, and very little. The reaction to that article of his has swollen his self-regard out of all proportion."

"Women," Ty grumbled, but the complaint was strictly for show. In truth, he was thrilled to see his sister so animated. "If you're going to gang up against me, I'm going to leave."

Shelby wasn't fooled for a minute. *You're welcome,* she replied cheerfully. *This is going to work, Ty. I can feel her responding.*

She joined Sukey on the bed. "So you're interested in witchcraft, huh? Why it works is, there are beings in higher dimensions—places that are real but beyond our senses—who are drawn to some of the chants and ingredients that are used. Some are playful and benevolent, and others are really malicious. If you get them in the right mood, they'll do what you want, but stick to the good ones, Suke. The bad ones are dangerous and unpredictable."

Sukey gazed at her uncertainly, then reddened and looked away. "That can't be true. I've never had any luck. You're making fun of me."

"Nope. It's the truth. Our experiments have confirmed their existence. They may be able to sense us where we can't sense them, but frankly, they're not the smartest folks you'll ever run into. About the other stuff—the time travel and telepathy—did you understand it?"

"I think so. I heard you in my mind, so I know what you can do. And nobody from 1865 would talk the way you do.'' A disgruntled pout took over Sukey's face. ''The language you use and the subjects you discuss . . . Doesn't your mother scold you? Doesn't Ty? He was always so strict when I went too far, lecturing me and sending me to my room. I never got away with a thing. But you—''

''Hah.'' Ty rolled his eyes. ''Not much, you didn't.''

''That's not the way *I* recall it. Well, Shelby? Don't you get in trouble?''

''Not really. My mom grew up in a more repressed era than I did, but everyone talks and thinks the way I do now, so she's gotten used to it. And your brother—he grumbled a lot at first, but his standards are ancient history, so I wasn't about to listen. In the end, I wore him down.''

''Only because you scare me to death,'' Ty said. ''That telepathic mind of yours—''

''I do not. When I really mess up, you let me know it.'' Shelby pulled up her legs and rested her chin on her knees. ''The truth is, we like each other a lot, Suke. I can see how people really are—you know, with my mind—and he's ethical and kind and—and a hundred other wonderful things. You're lucky to have him for a brother.''

''I know,'' Sukey said, but she thought far more, and the intensity was so great that Shelby overheard her.

A lump formed in Shelby's throat. More than anything, Sukey wanted her brother to be happy. She believed he was a man who needed a wife and family to be content, and she'd assumed Peggy would give him those things. Then Peggy had died, and Sukey had feared he would never get over the loss. Now, though, she realized that he loved Sarah far more, and that he would suffer far more when Sarah was gone. So she was sitting there, confused and distressed, wondering why he kept falling for women he couldn't have.

* * *

The dinner conversation revolved around Reconstruction and the future of the reunited nation. All those present had read Ty's article and looked forward to his lecture, especially Caleb Washburne, who had decided to cover the speech for his paper. "Is there any way you could come to Cleveland next?" he asked during dessert. "I know the *Herald* would sponsor you. Our readers are extremely interested in your views. There would be standing room only, I'm sure."

Professor Allen promptly weighed in, urging Ty to agree, telling him he had important things to say and said them calmly and clearly, a welcome change from the usual low level of discourse in the nation. "In fact, if one or two speeches would be valuable, a whole series of them would be even better. You're traveling to California anyway, so why not put together a lecture tour of the cities along your route? Cleveland, Chicago, St. Louis, Denver . . ."

Washburne chuckled. "It would be a marvelous trip. With any luck, I could get myself assigned to cover it."

Now Fairchild spoke up, bubbling with approval and enthusiasm. "A splendid idea! I could help with the arrangements, Ty. I have a wide circle of friends, and I could wire them on your behalf. What do you say? Shall we talk about a schedule?"

Any journalist worth the name would have jumped at the offer. It was a matchless opportunity to talk to people throughout the nation and write about their views. But with Ned out for blood, Ty feared a speaking tour might be dangerous. His schedule would be public knowledge, and Washburne's articles for the *Herald* might be wired all over the country. If Ned saw an account in the papers and put two and two together, he would realize that Stone was Johnston was Reid. An attack would almost certainly follow.

Ty pursed his lips. Then again, Ned might be tailing them this very moment. Shelby was only partially blocked and would sense his thirst for revenge if he got close enough, but he could still strike with only minimal warning. Since Ty had three women hovering around him, all of whom would risk themselves to protect him, a surprise was the last thing he could afford.

But there was a third possibility, he suddenly realized. Shelby's range was thousands of miles, so he assumed she could reach Ned whenever she liked. The question was, Could she do so without risk? Could she plant an irresistible urge in his head to meet them at a time and place of Ty's choosing?

He wanted to ask her, but Fairchild was gazing at him expectantly, waiting for a reply. "That's an extremely generous offer," he finally answered. "May I give it some thought? Discuss the matter with my traveling companions and give you a response in the morning? I, uh, I could pay their extra expenses, but that wouldn't compensate them for the time they would lose. They're . . . extremely busy women."

"But not so busy that we can't spare two or three weeks," Shelby said. "Besides, the tour will be exciting. No girl in her right mind would pass up the chance to watch." *I'll get him for you, Ty. Just tell me when and where.* "And Mr. Stone . . . I was just thinking . . . Having a singer entertain during your forums would add a special something extra." She gave him a winsome smile. "Don't you agree?"

I said without risk, Shelby. Can you contact him without endangering yourself?

Yes, if I zing in a suggestion and get right out, but I can't guarantee he'll receive it. He blocked me after Front Royal and he could do it again, even if I throw stronger bursts at him and do it repeatedly. But even if I fail, we're no worse off than before. So what do you think?

That it's worth a try. "If you're the singer," Ty said, "then indubitably, Shelby."

* * *

Ned began to listen on the day after George died. He had gone to church that Sunday morning, but only because his mother had dragged him. A God who would allow his brother to perish while Reid still flourished wasn't the sort of deity he wanted to pray to.

He was sitting there wishing he were elsewhere when the minister began droning about repentance and sanctification. The words rang so hollow to Ned's ears that he wondered if the old man believed them. After all, he had lost a son and two grandsons to the war. It didn't make sense that his faith could have survived not only his own three tragedies, but also the terrible suffering of his entire flock. Maybe he was just preaching to pay the bills. And then Ned realized that he didn't have to wonder about the answers. If he wanted the truth, all he had to do was plumb the preacher's mind, just as he had George's.

His heart began to pound fiercely, and he slowly lowered his defenses. A vague sense of concern came back, and then, as he exposed himself further, a profound anxiety.

Wanting to learn more, he stole into the minister's mind. He didn't know how he did it, only that when he pictured himself reaching and examining, alien thoughts and emotions entered his brain. He discovered a goodness in the minister that made him regret his earlier doubts, but there was more. A passionate determination to save people. An anguish over their suffering. Ned had never imagined that this haggard and prosaic old man was such a fervent servant of God. He was stunned and ashamed.

The minister swayed and grabbed his lectern, and Ned quickly withdrew. He didn't really suppose that his violent burst of emotion could have caused the man's actions, but given the timing, he couldn't rule it out, either. To find out, he waited until the preacher resumed his sermon, then directed a torrent of bitterness and doubt into his mind. To his amazement, the old man flinched and stiffened.

Ned retreated again, but not before he felt the pain he had caused. It was astounding, to know he could affect a person with the power of his mind. It appeared he would have to keep his emotions under control when he listened. He grimaced. *If* he listened. Perhaps he should refrain, since they said eavesdroppers heard little good about themselves.

He wrestled with the problem all day. His talents unnerved him, but he was desperate to understand them. As curious as he was about people's true thoughts, he feared what they might reveal. But as matters turned out, he could no more stop himself from listening than from seeing, hearing, or smelling.

Day after day, as callers paraded through the house on Chester Street to pay their final respects, he explored his abilities and practiced their use. Most often, he eavesdropped without invading. Only when people truly interested him did he delve into their minds, actively and deeply probing them.

And that was how he learned that the former judge who was considered a model of rectitude had made a mistress of his wife's Negro half sister. That the neighboring farmer who held himself out as a perfect husband and father lusted after his fourteen year-old stepdaughter. That the wealthy widow who was the town's chief benefactress held "ordinary people" like the Beechams in contempt. That the prosperous shopkeeper's son whose accusations had gotten a Negro strung up for thieving had stolen the missing goods himself.

Ned was appalled. He considered himself a sophisticated man who understood that people weren't always what they seemed, but these were his friends and neighbors. He hated the idea that neither prominence, wealth, nor success was proof against moral depravity.

On the other hand, he thought, these were isolated transgressions. Most of the people he perused, while not perfect, were decent and reasonably honest. Yet in the end, far from comforting him, that very discovery—and the thoughts, emotions, and abilities that led to it—turned his whole world upside down. On the deepest, most fundamental level, people were all the same.

True, some were good, others evil. Some generous, others cheap. Some kind, others cruel. Some complicated, others simple. Some bright, others slow. Some ambitious, others lazy. The list went on and on.

The problem was, you couldn't look at a person and tell what he was. His station in life proved nothing about his character or even his talents. Neither did his politics. Or which side he had taken in the war, since walking around town, Ned had listened to some Yankee soldiers and found that they were just like everyone else. But as much as these findings amazed him, they were unremarkable compared to the most staggering discovery of all. Neither did the color of a man's skin.

Ned had been around slaves all his life. His family had owned them, and he had been taught to treat them well. As with women and horses, he hadn't disciplined them unless they misbehaved. In his relations with them, he had always been strict but scrupulously fair.

So whenever any freedmen arrived at the back of the house on Chester Street to pay their respects, he received them graciously. And since he was curious about what manner of minds the creatures had, he always listened.

He could hardly believe it at first. These beings he had considered little better than intelligent animals were no different from any of his friends. Still, he knew what he had heard, and what he heard was always true. When he probed a Negro's essence, no color came through.

In traits such as intelligence, potential, and ambition, black men had the same general range as white men. Which was the same range, God help them all, as white *women* had, and black women, too.

And if that was so—if no group of people was different or better than any other—then what did that say about how society should be organized? That blacks should mingle with whites? That females should have the same rights as males?

Ned couldn't credit such outrageous notions—but he couldn't completely dismiss them, either.

Chapter 24

When the minister laid George to rest, he said it was one of the saddest days of his life—first George Sr., then Margaret, then George Jr.—and Ned could sense how deeply he meant it. His eulogy was about faith and salvation, and while the words were dull, the sentiments shone. Maybe God had a purpose after all, Ned decided, but even so, crimes had been committed and the perpetrator would pay the price.

He and his mother departed the next morning, stopping at the church on their way out of town so Caroline could say a final farewell. Ned never listened to her thoughts—the notion seemed indecent—but as he followed her to the spot where two of her children lay buried side by side, her anguish was so piercing that he couldn't help overhearing.

He felt a stab of remorse. His outburst Friday night had made her realize that George had gone to Washington to kill Reid and had fallen by Reid's hand, not as a result of random violence. She blamed herself for not guessing, for not stopping him. The only saving grace was that she thought Reid was dead. Ned had spared her the knowledge that the bastard had had the effrontery to show his damned face at the hospital.

He had spared her any talk about his plans, too, because she would have fretted about his safety. But as soon as he had attended to the farm, he meant to travel to Washington City, where Reid had lived and worked. Someone—a friend, a colleague, a superior—would know where Reid had gone. Then he could track the villain down, and the beauty part was, he wouldn't have to ask a single question. He could simply listen. There was no danger in *that*.

Caroline knelt to pray, and Ned did the same. Then, hearing her quiet sobs, he said in a low, earnest tone, "It's not your fault, Mother. Peggy wanted to serve her country. She was a strong-willed girl. You couldn't have made her come home, or even stopped her from spying. And George . . ."

Caroline's thoughts broke through, and Ned's voice trailed off. He hadn't meant to listen, but he found it impossible not to when he was focused on someone so emotive.

His mother's guilt, he realized, had nothing to do with Peggy's choices, only her own. Reid had never forced Peggy, not once, only responded the way any man would when a fiery woman teases him unmercifully, asking to be seduced. She had bedded him because she had wanted the pleasure he could give her, not just as a means to her spying. All along, he'd been willing to marry her, without even knowing about the baby. Caroline wished she had forced Peggy to agree. But Peggy hadn't loved him, hadn't wanted another Yankee husband, and hadn't wanted his brat. So Caroline had conspired in Peggy's lies and aborted the child. And now, because of her sins, both her daughter and her son were dead.

It was all Ned could do to keep his shock under control. Peggy had sworn to what she had said. Caroline had backed her up. How could their words have been lies? But they must have been, because he had heard Caroline's thoughts, and thoughts were the naked truth.

He struggled to his feet, wanting to question her, to demand more details, to rage at her for protecting her daughter in death at the risk of her sons in life. But that would have involved admitting to the talents he possessed, and he wasn't about to do that to anyone, not even to his mother.

And then, in a blinding revelation, he realized that he didn't hear the truth in people's minds, not beyond a doubt. He heard only what they *believed* to be the truth. Caroline's extreme grief might have caused her mind to fabricate this monstrous account because the alternative was even worse: to live with the knowledge that the daughter she loved had been raped and abused, over and over.

She looked at him, her face wet with tears, and held out her hand. He helped her to her feet, saying nothing, feeling as if someone had reached into his chest and squeezed his heart. He needed to discover the truth, but whatever it was, he wouldn't learn it from this bereaved and guilty woman.

She kissed his cheek. "At least I still have you, Neddy. Thank God. I love you so."

Words like that made him want to stay in Front Royal to shield her from the world, but George's last thoughts were etched into his soul: "Revenge me." The truth was well and good, he told himself, but ultimately irrelevant. He couldn't have held up his head and called himself a man if he had turned his back on the promise he had given his brother.

He took Caroline by the arm and led her out of the graveyard. "Yes, Mama. You still have me, and you always will. As I wrote George, unlike most in this area, I have money to invest. I'm going to make the farm thrive again."

"Then you'll run it yourself? You'll be staying in Virginia?"

"Yes, Mother." It was a good base for an ambitious man, a position as a prosperous and respected planter. His mother smiled, and he helped her into the carriage. She was calm and happy now. Sooner or later, he would have to tell her about his trip, and now was as good a time as any.

He climbed in after her and started down the street, then said matter-of-factly, "But first, I have some business to take care of in Atchison. But don't worry. I'll be very careful, and I won't be gone long."

"Atchison?" she murmured. "What's in Atchison, Ned?"

He glanced at her. "Excuse me, Mother?"

"I asked you what was in Atchison. Why you're going there. Did you ship something by wagon from Denver?"

She was right, he realized. He *had* said Atchison. He couldn't imagine why. "No. My mind must have wandered back to my trip here on the stage. I'm going to Washington City, not Atchison. With George gone—now that I own the farm in addition to my investments out West—I'm wealthier than Andy Johnson wants me to be. I'll have to seek a presidential pardon." Which wasn't the reason he was going, but he could take care of the matter while he was there.

Caroline knew that pardons for wealthy Rebels had to be applied for in person. She believed him and didn't object. They arrived at the farm in time for lunch, after which he reviewed George's records with the new foreman and inspected the damage to the buildings and fields.

He spent the next four days at home, and had never felt so restless in his life. He was itching to leave—for some damned reason, he kept thinking about Atchison, wanting to go there—but he forced himself to stay, drafting a detailed list of repairs and hiring the hands to carry them out. Finally, on Monday, he set out for Washington, arriving at Reid's old stamping ground, the Willard Hotel, late the next afternoon.

The clerk claimed that the only vacancies were four flights up, but Ned didn't believe him. If you were important enough, you always got something lower. Figuring he had nothing to lose, he entered the man's mind and delicately cajoled him. Within moments, a room on the second floor had miraculously materialized.

Ned had never expected it to work, not really. To learn he could affect people's actions . . . Plant ideas in their heads . . . It was incredible. Unconsciously, had he been doing this all his life? Was that why he always got his way?

A little dazed, he purchased a copy of the *National Intelligencer* and went upstairs to read it. On the front page, along with stories about the trial of Lincoln's alleged assassins, the last skirmishes of the war, and the problems in the occupied South, there was an article about a lecture in Cleveland. The speaker—and the splendid singer who had provided a musical interlude during the evening—evidently had that whole city talking. Tyson Stone and Shelby March.

The second name brought him up short. The singer at the hospital had been named "Miss March," and she had been *better* than splendid. Could it be the same girl? And if it was, who was Tyson Stone?

He continued to read. Stone was a journalist who had written an article about the future of the country that had been published in this very paper and reprinted just about everywhere. Ned hadn't seen it, probably because he'd been busy with his family. It had made quite a splash, it seemed, so he resolved to get hold of a copy. The story went on to say that Stone was headed to California and planned to lecture at many of the cities along the way.

The blood drained from Ned's face. The girl in Ohio—her name had been Susannah Stone. Could Reid really be Stone? Not Susannah's half brother, but her full one?

It all fit, Ned thought. The *Intelligencer* was a Washington daily. The article had appeared on May 30. Stone had evidently been here in the days before, talking to Union soldiers. So, in all likelihood, had Reid, who had faked his own death that same week.

Reid was going to California. So was Stone, on the Overland Stage out of Atchison, according to the story. Atchison, which he couldn't get out of his mind.

The conclusion was inescapable. Reid was indeed Stone. His mind was like Ned's, but stronger, because it could call to him from far-off Cleveland. He was trying to lure Ned to a final showdown, and Atchison was an excellent choice. On the frontier, unlike Virginia, it was easy to kill a man and get away with it.

Fear slashed through Ned at the power Stone wielded, but he was no coward. If his enemy wanted a contest in Atchison, he would go. But if Stone prevailed, he told himself, it would be by taking his life, not by destroying his mind. For the first time in over a week, he shut out the world.

Sarah made her choice in Chicago. She would return to the future with Shelby. As wrenching as it was to think about leaving Ty, once she got her emotions under control and looked at the situation logically, the decision was surprisingly easy.

Ty, after all, was an adult. He'd lived through many different hells, and he had always survived. And if this latest hell—learning about Peggy, loving and losing Sarah—was especially painful, she'd heard him lecture and she had watched him bloom. From Winchester to

Oberlin to Cleveland, his confidence had grown and his sense of purpose had increased. Then, in Toledo, he'd decided to talk about his past, hoping to connect with his audience in a more personal way, and found the experiment as cathartic as it was successful. His achievements pleased him, and so did his life, quite apart from any role Sarah might play in it.

Equally important, his fears about Sukey had been eased. She was sharing a room with Shelby during their travels, and after hours of conversation about the laws and mores of 2102 and some pointed demonstrations of Shelby's powers, she had come to see that Ned might as well have jumped her and pinned her as slickly seduced her. Whether physical or mental, coercion was coercion. While there was still a deep wariness in Sukey, a distrust of both men and herself, time and love would almost certainly heal her.

But if Ty was beginning to thrive, and Sukey was finally mending, Shelby was rapidly wilting. Unlike Ty, she was only a child, and an increasingly anxious, unhappy, and guilty one. Unlike Ty, the work she wanted to do wasn't the work society expected of her. And unlike Ty, she had no family at all. As wonderful as Sarah's friends were, they weren't blood. They weren't her mother. Sarah was all she had, the only one who loved her unconditionally, the only one she could count on to stand by her side and help her fight for the life she wanted.

So for Sarah, the bottom line was that her daughter needed her much more than her lover did, so she would return to the future with Shelby. And if she'd decided to take a small part of Ty back with her, she didn't say so. There was no point causing pain, no point inviting arguments.

He accepted her decision with a somber sort of grace, admitting that he doubted he could have lived with himself if he had taken her from her daughter. He would make the most of the time they had left, he said, and try to be grateful for it.

Deep in his heart, of course, he hoped Shelby would change her mind about staying, but Shelby already knew that. As a telepath, she felt what he felt and she saw what he saw. That she had a deep affection for him. That she wanted her mother to be happy. That Sukey was becoming a dear friend. That in 1865, nobody would tell her she couldn't be a singer. Quite the reverse, in fact.

But Shelby missed her favorite foods, clothes, programs, and music. She missed gossiping with her friends even more, and surfing on the net. Eighteen sixty-five meant appalling discrimination, perpetual discomfort, and incredible ignorance. She wanted to go home. And nothing that anyone said could stop her from feeling guilty and depressed about it.

Three days later, in St. Louis, she started to change the people she sang to, not unconsciously, but deliberately. Missouri, a slave state that had remained in the Union, had endured bitter guerilla fighting during the war. Ty's audience included people who'd been indifferent or even hostile to the North, but at least they'd been interested enough to show up. He spoke of his background, of the need for equality and tolerance, and of the nation's possible futures, and opened some eyes and hearts.

Shelby took it a step further. She sang with an intensity that blanketed her listeners' minds. They couldn't help but absorb her views. Without consciously knowing it, they grew less afraid. More open. Less bigoted. More rational. They were more reflective during the question-and-answer session that followed. More optimistic.

If Ty or Sarah noticed anything different, they didn't comment, and Shelby didn't tell them. In 2102, it was illegal to adjust someone without a court order or a signed consent. But then, she hadn't really adjusted them, only improved them a little, maybe by twenty percent. She wondered what would happen if she could sing to the whole country. Nudge them in the direction she wanted.

The notion was so intriguing that she repeated the experiment in Quincy and St. Joseph, perfectly well aware that she was looking for a larger purpose, an incentive to want to stay. Her mom had gone totally off the deep end with this baby stuff, but there was no sense mentioning something she didn't want to confront, or even urging her to stay with Ty, because it wouldn't have done any good. Sarah felt lousy about missing the last five years of Shelby's life. She wasn't going to miss any more of it.

Only one thing came easy to Shelby that week, her assignment to contact Ned. In Oberlin and Cleveland, she'd reached for him repeatedly, urging him to come to Atchison. By Toledo, she'd begun to listen, to see if it was doing any good. Given her earlier failures, she hadn't really expected to hear him, but she had. Every time she nagged him, confusion and agitation followed. Still, he was weak and far away. He couldn't harm them, either mentally or physically.

Then, on their first day in St. Louis, the emotions had disappeared, but Shelby suspected their absence was a sign of success. Looking back on it, she believed that whether she heard Ned or not was up to him, not her—that it depended on whether he was blocking her, not on whether her erratic ability to listen was functioning well. If that was so, then Ned must have unblocked himself for some reason, allowing her to pick him up, then realized what she was doing and shut her back out. She assumed he was on his way west now, since he wanted Ty as badly as Ty wanted him.

Each day, hoping to pinpoint his location, she

dropped her defenses lower and listened more aggressively, but to no avail. The guy was incredibly good for someone who was self-trained, she had to give him that. Still, none of them worried about the silence until Atchison.

Ty had chosen the town because frontier justice still prevailed there. Nobody had ever been convicted of murder for killing someone in the course of a fight. To make sure of the verdict he wanted, he would take the first bullet, or rather, the shield provided by his cameo would.

Sarah wasn't crazy about how he planned to accomplish that, but she had to admit to its logic. A barrage from Ned's revolver would have caused bullets to bounce every which way, which would have been as dangerous as it was mysterious. Because of that, Ty intended to roam around town looking for Ned and making himself visible. Ned couldn't shoot at him in cold blood, because if he did, he would be spotted and arrested, so he would have to provoke Ty before he fired.

Atchison, after all, was a madhouse. The annual westward migration was under way, and, day and night, the streets bustled with people, livestock, and vehicles. Shelby was amazed by how much merchandise was shipped across the country in 1865, mostly mining, military, and agricultural equipment, and food and other consumer goods. It came in by railroad and steam-driven ferry, and left on long wagon trains pulled by mules or oxen. And in the meantime, it all had to be kept somewhere, so that the only things Atchison seemed to have more of than warehouses and storage lots were saloons and gambling parlors.

And a saloon or a gambling den, Ty figured, was where Ned would pick a fight. That was the usual venue for such matters. It would be easy after that—everyone ducking for cover while insults filled the air, an exchange of shots, and a quick decision by the witnesses that the killing was in self-defense.

But if Ned was in town, Ty couldn't find him, and he wandered the streets and fleshpots for a day and a half, asking if anyone had seen him. Shelby repeatedly tried to hear him, reaching out hard, probing with her mind, and picked up exactly nothing.

Finally, since any information was better than none, she unblocked completely for the first time in weeks and sought out Caroline Beecham. As always, sending was easier than receiving, so she asked about Ned at the top of her voice, trying to evoke the strongest response she could. The poor woman panicked even worse than the first time, filling Shelby's mind with terror. It took every ounce of her skill, but she finally pulled out the information she needed. Ned had gone to Washington, then to New York, or so he'd said. He might have lied, of course, but at least they knew he wasn't at the farm.

Ty's lecture was scheduled for Monday at eight. Sarah grew more and more anxious as the hour approached, until, at seven-thirty, she literally begged him and Shelby not to go. She was sure something awful was about to happen, even though both would be wearing cameos. But they didn't want to disappoint the audience, and she couldn't deny that they would be as safe on the stage in Pioneer Hall as in Ty's room at the Massasoit House hotel. She finally gave in.

As for her and Sukey, Ned had arranged for their deaths in the previous version of history and would likely try it again. When Caleb Washburne stopped by Ty's room to walk the group over to the lecture as he always did, and asked why Sarah and Sukey weren't coming, Sarah blamed it on severe indigestion and wished she had another cameo. It was the hardest thing she'd ever done—watching Ty and Shelby walk out the door. Afterward, she sat beside Sukey on the bed, behind the security of a quantum shield, and trembled.

The hall was only two blocks from the hotel, and already two-thirds full when Ty and his party arrived. Ty turned on his cameo and climbed onto the stage while Washburne and Shelby sat down in front, in seats expressly reserved for them. Scanning the audience, Ty saw no sign of Ned. He was beginning to think the bastard had gotten himself killed, which would have been a boon to all humanity.

The lecture went well. Atchison was booming, and the citizens were filled with such confidence and ambition that Ty felt a little sorry for them. Sarah had mentioned they would lose the transcontinental railroad to Omaha, about 150 miles to the north. When the trains began running in four years, Atchison's place as the chief transshipment point between East and West would be lost.

As always between the lecture and the question periods, Shelby came up to sing. Washburne kept referring to her as the Magnificent Miss March in his articles, and the name had caught on. A stir of excitement rippled through the hall when she reached the stage. Her reputation had obviously preceded her.

Ty smiled at her as he set a chair in front of the lectern. *A less generous man might be jealous, my dear. Have you heard anything from Ned?*

Not a whisper. Maybe we should work out a signal. She grinned back. *If I hear him, I'll sing a song called "God Bless America." This crowd could use a little more patriotism.*

Ty assumed it was another of her tunes from the future. *This is no time for pranks,* he thought sternly. *If you hear anything, you're to throw up a block and stop. Say you're ill. We'll leave.*

She sat down in the chair. *Yes, Colonel Stone.*

Is your cameo on?

Yes, Colonel Stone.

Good. I mean it, Shelby. You're not to take chances. Ty gave mental growl to underscore the order, then left the girl to perform.

Shelby was halfway through her third number when a voice intruded. Ned's voice. And what it said was, *Please—whichever one you are—don't hurt me.*

Chapter 25

Ned was hiding in a warehouse in the north end of Atchison, trying not to shake. He had arrived in town over an hour before, even before Stone's lecture had begun. He had known from an article in the St. Joseph paper just where and when it would take place, but he hadn't been able to bring himself to attend. He had read too much . . . thought too much . . . heard too much with his mind. And if everything he had learned was true, then he feared for his immortal soul.

According to an account in the *Chicago Tribune*, Reid—or Stone—had fought for the North until Chancellorsville, then reluctantly accepted an assignment as a Yankee spy. Having been a soldier himself for over two years, Ned had come to respect the men on the other side. When Stone spoke about justice and equality, he did so from a background that compelled a fellow to listen to his words and consider his arguments. The more Ned did so, the more he suspected that Stone's statements conformed exactly to the shocking reality he had sensed in people's minds.

He thought of Stone's sister, and grew physically ill. Suppose he had corrupted the girl with his mind? Induced her to engage in the very behavior he had later disdained her for? And why had he involved her in the first place? What had made him think he had the right? She'd had no role in Peggy's death, and neither, from what he had sensed, had Stone. Both Peggy and his mother must have lied.

In retrospect, he didn't understand why Stone hadn't challenged him in Front Royal. He'd certainly had sufficient cause, along with a sterling enough reputation to survive any subsequent inquest, so why had he come there only to leave? Why had he preferred a showdown in the wilds of Kansas?

And who had summoned Ned to arrange it? The more Ned thought and remembered, the more certain he was that it wasn't Stone, but the singer, Shelby March.

After all, Stone hadn't dominated Peggy, not really, or even juggled both sides during the war. And at the hospital in Front Royal . . . Ned recalled lashing out against the tingling, then collapsing, and the singer had evidently done the same. Struck back hard at him, then fainted. Each of them must have attacked the other, with the result an exhausted draw.

But even if he had matched her on that one occasion, he was still fearful. From Chicago to St. Joseph, he had tried hearing the people he knew in Front Royal, with no success. Yet the singer had reached him from equally far away with no difficulty at all. She was stronger than he was.

Perhaps he could block her enough to be safe, or expel her whenever she entered, but he no longer wished to do so. It was deeply lonely, to be the way he was. So far as he knew, she was the only one like him in the world. He wanted to understand her mind, to ask her what he was.

So he had remained in this warehouse for almost an hour, afraid he would be challenged if he showed his face at the lecture but no longer wanting to kill or even to fight, longing to reach for the girl with his mind but afraid that the consequence might be madness or even death.

Finally, though, his yearning defeated his fears. He marshaled his courage, dropped his defenses completely, and hesitantly reached out. *Please—whichever one you are—don't hurt me. I didn't understand what I was, or that people are all the same, but I've been listening to everyone and everything, and it's changed me.*

A commanding voice came back at him. *I'm Shelby, the singer. Don't think at me, Ned. Just keep your mind open. I want to examine it for myself. I swear to God, if you come anywhere near me—*

I won't. I promise. Just do what you have to do.

He felt an incredibly delicate tingling. If he hadn't been focused intently on his own mind, he never would have known she was listening. He shuddered with a mixture of hope and dread, feeling that his whole future, and perhaps his very existence, depended on whether or not this girl approved of him.

Ten blocks away, Shelby was carefully probing. Ned was allowing her total access, so analyzing his mind was as easy as reading a map. What she sensed left her amazed and awed. She'd never felt such changes in her life.

The bitterness, the narrowness, the arrogance, the suspicion . . . They were gone now, and more than anything, he was frightened and confused. True, he had listened widely, but he hadn't totally assimilated what he'd heard. Nobody, not even a telepath, could reverse his deepest beliefs in only two weeks. He was shaken by his own nature, bewildered that the world was so radically different from what he'd supposed, and terrified he'd committed sins that would see him burn in the fires of hell forever.

You're right. You've changed. Her tone was gentle and reassuring. *But you don't have to be afraid, Ned.*

I want you to listen to my mind, and you'll hear the truth about what we are and what we can do. But go slowly, and be very careful. You could hurt me otherwise. Do you understand?

She felt his relief and gratitude. Communion with her fellow telepaths had a special intensity. She'd missed it, she realized.

Yes, he thought. *I swear you can trust me.*

She relaxed and let him in, wincing when he began to examine her. She was extremely sensitive to other telepaths, and Ned lacked the finesse that came with formal training. As he probed her, she absently listened back, and picked up mounting astonishment, humility, and excitement. His emotions grew so intense that she started to echo them, and they stole their way into her singing. She finally had to caution him to extract what he wanted more gradually, and to use the lightest touch he possibly could.

Back at the warehouse, Ned blinked in confusion, then shook his head to clear it. *I'm sorry,* he thought contritely. *Your mind—it's so extraordinary, I got carried away just from listening. But I'll be more careful from now on, I promise.*

He began to listen again, forcing himself to exercise more restraint, to maintain greater control. Shelby March—Maravich—had the most organized mind, the most generous mind, the most artistic and vibrant mind, he had ever sensed. Probing her was like making love to a goddess. And the knowledge she possessed . . . ! The secrets of heaven and earth were stored in her brain. He wanted to suck them all out, to learn what she knew, to understand on the deepest level what the true nature of humanity really was.

As if from a distance, he heard her tell him to stop and get out—that he was seeing more than she wished, and doing it far too quickly. He tried to break the contact, but he might as well have attempted to pull out of the most seductive woman on earth within a thrust or two of his climax. Her mind was too fascinating. Too brilliant. Too compelling. Total perfection. He couldn't let go.

In the lecture hall, Shelby stopped singing. Ned was too insistent, too needful. He was learning things he wasn't supposed to know, like who she was and where she was from. She kept telling him to stop and leave, but he wouldn't. Couldn't.

She swayed. He had the most enormous potential she'd ever encountered, and she didn't want to hurt him. She begged him to get out, but it was no use. In the end, she had no choice but to force him.

It took an enormous mental effort, but she found and used the smallest level of power possible, expelling him without damaging him in any way. Her guitar slipped from her hands, then crashed to the floor. She felt herself going under, and called out to Ty. *Help me . . . I'm in trouble . . .*

But Ty was already on his feet, leaping onto the stage. Watching Shelby, he had sensed something different about her singing, even before she had stopped and swayed. She touched her cameo to turn it off, then thought weakly, *Ned . . . Don't . . . harm him.* She appeared to be teetering at the edge of oblivion. *He's different . . . now.*

She slumped over just as he reached her. He screamed into her mind as he lifted her up—*Shelby! Are you all right?*—but nothing came back.

He quickly examined her. This wasn't like the last time, at the hospital, when she'd been unconscious for only a few seconds. She showed no signs of rousing. Her skin was cold and clammy, her breathing was shallow and erratic, and her face was an ashy white. God only knew what the bastard had done to her. Ty was terrified she was going to die.

As the audience buzzed with shock and concern,

Caleb Washburne jumped onto the stage and asked if he could help. But if Ned had attacked Shelby's mind, there was no medicine they could give her to bring her back, no operation they could perform to revive her. Not in Sarah's strongbox, and not in Atchison in 1865.

And that told Ty what he had to do. "Listen to me very carefully," he said to Caleb. "I want you to go over to the telegraph office. Dictate your story to the operator. I don't care if you have to hold a pistol to the man's head—have him wire it to the *Herald* at once, to be run in tomorrow's paper. Say that Shelby collapsed. Say it was a fever of the brain. Put in exactly when it happened, and note that it was Atchison time. Say that I carried her to my room at the Massasoit House hotel to recuperate. Do you understand all that?"

Washburne nodded. "Yes, if that's what you want, but shouldn't a doctor—"

"No. Do exactly as I've said, Caleb, and now. Insist that they print precisely what you send, word for word. I can't explain why, but Shelby's life depends on it."

Washburne agreed, and the two men hurried out of the hall through a side entrance. Holding Shelby close against his chest, Ty raced down Main Street to the hotel and bolted up the stairs to the second floor. He called out to Sarah as he ran down the corridor toward his room, yelling for her to open the door.

The stricken look on her face as he dashed into the room made him burn with guilt, even though Ned could have attacked Shelby just the same had they remained at the hotel. "It was Ned," he said as he laid her on the bed. She was warmer now, he realized, and her color was noticeably better. "He contacted her while she was singing. I thought she sounded distracted, but I wasn't sure. It all happened so fast. The next thing I knew, she swayed and dropped her guitar, then called to me for help. I reached her just as she passed out.

She was pale. Clammy. Cold. But she appears to have rallied since then, thank God.''

Sarah sat by Shelby's side and cupped her face. The physical improvement was a good sign, but still, she looked fragile and vulnerable. Sarah was shivering with anxiety by now, but her mind remained calm and focused. She couldn't afford to panic. First and foremost, she had to ascertain Shelby's condition. Then she would know how to proceed.

Her eyes were brimming with tears when she looked back at Ty. Their time together might be very short. Shelby was in a telepathic shutdown—a protective block that provided protection against a violent mental attack. It would be safest if she emerged on her own, but if she didn't within twelve hours, a Class A telepath would have to pull her out. And even then, the process could damage her psychic talents.

''I told Caleb to wire in his story,'' Ty said. ''I told him what details to include. What happened to Shelby, what the exact time here was, where I took her to recover . . .''

Sarah felt as if the whole world had been yanked out from under her. They could have waited until morning. Waited and hoped and said their good-byes. But by now, the story would be on its way. ''When they run it . . . Do you realize what you've done?''

''Of course I do. There was no other choice. She needed help we couldn't give her. How long . . . ?''

Sarah got to her feet, crying openly now, and put her arms around his waist. They could tell Caleb to withdraw the story, but if he did, and if Shelby didn't emerge, he would only have to send it all over again. He would ask questions she wasn't supposed to answer. She considered Shelby's odds, her own obligations as a tempronaut, and the fact that she was going to leave in the end anyway, and knew that the only ethical choice was to do nothing.

"I don't know," she said. "Very soon. They would have allowed a few minutes for you to get her here, so that as few people as possible would see us vanish." She gave him a fierce hug. "Good-bye. I love you. If I could come back to you someday—"

She was interrupted by a blackness darker than night. She clung to Ty frantically, wanting to memorize the feel of him holding her. Yet when the light reappeared, she was still in his arms. She jerked around. There was nothing on the bed but the clothes she had bought Shelby in Washington. Shelby herself was gone, and so were the personal possessions she'd left scattered around Ty's room.

Sarah and Ty simply stared at each other, too stunned to speak. It was Sukey who finally got out the question on everyone's minds. "But—but why didn't they take you, too, Sarah?"

Sarah didn't know. Only one possibility even occurred to her. "Even with two jump chambers, they can't reverse two different jumps from the exact same time in the future. There's only one technical team, so now that they've performed the first retrieval, they'll need to run through their countdown before they can perform the second. That will take them at least an hour."

Ty looked puzzled. "But what time it is in the future has nothing to do with what point they take you from in the past."

"That's true, but with a shutdown like Shelby's, intervention isn't always necessary. It's possible she came out of it almost immediately, and if she did . . . You know how guilty she felt about taking me away from you. She might have told them to leave me in the past."

"And she's a telepath," Sukey murmured. "She has a talent for getting her way."

"Yes." But Shelby's wishes in the matter weren't the deciding factor, Sarah thought. The choice was still hers. If she wanted to go back, all she had to do was run a message in the *Intelligencer*. That was still the paper of choice for her mission, and not even Shelby's telepathic pushing would stop the Wellsians from remembering that and displaying their usual thoroughness. They would look for instructions from her for at least another few months.

Ty knew it, too. She could see it in his face. He put his arm around her, then said quietly, "You'll do what you feel is right, Sarah. I understand that. But I've been thinking . . . If you leave, and if the time comes that Shelby doesn't still need you . . . I don't care how old you are—forty, fifty, sixty—I want you to return to me in 1865."

She shook her head. There was no point giving him hope where none existed. "A jump is so expensive . . . They won't pay for it, Ty. Not just to reunite us."

He gave her a pained smile. "Then I suppose I'll have to wreak havoc with history again"—his voice cracked a little—"if that's the only way to force them to—"

A wave of agonizing remorse and anxiety crashed into him, and he gasped and stiffened. Sarah staggered slightly, then clutched his arm for support. Sukey dropped numbly into a chair, then said dazedly, "Those emotions . . . Where did they come—"

She was interrupted by a violent pounding on the door. It was slightly ajar, Sarah noticed. Someone had opened it, then been stopped by the quantum shield. He began to scream at them. Ned Beecham.

"I'm sorry. I didn't mean to. You have to let me in." He was panting with exertion and hysteria. "I ran here as fast as I could. I couldn't reach her from the warehouse, but maybe if I was sitting right next to her, actually touching her . . ."

Sarah wanted to strangle the man with her bare

hands. "You filthy bastard . . . After what you did to her, how in hell do you have the gall—"

I swear to you, Dr. Maravich, I didn't mean to. Ned's guilt was so excruciating that Sarah grimaced. *But your daughter . . . Her mind was so perfect, so beautiful, and she was letting me listen, and I knew I should stop but I couldn't. She had to make me go. Knock me unconscious. I'm sorry. Please, just let me try to help her. I reached my brother before he died, and he wasn't even like Shelby and me, so maybe I can bring her back.*

Ty gave Sarah a gentle shake. "Sarah? Is he talking to you? What is he saying?"

She summarized Ned's words in a stunned mumble, then grasped their implication. "He—he called me by my real name. He knows I'm Shelby's mother. And he sounded so different. Like he'd changed. Like he cared. Do you think—could it be possible?"

Ty didn't know. Too many things had happened tonight. Too much horror. Pain. Fear. He felt drained and raw. "Maybe. That was—it was what Shelby thought before she fainted. That Ned was different. I think—she obviously examined him at some length. She asked me not to harm him."

Then Ned spoke again, and he sounded bereft. "Shelby is gone? But how can that be? Where did you take her?"

He'd listened to their minds, Sarah realized, and he'd learned what had just happened. She struggled to come up with an explanation, but Ned was two steps ahead of her. "Is she home, then? Back in the future? Will they be able to help her there?"

Ty and Sarah gazed at each other for several seconds, then reached the same conclusion. "He wasn't surprised," Sarah said. "He must have learned all that from Shelby's mind, not from ours. We have to let him in. He knows too much. We have to deal with it."

"Yes, but God only knows how." Ty reached into

Sarah's carpetbag for her pistol, then walked to the quantum cube on the floor and moved it back about four feet.

After a moment, Ned opened the door, closed it behind him, and slowly walked forward—smack into the shield. He rubbed his nose, looking more bewildered than hurt. "This invisible barrier . . . It's astonishing. How does it work?"

"We'll get to that later." Ty aimed the pistol at him. "Right now, I want you back against the wall. Put your hands in the air, straight up. And then don't move."

Ned did as he was told, watching Ty through anguished eyes. "I'm truly sorry, Stone. I was wrong. Wrong about everything. The ideas in your lectures . . . I've listened to people—listened to Shelby—and I know they're the truth. You have to believe that."

He wasn't afraid, Ty realized. He knew he wasn't in danger. "Fine. I'm thrilled you've seen the light. Now shut your damned mouth and stop your damned eavesdropping. It's rude."

But Ned's attention was suddenly elsewhere. He was staring at Sukey with aching regret, and Sukey was staring back with a mixture of revulsion and anger. Still aiming the pistol at Ned, Ty crouched to turn off the field.

"Susannah . . ." Ned whispered. "I swear to God, I didn't understand—"

"You tried to rape me, you son of a bitch. What is there to understand?" She threw herself out of her chair, hands on hips, glaring at him. "You wanted to kill my brother. I'd like to thrash you senseless, then leave you to die by inches."

Ty fired the pistol, and yellow light filled the room. Ned crumpled to the ground, his muscles useless now, his body close to paralyzed. Ty tossed the pistol to Sarah, fetched a pair of handcuffs, and pulled Ned's wrists behind his back to lock them together. He was none too gentle about it, nor was he gentle about the way he hauled Ned up and dumped him on the bed.

Ned neither objected nor panicked. Clearly, he had picked up Ty's memories about the effects of the yellow light. Still fixated on Sukey, he said in a labored rasp, "Please, Susannah . . . I didn't know . . . I was forcing you. And then . . . I believed . . . whatever I wanted . . . I should have. I was insane . . . I think. Warped. Until I began . . . to listen."

She took a step forward. "I liked you. Trusted you. I had nothing to do with your stupid vendetta against my brother. How could you have hurt me that way after all the time we spent together? After the way we talked?"

"I don't . . . know. I was someone . . . different. Blind . . . and deluded. But that other . . . man—"

"You weren't someone different at all," Sukey snapped, and strode to the bed. "No matter what you call yourself, you're the exact same person, and you're responsible for what you did. I don't care if you've changed into a bloody saint—you have to pay."

Sukey curled her hand into a fist and raised it, and Ty made no attempt to stop her. Personally, he wanted to beat the man to a pulp, then tar and feather him, but he would do neither. Shelby had said not to harm him, and she'd known what was in his mind and heart. Obviously she had wanted him spared. She had believed he could be redeemed.

Sukey punched him as hard as she could, right in the nose, and his blood began to flow. Hitting him evidently hurt her as much as it hurt him, because she winced and shook her hand. Still, a little of the fury seemed to leave her.

Sarah set down her pistol, pulled a handkerchief out of her carpetbag, and calmly walked to the bed. Holding it to Ned's nose, she said crisply, "You should be grateful you're in 1865 and not 2102, Mr. Beecham. If

Shelby had decided to hit you, she would have pulled your legs apart and slammed her foot into your testicles.''

Sukey's eyes narrowed. ''Now *there's* an idea . . .''

Ned paled. ''Susannah, please . . .''

But she was already yanking at his legs, first one, then the other, pulling them into a wide *V*. She stared at his crotch, then scowled at him. ''Why are you filling my mind with your damned remorse, Ned Beecham? You can make me not want to kick you, so why don't you just do it?''

''Because . . . I don't want . . . to control people. I don't want . . . to hurt anyone . . . ever again. I just want . . . to go back . . . to my farm.'' His eyes drifted closed. ''I can't seem . . . to stay awake.''

Within seconds, Ned was fast asleep. Ty assumed it was a combination of the effects of the pistol and the exertion of exploring Shelby's mind. He was about to ask Sarah how long Ned would be out when the room was once again thrown into pitch blackness.

Five seconds later, when the light returned, every vestige of Sarah Maravich—her baggage, her devices, the woman herself—had vanished from sight.

Chapter 26

Calistoga, California
September 18, 1865

Ty laughed, and Sukey realized that it was the first time in three months that she had heard the sound. The two had been traveling all that time, first across the country, then within California, as if constant movement would make Ty forget. But it hadn't, of course.

Finally, he had agreed to stop in San Francisco to call on some old friends, Comstock mogul Thomas Wyatt and Chinese businessman Shen Wai and his family. To the Stones' delight, they had found Thomas's daughter and her husband, Melanie and Alex McClure, at the Wyatt mansion on Hawthorne Street. They were visiting from Hong Kong with their children, Wyatt Tyson, three this past June, and Elizabeth May, who had been born in March, and were enjoying the postwar social whirl while showing off their progeny to the city. Ty's arrival made a wonderful visit perfect.

Thomas, having doted on his grandchildren for two solid weeks, had announced he had business to attend to, then shooed away his guests to his vacation retreat in Calistoga. This "business," he had admitted, included a visit from the woman he loved, a spirited widow from Virginia City. She was recalcitrant enough about giving him her hand, he'd said, without his having to cope with a houseful of people running about, interfering with his courting.

The company arrived in Calistoga on Monday afternoon. The resort had been built by entrepreneur Sam Brannan and opened in 1862. It included a large hotel, twenty-five cottages, a racetrack and stables, a pavilion for dancing and skating, and of course, luxurious facilities for bathing in the medicinal hot springs.

As soon as they had settled themselves in Thomas's cottage, they changed into their costumes for swimming. Only Ty demurred, saying he wanted to write. He had taken copious notes during their travels in California and hoped to turn them into a book about the state.

Nobody pressed him to go along. Melanie and Alex knew he had fallen deeply in love, that a problem had arisen concerning the woman's daughter, and that the affair had recently ended. They knew he was trying to pull his life back together, and that Sukey had taken a leave from school in order to look after him. He would confide the rest if and when he was ready. As for Sukey, she was pleased to see him take an interest in his work. He hadn't delivered a single lecture or written a single word since Atchison.

When they returned several hours later, he was sitting at the table on the veranda, writing letters. Sukey had hoped to find him working on his book, but told herself any writing was better than none at all. Two of the letters were finished and sealed, one to Secretary Stanton, the other to the Reverend Fairchild. The return address read simply, "Comstock Cottage, Calistoga, California." Ty thought he would settle in San Francisco eventually, but he wasn't yet ready to be in one place for any length of time.

He finished the final letter, to Joseph Gales of the *Intelligencer*, then joined the group in a stroll around town, leaving the mail at the Hot Springs Hotel to be posted. They purchased a picnic dinner there, eating it in the park across from their cottage. Finally, after the children had been put to bed, the adults retired to the parlor to talk.

Seeing how somber Ty was, the McClures set out to amuse him, plying him with wine and telling exaggerated stories about their exploits as detectives in Hong Kong. His spirits did lift, and he often smiled. But it wasn't until long past midnight, when Melanie launched into a tale about how Alex had concocted an elaborate but fictional adventure for her to engage in, complete with arcane clues, mysterious meetings, and breathless escapes, that he burst out laughing.

"And you mean to tell me you actually fell for it?" he asked incredulously. "How could you have been so gullible?" Restless as always, he crossed to the window and leaned against the wall. "You were eight months along with Beth at the time. Alex wouldn't have allowed you to risk yourself on a real case."

She made a face at him. "I wasn't myself. My usual flawless logic had deserted me. Anyway, I had a grand time, Ty. The weeks had been dragging, and they flew after that."

"The only problem," Alex said, "is that I won't be able to get away with it twice, and we'd like another child. Frankly, Ty, I'm not sure I can survive the nine months. I don't know what it is about women and having children, but they become wildly emotional and completely irrational. Some sort of fever of the brain, I suppose."

Ty gazed out the window. "It's hormones." It was a crisp, clear night, and the whole sky was ablaze with stars. "Just normal biochemical changes, Alex." He could never look at this sight without recalling what

Sarah had said about the light and air pollution in the cities of the future, and how they blocked out the stars.

But, of course, it wasn't just the stars that reminded him of Sarah. Everything did. He knew he had to stop indulging himself, that he had a responsibility to lecture and write, but he couldn't seem to get started. Not a day went by that he didn't ache for her.

"I'm afraid your vocabulary far exceeds my own," Alex said a little testily. "Perhaps you'd like to define that word. Explain what the hell you're talking about."

Ty turned around. "To define . . . ?" He realized he'd used a term from the future. "Oh. The, uh, the body produces certain chemicals during pregnancy that affect the brain. It's—a recent scientific discovery."

Sukey rolled her eyes. "And when did it take place, Tyson? The twentieth century?"

"Suke, I really don't think—"

"Why not, for heaven's sake? They're your closest friends. You should tell them everything. Talking might help you get over her."

"Tell us what?" Melanie asked. "And what was all that about the twentieth century?"

"Nothing." Ty closed the drapes and turned away from the window, then forced a smile. "I believe we were discussing your confinement, Mel. Correct me if I'm wrong, but I believe I detect about ten extra pounds—"

"Do you want them? You can have them." She looked him up and down. "God knows you could use them."

"What I could use is some sleep." He yawned unconvincingly. "It's almost two. We should go to bed."

"In other words, you don't want to be nagged about your health or asked about the woman you love." Melanie rose from the sofa and pecked him on the cheek. "Good night, Ty. I think Sukey is right—it would do you good to talk—but if you don't want to, I certainly won't—'' She suddenly gasped. ''What in the world . . . ?'' The whole room seemed to be bathed in sparkling blue-violet light.

Ty's heart almost jumped out of his chest. He was so excited, so filled with wonder and joy, that he couldn't have gotten out an answer to save himself. A split second later, the shimmering stopped, the light disappeared, and Shelby and a very large trunk materialized in the room. But only Shelby, not Sarah. Ty was seized by the most excruciating anxiety of his life.

''Hi, Ty. Absence made the heart grow fonder.'' Shelby grinned at him, then ran into his arms and hugged him. *She's coming, she's coming. Be patient, for God's sake. There was too much matter to send us through at once.*

He would have wept from pure happiness, but Shelby's outfit threw him into a state of gaping shock. It was scandalous even for her, a costume made of a shiny fabric that was striped like a zebra, clung to her like a coat of plaster, and dipped low enough in front to reveal a salacious amount of cleavage. The only saving grace was that it covered her from ankle to wrist, but he still wanted to wrap a blanket around her to cover her up.

She disentangled herself, hugged Sukey hello, and twirled around. ''What do you think, Suke? Isn't it fabulous?''

''It's indecent,'' Ty muttered. ''Are you wearing any undergarments beneath that—that—whatever it is?''

''Skinsuit. It's totally in style.'' She struck a pose. ''And no. I'm young and firm. I don't need to.''

''Personally, I rather like it,'' Alex drawled, and leered at his wife. ''Would you have another one with you?''

''Sure.'' She winked at him. ''What'll you give me for it?''

He laughed. ''My undying gratitude.''

''You always were good at making an entrance,''

Sukey said. "You can't imagine how glad I am to see you. Ty has been utterly miserable. Meet our friends, Melanie and Alex McClure. This is Shelby Maravich. When's Sarah coming?"

"Sarah would be—your daughter?" Melanie asked, glancing furtively from Ty to Shelby and trying not to look appalled.

Now Shelby burst out laughing. "God, no. I'm the daughter. Sarah's the mother. She'll be here soon. You're right that I'm not Ty's type—too impulsive, too flashy, too mouthy—but he's not mine, either. He's kind of stodgy, you know? But perfect for the strict-older-brother role. After all, he's had so much practice with Sukey."

Shelby studied Melanie for a moment. She had gotten over her shock and was sending out the most interesting vibes. "Oh, right. You're the clairvoyant. How totally cool. You have a fascinating mind. Since you were wondering, I'm eighteen and my mom is thirty-one. We're from Virginia City, but in the year 2103. And yes, I *can* hear what you're thinking. Ty didn't tell you very much, did he?"

Melanie shook her head. "No, but I would have thought he'd gone mad if he had."

"It was a rhetorical question," Ty said. "Shelby knew the answer. It's a bad habit of hers—listening to people's thoughts." He kept waiting for another blue flash, and it wasn't happening. He was impatient with the delay. "Where is she, Shelby? When will she arrive?"

"In about ten minutes. Right after I left the future—the first time, I mean—they figured out why jumping twice in rapid succession damages the human brain." Shelby explained that it had to do with tearing the fabric of space-time twice in too short a period of time. The waves from the disturbance rippled through everything in the vicinity, not just the jumper, so if Sarah had come here right away, everyone in the room would have been harmed. But in only a few more minutes, the waves would subside and space-time would finish repairing itself.

She proceeded to give Melanie and Alex a rapid-fire telepathic summary of what had happened in May and June, then turned to Sukey. "About Ned . . . Mom told me he came looking for me after I left, and what everyone said and did. History says he was at his farm for the rest of '65, so obviously you set him free. But I wondered—are you okay with letting him off? Can you look at him as a different person now?"

"I think what you're really asking is whether I've gotten over what happened. The answer is no. I don't think I ever will. I can't be the same as I was before, not after what I went through, and not after learning about the contributions I'm supposed to make." Sukey sat down on the sofa. Shelby had never seen her so soberly self-possessed. "But I'm not angry anymore, Shel. Ty and I have talked about this for hours. Mentally, Ned was a child in the body of a man. He had enormous abilities that he didn't understand. The more he got his way, the more he thought of himself as a god. If he was filled with prejudice and bitterness, it was because of how he was raised and what he was taught. I do understand all that. I truly believe he's changed. I'll never forget, but I *have* forgiven."

Shelby was relieved. "I'm glad, Suke. It's awfully important to get past what he was, because if I do my job right, the two of you will be working toward some of the same goals. You might run into each other." She paused. "Part of the reason I came back here was to talk to him, to train him, so I'd like to say hello, but it doesn't have to be right this minute. I mean, if it would bother you—"

"Of course not, but . . . You're willing to work so closely with him? After what he did to you?"

"It wasn't on purpose." Shelby smiled slyly. "It's just that my mind was so completely awesome, he couldn't tear himself away."

Ty took her by the arm. "I refuse to allow it. He almost killed you a few months ago—"

"It was a year ago," she corrected, and then sighed. "A year of twelve-hour days, six days a week, filled with telepathic training. What happened before, couldn't happen now. I'm too strong. Too skilled. But thanks for helping me last June. For caring enough to send me back, even though it meant losing Mom. In the end, I didn't need a Class A telepath to intervene. I came out of it in about six hours. If it would reassure you, I'll let you listen, but you have to understand . . . It's terribly lonely, to be the only one of your kind. I want him to know I'm back—for both of us."

Ty knew his eavesdropping wouldn't help Shelby if she ran into trouble, but he stifled the urge to keep objecting. She was as outrageous as ever, but she also had a new poise and presence that told him she'd grown up in the past year. Besides, if her trainers in the future thought she could handle Ned Beecham, she undoubtedly could.

Shelby cast out her mental net, searching for Ned's mind. As she'd expected, he was still asleep, so she woke him with a piercing mental blast. *Hey! Beecham! It's past five already. I thought you were supposed to be a farmer. Shouldn't you be out feeding chickens or something*?

He was groggy at first, then stunned, then ecstatic. *Shelby? You came back? Are you all right?* Every word was crystal clear. She was much better at listening now.

Yeah, even though you've got a mind like a damn stamp mill. When I got home— She felt his intense remorse and wished she'd played it straight. *I was only kidding, Ned. It was the effort of ejecting you without hurting you that made me close up, not anything* **you** *did. But I've been studying hard, and you couldn't hurt me now even if you tried. I'll be coming to Virginia later this year. We all agree that you're much too powerful to be let loose without formal training, so—*

No, Shelby, no training. He was suddenly very tense. *I don't use it anymore. I want to be a normal person.*

She answered as gently as she knew how. *You can't be. We're stuck with what we are. But I'll teach you to use your abilities to help people instead of to hurt them, and you'll find that being normal is pretty boring by comparison. Okay?*

I don't know. Maybe. I'm afraid.

You don't have to be. You have me here now. We can talk more tonight, but I've got to go now.

Ned reluctantly said good-bye, and Shelby turned to Ty. "You see? It went fine."

"Yes. It did. Uh, Shelby . . . You said working with Ned was *part* of the reason you'd come back. What was the rest?"

She slid her arm around his waist. "Besides missing you and Suke? And watching Mom go crazy without you? Two things, I guess. The future wasn't as perfect as I remembered. I'll miss the technology and the physical comfort, but there's a challenge in 1865 that doesn't exist there. Before I left, I'd started to push people when I sang—"

"I'd noticed."

So had her mother. Neither of them missed much. "Well, I've got official permission now. In 1865, I can combine my talents in a way I can't in 2103. I still don't like the bigotry and discrimination, but I'll be working to end them. It's really exciting, to think of being useful on such a grand scale, especially to all my sisters. And let's face it, Ty. Given the powers I have, the discrimination won't touch me. Running for president doesn't interest me, and most anything else I want,

I can have.'' She gestured toward her trunk. ''There's more of 2103 in there than the Wellsians wanted, but I insisted, and they had to give in. We were destined to come back here. They didn't dare not send us. Anyway, what I do in the privacy of my own home is nobody's business but my own, right?''

''Right.'' And if anyone saw too much, she could excise the memory from his mind. ''You said *two* things. What was the second?''

She broke into a huge grin. ''A kid should have a father. I should know. John Shelby hardly ever checked into my life, and I missed having him there.''

He looked at her quizzically. ''Your father? I thought we'd already established that I'm to play the role of the overbearing older brother.''

''Just watch,'' Shelby said.

About thirty seconds later, the room began to shimmer with blue-violet light. Ty couldn't wait to scoop Sarah up and kiss her until she was breathless, but when she appeared, she was holding an infant in her arms. She was also dressed in the same sort of garment as Shelby, in black. She filled it out to perfection, but he was too transfixed by the baby either to scold her or to ogle her.

''I couldn't bear to leave without taking something of you with me,'' Sarah said softly. ''I named him Benjamin Barrett, after your parents. I hope that's okay. He's three months old. What do you think of him?''

''That he's beautiful. Perfect.'' Ty's eyes filled with tears, and he put out his arms for a hug that included both Sarah and his new child. ''You came back to me. I can hardly believe it. You said they would never send you.'' He stroked the baby's face. ''I can hardly believe *this*. A son.'' He smiled stupidly, then took Ben from Sarah to hold and cuddle. ''Hello, there. What do you think of your pop? You look like me, you know.'' He shot Sarah a teasing grin. "You're lucky there. I'll bet you're smart as a whip, too . . ."

Sarah listened to Ty's cooing and bragging for several minutes more, then rolled her eyes and took the baby away, handing him to Shelby. Unlike Ty, she'd known almost from the start that they would meet again tonight, but that hadn't made the waiting any easier, or the reunion any less blissful. She put her arms around his neck, then demanded, "Aren't you going to ask me why I'm here?"

"Shelby said it was destined. I assume you're here because that's the way it happened."

She scowled at him for being so smart. "Yes. Things got much better after Shelby came the first time, so they checked out history, and there we were—except for three months in 1865. They were afraid if they didn't return us, the past they knew wouldn't be created again. That deterioration would take place."

Ty and Sarah shared the kiss that Ty had imagined, retreating into their own private world. They only came back to earth when Alex said irritably, "Sukey . . . Do you mean to tell me that between June and now, your brother has gotten himself a three-month-old son, and he didn't even have to suffer through the damned pregnancy?"

Sarah turned around. "Or even put up with the colic Ben had for the first two months, since I didn't want to leave without Shelby, and she needed to finish her training." She gave Ty an accusing look. "Would you mind telling me where you've been for the past three months? Oh, crossing the continent, I know that, but I couldn't make such an arduous trip with a brand-new baby, and then, poof! Between Atchison and now, no articles, no letters, no Ty. Really, this habit you have of disappearing from the pages of history . . . If you hadn't finally written some letters, and we hadn't been able to pinpoint the exact location of Comstock Cottage, you would still be waiting for me.''

''I was traveling around California,'' Ty said, gazing at her as if he could have watched her for the next hundred years and not grown tired of the sight. ''Trying to put myself back together. But it wasn't possible, because when you left me, half of me went with you.''

Sarah promptly melted. ''I know. Me, too. This has been the longest year of my life.''

Sukey, meanwhile, had taken charge of Ben and was fussing over him, telling him she was his aunt and assuring him he was the most brilliant and beautiful child who had ever been born, doubtless because he took after his mother.

''You said the exact same thing to Wyatt and Beth,'' Melanie pointed out. ''They can't all be the most beautiful and brilliant, Sukey.''

''Of course they can, if they're McClures or Stones.'' She nuzzled Ben's cheek. ''Isn't he precious? I do adore children.''

''It's a good thing,'' Shelby said with a yawn, ''because you're going to raise six of them.''

Sukey's eyes widened. ''Six? Good grief. Are you sure?''

''I only know what I read in the history books,'' Shelby drawled.

''Which was actually very little,'' Sarah said. ''Our lives would be a total bore if we knew what lay ahead, but our scientists also believe that if we were told what would happen, and tried to duplicate everything we'd done, we would only make changes and mistakes that would mess everything up. So spontaneity isn't only better; it's inevitable. Free will does exist. But we did make one exception, Suke. You.''

Sarah rested her head on Ty's shoulder, then continued, ''I knew you would ask, so I had someone check. Your sister won't be quite the firebrand she was the first time around, but with a husband and all those kids, who can blame her?"

"And her husband?" Ty asked. "He'll love her? He'll be good to her?"

"Absolutely. They say he's the dearest man, Ty. Strong but tender. Honorable and patient. A wonderful father. Smart but not arrogant."

"And fantastic in bed," Shelby added blithely, paying no attention to the way Sukey blushed.

Mother and daughter exchanged a look. Leaving Shelby's postscript aside, both of them knew that when Sukey first met her future husband, she would never recognize him as the man Sarah had described. Never in a million years. But her memoirs had made it clear that she'd believed him to be a total devil at first, and it was the so-called devil who had penetrated her defenses before the angel had won her heart. When it came to history, sometimes it was best to leave well enough alone.

Author's Note

Dear Readers:

Some of you may have noticed that the world Sarah comes from is not the world we exist in. For example, the Supreme Court decision legalizing racial segregation was *Plessy* v. *Ferguson* in 1896, not the fictional *Wallace* v. *Robinson* in 1878. Plessy was overturned in 1954, not in 1971, and the "sexual revolution" of Sarah's 1980s took place in our own 1960s. In general, her world had more inequality and greater problems than ours does. The world we live in is the world she and Shelby brought into existence.

The next book in the series, *Runaway Magic,* finds Sukey in Hong Kong, running a girls' academy at the behest of the McClures. For six years, she's been waiting to fall in love, but she hasn't yet met the paragon Sarah described. So when Alex returns from a trip to London with two young children in tow, the offspring of a widowed English aristocrat who is touring China before taking over as the taipan of a local trading house, Sukey wonders if *he* might be the man. After all, Luke Wyndham is said to be educated, brilliant, and handsome, and she adores his children on sight, especially his daughter Ellie, whom Alex enrolls in her school.

Then Wyndham arrives, and he's the last man Sukey would agree to marry—aloof and arrogant, condescending to females, and icily stoic about the circumstances that have forced him to abandon his life as a scholar and enter the undignified world of trade. He also has a slew of relations who have died under bizarre circumstances, leaving him with both a fortune and a title. In fact, his shadowy past results in so much gossip, even among Ellie's classmates, that he withdraws the girl from Sukey's school in order to shield her.

Missing the child, and vehement about the value of educating females, Sukey resolves to get Ellie back. She's been dabbling in magic since her teens, so when Luke dismisses her as a brazen and meddlesome nag, she casts a spell to make him accede to her wishes. But her magic goes hopelessly awry, and instead of returning Ellie to school, Luke develops a grand passion for her—a passion that appalls both of them.

In the meantime, Sukey has observed odd goings-on at her school, and Luke has been implicated in a puzzling murder plot while looking into mysterious losses at his company. As a result of their investigations, they make enemies who are far more skilled at magic than Sukey is. Unknowingly bewitched, they're trapped by a sexual scandal that leaves them no choice but to flee Hong Kong in disgrace—or marry each other. They select the latter, but in name only, and only until their enemies are unmasked and punished.

But Luke, to his chagrin, can't seem to keep his distance from his unruly but beautiful wife. He grows impatient with her irrational insistence that he's not the husband she's been waiting for, but a narrow and wrongheaded autocrat. And he can't help but wonder what it would take to tame her—and to lure her into his bed.